The Jagged Orbit

KT-144-150

COLLECTORS' EDITION

GOLLANCZ **SF** GOLLANCZ

SPARTAM · NACTUS
HANC · EXORNA

LORETTO SCHOOL LIBRARY

*Also by John Brunner
in Millennium*

Stand on Zanzibar

The Jagged Orbit

JOHN BRUNNER

VICTOR GOLLANCZ
LONDON

Loretto School

10682

Copyright © Brunner Fact and Fiction Ltd 1969

All rights reserved

The right of John Brunner to be identified as the author
of this work has been asserted by him in accordance with
the Copyright, Designs and Patents Act 1988.

This edition published in Great Britain in 2000 by
Victor Gollancz
An imprint of Orion Books Ltd
Orion House, 5 Upper St Martin's Lane,
London, WC2H 9EA

To receive information on the Millennium list, e-mail us at:
smy@orionbooks.co.uk

A CIP catalogue record for this book is available
from the British Library.

ISBN 0 57507 052 8

Printed in Great Britain by
The Guernsey Press Co. Ltd, Guernsey, C.I.

FOR CHIP

—the only person I know who really can fly
a jagged orbit.

ONE   PUT YOURSELF IN MY PLACE

I –

-solationism.

So what shape was the world in this morning? Even flatter than yesterday. In every office of the Etchmark Undertower the air was at a comfortable 65° but there was sweat on the brow of Matthew Flamen the last of the spoolpigeons. By noon, a fifteen-minute show to be compiled, processed, taped, approved, amended and slotted into the transmitters, and at this late stage nothing ready bar the two minutes and forty seconds of advertising. Item after item from the list he had set to simmer overnight was being comped out as unusable, and his contract still had nine months to run.

It was the climax of a long-recurrent nightmare. The planet had closed up like a weary clam and he, a starving starfish, lacked the strength to pry it open again. Open? Pry open?

With a convulsive effort he managed it; his eyelids parted and there was blue sky bright above the one-way armored glass of his bedroom ceiling. He was alone in the room; he was alone in the house. He was profoundly glad of that. His heart was hammering on his ribs like a lunatic demanding to be let out of Bedlam and he was gasping for breath so violently he could never have framed a coherent sentence, not even a simple good morning. Though nobody could in reason be held responsible for the content of a dream, he felt horribly and unspeakably ashamed.

Piecemeal, he grappled together the dispersed fragments of his personality until he had enough control over his limbs to get up. Superficially noted long ago, categorized as a quotable quote because it touched so directly on his line of work, a dictum by Xavier Conroy drifted out of his subconscious: "Western culture is undergoing a process of transition from guilt-oriented, with a conscience, to shame-oriented, with a morbid fear of being found out." Lately the words had been festering in his brain, like the mark of a brand applied at too low a temperature to cauterize and sterilize the site of the burn.

He looked around with bleary eyes at the luxury, the comfort, the security of his home, and found the place repulsive. He stumbled into the bathroom and swallowed a trank from the dispenser. It took effect while he was emptying his bladder and the world seemed marginally less threatening. He was able to reassure himself that so far he was managing to keep going, he was still in business, he was as yet continuing to lever the lids off countless secrets intended to stay hidden. . . .

Nonetheless, before thinking about showering and eating and the other minutiae of civilized existence, he exorcised the ghosts of nightmare by going to the comweb and punching a direct line to his office computers. Watched by the looped-tape cut of Celia playing over and over in its niche of honor, he sat naked in a clammy rotachair and struck head after head from the hydra of his apprehension. It was local-early yet—oh-seven-ten EST—but the small and shrunken planet nowadays existed in a zone of timelessness. The items he had set to simmer while he slept had come along nicely: some cooked enough to be used today, some exuding juices with a promising smell.

Gradually confidence returned to him. It was always a better medicine than tranks to realize that he was looking into the not three- but four-dimensional world deeper than almost anyone else. He forced himself to disregard the sniggering demon of doubt which kept quoting that remark of Conroy's and pointing out that if it were true sooner or later the whole western world would be conspiring to keep their shady actions from him. Ten, eight, even six years ago all the major networks had had their respective spoolpigeons; one by one they had faded away, some for making charges that could not be proved, others merely because they lost their audience, ceased to be able to irritate, provoke, excite.

Was it because the world no longer admired an honest man as much as one who contrived to get away with dishonesty? And how honest is the man who makes a living by unmasking those who haven't completely succeeded in covering up their deceit? As though the questions had been put to him by someone else, Flamen glanced around uneasily. But all he saw move was the picture of Celia, going through its endless cycle. He turned back to the comweb screen, and selected the first and biggest of the dozen-odd items he had assigned for overnight comping.

Yes, indeed, it was true that Marcantonio Gottschalk had been snubbed by the absence of Vyacheslav Gottschalk and a number of other high-level pollies from his eightieth birthday celebration. It was hardly news that yet another power-struggle was going on within the cartel, but up till now details of who was taking whose side had been efficiently suppressed.

Dare he risk a guesstimate as to which of the conventional protestations of illness—the Gottschalks were curiously conservative in a great many ways—had actually been lies? The computers warned him not to; the cartel was far too big to tackle without really solid data. And yet his heart yearned for something big. It wasn't so much that his contract still had nine months to run, as his dream had warned, but more that it had *only* nine months to run, and unless he gaffed somebody really spectacular before the end of the low-audience summer season he would be one with Nineveh and

Tyre. He put a hi-pri on the story and instructed his computers, not with any real hope, to have one more go at finding out whether he could buy a key-code for the Gottschalks' information bank at Iron Mountain.

Waiting for the evaluation, he moved on to other subjects. The mere idea of attacking the Gottschalks seemed to have restored him to complete normality, and he tabbed items old and new with assurance.

Lares & Penates Inc. is almost certainly what rumor claims: a college-educated front for Conjuh Man, exploiting the blank flight from rationality with the same enthusiasm as knee ignorance of it. Mark for maximum detail and use when the reading breaks eighty in favor; so far, only seventy-two. The refugees converging on Kuala Lumpur must be being culled according to a pre-set plan requiring reduction of their number by at least two-thirds and not as official releases would have it by division into loyalists and subversives. Reading eighty-eight in favor, hence usable today. But worth the risk of provoking an international incident? Who in the English-speaking world could give a damn about the fate of never mind how many people with brown skins speaking an alien language?

While he was still hesitating over whether to use the item or keep it in reserve, an interruption. Sixty-plus in favor of his being able to buy a code and unlock the Gottschalks' data bank at Iron Mountain. Estimated price between one and two million. That put it out of Flamen's orbit anyway—there wasn't enough cash in the informers' fund—but instantly his professional suspicions were alerted. On all the previous occasions he'd made that inquiry the computers had immediately rung up a NO SALE sign. Instinct told him the right question to ask next: are they planning to get along without that particular facility?

Meanwhile, continuing: something big brewing among the X Patriots. The routine reading carried him straight back to the Gottschalks and the superficial verdict that they were once more fomenting discontent among knee extremists to ensure good sales for their latest product among frightened blanks. But there was a secondary possibility only five points lower on the scale which caused him to finger his neat brown beard and frown.

A breakthrough in the matter of Morton Lenigo? Rational judgment decreed that that was nonsensical. No immigration computer would conceivably issue Lenigo a visa after what he'd done in British cities like Manchester, Birmingham and Cardiff. Nonetheless, for a reading which had been hovering in the middle forties for three years suddenly to jump into the high sixties was certainly a danger signal. And it would be a hell of a story if it turned into a story at all! He flagged it for intensive evaluation and reverted to the Gottschalks.

Yes, said his computers, the Gottschalks may very well be planning to dispense with Iron Mountain. They've been buying data-processing equipment in quantities too large to be explained away as tracking or range-finding systems.

Logical conclusion: if they were thinking of opting out of Iron Mountain the sale of one of their access codes would be an on-the-side fund-raising venture and they'd sit back and laugh like hyenas when the gullible purchaser found how he'd been cheated.

Sometimes I hate the Gottschalks, Flamen thought, not so much for what they are as for what they think other people are. Nobody likes being treated as a myopic idiot.

After some cogitation, he instructed his computers to look for three things: the site to which the Gottschalks were having all this equipment delivered, which would itself be illuminating; notice of any recent technical breakthrough which might lead to the marketing of a brand-new product; and every single clue, no matter how tenuous, regarding the current quarrel within the cartel. Since there was absolutely no hope of anything turned up by such a blanket order being comped and usable by show-time today, he flagged the subject for overnight holding and turned back to immediately exploitable material.

Rumor-trapping, like running after butterflies with a muslin net, was one of his chief professional talents, and that he was good at it was proved by his show having survived—mutilated, one had to concede, but the loss of a leg was better than being put in a shroud for cremation. Nonetheless this patent truth did not greatly reassure him as he looked over the final selection of seven items, with three held in reserve against the risk of something being comped out at network HQ. Before making any kind of a charge against anybody his contract obliged him to let Holocosmic's own computers review the background data, and sometimes they downgraded a reading past the limit fixed by the firm which insured them against losing libel suits. Recently about one item a week had been being rejected, far too many in Flamen's view; still, there were good reasons for suppressing the urge to complain.

It was a lean harvest today. At least, though, he now knew he was going to have a show. It was safe to spend the time needed to ingest some breakfast. But the food tasted of ashes as he forced it down.

FOUR

Q. WHO WAS THAT SERPENT I SAW YOU WITH LAST NIGHT? A. THAT WAS NO SERPENT, THAT WAS MY CURRENT MISTRESS WHO HAPPENS TO BE A PYTHONESS

The mechanism of the flotabed was beginning to go home. It had been bought secondhand, and in any case even though it was a meter thirty wide it hadn't been designed for use as a double. So the first thing Lyla Clay was aware of on waking was that as usual she had remained rigid in her sleep to avoid the top left corner where the support was weakest, and by lying on her right arm had cut off its circulation. From elbow to fingertip it rang like a bell with the agony of returning sensation.

Annoyed, she opened her eyes to find a man she didn't know grinning at her. His lips were writhing in complete silence, but the implications of that did not at first strike her.

She was completely naked; however, she had no reason to be ashamed of her body, which was lean, youthful and evenly tanned, and the reflex left over from her somewhat old-fashioned childhood which impelled her to reach for a nonexistent blanket—the heater circuits of the bed, at least, were still working properly—ran foul of the stiffness of cramp. Anyhow, it wasn't the first time in her twenty years that she had woken up to find herself being admired by a man whose face and name were alike unknown to her.

Then the stranger dissolved in a shower of pink and purple snowflakes, and she remembered the vuset Dan and his friend Berry had trolleyed along the corridor from the elevator yesterday with so much sweating and cursing. They hadn't had a vuset in the apt before—only an ancient non-holographic TV which offered nothing more interesting than the three surviving 2-D satellite transmissions insisted on by the PCC. Since those were beamed primarily at India, Africa and Latin America, and she and Dan spoke neither Hindi, Swahili, nor more than a smattering of Spanish, they had seldom bothered to switch on unless they were orbiting. Then, it didn't matter that the programs were chiefly concerned with latrine-digging, fish-traps and the recognition of epidemic disease symptoms—in fact, as Dan had once pointed out, if they'd had a plot of land to dig latrines in, the information might have come in useful next time the toilets were blocked.

She looked around for Dan and found him on the other side of the bed. Rozar in hand, he was feeling for a spot on the wall where the magnetized leech on the end of the flex could pick up some power, rather like a mainliner hunting for a usable patch of skin. He located a section where the induction wire was still uncorroded, the rozar hummed into life, and he set about making good the defects in his beard. He was cursed with large round bald patches on both cheeks.

A couple of heartbeats later the vuset miraculously reverted to proper synchronization. Beaming and gesticulating, the man in the screen resumed his unheard diatribe.

Lyla sat up and cradled her stinging arm across her bosom, rubbing it with the tips of her opposite fingers. "Why don't you make a mark on the wall there so you don't have to feel around for it next time?" she said, not looking at Dan but allowing her eyes to rove distractedly over the contents of the room. In the Benares brassware tray before the Lar's shrine there was a sludgy pile of pseudorganics; clearly someone had remembered just in time to dump in it the books whose expiry date was approaching, and since she didn't recollect doing so it must have been Dan. There was a thread of dried red wine running down the wall from the corner of the table, which had been folded back without being wiped. The shelf which held their genuine twentieth-century seven-branched candlestick was covered in powdery ashes, because she had insisted on burning seven different types of *agarbati* in it all at once—her nose wrinkled at the memory.

In short, the place was a mess.

Dan paused in his task of applying, strand by strand, synthetic hair to the adhesive he had smeared on his cheeks. "You finally woke up, hm? I was just about to start shaking you. Don't you know what the time is?" He gestured towards his new acquisition, the vuset, as though it were a clock.

Lyla stared at him blankly.

"Don't you recognize Matthew Flamen? Hell, how many spoolpigeons are there *left* on three-vee? That's his noon slot, and it's better than halfway through. Listen!" He raised one bare leg and jabbed it towards the sound control on the low-built cabinet from which the centimeter-thick holographic screen jutted up like a sail from the hull of a yacht. Misjudging his balance, he sat down plump on the corner of the bed. The sudden load was too much for the worn mechanism, and Lyla found herself deposited on the baseboard to the accompaniment of a whine of escaping gas.

Flamen's ingratiating voice said, "In this world which is so often terrifying, aren't you envious of the security people feel when they've installed Guardian traps at their doors and windows? You can't buy better, and you'd be a fool to buy anything less good."

He vanished. A tall scowling kneeblank marched for-

17

ward in his place, and before Lyla had had time to react—she was still not awake enough to have convinced
herself that the three-dimensional full-color image was
going to stay buried in the screen—spiked metal bands
had clamped on him at neck-, waist- and knee-height.
Blood began to ooze from the points where the cruel
metal prongs had sunk in. He looked briefly bewildered,
then slumped unconscious.

"Guardian!" sang an eldritch castrato voice. "Guar—
dee—ann!"

"I guess maybe we ought to invest in some of those,"
Dan said.

"What in the world do you think we're going to have
left that's worth stealing if you go on like this?" Lyla
demanded crossly. "Don't you realize you just broke the
bed?" Jumping to her feet, she hit the off switch of the
vuset. Nothing happened.

"Forgot to tell you," Dan muttered. "The off switch
doesn't work. That's why Berry gave it to us."

"Oh, for—!" Lyla sought the power-cord with her
eyes; finding it, she yanked the leech free of the wall
and the renewed image of Matthew Flamen collapsed
into a welter of blues and greens. "Do you want to sleep
on a hard plain board tonight? Because I don't!"

"I'll call someone and get it fixed," Dan sighed. "Right
now you get a move on, hm? Have you forgotten we're
booked for the Ginsberg this afternoon?"

Sulkily Lyla picked up the clothes she had discarded
last night: gray and olive Nix and a pair of Schoos. "Any
calls or mail?" she asked as she began to put them on.

"Go look if you're that interested." Dan touched the
flock on his face gingerly; satisfied that it was presenta-
ble, he detached the rozar from the wall and returned
it to its case. "But you're supposed to do duty to the Lar
first, aren't you?"

"We only have it on seven-day appro," Lyla said indifferently, snugging the Nix into position around her
hips. "If it's that keen to stay in a crummy hole like this,

let it do the work. Besides, what possessed you to stack a heap of expiring books on its tray? Expect it to take kindly to being used as a garbage-disposer?"

"Matter of urgent necessity," Dan muttered. "The drains overloaded again."

"Oh, no!" Balanced on one leg to slip her toes into the first Schoo, Lyla stared at him in dismay.

"It's all right—the toilets are still working. But I didn't want to risk blocking them too by dumping down a load of books, did I?"

"Talk about hardening of the arteries," Lyla sighed, recalling a favorite metaphor from Xavier Conroy's *The Senile City*. "When it's not the sewers it's the streets, and when it's not the streets it's the comweb. . . . I'll go check our slot anyway. You never know; there might be something interesting."

She moved to the door and began to strain against the handle of the winch to lift clear the hundred-kilo deadfall block that closed it against intruders overnight.

"Put your yash on," Dan said, stepping into a pair of green breeches and belting them tight around his waist.

"Hell, I'm only going to the comweb!"

"Put it on, I said. You're insured for a quarter-million tealeaves and it says in the policy that you have to."

"It's all right for you to talk," Lyla countered mutinously. "You don't have to wear the horrible thing." But she reached obediently for the yash where it hung on its peg adjacent to the door.

Making to slip it over her head, she checked. "Say—uh —I won't have to wear this at the hospital, will I? It'd be awfully hampering while I'm thrashing around."

"No, not while you're actually performing. Come to think of it, though . . ." Dan bit his lip, eying her doubtfully. "The patients are segregated at the Ginsberg, and the sight of you like that might not be a good thing. Got anything less revealing?"

"I don't think so. All my February clothes have expired by now, and the March ones are getting pretty shabby. And of course in April I went over to transparents."

"Skip it, then," Dan shrugged. "If they insist, you can ask for something at their expense, can't you? Like a dress, maybe. How long is it since you last had a dress —was it in November?"

"Yes, the one I bought to go home and see my folks at Thanksgiving. But it was cold then, and right now it's sweltering. . . . Oh, I guess I could put up with it in a good cause. Provided they pay for it—dresses are horribly expensive this season." She ducked into the yash and opened the door. Having made sure with a cautious glance in each direction that the corridor was deserted, she added, "I won't lock it—I'll only be a moment."

FIVE

MAKING READETH A FULL MAN,
SAVING YOUR BACON'S PRESENCE

"The name is Harry Madison, not Mad Harrison!"

"I'm sorry?" the computerized desketary said, with exactly the right interrogative inflection; it was one of IBM's ultra-advanced models with fully personalized vocal communication, and abode by articles of faith in its mechanical existence. One of them stated that hospital staff alone in a room who uttered audible words desired a reply. This did not apply to patients. To enable desketaries and other automatics to distinguish them the latter were compelled to wear oversuits with a metal thread woven criss-cross on back and chest.

"Not important," Dr. James Reedeth said wearily, and clamped his jaw so tightly shut he heard the singing tension of the muscles. Silently now after that careless peaking into speech: *He was committed for a reason, damn it, by experts whose judgment is at least as sharp as mine! He's not even one of my own patients. So what makes me take such an interest in his case—subconscious resentment at the presence of a knee in an otherwise all-blank hospital? I don't believe it. But it's completely pointless to keep coming up with the sane answer.*

For the latest of so many times he would not have dared to count them if he'd been able to, he found himself wondering what had driven him into this Minotaurhaunted labyrinth. Was it in order to become a doctor, whom men might consult *re death* . . . ?

"Ariadne! Ariadne! Where art thou now that I need thy clew of string?" On impulse, he chose to utter that aloud too, and an instant later was not sure whether he had glossed the decision with a veneer of voluntarism in order to delude himself. The desketary emitted electronic complaints as it matched and discarded partial resemblances, and finally produced the response he had expected.

"Assuming the reference to 'Ariadne' connotes an inquiry regarding Dr. Spoelstra, her location is at present on Floor Nine of Wing Four and she is subject to a Class Two interdiction on being disturbed. Please declare the urgency of your requirements."

Reedeth gave a humorless laugh. When, after half a minute or so, the desketary had heard nothing further, it added with a convincing tinge of artificial doubt, "No reference can be found to her possessing a piece of string whether in the form of a clew or otherwise. Am I authorized to add this to my stock of data concerning her?"

"By all means," Reedeth assured it cordially. "You may record that she alone knows the way out of the maze. You may furthermore store the fact that she has skin smoother than synthosilk, exceptionally beautiful breasts, the most sensual mouth ever divinely wished on a mortal woman, thighs which probably correspond to an equation that would blow all your circuits, and—"

He had been going to add that she had a heart of Ice-V, but at that point an unhappy grinding noise emerged from the bowels of the desketary and a flashing red light came on to signify that it was temporarily out of service. Furious, Reedeth jumped to his feet. What in the world was the good of letting the contract for the Ginsberg Hospital's computing system to a firm which was currently hiring as many neo-puritans as was IBM? When at least eighty percent of the patients he was trying to cope with were suffering from sexual hang-ups, it was a constant source of irritation to have these censor-circuits expressing reflexive mechanical Grundy-ism all the time.

And yet, in a way, it was a relief to be deprived of the desketary's company. Reconciling the web of information-channels that permeated his working environment with the principles he gave lip-service to was a paradox he had never really solved.

He walked over to the window-wall of the office and stared out at the vast bulk of the Ginsberg Memorial State Hospital for the Mentally Maladjusted. Fortress-like, with tall maxecurity towers distributed around its perimeter and linked by curtain walls as though some drawing of a fairy-tale castle from a children's book had been unsympathetically interpreted in modern concrete, it was a structural analog of that chance to "retire and regroup" which Mogshack advocated as a perfect anti-dote to almost any problem of personal adjustment. There were windows only on the low-built administrative wings; the towers themselves were featureless. The sight of them—so the argument ran—offered to a fearful newly-committed patient the promise of ultimate immunity from the intolerable challenges of the outer world.

But the view from here always made Reedeth think of the medieval castles that were rendered obsolete by the advent of gunpowder. And in an age of pocket nukes . . . ?

He sighed, recalling the query posed in a mild voice by Xavier Conroy, under whom he had worked while preparing his doctorate thesis. The plans for the Ginsberg had just been published, together with a persuasive summary by Mogshack of the underlying principles.

"So what provision has Dr. Mogshack made for the patients whose recovery is likely to be delayed by their inability to discern any way of getting out again?"

It had taken him two years' work here to appreciate

the full force of that criticism, and indeed only his un-expected recognition of Harry Madison's plight had brought it home to him. At the time, he had chuckled along with everyone else at Mogshack's curt and pointed reply.

"I'm grateful to Dr. Conroy for yet another demon-stration of his ability to jump his fences before he comes to them. Perhaps he would care to favor us with his company at the Ginsberg, when he will be accorded ample opportunity to figure out the solution to his prob-lem—which, incidentally, I suspect to be one of many."

Reedeth shook his head. "Retire and regroup!" he quoted aloud, glad of the chance to speak without me-chanical eavesdropping. "If I'd known what limits that precept could be pushed to, I swear I'd have gone to work anywhere rather than here, where that abominable woman can bounce me up and down like a kid batting a ball because 'love is a dependent state' and how can a therapist at the mercy of his emotions help patients to regain their own rational detachment?"

He scowled at the desketary, epitome of Mogshack's impersonal ideals, and suddenly noticed that although the red light was still on it had ceased flashing and now shone with a steady glow. Silently cursing, he realized that that meant he was about to be brought face to face with the very person whose predicament was preying on his mind even more persistently than was his own.

SIX

THE WHERE IT'S AT AND THE
WHYFORE IT SHOULD BE THERE

"It is not so much that the nature of mental disturbance has changed, as a layman might assume from the observable fact that nowadays a higher proportion of our population can expect to be temporarily committed to a mental hospital than—let us say—would ever have been committed to a tuberculosis hospital or a fever hospital in the days when mere organic diseases were the prime concern of a public health authority.

"No, rather it is that the nature of normality is not now what our ancestors were accustomed to. Is that surprising? Surely one would not expect social problems to remain unchanged, static from generation to generation! A few get solved; many—indeed the majority—develop along with the society as a whole. I hardly need to cite examples here, for several are available in the news each day.

"What is far too seldom stressed, however, is the positive aspect of this phenomenon. For the latest of uncountably many times, humanity as a species has presented its individual members with a challenge which— like a mathematical limit—can never be fulfilled but which can always be approached more closely. In former ages the challenges were philosophical, or religious: *abjure desire; defy the world, the flesh and the devil;*

be ye perfect, even as your Father in heaven is perfect . . . and so on.

"But this time the command is psychological: *be an individual!*"

—Elias Mogshack, *passim**

"What people want, mainly, is to be told by some plausible authority that what they are already doing is right. I don't know of a quicker way to become unpopular than to disagree."

—Xavier Conroy

*Or, as some would put it, *ad nauseam.*

SEVEN

(THIS SPACE RESERVED FOR
ADVERTISING)

Kicking the door shut with her heel, tossing aside her yash, Lyla grimaced at the wad of envelopes she had collected.

"Practically all satches, same as usual. I do hate saturation mail! It clogs the comweb same as garbage does the drains, and I swear ninety percent of it goes straight *into* the drains without being read. . . . Oh, this one isn't satch. It's from Lairs and Pen-eights Inc. Must be the reminder about old whoozis." She jerked her head at the impassive Lar.

"Laireez and Penaiteez," Dan corrected her. "You must get things like that right." He hesitated. "It's French, I guess," he concluded lamely, holding out his hand for the letter.

Flicking through the rest, Lyla muttered, "Same old names—won't they ever learn to take a hint?" She pantomimed tearing them across, but they were reinforced against that; they could only be torn along the line which would liberate the chemicals powering their in-built speakers. Satch mailing campaigns were too expensive to let illiterates escape.

27

"Stick 'em in the used books pile," Dan suggested. "The reagents sometimes last long enough to attack extra paper."

"Good idea." Lyla complied, wedging the unopened envelopes into the sticky mound on the brass tray like so many pieces of toast in a rack. Obligingly two or three of them started to decay at once.

Meantime, Dan had ripped along the sealing strip of the one from Lares & Penates Inc., and at once the room was full of a familiar high thin voice.

"You can't afford to be without a cult tailored to your private needs in this age of the individual. Consult Lares & Penates for the finest specialized—"

It took him that long to locate the power-capsule driving the speaker and break it between finger and thumb. Promptly, he dropped the envelope with a yelp, shaking his hand.

"It burned me! That's a new one! They must have got wise to people cracking the capsules."

"Is it serious? Has it left a mark?" Lyla was instantly solicitous.

Dan inspected his forefinger, licked it, and finally shrugged. "No real harm done—just a few volts shorted through the paper, I guess. But from now on I open their envelopes with Schoos on so I can crack 'em under my heel!" He scanned the letter he had withdrawn from the envelope. "And it's only what you expected, a reminder to pay up or send back the Lar."

"Which are we going to do?"

"I guess we'd better make our minds up later, don't you? After all, it did get us this booking at the Ginsberg, and that's a breakthrough, you know. I asked round, and apparently this is the first time they ever engaged a pythoness. It could be very big. In fact I—"

There was a loud bang on the door. Lyla spun around. Realizing she had forgotten to wind down the hundred-kilo barrier again, she dived for her yash. It was a good one; it had been dreadfully expensive, but as Dan had truthfully pointed out it was insisted on by her insurers. Heavy and clumsy though it was, the guarantee did promise protection against solid shot up to 120 grams, laser-beams up to 250 watts and virtually all kinds of acid.

"Who the hell?" Dan muttered, and strode over to set the deadfall catch on the over-door barrier. That attended to, he shouted, "Yes, who is it?"

"Morning!" the invisible caller replied. "Or afternoon, rather! My name's Bill and I'm your new neighbor in Apt Ten-W. Sorry to disturb you, but I understand you lack a citidef group on this block! Well, of course nowadays"—here the voice dropped solemnly by half an octave—"in a district like this one never knows when the knees may choose to strike. So I thought I'd be public-spirited and all that sort of garbage and see what I could do to whip up interest in organizing a group."

"Another Gottschalk?" Lyla whispered to Dan. He nodded.

"Lay you fifty in favor. And pretty raw, too. I'd even make bets on what he'll say next."

The voice from outside resumed. "You see, I happen to have some contacts which can get me the necessary at very favorable prices, such as guns for a mere sixty-three with maker's warranty, gas of assorted types at prices as low as three-fifty the liter—"

"Oh, for heaven's sake," Lyla said wearily, letting fall her yash.

"Want me to ask you in?" Dan shouted with a wink at her.

"Well, naturally, if you'd care to discuss my proposals . . . !" The voice was suddenly tinged with optimism.

"Sure! Come right ahead! There's only a hundred-kilo deadfall to stop you."

There was an interlude of silence. With cheerfulness that was now distinctly forced, the Gottschalk said, "Ah —I guess maybe if you're busy right now the best thing

I can do is leave some literature in your comweb slot.
Be seeing you, friends."

"Tell him some knees took over the apt," Lyla suggested softly. Dan shook his head.

"No point. This one may sound like an idiot, but the
Gottschalk pollies are much too smart to turn a new
recruit loose without going over the ground for him
first." Glancing at his watch, he added, "Hey, we'd better move. I don't recall you eating last night, so I'll have
to get some breakfast down you on the way to the Ginsberg. I sure as hell don't want you fainting during the
show."

Humidity index in New York in excess of previous high for the current date, a factor ascribed by officials to the effect of the city's five and a half million air-conditioners. The insurrection probability index slipping ahead of schedule into what is nicknamed "the sweaty season downturn" (for which heartfelt thanks among those who were half afraid they might not get one this year). Over most of the eastern seaboard of North America a warm close summer day with slight precipitation in inland areas. Snow on high ground in South Island, New Zealand. Owing to information transmitted from the Bureau of State and Federal Relations computers at the Immigration Dept. this morning had to ease the reading on the Morton Lenigo application south of the fifty-fifty line but simultaneously and for the same reason computers at ISM canceled their sweaty season downturn weightings. The new government of Trinidad & Tobago broke off diplomatic relations with (in order of importance) South Africa, Australia, New Zealand, Russia and the USA. The kneeblank city council of Washington DC ignored the thirty-third request from the DAR to remove the paint from the façade of the Black House.

All in all a pretty ordinary day.

Reedeth's office door buzzed and he told it to open
and there indeed was Harry Madison in his patient's
oversuit of the bright green shade which signified mini-
mal disturbance and, ordinarily, impending discharge.
Seeing him around the hospital for such a long time
after he had—as the phrase went—"gone to green" was
not, of course, the first thing that had attracted Reedeth's attention to him, but it was the factor which led to
the alarming discovery that he was trapped here in a
tangle of legalisms.

He had been committed by the Army, following conscript service in a brushfire war in New Guinea, at a
time when the subject of kneeblank draftees was rather
a sensitive one and it was politic to send him to a civil
instead of a military institution. Naturally that made the
Army his legal guardian, for he appeared to have no
surviving relatives. However, by the time he was handed
his new green suit, the Army no longer wanted to know
about him. They'd given up accepting knees even as
volunteers, and they certainly would not admit responsibility for a former conscript whose medical discharge
had removed him from the reserve. That meant that he
automatically became a ward of New York State, and
directly his personality profiles matched the computerized ideal laid down for him he should have been turned

loose to fend for himself subject only to restrictions on things like his credit rating, getting married and moving out of the state to reside elsewhere.

However, his personality profiles, though stable, had continued to deviate from the predetermined optimum for a man of his background, race and abilities, and moreover a stern directive from the Bureau of State and Federal Relations decreed that no kneeblank patient should ever be released with the least shadow of doubt still hovering over his case. News of such an action, blown up by some skilled propagandist such as Pedro Diablo, could far too easily be turned into a legitimate *casus insurrectionis* and bring down black wrath on all their heads.

Yet it seemed damnably unjust to Reedeth that Madison should be cooped up indefinitely for what amounted to no more than eccentricity. . . .

He grew aware that Madison had made a formal reference to the desketary being in a mechanical double bind and asked permission to fix it. Belatedly he nodded, and Madison wheeled in the obese reparobot on its eight soft wheels and deftly connected its terminals to the faulty appliance.

Watching, Reedeth wondered what the directorate of IBM would say if they knew their expensive, elaborate installation for the Ginsberg Hospital was being serviced by one of the inmates.

He let some time pass in silence, not being in the mood for casual chat, but eventually he forced himself to speak at random. It couldn't be very pleasant for Madison to be the only knee in the entire hospital; he deserved to be talked to whenever the chance arose.

"Ah—Harry!" Reedeth picked on the only subject he could call to mind. "That damned machine you're fixing: know why it quit on me?"

"Well, you gave it something it couldn't handle, I guess." Madison didn't look up from his work.

Reedeth snorted. "I was describing Dr. Spoelstra to

33

it, and some damned censor-circuit must have cut in. It's ridiculous!" He heard his tone growing heated and was unable to prevent it. "Who's supposed to be in charge around here, me or some arrogant computer with a load of its designer's prejudices built in? I mean, I hadn't said anything more—more detailed about Dr. Spoelstra than you could see by just looking at her!"

He caught himself, gave an embarrassed grin, and turned back to the window. Did Madison ever talk about his therapists with the other patients? It wasn't likely, in view of the high-order segregation Mogshack insisted on: not only racial, religious, sexual and all the other commonplace social boundaries, but also categories of mental disorder formed dividing lines within the hospital.

If he did, though, so what? He'd only be discussing a shared area of experience. Even if it constituted an invasion of privacy—a view which on the intellectual level Reedeth would have been prepared to contest after his third or fourth drink—the staff members were necessarily of object status to the patients, part of the environment like furniture and lamp-posts.

Another minute or two passed, he grumpily gazing out of the window, Madison occupied with supervising the reparobot. Finally there was a discreet cough, and Reedeth turned to find the kneeblank standing by the door awaiting re-admission to the corridor beyond. The automatics permitted staff members to leave an office without waiting for the assigned occupant's authority— something Reedeth had frequently found a nuisance when Ariadne Spoelstra chose to cut short one of their all too frequent arguments—but an inmate had to be let out, to prevent him running away from therapy.

Sighing, Reedeth gave the necessary order; the door slid aside, and man and machine departed.

Abruptly yielding to an impulse that was likely to involve him in arguments not just with Ariadne but with Mogshack himself, he said to the now functioning desketary, "Damn it, I hadn't finished telling you about Dr. Spoelstra when you went on the blink! Now you just sit there and listen, hear?"

Without allowing time for a response, he categorized those other anatomical attributes of his colleague which he so violently craved and so seldom enjoyed as he would have wished, until at last he ran out of breath in a welter of crude Anglo-Saxon terminology. At the back of his mind was the vague idea that he could make the red light flash again, and armed with this incontrovertible evidence he could make a formal complaint to Mogshack about the inability of the automatics to cope with the regular language of an abreactive therapy session.

But the lamp remained dark. The desketary merely said in its ordinary voice, "Very good, doctor. I have stored those data. Are they for general release to the staff or to yourself only?"

"Myself only!" Heavens, if Mogshack were to take it into his head to review Ariadne's file and found that outburst on it duly credited "authority of Dr. Reedeth" ... !

But how come the machine had accepted the unashamed obscenity of what he had just said, whereas before it had broken down under what was actually no more than a bunch of compliments? He felt sweat prickle on forehead, nape and palms. The reparobot couldn't have intervened; it was strictly programmed to restore the authorized status quo. So it could only have been ...

Excitement gripped him. He sat down hastily behind the desketary and set about establishing whether that was the only improvement Madison had carried out.

It wasn't.

Twenty minutes later, tugging at his beard in a repeated gesture of impotent anger, he came to grips at last with the suspicion that had been haunting him for months.

It's a monstrous injustice, keeping Harry Madison here. It isn't that he's crazy. Maybe he never has been crazy. We just don't understand the peculiar way in which he is sane.

TEN

THE BLACKER THE BURY THE NEATER THE RUSE

Waiting for clearance at the frontier, Fredrick Campbell held his briefcase—symbol of official status—before him like a ridiculous cardboard shield. The hands which gripped it were slippery with sweat. Overflights were not in the city-federal contract here; he had had to ground his skimmer a hundred meters back along the decaying concrete of the ancient freeway and walk to the point where he now stood among a kind of mushroom-forest of lidded concrete tubs. From slits around their rims dark suspicious eyes focused on him, and he knew that invisible hands were poised to let loose a landslide of destruction on him if he made one unprogrammed move.

Looking straight ahead, he contrived to shift his eyes enough to determine that one of the Gottschalks had been here since his last visit—and a senior polly at that, perhaps one of the really top-level reps like Bapuji or even Olayinka. No monosyllabic would be entitled to dispose of the kind of equipment which betrayed itself to his trained scrutiny. But weaponry analysis wasn't in his official brief; Bustafedrel was careful to maintain the traditional fiction that armaments were irrelevant to their negotiations with municipal co-contractors. Doubtless, of course, during the next few days someone from ISM would drop by —casually—and raise the matter while chatting to him, but he wasn't expected to bring back detailed information.

He was profoundly grateful. He felt horribly naked out here. He felt, in a word, flayed. Which was exactly the effect Mayor Black must have wanted to produce. This whole transaction could far more easily and quickly have been conducted by comweb, but then it would have denied him the opportunity to gloat.

Lonely, perspiring in the cruel summer sunlight, he found his eyes settling once more on the signs adjacent to the main guardpost. They said: BLACKBURY, FORMERLY BROWNBURY.

One of them also said (but this was not part of the original wording, only a scrawled addition in hard-gloss paint): *Honky dont let the sun shin on you head it make you an easy target.*

"Talk about a Red Queen's Race," Matthew Flamen said moodily, dialing a drink from the liquor console in his compulsorily well-appointed office deep in the Etchmark Undertower.

"What?" The round face of Lionel Prior, which had appeared one moment earlier in the lifesize comweb screen, stared at him blankly. Prior was Flamen's manager, agent, chief confidant and universal dogsbody. He was also his brother-in-law, but that was the least important part of their relationship.

"Lewis Carroll," Flamen said. "Running as hard as you can and only managing to stay in the same place."

"You mean it's from a book?"

"Sure it's from a book. Don't tell me—don't tell me!" Flamen raised a weary hand; finding it had picked up the waiting drink on its way, he sipped. "You don't read books because they contaminate the purity of your approach to the medium. One of these days it's going to dawn on you that it also makes you ignorant and ill-educated. What the—?"

In the middle of his last utterance, Prior had disappeared and a swirl of multicolored blobs now filled the screen, accompanied by a very faint but disturbing howl as of a mad dog lost in fog far off across a haunted marsh.

On the wall of the duplex penthouse home of Michaela Baxendale, nineteen-year-old sensaysh—still; only just still; it had been a long run since age fifteen—a large automatic meter displayed a swinging needle which this morning had edged into the red zone of the dial. Time for another spell of work.

Cursing, she walked naked around the eleven rooms into which the current party had spread, kicking as many bodies as she could into wakefulness, ordering them to drag out the ones which were completely inert. Having dialed the robots to clear away the broken furniture and the soiled rugs and fetch some new ones, she started gathering up the material that came to hand. There was a satch filter in the comweb slot which routed advertising circulars directly to the sewers, but one item had evaded it: yet another stern letter from the city sanitation authority complaining about the lack of toilets in the apt. She'd had them taken out and enjoyed watching them crash forty-five stories to the street.

She re-composed her standard reply: "I was picked out of the gutter, wasn't I? You can't expect me to lose my gutter habits overnight!" It had been a clincher four years ago when Dan Kazer launched her upwards towards penthouse level. It made a mess of things, but what the hell? There were always more things. Besides, some troubledome out in Omaha was compiling a thesis on the significance of bodily effluents in the later works of Michaela Baxendale. It wouldn't be fair to undermine him.

Along with the letter, then: a 1979 Johannesburg phone directory, a pre-pseudorganic edition of *The Golden Bough,* a Krafft-Ebing which retained the original Latin passages—that would do. She spliced chunks of them together and by nightfall the meter on the wall was healthily back into the green.

Prior's picture came back and he was scowling. "That
settles it!" he fumed. "Don't we have enough trouble already without our own comweb right here in the Etchmark going into some crazy orbit?"

"You want to talk without being interrupted, darl,"
Flamen said wearily, "you just shift your butt over here.
Hell, you're only the other side of that wall!" Not that
that invitation was likely to be very well received, he
glossed silently. Prior was a totally different personality
from himself, with strong neo-puritan leanings, and his
commitment to the principle of keeping a spoolpigeon
show on the beams seemed to be rooted not so much in
an abstract dislike of hypocrisy—which was what Flamen liked to think of as his own standpoint—as in a wish
to improve the mask of proper social behavior, the im-
pervious coffin to hide the corruption within. Hence he
kept his distance, dealt with people by choice via a comweb screen, feeling face to face contact a waste of the facilities which financial success had brought to him. It
made him a perfect buffer in negotiations between Matthew Flamen Inc. and the Holocosmic directorate, but
sometimes it became ridiculous.

For example, now.

Exactly as predicted, Prior said huffily, "Matthew, one
doesn't expect to have to—"

Abruptly Flamen ran out of patience. "On the contrary, one *does* expect to have to! Unless one does something to cure the trouble! How many breaks did we have on today's show—five, was it?"

"Ah . . ." Prior swallowed. "Yes, I'm afraid so. And the longest ran nearly fifty seconds."

"And in the face of that you think it's surprising when our comweb goes wrong? Come off it, Lionel, you aren't that naïve! Or—well, come to think of it, maybe you are, the way you abase yourself by kowtowing in front of that lump of plastic you call a Lar!"

"Matthew, a man's personal choice of religion is—"

"When did you last bother to check our own computers? We have seventy-plus in favor of L&P being a college-educated front for that kneeblank outfit Conjuh Man Inc. Pickings from the black enclaves apparently aren't enough for them, so they've decided to expand and milk some gullible blanks as well. If you're anything to judge by, they're going to be a roaring success on a par with the Gottschalks!"

Prior's eyes bulged. Cruelly Flamen gambled on his habitual unwillingness to be seen giving way to emotion even in the presence of someone he had worked with for years. He let silence stretch elastically; then, at the last possible moment, brought up the *important* subject again.

"What did you call me about, anyway? Got some brilliant idea for tomorrow's slot which will drag the viewers back by the millions?"

Recovering with an effort from the shock Flamen had administered, Prior mumbled, "Well, the audience figures are holding up pretty well, considering. And that's mainly what counts, I guess."

"So if they're holding up why do the interruptions make you so furious? Darl, you know as well as I do that if someone carried out a physical check of the sets that are nominally tuned to my show, they'd find that half of them have the color and hold controls deliberately set adrift. Who watches three-vee at midday nowadays except while they're orbiting? Hell, the viewers probably even like the interference!"

Looking anxious, Prior came back with a reflex answer. "Matthew, you're too modest. You're one of only a handful of people who can still hold an audience for a talking show. You mustn't run down your own talents."

"I don't have to. It gets done for me." Flamen sent the rest of his drink down in one long gulp; when it struck the pit of his stomach he felt marginally better. "Do me a favor, darl—think for a moment, hm? Does this mysterious interference ever hit during a commercial? It does not. Does it even hit when we have a good juicy piece of tape from the site and scene of some nauseous scandal? Uh-uh. It hits when I'm on camera and at no other time. Truth, darl?"

Prior would have liked to contest the statement, by his expression, but the facts were self-evident. He nodded sadly.

Flamen set his glass in position for a refill and hit the console stud. "So what you want I should do?" he said. "Have the situation comped? Darl, why should I need to? Recall the background: they eased us out of prime time with the bribe of fifteen minutes daily instead of ten, didn't they? Then they chopped down the bonus with extra advertising. Fine, it's a convincing argument—here's this fabulous audience that more and more sponsors want to reach—but the fact stands that our fifteen-minute slot is down to twelve and a half and apt to get shorter still. Meanwhile the number of items we have comped out on network say-so rises steadily. Don't you think they're being a trifle over-sensitive for people who want to hold an audience?"

He paused, but Prior didn't say anything.

"I read it this way," he resumed. "They can't afford to simply show me the exit—I'd collect a palladium-plated handshake for breach of contract. So they're merely hoping I'll get annoyed enough to start yelling, when they could clobber me for like insulting the Head of Programming and the PCC wouldn't be able to touch them. So I suggest you make like me and hang on as long as you can. A hundred thousand tealeaves a month isn't something you can collect by knocking on the first door you pass."

Halfway through the last sentence Prior stopped paying attention. Flamen deduced from his expression that at his end the screen had either switched to another picture or blurred out altogether again. He made to cut the circuit, but changed his mind. It was amusing to watch the normally imperturbable Prior mouthing curses which couldn't be heard because at the same time as the vision outward had failed so had the sound inward.

But his enjoyment was short-lived. His smile vanished as he reverted to contemplation of the truth which Prior was resolutely declining to face for some such superficial reason, perhaps, as the idea that the directors of the Holocosmic network were—like Brutus—"honorable men."

"A man can smile and smile and be a villain," he murmured, briefly pleased with the aptness of the quotation but almost at once dismayed by the image of the smiler with the knife. What other explanation could there be for the interference which was cropping up daily on his program and on no other transmission from the Holocosmic studios? It simply *had* to be sabotage.

Worse yet, it must be connived at by the directorate. Had it been due to infiltrators, Holocosmic would have stopped at nothing to eliminate it; they were as concerned as any company in the world about maintaining internal security. Instead of which, again and again the engineers had fobbed him off with declarations of their inability to trace the trouble.

The logical conclusion was that they wanted to move his slot over and make room for yet another all-advertising segment. It was against the regulations laid down by the Planetary Communications Commission, of course, to run more than twelve hours' continuous advertising out of the twenty-four, and getting rid of their last spool-pigeon would take Holocosmic over the prescribed limit. But the PCC was a bad joke and had been for years: an ancient watchdog without any teeth.

It wasn't the first time they'd attempted to mislay him, moreover. They'd tried it directly following Celia's breakdown, hiring a venial psychiatrist to testify that her resorting to sykes was due to her husband's systematic disregard of her needs and preferences, this constituting sadistic cruelty. A person capable of such behavior, they'd argued, was unfit to perform before the great viewing public. (Horse laugh—if you dug into the private lives of the Holocosmic directorate you'd come up with material for another *Hundred and Twenty Days* without the need to plagiarize, and long ago Flamen had made himself a quiet promise that if they ever squeezed him hard enough he'd go out in a blaze of glory by swapping his last-ever taped show, duly approved by the network's computers, for another in which he gave chapter and verse on the directorate's vices.)

Their real lever, though, had been fulcrumed on her commitment to the Ginsberg, a public hospital, instead of to a private sanitarium, and that Prior had miraculously undermined in the shocked tones of an adoring brother: whose reputation stood higher in the contemporary world than that of Elias Mogshack its director, universally acknowledged field-leader in remedial psychiatry—who here among admitted laymen would question the brilliance of one appointed to oversee the mental hygiene of populous New York? So, a rapid compromise whereby he undertook to meet the cost of her incarceration himself instead of leaving her as a charge on public funds, and consequent inevitable disaster.

At the time Flamen had wondered why the directorate gave ground so swiftly. He stopped wondering the moment the first of the swingeing monthly bills arrived, together with the unchallengeable State-comped contract to which he had carelessly committed himself. He didn't have to consult a computer to discover that he was cornered. And he couldn't provide a cushion by, say, moving to a less expensive house. He was compelled to maintain that standard of living which was quote appropriate unquote for a person to whom Holocosmic allotted five slots a week. His accountants were first-rate and his tax demands were laughable, but he couldn't weasel out of his obligatory expenditures. He was defeated before he started by the scale of Holocosmic's computers; his own were good, but for equipment like theirs you had to hire computers like his to write the programs— no human being could manage it.

So knowing the knife was in: what to do? Make overtures to a rival network? Suicide—apart from the obvious truism that when only one spoolpigeon had managed to stay in business no network was likely to be interested in hiring a newcomer, he'd be dropped on his butt within hours on some specious but adhesive charge such as disloyalty to his employers. Also he would instantly stop being able to meet Celia's hospital bills out of income, and the penalty for premature removal was colossal. Though Mogshack's last report had been cautiously optimistic, it was clear that Celia was not by any means fully recovered. So that left one possible solution: hold his audience. Somehow. Anyhow. It was his only resource, the computer factor which showed a higher rating for him personally, Matthew Flamen, than for an all-advertising segment.

And in an age when people were far too preoccupied with their own business for even the most savory scandal and gossip to attract their attention . . .

Definitely a Red Queen's Race, he told himself. *And I'm running short of breath.*

47

FOURTEEN AN OBJECT LESSON CONCERNING A VERY IMPORTANT SUBJECT

Eugene Voigt didn't go quite so far as to turn off his screen, but he did disconnect his ears after the first minute or so of the eager-beaver's diatribe. They were an excellent design, by far the best he had ever worn, and he liked the location of the silence trigger particularly; it was concealed under the drooping eaves of his moustache and could be inconspicuously activated by a mere touch of the tongue. Besides, it was offered as a regular feature instead of as a customized option. It would be worth sticking with this brand for a while—at least until rival manufacturers overtook it. And it was hard to discern what room was left for improvements short of direct sub-dermal implantation.

The eager-beaver (his name was irrelevant but he held a resonantly-titled post in the lower echelons of the PCC) kept talking for a full quarter of an hour, but Voigt had realized what he was going to say within the first few seconds and none of the phrases he caught by idle lip-reading contradicted his first guesstimate. When the tirade finally subsided he said, "Forget it. It won't work."

"But Holocosmic clearly intends to—"

"You won't make it stick," Voigt told him firmly. "You won't make anything stick. The subject of communications, on this planet of ours, is dead."

FIFTEEN   IT'S A COMMON PLATITUDE THAT
KNOWLEDGE IS NEUTRAL BUT EVERY
NOW AND THEN IT WOULD BE USE-
FUL IF IT WERE ON YOUR SIDE RATHER
THAN THEIRS

It was hot outside; it was much hotter inside because
the lighting was old-fashioned and there had to be a
hell of a lot of it. Pedro Diablo's dark skin shone with
perspiration. But his white teeth shone even brighter.
He was enjoying himself.

"One final time!" he coaxed. "I swear they're going to
lap this up in Conakry and Lumumbaville!"

The actress playing King Leopold of the Belgians
sighed and replaced her pale, effeminate, beardless
whole-head mask, then trotted obediently across the
studio floor to her place for the scene, her bottom wag-
gling as she went. Down to her waist she was wearing
a full-dress military uniform jacket, the breast ablaze
with orders and decorations, but her steatopygous buttocks were concealed by nothing more than a sort of
docked horsetail of grass-stems. It was a great image,
especially for areas where there was strong Muslim influence and the concomitant view prevailed that women
had no souls.

"Got those fetters ready?" Diablo called to the props
man. "Remember I want them to break a sight easier
this time than they did last! Bad associations if they

take longer than five seconds—out of time-scale with the rest of the show. What the hell?"

He stopped dead in the very middle of the floor, on his way back to the control bubble, and realized that there were two armed macoots facing him.

"The Mayor wants to see you," the one on the right said. His tall plastic mask—black-grounded, but with slashes of red, yellow and brown on the cheeks—made his voice resonate eerily.

"Tell him to wait!" Diablo snapped. There were very few people in Blackbury who could say that sort of thing to a macoot, but he'd been doing it for years. "I'm right in the middle of a show—can't you see?"

The second macoot drew a casual smoking line on the floor with a low-powered beam from his laser. "He said now, white trash. You coming on foot, or as butcher's meat?"

"*What* did you call me?" Furious, Diablo took half a pace forward, then canceled the movement as the laser's muzzle jerked upward significantly. Those guns were the legacy of Anthony Gottschalk's last visit; he'd recently canned a show about them—in which for obvious propaganda reasons they were reported as having been developed right here in the city—and he had no illusions about the effect of concentrating two hundred fifty watts in a space no larger than the tip of a sewing-needle.

There was an eternal pause. Eventually he said, "Okay. *O*-kay. But I sure hope he doesn't hang me up too long." And he added to his cast and technicians as he moved towards the door, "See you back here after lunch, you-all!"

Awaiting him at the studio entrance was a black official Voortrekker convertible, the Capetown-built skimmer-cum-groundcar which was the world's most expensive means of private transport. Mayor Black owned six of them personally, a matter about which Diablo had

never been entirely happy despite the rationalization
that the South Africans and the American knees were
allegedly on the same side in the ultimate analysis;
the argument smacked too much of the similar one
which had justified the admission of Black Muslims to
meetings of the Ku Klux Klan back in the last century.
He scowled more deeply still as he was forced into the
back seat of the Voortrekker by the macoots, who joined
him, one on each side. The vehicle hummed off in the
direction of the Mayor's palace, the way ahead being
cleared by the remote override which put the stop
lights to red on all the cross streets at the touch of a
button on the dash.

In spite of everything, Diablo sat with his mouth
firmly shut. He had no idea what could have led up
to this, but his best guess was that Mayor Black had got
out of bed on the wrong side this morning. When he
was in that sort of mood, he tended to enjoy re-asserting
his authority over anyone who contributed to the econo-
my of Blackbury, and Diablo certainly fell into that
category. His canned vushows were among the city's
chief sources of foreign exchange, quite apart from their
propaganda value, and it had revolutionized their relationship with the American Federal authorities when
they started to be able to pay their power and water
taxes in hard currency like cedi and riyals.

He made a mental note to trace the macoot who
had publicly insulted him and make sure his future
was blacker than his backside. It would be difficult, in
view of his issue mask, but in a small community like
this one it wouldn't be impossible.

Regardless of that, though, he kept telling himself,
someone with Pedro Diablo's status had no reason to be
afraid of a fit of bad temper on the Mayor's part.

He kept on telling himself so until he was actually
shown into the Mayor's presence—if you could call being
herded into a room at gunpoint "being shown." For
Mayor Black was not alone. Seated next to his enormous

desk was a honky: a thin man with a straggly apology for a beard supplemented by mismatched rozar flock, very pale hair combed carefully across the pink baldness of his crown, knees primly together and hands folded on his lap.

Then Diablo's heart sank like a stone in a deep well. He knew that stern, thin-lipped face. The features of Herman Uys, top South African expert on race, were perhaps as well known as any in the modern world.

He was still struggling to work out why Uys's presence in Blackbury had been kept secret from him, Pedro Diablo, when the Mayor uttered his only statement of the interview.

"Out of town, mongrel. You have three hours."

SIXTEEN

THE POINT AT WHICH THE OUTLAY
ON MAINTENANCE BEGINS TO EX-
CEED THE COST OF CHANGING TO
A REPLACEMENT

Without warning Flamen's comweb circuit reverted
to normal and he found himself back in touch with Prior.
The moment he realized, the latter's face took on a
shifty expression which Flamen recognized from years
of close association: the look which signified that he was
about to put over some really monstrous con job on the
assumption—almost always justified—that the person
he was dealing with had overlooked some very subtle
trap. He might be naïve in some matters, as witness his
ready acceptance of a Lar as everything the advertising
claimed, but when it came to closing a deal weighted
in his own favor he was brilliantly devious. That, chiefly,
was why Flamen put up with him. He had never dared
tarnish his own image of himself by learning the whore's-
trading skills required to keep afloat in the cut-throat
ocean of modern business, yet he correspondingly did
not dare to forgo them altogether. Prior was a perfect
compromise: the epitome of self-deluded honor, who
could dismiss the most flagrant kind of cheating from
his conscience on the grounds that *he* had thought of it
and *he* could not possibly be a dishonest man.

Flamen tensed. If he, now, was to become the target
for Prior's personal talent . . .

"Matthew, as far as I can comp it out," Prior began, "you just made a very serious charge against the directorate of Holocosmic."

"I don't recall making any sort of charge against anyone," Flamen said hastily. "But if you have something important and urgent to say, why not . . . ?"

He cast around in his mind for a chance of privacy. Everything said over the comweb in these offices, as in the offices of any firm contracted to the Holocosmic network, was monitored, analyzed and if necessary relayed to the directorate. Ah yes!

"Why not ride out to the Ginsberg with me and call on Celia?"

"Not this afternoon," Prior said.

"Oh, come now! She's your sister as well as my wife, remember." A hamhanded attempt to get something discreditable on the record; it failed.

"I'm booked for exercises with my citidef group," Prior said, ever the solid, responsible member of society. "Besides, you know that Dr. Mogshack disapproves of intrusions from his patients' former environment, and I wouldn't care to go against his judgment."

"I regard contact between husband and wife as highly normalizing, even if he doesn't." The juiceless old stick, Flamen added to himself—but it wouldn't do to utter the comment aloud, not when he had so narrowly scraped under the blade of Holocosmic's guillotine by appealing to Mogshack's reputation.

"That's as may be," Prior shrugged. "Nonetheless, the point I'm getting at is this." He hesitated, with an air of calculation. "Matthew, to be blunt, I think you're becoming a trifle paranoid about this trouble we're having on the show. While I concede"—switch to reasonable concession-making tone—"it's debatable whether Holocosmic can be said to have afforded us maximal cooperation in our attempts to eliminate the interference fouling up our transmissions, it's something else altogether to associate that with failures of our internal comweb here at the Etchmark." Back to stern, fatherly manner, though he was only three years Flamen's senior: the standard rôle of the knowledgeable worldly manager protecting the admirably idealistic star of the show from his own lack of cynicism.

"So I suggest," he concluded, "you authorize me to call in an outside expert to substantiate these suspicions of yours. They're far too grave to be allowed to pass unchallenged."

Flamen stared at him incredulously. Outside expert? Had Prior taken leave of his senses? What "outside expert" could outfox Holocosmic's own computers—what court could anyone persuade to believe in the fantastic notion of a major network sabotaging its own transmissions? Only one explanation occurred to him for Prior's extraordinary behavior, and before he had time to think it over the pressure of anger had driven him to blurt it out.

"What happened to put *you* on Holocosmic's side all of a sudden? Did one of the brass take you out of bugging range and make you a proposition? No matter what kind of a minefield I'm driven into, *I* can't jump clear! I have bugs keeping watch on my bugs!"

He was distantly aware that the look on Prior's face had shifted from smugness to pure horror, but he plunged on anyway. "And if I could afford bugging to that standard, you're the first person I'd sic 'em on! Not wanting to go visit your own sister when she's in the hospital!"

He cut the circuit with a trembling hand before he said anything more damaging to his prospects. If that particular exchange ever came up in court, he reflected bitterly, he'd be hard put to it to argue that concern for Celia had motivated his temporary loss of control. The suggestion of calling on her this afternoon had been strictly a spur-of-the-moment improvisation so that he could talk to Prior out of eavesdropping range.

But it would have to be done now, of course. Scowling, he headed for the door.

Almost immediately, to his horror and dismay, he realized just how over-hasty his reaction to Prior had been, but he put off facing the consequences as long as he could.

SEVENTEEN   IF "MEDIA" IS THE PLURAL OF "MEDIUM" THE QUESTION IS: HOW MANY OF THEM ARE FRAUDULENT?

"Have I ever watched a pythoness perform?" repeated Xavier Conroy, over the border up Canada way. This was a crummy run-down poverty-stricken sort of a college, but living far enough in the past not to mind that his reputation was a horse-drawn hearse for his career. "No, I never have. But the phenomenon is interesting, and well worth discussing. How do you view it?"

The boy who had asked the question stumbletongued. "I—I guess I don't really know."

"You ought to have formed at least a tentative conclusion, though. It's a subject which fans out with all kinds of stimulating and provocative implications. Come to think of it, there's one place at which it touches directly on what I've been saying recently about the increasing reluctance of people to commit themselves to anything without a watertight contract, preferably computerized. So we could do worse than make it the class assignment for the week. I'll give you a few guidelines first." Conroy combed his grizzled beard with his fingers and corrugated his brow deeply.

"One might well start by considering the nineteenth-century cult of spiritualism, table-rapping and table-turning, attempts to commune with the dead and the readiness of the public to go on believing in patently charla-

tanous mediums. Now that was effectively conditioned
by the rigid propriety of Victorian society. What started
off as a perfectly proper and indeed quite scientific
investigation of certain improbable phenomena developed
in an age of tight corsets and strict social etiquette into
a desperate, irrational yearning for direct contact between individuals. Yes?"

A girl in the front row, whose name he knew to be
Alice Clover because it was on the illuminated reference
board before him but whose face he was completely
ignorant of because at every class since the beginning
of the year she had kept her street yash on, had raised
her hand.

"Do you mean that it's irrational to pay attention to
pythonesses?"

Conroy hesitated, looking over the array of students
and taking especial note of the girls. About a quarter
of them were in street yashes, like Alice who had just
spoken; the remainder wore a fantastic galaxy of cos-
tumes ranging from a height-of-last-year-fashion oversuit with inflated bosom and buttocks to a waist-length
orange wig and a pair of shabby Nix.

"Who am I to define what's rational?" he said wearily.
"I mean no more and no less than I say. You comp it
out for yourselves."

EIGHTEEN   THE DRAWBACKS OF AN INVENTION
INTENDED FOR A RATIONAL SPECIES

Seeing Reedeth awaiting her at the point where this and another corridor joined, Ariadne Spoelstra would have liked to turn around and go back. Currently her planned program for the relationship between them was at the stage where physical proximity was being discouraged—and that, of course, was why he had chosen to waylay her. "Lying in ambush" was the term that sprang most readily to her mind; the bastions of the Ginsberg were conducive to imagery of snares and pitfalls, traps and gins.

But she was on a pediflow, and—like so many of the devices which twenty-first century ingenuity had made available to mankind—that was something which seemed to have been destined for an altogether more rational species than the one she belonged to. It did not afford the opportunity to change one's mind. Once riding it, one was compelled to stay with it until it reached the quiescent area at an intersection and the monomolecular flow level on the upper surface eddied out into a random pattern equating to stillness. There was no going back, only continuing to one's starting point by a different route.

In the course of the ten years they'd been in use, how many affairs had been conditioned by the direction the pediflow happened to take outside one's office or apt? How many acquaintanceships, how many marriages . . . ? How many perfect lifetime partners had been on the flow heading the other way?

Stifling that train of thought with an almost physical effort, she composed herself for the properly curt nod and the unmistakably formal smile which were appropriate to the down-phase of the cycle of their intimacy. Reedeth, however, was clearly not in a mood to abide by other people's rules. She had to suffer him to kiss her, though she did manage to avert her mouth.

"Finally!" he exclaimed. "I've been wanting to talk with you, and—"

"I've been on call all morning," she countered frigidly.

"Sorry, but that isn't true. You put up a Class Two interdiction at ten-ten, according to my desketary, and it wasn't lifted until a few minutes ago. Hmmm?" He cocked one eyebrow and looked parentally reproachful.

Bastard! But the gamble had failed. She had hoped the dialogue might go:

"Yes, but I wanted to say this personally!"

In which case she would have answered, "What's the good of having a comweb system if you won't use it?"

And walked briskly on, having gained a major point.

Instead of which she'd been caught in a downright lie. She sought the least damaging escape route, like a chessplayer trying to reconstruct a weak attack to provide emergency protection for the king.

"Well, if it was really important you could have overridden, and if it wasn't why come bothering me now?"

"That's just it," Reedeth shrugged. "I don't know if it's important or not—that's what I wanted to ask you. This pythoness you've engaged for this afternoon: who is she, anyway, and what's the idea?"

Chance for a counterblow. "That's something you could have asked your desketary. The information was minuted to all staff members three days ago."

"As a *fait accompli*. With his customary secretiveness

Mogshack failed to make his discussion with you available for consultation by the staff."

"He probably didn't think it was necessary—any more than I would have. Just what is it that you want to be told? What a pythoness is, what she does, how she does it?"

"Oh, for God's sake, Ariadne!" Reedeth's affability vanished like smoke before a gale. "Don't you have a better peg to hang your life on than making men dance up and down like yoyos? If you're that badly obsessed with your own emotional dependence, you'd better take a vacation and get over it before you communicate the problem to your patients!"

She stared at him blankly, unable to believe that it was Jim Reedeth who had uttered such words. They were more typical of Mogshack himself, whose single-minded dedication to the principles he preached was sometimes terrifying, even though in arguments she had often enough compared it to the attitude of a Buddha voluntarily renouncing the bliss of nirvana in order to share the chance of perfect enlightenment with less fortunate beings.

It didn't take a trained psychologist's insight to deduce that something had happened to drive Reedeth a long way out of his customary orbit.

Reluctantly answering his former question before he had a chance to say anything else as cruel as his last gibe, she said,

NINETEEN

THOUGHT PASSING REPEATEDLY THROUGH THE HEAD OF MORTON LENIGO, FIFTH GENERATION EXPATRIATE WEST INDIAN, FOURTH GENERATION BRITISH SUBJECT, THIRD GENERATION PAN-MELANIST, WHILE IN TRANSIT ACROSS THE ATLANTIC AFTER SECURING A VISA FOR THE UNITED STATES BY PULLING THE STRING WHICH LED TO THE KNEEBLANK CITY GOVERNMENT OF DETROIT THREATENING TO WITHDRAW THEIR WATER TAXES AND INSTALL AN ATMOSPHERIC CONDENSATION PLANT

"*Festung Amerika,* you monstrous Aryan bunker, it's time for the twilight of the sods!"

"Oh—very well. The underlying thinking goes like this. Whatever it is that pythonesses actually do, it seems they get results of some kind. The evidence is overwhelming. And the only way they could achieve the success that's ascribed to them is, presumably, because they display exceptionally high empathy with people who are relative strangers to them. I want to find out if the degree of 'strangeness' they can cope with extends to the mentally deranged. And since I'm assured that this girl Lyla Clay is one of the most talented of them, she's a logical choice for the experiment."

Reedeth rolled a strand of his beard absently between his fingers. "On the face of it, that's an excellent idea. It might lead to a whole new diagnostic technique if it pays off. But isn't three days rather short notice to put together such a potentially significant operation?"

"I contacted her mackero and this was the only date he could offer me until seven weeks from now. Apparently she's very much in demand."

She added caustically, "I'm flattered that you approve of the idea, I must say!"

"Oh, give it a rest, will you?" Reedeth snapped. "You may have quit trying to keep your private emotional entanglements from interfering with your work, but I'm at least still making the effort." And continuing with-

63

out giving time for a counterblast: "What does Mog-shack think of it? Obviously he gave approval in the end or you couldn't have set it up, but I'm surprised he didn't balk at packing a number of patients together in conditions—now how would he have put it? Ah yes! —in conditions that are not only medically insanitary but psychologically so perilous as to prejudice many of them on the road to recovery!"

"You bastard! You *have* been checking on the talk I had with him!"

"No, I told you: it isn't available. I just . . . Well, I just tried to pick the words he'd have been most likely to use."

For a long moment they stared at each other, face to face and much less than arm's length apart. Suddenly, quite against her will, Ariadne felt her mouth straining upwards at the corners. She resisted for a second, then gave in. *Il faut reculer pour mieux sauter,* she told herself, quoting one of Mogshack's own favorite aphorisms. One must go back to make a longer jump. And next time she jumped, she promised herself, it would be out of Jim Reedeth's reach.

"I still think you're a bastard, Jim. But there's no doubt you're a clever one. 'Psychologically perilous' was his exact phrase. . . . Mogshack can be a bit predictable sometimes, can't he? Though I suppose anybody who pursues one goal with unswerving determination is vulnerable to that charge."

Once more refuting her expectations, instead of answering her smile with one of his own, Reedeth frowned. "Yes, but I do sometimes wonder where singlemindedness shades over into fanaticism. . . . Never mind, though. At least he's shown flexibility in this matter. Like I said, I think it's a very promising idea. Anything which will tend to reinforce the broken bridges between one personality and another has my support."

Piqued at his failure to acknowledge her gesture of surrender, she said sharply, "That's a very Conroyan remark, Jim. And it isn't the purpose of the project, anyway."

"I'm being driven to the conclusion that the only way some people can be made to understand—"

But the expostulation, which had begun heatedly, lost its impetus and died away. Reedeth grinned. "Ah, hell. I'd rather compliment you on a bright idea than have a fight with you. Suppose we continue the conversation tonight, hm? I think it's about time for your winter to come to an end."

"Well . . ."

"Good, that's settled. And do you mind if I attend this afternoon's performance? I assume Mogshack will be there."

"No, he will not. He'll be witnessing it, of course, but from his office. And I think it would be better if you did the same."

"But there's a question I'd like to ask this pythoness myself, since you recommend her so strongly. And I understand pythonesses can't react to people unless they're actually in the room."

"A question? What about?" And her eyes said more loudly than words: *Not about us—you wouldn't dare!*

"Why, Ariadne!" Reedeth said in a mocking voice. "You're blushing! I've never seen you do that before. And it looks great on you!"

While she was still struggling to formulate her reply, there was a sweet shrill buzz from the personal communicator strapped to her left wrist. She raised it reflexively, looking daggers, and muttered, "Yes?"

"A visitor for a patient under your care, Dr. Spoelstra. Just landed on the roof in a private skimmer. Not at all cooperative. Demanding a Class A disruption of the programmed schedule."

"Hell. That is absolutely all I need right now!"

Not without malice, Reedeth uttered a deliberately loud chuckle.

"Oh . . . ! Very well, I'll come and see about that in a

moment!" She shut off the mike and raised blazing eyes to Reedeth's face.

"No, I won't have you attending the session this afternoon! You want to consult a pythoness, you go hire one of your own. And you'd better get a good one. Empathy's wasted if it doesn't work both ways, and *I* don't know anyone who could get through that armor-plated hide of yours!"

"Try," Reedeth said softly. "That's all I'm asking, you know. If you're scared to walk through a wide open door because you think something's going to fall on your head as soon as you cross the threshold, you're in trouble, darl!"

He spun on his heel, stepped over the boundary of the intersection. In a moment the pediflow had carried him out of earshot.

Not—Ariadne swore it to herself, barely preventing her foot from stamping—not that she had the least intention of calling after him. Not, in fact, that she ever wanted to speak to him again.

TWENTY-ONE   CLOSE THE DOORS, THEY'RE COMING
                          IN THE WINDOWS!

The jocular paranoia of the last-century song had at
first seemed apt to Celia Prior Flamen following her
commitment. Possibly it still was. But nowadays she
merely hummed its tune to herself. Singing it aloud was
pointless. No matter how much she raised her clear high
voice, the sound was soaked up by the layers and layers
of insulation on the walls of her luxurious retreat.

That was what they called the cells in the Ginsberg:
retreats.

She was thirty-five, a year younger than her husband
and four years younger than her brother, though Lionel
always looked, acted, and apparently felt at least a
decade her senior. She was also rather beautiful, having
a casque of sleek brown hair which she had never dyed
or patterned despite the dictates of fashion, framing a
heart-shaped face with an over-large but delightfully
mobile mouth, and a taut slim body which at one moment could suggest sensual languor, at the next nervous
tension barely held in check by sheer force of will.

But her mind, like a scalpel designed for healing and
used for murder, had gone too deep into a place it was
not intended to enter.

Watching her thoughtfully over the concealed comweb link—the camera was behind the mirror on the
dressing-table at which she spent much of her time cur-

67

rently, inventing new faces for herself from the lavish range of cosmetics with which she had been provided— Elias Mogshack fingered his beard. He was in a dilemma. It was not the first such, and doubtless it would not be the last. But to depart even for a moment from the transcendent certainty which the public at large associated with his name was an affront to the aura of authority that had gained him his present influence.

Paradox: on the one hand, the overriding command to "be an individual" which he, personally, had put into common speech as a taken-for-granted byword, with the concomitant implication that a schizophrenic, for example, was obeying that command to the letter; on the other, the all-too-obvious fact that someone who was *that* much of an individual was (a) nonviable because he might forget to eat or turn to sykes or do any of a score of other ultimately fatal things, and (b) excessively demanding of other, competing individuals, as for example insisting that they listen for hours and days to some universal insight which, boiled down, amounted to something most adults had worked out for themselves in their early teens.

He had a case of it right now; there were a dozen other subjects he would have deemed more worthy of his attention had he not been snagged by the question of Celia Prior Flamen.

In principle the methods which had so caught the imagination of the public that he had been railroaded into the post of director for the Ginsberg, willingly enough of course because he wanted to see as many unfortunates as possible benefit from his teaching, were very simple. In every retreat there were data-collecting devices that monitored the sewage, the surfaces of the bed and the chairs, the very air that the patient exhaled —parameters for the construction of a computerized curve calibrated against standard examples of all the known kinds of mental disorder. Causeless anxiety, self-induced stress-response, every possible type of deviation from cool was measured and projected into the future and interpreted as therapy: drugs, hypnotism, analysis, anything available. The target was likewise simple; one might define it as the production of a personality capable of functioning viably despite the pressures of other members of the species. An ideal personality profile was raised for each patient, a beautiful symmetrical curve, and when the observed profile matched the optimum the patient was discharged. Easy.

Except that in practice it wasn't easy at all. . . .

Take this case, for example. In theory it ought to have been absolutely straightforward. Celia Prior Flamen—like the majority of the patients here and in all other mental hospitals in the western world—had turned to sykes as an escape from intolerable reality, starting with relatively mild ones such as natural peyote and mescal and graduating to that fiercest of synthetics, Ladromide. Shattered to bits, wetting herself like a baby for the delirious pleasure of moist warmth between her legs, she had been carried here ignorant of the world.

And responded well to treatment.

?

Mogshack frowned. He looked again at the comparative curves his desketary projected for him: the green ideal, the red observed profile. There was a dent in the latter and there was no known therapy that would flatten it out. But the word was humming down the grapevine that her husband might not be able to meet the monthly bills much longer, and it was bad for the image to discharge a patient for financial reasons and then have him or her re-admitted as a charge on the state because the condition hadn't been cleared up permanently.

The dent reminded him of another similar problem—Madison's—but he preferred not to consider that. With a shrug he compromised by giving orders for Celia to be issued with a green oversuit in place of her previous pale blue one, and realized in passing that it would go much better with her dark brown hair.

TWENTY-TWO THE MORTON LENIGO STORY PART TEN THOUSAND (APPROXIMATELY)

The Boeing Sonicruiser this morning operating Pan Am Flight 1201 London-New York, having dutifully spent its bang over the ocean, stood on its jets and began to climb down the ladder of the air towards the ground. Six hundred and two of its seven hundred and five seats were taken this time, and one of the passengers had found the legend painted over the entry door ("Soniclipper Friendship") excruciatingly funny.

He was occupied in unpicking the stitches along the handle of his traveling bag. It would save the American customs the trouble.

Landing on the skimmer-park of the Ginsberg, Matthew Flamen thought as he glanced up at the tall maxecurity towers, was like parachuting among the stakes of some Brobdignagian picket fence. To picture human beings existing within those colossal blank pillars was to reduce them to the status of nematodes, burrowing under the bark of trees in utter ignorance of the greater world outside.

He was taken aback at the violence of the repulsion with which they filled him. On his former visits—few of them, granted, and the last one already months in the past—he had been inclined to envy Dr. Mogshack, wondering what it felt like to conceive an abstract principle and see it so splendidly interpreted in the form of a building.

Reaching in through the side window of his skimmer, he tapped the dispenser key on the underside of the dash. A small white trank dropped into his waiting palm, and he gulped it down. A nasty sneaking suspicion had been developing in his mind during the flight out to the hospital. He had jumped on Prior as though accusing him of treachery—as witness that gibe about one of the directorate taking him out of bugging range and making him a proposition—and the idea simply didn't stand up. Prior had at least as much to lose by the cancellation of the show as he did himself; in one sense he stood to lose even more, for he had children and Flamen didn't.

So the idea of calling in an independent expert to evaluate the trouble they were having with their internal comweb at the Etchmark Tower was in fact a damned good one. The investigation could convincingly be made to lead into a check on Holocosmic's own circuitry; for what it was worth, PCC backing could probably be obtained, and . . .

But it was a pipe-dream anyway, Flamen assured himself. Grant that it could be done—which was debatable, for what "outside expert" could be found to match Holocosmic's own computers?—grant that he could prove his case, be awarded damages, survive the nine remaining months of his contract . . . so what? Where else was there for a spoolpigeon to go? He belonged to a dying species. People were too busy minding their own business to care about anyone else's. They were turning inwards, to the ultimately private entertainment of subjective hallucinatory experience. They were each constructing a maxecurity tower, windowless, unbreachable.

Maybe Prior wasn't so wrong after all to have resorted to Lares & Penates Inc. In the face of this incomprehensibly complex modern world where the forces of economics and macroplanning reigned with the impersonal detachment of storm and drought, it might well be better for an individual to delude himself into believing that he could cope. Feigning confidence might indeed be superior to merely resigning oneself to one's own inadequacy.

What sort of a cult would L&P dream up for him? One like Prior's, involving elaborate posturing and ceremonial? Flamen shook his head. Regardless of whether L&P were really a blank-targeted subsidiary of Conjuh Man, there was no doubt they were excellent pragmatic psychologists. For him, therefore, they'd likely suggest a complete contrast: something rather nasty, demanding that he chop the heads off chickens and smear his face with their blood. Doing duty to one's Lar was supposed to externalize one's inward characteristics, and for somebody who had originally established himself in his career by systematically slaughtering reputations there was bound to be an element of sacrifice. . . .

The trank took hold. His mood lightened. But his irritation didn't pass away completely. How much longer was he going to be kept out here in the clammy heat of midsummer? No doubt it was decently cool inside, but here he was suffering the output from the conditioners beneath the skimmer-park, and one could almost have taken the air in one's hands and wrung it out like a washrag.

Getting into the Ginsberg, apparently, was on a par with getting out of it. There was only one means of access to the interior from this parking lot, and that was guarded by horribly logical automatics. His brief and frustrating dialogue with them had convinced him that they must divide the human race into three categories: staff, patients and potential patients. Short of throwing a crazy-looking fit, he couldn't see any alternative to staying put until this therapist—what was her name? Oh yes: Dr. Spoelstra—got to a comweb and talked to him.

Grumpily, he went on waiting.

Arriving at the Ginsberg's rapitrans terminal was like
being one dose of a drug administered orally in capsule
form. Rapitrans trains were segmented, tapeworm fashion, into compartments each seating one person; they
could be separated, shuffled, connected and discon-
nected to follow—according to the operating authority's
publicity—just under ten million different routes, dic-
tated by the electronically active tickets the travelers
had to insert into a slot in the arm-rest of each seat.
Once launched into the tunnels, they were hurtled along
by forces as unquestionable as gravity. There were no
windows to reveal whether there was another compartment ahead or behind, because at the speeds these things
traveled some people suffered from horizontigo—the
same as vertigo but at right angles—and the concomitant
nausea made a filthy mess of the seating.

Tickets for the rapitrans had come as part of the down
payment on the contract Dan had signed with the Ginsberg's management. Doubtless they wanted to ensure
that the cost of skimmer rental—which was very steep
these days—wasn't added to the bill for incidental expenses. But after the next-to-last stop Lyla's ride seemed
to go on and on and on. Clinging for comfort to the
recorder they employed to fix the cryptic oracles she
uttered during trance, she wondered if she were really
plunging alone into nowhere.

74

TWENTY-FIVE

A MODEL CITIZEN AND A CLIENT GREATLY VALUED BY HIS AREA GOTTSCHALK

Qty. 1 Mark XIX oversuit, insulated, with integral boots and gauntlets

Qty. 1 Helmask with integral respirator and aeration pack

Qty. 1 350-watt laser-gun with 50-shot accumulator rechargeable from domestic current

Qty. 1 Projectile side-arm caliber 9 mm., automatic

Qty. 3 Spare magazines for foregoing

Qty. 6 Untimed self-fragmenting glass emetic gas-grenades

Qty. 1 Baldric for grenades with attached pouch for magazines, etc.

Qty. 1 Sheath-knife with 18-cm. blade

Qty. 1 First-aid kit

The children were away in boarding-school and Nora was out calling on a neighbor so Lionel Prior collected his equipment and went to join his citidef group for their afternoon exercise.

TWENTY-SIX

THE ASSASSINATION OF THE MARAT/DE SADE BY THE INMATES OF THE ASYLUM AT 2014

At long last a human voice emerged from the speaker adjacent to the exit of the skimmer-park. The compatibility of the automatic voices was as good as any Flamen had ever heard, but his nervous sensitivity to subtleties of this order was among the talents which had kept him afloat, albeit precariously, in the world of vu-transmission long after his former rivals had capsized. In fact he had once broken open a major bribery scandal through recognizing that a custom-tailored automatic was answering calls for a man who ought not to have been able to afford such equipment.

"Dr. Spoelstra here, Mr. Flamen—what can I do for you?"

"You can let me see my wife," Flamen snapped. Somewhat to his surprise, he realized as he uttered the words that he really did want to see Celia, very much indeed. Their marriage had worn threadbare long before her actual breakdown, but in spite of falling out of love with her he had gone on liking her as a person. She could never, for example, have become boring, even though towards the end the way she stimulated him had narrowed down to one single channel: a gift for making him angry.

Better that, he told himself, than the kind of drab

pretense at respectability which Lionel Prior and his wife Nora maintained. And—more cynically—if it turned out that he really had mortally offended Prior this morning, he wouldn't want to be wholly without allies and confidants.

"You should have warned us to expect you today," Dr. Spoelstra responded equally curtly. "A comweb message has been sent to your home informing you of the good news that your wife has gone to green, as we put it—in other words, she's been upgraded to the status enjoyed by patients approaching the temporary discharge point—and in consequence she's been invited to be among the audience this afternoon at a performance by the well-known pythoness Miss Lyla Clay. I'm—"

"So that takes precedence over seeing her own husband?"

Stiffly: "There's no compulsion about it, Mr. Flamen! I was merely about to say that I'm sure she would be disappointed to have to miss this unique occasion. However, if you *insist* . . ."

"No, of course I don't insist," Flamen assured her hastily. Apart from other considerations, he couldn't afford to; Celia was in the Ginsberg on a monthly contract which ceded his legal guardianship of her to Dr. Mogshack, and the swingeing penalty clause for premature discharge was matched by one for premature reclamation of responsibility.

But something had gone click in his subconscious at the news he had just been given, and during the next few seconds an idea emerged that almost made him shake with excitement. A pythoness performing in a mental hospital . . . ? There had been that last-century classic about the assassination of the Marquis de Sade as performed by . . . No, that couldn't be right. But "by the inmates of the hospital at Charenton," anyway. Hmmm . . . !

It took him half a heartbeat to consider and discard the possibility of sending for extra cameras; the meterage he could collect with the equipment he always kept in the skimmer would probably do very well.

He began to talk again, rapidly and persuasively, laying maximum stress on the degree of imaginative insight which must have gone into mounting such a significant project.

TWENTY-SEVEN

THOUGHT PASSING REPEATEDLY THROUGH THE MIND OF AR-THUR J. HODDINOTT, UNITED STATES IMMIGRATION SERVICE OFFICER, ON DUTY AT KEN-NEDY INTERNATIONAL AIRPORT WHEN MORTON LENIGO AR-RIVED

"So the computers must have said it was okay but can't computers sometimes lose their marbles too?"

TWENTY-EIGHT   PROOF POSITIVE FOR THE ASSERTION THAT IT IS NOT IMPOSSIBLE FOR A GUTTER TO RUN AT PENTHOUSE LEVEL

Lyla Clay emerged onto the rapitrans platform, trembling. The tunnels themselves were under low pressure —had to be, or air resistance would have rendered their designed operating speeds impossible. So there was just this one access door, and the space beyond it was constricted, the very roof seeming to lean on her head. She had seen pictures of the Ginsberg, and knew that perhaps as much as two hundred meters of concrete and steel might be directly between her and the open sky. She bit her lip. The talent which had made her a pythoness with a growing reputation had its drawbacks, and excessively vivid imagination was one of them. For an endless moment she pictured herself being trapped here. She couldn't get back into the train compartment and hurtle away with it, for this was as far as her ticket carried her and the tickets for the homeward journey were in the pocket of Dan's breeches. So too was the pass which would get them through the barrier blocking access to the elevator for the upper levels.

Suppose his compartment had been misrouted? Once in a few million times that did happen, for all the reassuring propaganda to the contrary. He might have been sent to Far Rockaway or somewhere, and she'd have to stay here for hours and hours and . . .

But the door sighed open again and there he was, only a few seconds behind her. With perfect aplomb he marched towards the elevator; glad that her yash concealed her expression of relief, Lyla followed, wondering what it would be like to be thirty instead of twenty. Would she too gain that extra confidence after fifty percent more aware existence?

Waiting for their pass to be read by the scanners, she felt a desperate need to speak, and seized on the first words which sprang to mind.

"I don't like the atmosphere of this place," she said.

Dan glanced at her. "I'm not surprised. The air's probably permeated with the skin-secretions of schizophrenics. I hate the stink of mental hospitals, and I'm not what you'd call a sensitive type. Just put up with it for a while, though, darl. All kinds of things may come of this. According to what Dr. Spoelstra told me, we're setting a very important precedent this afternoon."

He chuckled. "Never had anyone so eager, know that? She was practically climbing down the comweb line to make sure she got you here today. I hate to think of all the other bookings we're going to have to postpone to accommodate her repeat orders!"

Other bookings? What other . . . ? Oh. Of course. A typical Dan Kazer con job, no doubt involving the later faking of contracts including penalty clauses and kickbacks to the cooperative acquaintances he'd persuaded to invent bookings purely in order to cancel them. One could easily add fifty percent to the proceeds from an engagement by setting it up that way.

She shrugged. It worked, and it was no more dishonest than half the "respectable" business deals put through in the course of an average year. Look what it had done for Mikki Baxendale, for example, four years ago when Dan was still macking for gutter poets instead of pythonesses.

Impulsively she said, "Dan, you never did tell me—what separated you from Michaela?" And, as she recognized the emerging expression on his face, the mask of stony anger colder than arctic ice, she added hastily, "It's my good luck, of course, but—well, I would like to know how I got it."

There was a pause. During it, the automatics conceded the validity of Dr. Spoelstra's signature on their pass, and the barrier before the elevator car slid aside.

Not moving to enter, Dan thought for a long moment, and finally spread his hands.

"Okay, I'll tell you. It's not the sort of trick anyone will pull on me twice. There was another mackero after her—a poacher. Bought a few bugs, planted them, got the evidence, came around one day and said if I didn't dissolve my contract with Mikki he'd sell me for a five-stretch because she was only fifteen." Jaw-muscles lumping at the bitter recollection caused ripples in his dark beard, the artificial flock faithfully parodying the movement of the natural hairs. "He wasn't interested in bedding her. He didn't care for girls."

"And . . ." Lyla swallowed hard. "And could he have done what he threatened?"

"Sure he could. But I'm not apologizing. By age fifteen Mikki knew more about that side of life than most people do by age fifty! The bastard's still using some of the publicity material I compiled for her. You must have seen it—her brother at nine, her uncle at twelve? It's all true."

"And that was okay, huh? But you at fifteen wasn't?"

Dan drew a deep breath, his face etched with a scowl like the traces of a heavy truck in soft ground. "Darl, if you can't answer that, you'll never get the measure of this planet of ours. Come on, they're waiting for us upstairs."

"I guess it was naïve of me," she agreed meekly, and complied.

TWENTY-NINE   IT IS ONE THING TO TALK GLIBLY
ABOUT THE DETERMINISM OF HIS-
TORY BUT ANOTHER THING ALTO-
GETHER TO FIND ONESELF CAUGHT
UP IN HISTORIC FORCES LIKE A
DEAD LEAF ON THE GALE

As the sun tilted away from the zenith, so the sus-
taining anger leaked away from Pedro Diablo's mind,
and he was suddenly brought face to face with an ap-
palling truth.

It's not hate. It's terror.

He looked at his own dark-skinned hand and watched
it shaking, detachedly, because he could not really accept that a trembling due to fear had its origins in the
mind that he Pedro Diablo was used to occupying. He
was a maker of fear, not a victim of it.

Here I am. How? Why?

The reasons were as many-layered as a constructional
sandwich of industrial plastics. Superficially one might
say—but what was the good of superficialities? The Diablo reputation was founded on the ability to look far
deeper into any given situation than most people could
manage without a computer handy to consult. An atavis-
tic talent, on a par with being able to multiply six-
figure numbers in the head because it was too much
trouble to go find the log-tables, but in a context like
Blackbury very damned useful indeed.

Out here, in the open so to speak . . . ?

He shook his head. It was no good trying to guess about his personal future. He could draw analogies with people in similar predicaments in the past—mainly in the far past—but nothing more. He could for example compare himself to a Jewish physicist thrown out of Nazi Germany, or one of the South African intellectuals deported during more recent crises by the Afrikaners, but it didn't help. Until this very morning he had been a loyal, cooperative, and indeed an admired and respected proponent of the ideals which Blackbury stood for. To be kicked out on the say-so not of one of the resident knee geneticists but of some stinking foreign honky—that was just too much for his mind to digest.

His hands folded into fists so abruptly there was a faint clapping sound. For an instant his mind had been dominated by lust for revenge. He was a master propagandist; his work at the insignificant Blackbury vu-station had had repercussions far beyond the range of the antennae, being rebroadcast by half a score of black-owned, black-financed satellite relays. With his long-term intimate knowledge of the private lives of Mayor Black and his counterparts elsewhere, he could make the whole notion of Negro enclaves into a bad joke. It would take a week.

But the desire was fading as rapidly as it had come. To turn his coat was beyond his powers of adaptation. Right now he almost regretted having been so dogmatic with the Federal rep who had been compelled to carry him out of black jurisdiction. Better, surely, to have taken time to think things over, perhaps look for employment outside North America . . .

Still, there it was. He had insisted on making it a matter of official record that the Blackbury-Washington contract be fulfilled, even though the very term made it certain that the contract must be an anachronism. This was still a honky country, but Washington had been a black-majority town for decades, and identifying it now with the Federal government was a mere symbol—the real seats of power were to be found in the dispersed centers set up during the war scare of the nineties, mostly in the Deep South where Mister Charley could be relied on to come running with gun in hand at the least threat of a knee revolt. Who should know that better than a man who'd exploited it often and often in his own programs?

His mind teemed with new possibilities. It wouldn't stop, and why should anyone expect it to? For ten years he'd fostered his talents; they couldn't be switched off like a vuset. Perhaps the cruelest thing Mayor Black had done to him, apart from taking a honky's say-so in deporting him, was depriving him of an outlet for his ideas. As though he were a time-traveler who'd spent years perfecting his Latin only to misfire and find the target city had been overrun by the Goths last week. . . .

On the other hand—and he brightened a trifle at the realization—he had been spared what would have happened in the inverse situation. Suppose some dark-skinned misfit had been deposited at the outskirts of Blackbury: instant directives would have come down telling the local vu-station to get him on the beams right away, coax him into virulent denunciation of his former friends before his wrath had cooled. It was as much to guard against that risk as because he was genuinely afraid of the way he might be treated that he had insisted on full compliance with the Blackbury-Washington contract.

But, as a mercy, he had been spared the expected siege of cameras and mikes, interviewers and political agents. He might have said, in his first outbreak of fury, things he couldn't have lived down. And after all it was Uys, the white Afrikaner, who had been at the bottom of his trouble. Venial, power-hungry, oversexed, whatever his faults might be, surely Mayor Black was too intelligent to go on undermining his own position! Sooner or later he was bound to realize that in dispensing with his internationally famous vu-man Pedro Diablo he was throwing away one of his most valuable weapons, and that that must be exactly what Uys had wanted in the first place!

There was a shrill buzzing sound. He jumped, then made the automatic mental correction. That was the noise a comweb made out here when someone was calling up. Back in Blackbury, of course, the call-sign was the thump of an African speaking drum uttering the Yoruba phrase for "come and listen." He was going to have to rid himself of a hell of a lot of ingrained reflexes, like a typist changing to a machine with a different keyboard layout. But he would just have to suffer in silence.

Sighing, he announced that he was ready to accept the call.

THIRTY

I AM BECOME AS A GOD, AND SEE
ALL THAT PASSES WITH THE EYE OF
AN EAGLE

It was almost surprising that a room large enough to
hold an audience of forty for the performance by the
pythoness had been incorporated in the design of the
hospital. The emphasis Mogshack placed on unbreachable privacy was so intense that there were no assembly
halls, open sitting-rooms nor even a gymnasium. Mogshack himself preferred not to deal with his staff face to
face; he "retired and regrouped" so frequently that weeks
might pass without even his senior assistants encounter-
ing him in the flesh.

However, worried for fear his plans might later need
to be altered in the light of experience, the architect
had insisted on some areas of the hospital being fitted
with retractable walls, and taking away half a dozen
of these in a sector temporarily not occupied by patients created a space adequate for the performance.

The audience had already begun to assemble when
Reedeth switched on his comweb screen to watch the
proceedings. He had never had the least intention of
insisting that he be physically present, but he had been
unable to resist the chance of making Ariadne blush.
He chuckled as he glanced over the green-clad patients
entering the room, but his amusement faded the instant

he realized that among the first of them was Harry Madison.

There must be some way to return that man to the outside world! Mogshack ought to have done it months ago; why he hadn't was hard to understand . . . unless (and a familiar demon rode the concept, snickering) he was indeed hoarding his patients like a miser. Perhaps one could confront him and argue that having one solitary kneeblank under his care was a potential source of disturbance for his other patients?

Reedeth sighed. If one were to pursue the implications of the Madison case to their ultimate conclusion, one might far too easily decide that anyone so totally unpredictable must be, by definition, unsuited to ordinary society. Those modifications to the desketary, for instance: could a normal person have done them so deftly and rapidly? Without being an expert, Reedeth was better grounded in cybernetics than the average layman—had to be, since so much of modern psychotherapy depended on computerized insights—and he was prepared to swear that the designer couldn't have envisaged these changes.

Additionally: asked to guess whether Madison would be interested in watching a pythoness, he would at once have answered in the negative. All the psychoprofiles ever raised for him had indicated strong opposition to anything that smacked of the unscientific or the supernormal. Yet here he was not only turning up but arriving ahead of time, as though eager.

So what had persuaded him to accept the invitation —mere boredom? That alas was all too likely. Madison's impassive demeanor, Reedeth noticed, was a complete contrast to that of the other green-clad patients. They without exception were visibly nervous. It was plain that they were relieved at this breach of their customary isolation, but at the same time alarmed at being in the real-life company of so many other people after weeks, months and in a few cases possibly years of contact via comweb screens.

Come to think of it, that meant—and Reedeth clapped his hand to his forehead as the point struck him—he was witnessing an event unprecedented since the foundation of the Ginsberg. And it was Ariadne, of all people, who had brought it about.

"That girl must be a Conroyan at heart!" he said to the air, remembering to add a rider and instruct the desketary not to store the comment.

So who was this girl Lyla Clay whose reputation had sustained Ariadne through what must have been a long and difficult argument with Mogshack? He had a vague general idea of what pythonesses were supposed to do and why people liked to watch them doing it. One could hardly live in twenty-first century America and not number a handful of pythoness-fans among one's acquaintances—not to mention hi-psi fans, Lar-worshippers and people even further off the traditional western orbit. But he had never actually watched a pythoness at work, and the name of this particular girl was strange to him even though Ariadne had assured him that she was among the most talented of all. Abandoning the room where she was scheduled to perform, he switched from one to another of the more than three thousand cameras he could pipe into his screen, wondering if he could spot her on the way up.

Shortly he caught the image of a dark-haired young man riding a pediflow in the right direction, accompanied by a girl in a bullet-proof yash. The pythoness and her mackero, presumably—yes, it must be, for Ariadne herself was coming to greet them at the next intersection in due compliance with Mogshack's code of good manners. That prescribed condescension from those who were wealthy enough to afford privacy towards those who were not, in such matters as appearing personally to welcome visitors from below the poverty-line.

In spite of the obscuring yash, it was possible to discern that the pythoness was young and graceful in her movements. Reedeth found himself hoping that she wouldn't be compelled to keep the yash on in front of the patients.

Mackero (*MAK-uh-roh*) [Fr. *maquereau* mackerel, col-
loq. pimp; cf. "mack"] Manager, agent (e.g.) for young
self-supporting female (photographic model, freelance
singer, pythoness, e.g.); specif. male, not derog. unless
abbr.

"Is everything as you like it, Mr. Kazer?" Ariadne said, unable to stop herself giving occasional nervous glances towards the omnipresent cameras. As well as Reedeth and Mogshack, she suspected that virtually every member of the staff was likely to be watching the show. It had damned well better be a success.

Dan bent down and felt the wide thick mat which had been spread out to prevent Lyla hurting herself during her convulsive thrashing about. "That looks fine," he said. "Where can I connect my recorder?"

"We'll be recording everything ourselves, naturally," Ariadne said. "And we have first-class facilities."

Dan gave her a brief professional smile. "I'm sure you have. I'd still like to make a tape of my own. Copyright, you know."

"Oh. Oh, yes—of course. Well, anywhere on the wall, then." Once more Ariadne's eyes flitted around the room. Watching, Reedeth had the distinct impression that she was stalling, delaying the start of the proceedings. Had she had second thoughts about her plan?

Suddenly she relaxed, and in puzzlement he changed cameras for a more general scan. Just inside the door, which was still sliding closed, was standing a newcomer who looked as though he had three heads. On his shoulders he was wearing a pair of eye-following stereovision cameras like extra skulls of polished metal. And the half-concealed face between them, crossed by a tonguetip-controlled switchbar, belonged to . . .

Matthew Flamen! Reedeth jolted forward in his chair. Although he was seldom able to watch the Flamen show, being at work on all the five days when it was transmitted at noon, he had met the vu-man twice directly following his wife's commitment.

Was she here? Reedeth scanned the audience and at once spotted her familiar casque of dark brown hair, far to the back in an end seat. He saw Flamen wave to her, but she gave him a perfectly blank stare, and after a moment of astonished hesitation he continued towards the front of the room. There Ariadne presented him to the pythoness and her mackero, and words were exchanged which were tantalizingly out of range of the pickups.

Turning away, Flamen began to discharge self-seeking mikes like so many kids' balloons, adjusting each to the flotational index of the air so it would maintain a constant height below the ceiling. Was his arrival chance or premeditation? And what did Mogshack think about a spoolpigeon turning up fully loaded with outside broadcasting equipment?

Reedeth gave a sudden cynical chuckle and asked his desketary both questions. The answers—especially the one concerning the motives which had driven Mogshack to seek the publicity—proved beyond the slightest doubt that Madison had eliminated all the censor-circuits while he was at it.

He was still chuckling when the dismaying thought crossed his mind that perhaps he wasn't the only person on the staff whose desketary had been unexpectedly modified by Madison. He asked about that too, and was assured that so far this one was unique. Greatly relieved, he turned his attention back to Ariadne.

"I hardly need to introduce Mr. Matthew Flamen," she was saying loudly and clearly; she must have turned the pickups to full gain. "His face and voice are probably familiar to you from his five-times-weekly spool-pigeon show on the Holocosmic network. He's asked permission to record this afternoon's performance by Lyla Clay for possible eventual transmission on his show, but naturally I must ask whether anyone here objects to—"

The sound dropped suddenly and the desketary said, "Dr. Mogshack is canvassing the staff also to see if they have any objections. Do you, Dr. Reedeth?"

Reedeth hesitated. "No objection," he said after a pause. It was the safest course. If Mogshack had already consented there was no point in starting an argument.

Evidently no one else registered an objection either, for the next thing that happened was that Lyla Clay said something very softly to Ariadne, fingering her yash, and Ariadne glanced at two or three of the patients, seemed to debate a point with herself, and finally shrugged. Lyla tossed the yash aside with what appeared to Reedeth to be a moue of distaste, and stood revealed in nothing but a pair of abbreviated Nix.

"Hmmm . . . !" Reedeth muttered. "That mackero of hers is a very lucky man!"

Several of the male patients, and two lesbian ones, fidgeted in their chairs in a way that suggested they were equally impressed.

The next thing that happened, however, was merely that Lyla set off on a tour of the room in total silence, briefly studying each of the people present—including, to his obvious dismay, Flamen. She seemed nervous, Reedeth judged, and took a long time about her task.

His mind wandered off down a side alley when she reached Madison. Perhaps the answer would be to get in touch with the IBM directorate and tell them there was somebody in the Ginsberg who displayed an absolutely unbelievable gift for servicing complex automatic circuitry?

No, that wasn't the solution either. As well as hiring far too many neo-puritans, Inorganic Brain Manufacturers Inc. were notorious for having rid themselves of all their kneeblank employees, down to humble sales reps.

Could he become a Gottschalk? The arms traders were among the nation's largest consumers of high-order automatics, and no doubt they would find knee repairmen handy in their dealings with the black enclaves.

On reflection, however, Reedeth doubted whether that would be suitable employment for Madison. His Army experiences had been successfully brought under control in his mind, but it was a matter of record that his period in combat had thrown him completely off his gyros, and who could say that exposure to close contact with modern armaments would not trigger a renewal of his trouble?

How convenient it would be, he thought, if Flamen were to take up the Madison case, make a grand fuss about the plight of a knee stuck in a hospital long after he had qualified for discharge. . . . Come to think of it, it might be possible to leak the story to one of Flamen's knee counterparts, who enjoyed far bigger audiences and what was more mainly overseas.

Reedeth brightened, and made a mental note to see if he could locate a tendril of the grapevine leading to, say, Pedro Diablo. It would have to be done discreetly, but properly handled it might very well result in someone volunteering to act as his legal guardian and enabling him to get out at long last.

But there was no time now to follow that up. Lyla had completed her survey of the audience and returned to the edge of the mat they had spread out for her. She nodded at Dan, who was standing by with his recorder poised, and reached for the hip pocket of her Nix. Producing a small flat bottle which Reedeth only caught a glimpse of, she shook from it a little red capsule. Flamen tongued the switchbar of his cameras to a closeup setting and captured her swallowing the pill.

Whatever it was. Reedeth hadn't realized that pythonesses took anything to help them go into trance. Was that a commercial product, or something alchemically home-cooked from a cut-and-try formula? Once more he consulted his desketary, and this time what he learned made him stare at Lyla's slender body in sheer incredulity.

For a moment or two she stood stiffly vertical, eyes closed. A heartbeat later she fell to the mat, writhing. Her back arched as though in orgasm. Spittle leaked from the corners of her mouth as she began to pant and gasp. Her hands contorted into claws and snatched at the air as though fighting off an invisible attacker—*slash, slash!*

The watchers, including Reedeth who had been prepared for such an event because the desketary had told him about sibyl-pills, tensed in alarm. The girl's muscles, contracting more violently than an epileptic's, seemed likely to tear her apart at the joints; her breasts bobbed on her torso like a pair of buoys on a rough sea. Flamen was continuing to record, but from his expression it was plain he didn't expect to be able to transmit this footage. If he tried, complaints from neo-puritans would almost certainly get him banned.

Only Dan Kazer stood by calmly, glancing every few seconds at the watch on his left wrist, his other hand holding the pause switch of his recorder. Flamen turned the cameras on him just in time to catch his look of expectancy as he let the switch go, and almost in the same instant Lyla's eyes jarred open, two deep wells into the remotest regions of her subconscious mind. From her mouth emerged a dreadful loud forced voice, baritone and masculine.

"*Ghnothe safton!*" she boomed.

"That's not English," Reedeth snapped at his desketary. "What is it—Hebrew?"

"Classical Greek with a Demotic accent," said the desketary in a faintly patronizing tone; Reedeth had often wanted to get back at the smug bastard who had

programmed the linguistic section of their data banks.
"It's the motto from the temple of the Delphic oracle
and it means 'know thyself.' "

Meantime, her muscular frenzy ended, Lyla had risen
to a sitting position without using her hands, eyes still
very wide and focused on nothing. She crossed her legs,
turned by scuffling with her toes against the mat so that
she was facing the audience, and placed her palms together before her face in a sketch for the Indian gesture
of *namasthi*.

There was a pause. Eventually Ariadne said, speaking
directly to Dan in a near-whisper but with her head
close enough to a wall pickup for Reedeth to catch the
words, "Do we have to ask questions now?"

"You have to with some pythonesses," Dan responded
equally softly. "Not with Lyla, though. I told you when
you hired her: this girl is very damned good."

Regardless of what she might now say, Reedeth had
made his mind up about one thing already. Lyla Clay
must be one of the most amazing people in the world,
capable of a feat he had never even dreamed of. If
what the desketary had said about sibyl-pills was true,
she ought not now to be able to even sit up straight.
She ought to be in raving delirium.

Tension mounted. The moment before it became un-
bearable, Lyla said in a high clear voice like a child's,
"Mother Superior couldn't be drearier! Life is oppressive and lonely and dun! Little Miss Celia envied Ophelia
—Hamlet ignored her and then there was none! Rat-
ta-ta-ta, rat-ta-ta-ta, rat-ta-ta-ta-ta-ta-ta-ta-ta-ta. Penny
a look, gobbledegook, you can't live the life that you read
in a book. Pouncing and bouncing hear what I'm an-
nouncing—it's true and you'll never hide from it. You
may think you're knowing in coming and going but you
can't take the 'come' out of 'comet.' As I was going
down the drains I met a man with seven brains. Every
brain had seven lives, every life had seven wives, every
wife told seven lies, who will win the liars' prize?"

She hesitated. Seizing the chance to take a look at the audience, Reedeth noticed that apart from Dan, who seemed rather pleased, everyone in the room wore a baffled frown.

"As I was—" Lyla resumed, and checked. "No. Back in— No. As I was rolling round the sphere I met a man who isn't here. As I was going down the stair I met a man who's everywhere. Hrr-*hum*. Back in—"

Once more she interrupted herself, and a shadow of worry crossed Dan's face. Her voice grew louder and rather frightened.

"As I was sitting on the floor I met a man who's much much more! As I was lying on my bed I kissed a man who wasn't dead! As I was crying out aloud I met a man who's not allowed! As I was—as I was . . ."

Her mouth worked, her hands folded and unfolded in naked terror, and she tried to hop across the soft mat frog-fashion, eyes rolling wildly in search of escape from some unimaginable predicament. Reedeth was half out of his chair. Something must be done about this—the sight of the poor girl's panic was intolerable!

But before he could do anything, Dan had shut off his recorder with an angry gesture, closed the gap between himself and Lyla with a single long stride, and slapped her on both cheeks. As though miraculously called back from a million miles away, she became herself again and looked up at him docilely.

"Was it all right?" she said in her normal voice. "What did I say?"

At thirteen-seventeen the computer which maintained Flamen's around-the-clock news monitoring service, ever alert for hints of corruption, maladministration, yielding to blackmail pressure or other juicy scandal, logged the announcement that a large group of X Patriots was demonstrating at Kennedy Airport against the by now 95-minute delay suffered by Morton Lenigo on his way through Customs and Immigration. Police were standing by with riot guns, gas and flamethrowers and Flights 1205, 1219 and 1300 were tentatively scheduled for diversion over the Canadian border.

At fourteen-thirty it logged an all stations from the South African Broederbond recommending that Lenigo be shot immediately and Detroit be taken out with a suitably sized nuke as necessary preliminaries to the impeachment of President Gaylord.

THIRTY-FOUR   IT'S OKAY TO BE A RESPONSIBLE MEMBER OF SOCIETY IF ONLY YOU KNOW WHAT YOU'RE GOING TO BE HELD RESPONSIBLE FOR

Fuming, Lionel Prior let himself through the elaborate series of barriers which guarded the entrance to his home. It would have been far better to fall in with Flamen's suggestion and fly to the Ginsberg this afternoon, he told himself, regardless of how angry he had been at that bitter and unjustified gibe about selling out to the Holocosmic directorate. He'd have been spared one of the most embarrassing episodes of his entire life.

Attracted by the noise as he stowed his fighting gear in its rack, his wife Nora appeared on the internal com-web screen in the hallway. By the look of it she was lying out on the patio at the back of the house catching some sun, but after a first curt glance he turned his back to the camera.

"Did you have a good exercise, dear?" she asked in the formally polite tone he had grown used to over the past few years.

"A good exercise?" Prior repeated, his voice shrill. "No, it was a stinking awful exercise!"

Her manner changing on the instant, Nora said, "Well, you needn't take out your bad temper on *me!*"

"Might as well give you a foretaste of what's coming,"

Prior snapped back. "We're due for the pariah treatment for the next few weeks, I can assure you of that. Those *nice* neighbors of ours!"

"What on earth do you mean?"

"Let me get a drink." He slung the last of his gear on its peg and headed for the living-zone; she switched cameras to follow him, looking alarmed.

"It went like this," he resumed when he had swigged the first gulp of a strong vodka rickey. "And all because I treat my citidef responsibilities seriously compared to some people I could name! You take the knee-blank part today, Phil Gasby says when I show up—you're good, he says, you'll sharpen our wits a bit. So I said all right. If he put it like that how could I refuse with them all staring at me? And then he pulled the drop on me. There's a man from ISM waiting at the junction of Green and Willow, he says. Captain Lorimer. He'll give you your attack program."

Savagely he poured the rest of his drink down his throat.

"I don't understand," Nora said after a pause.

"Don't you? Do you know where you are right now on the analog screen? Buried under a pile of smoking rubble, that's where! Phil's defense plan that he's been boasting about so long collapsed like a pricked balloon! I had to take him out three minutes after the start. I mean *had* to. I stalled as long as I could but the idiot was right there in plain sight and nobody, blank or knee-blank, could have failed to realize he was in charge the way he was shouting and waving. So then Tom Mesner took over and made a stand on the line of Willow Road, and Lorimer told me to go in by way of Orange and that was that. Sixty-eight percent casualties in under an hour and twenty-two houses afire including ours. So then he canceled the exercise and called everyone together and told us off like—like naughty children! Tom and Phil deserved what they got, of course, because lives are at stake in a thing like this and there's no excuse for carelessness. But you know who's going to be blamed for them being scolded in public? I am, that's who!"

"But I thought we had a good ISM rating here," Nora said, "That was one of the reasons we decided to move into this district!"

"I don't know whether they had a good rating before that bastard Phil Gasby took charge," Prior grunted. "But we certainly don't have one now. Listen!" He tugged a folded paper from his pocket and spread it out. "Internal Security Maintenance, exercise report number blah, district citizens' defense group number blah-blah . . . Ah, here we are. Rating for Lionel Prior Class Four, rating for group as a whole Class Six, *not* adjudged competent to maintain order in assigned zone in event of civil disturbance. Remarks: the group—no, I won't read that out. It's downright libelous!"

"At least you got a better rating than the group average," Nora ventured.

"Class Four? It's ridiculous! If I hadn't tried to do Phil a favor I'd have got at least a Class Two, but Lorimer bawled me out too for not shooting him as soon as I got the chance. Think I'm going to get any credit for that, though? Not in a million years!"

He threw himself into an inflatable chair and scowled at the big picture-window. Currently it was set for a broad arid stretch of veldt with a herd of antelope browsing in the distance.

"Has Phil got picture-windows?" he concluded ferociously. "The hell he has! Those poor kids of his could be cut to mincemeat by shards of flying glass!"

There was a moment of silence. Then Nora said in the self-righteous tone of someone winning an argument through a careless admission by the person on the other side, "And you spent a hundred and fifty thousand on that Lar of yours?"

For an instant Prior was on the verge of exploding. But instead he gave a sigh. "Okay, I was conned. Every damned thing that could possibly go wrong today *has* gone wrong. If you bothered to watch Matthew's show—"

"I started out to, but the picture went fuzzy and I had to switch to something else," Nora said.

"That's exactly it. That's what I've been trying to get him to show some reaction about! But he doesn't seem to care any more! Know what the idiot did? He practically came out with the accusation that Holocosmic is trying to get rid of him, and when I tried to pick the pieces up by suggesting we call in an unquestionable expert to study the problem he blew all his fuses and said I was selling out! Damn it, of course we're being sabotaged, but that's not something you say in range of a bug without having the evidence lined up! If this is what having a Lar leads to, I'm going to tell them right now what I think of their service!"

He drained his glass and marched over to the comweb. Nora disappeared, plainly not caring to continue the conversation after having won her point. Prior scowled at the blanked screen where her face had been a moment ago.

If only he could get her into an asylum—or any place out of earshot . . . !

Reaching for the board to punch the code for Lares & Penates Inc., he checked. There was a flag up over the message slot. He jabbed his hand in to retrieve the fax paper, and read it with dismay.

Eugene Voigt of the PCC needing to get in touch as soon as possible. That old fool! But right now his situation was too precarious to risk offending anyone who might later be of use. Sighing, he put through that call first.

Waiting for an answer, he looked around at the handsome expensive home he had worked for years to achieve: splendidly furnished, with real hand-painted pictures on the walls, hand-woven rugs on the floor protected by an invisible film of plastic against the scuffing of children's feet, antique ornaments thirty, forty, even fifty years old . . .

"Doesn't Matthew realize what I stand to lose if he throws his contract away?" he said to the unheeding air.

THIRTY-FIVE

A FIASCO IS A BOTTLE IN WHICH ITALIAN WINE IS SOLD

"Well, that was a fiasco and no mistake!" Dan muttered to Lyla the moment he had the chance to abandon his professional good manners and could speak to her without anyone else overhearing.

Bewildered, she stared at him. The patients were being shepherded from the room under Ariadne's supervision; Matthew Flamen, having covered several of them in closeup from near the door to wind up his reel of tape, had doffed his recording equipment and was now engaged in conversation with one of the last of the audience to leave, a singularly lovely girl with her mouth in a sulky pout. The conversation seemed to be completely one-sided.

"But—but why?" Lyla whispered.

"The biggest break you're ever likely to get in your life, Flamen turning up to cover the performance, and how long do you run? Eleven minutes, that's how long! Think they're going to be pleased at getting such a short show? You let me down, darl, and that's all there is to it."

She went on staring at him in disbelief for another few seconds. Suddenly, as though the nerve-signals had this moment reached her brain, she put up her fingers to touch her cheeks.

"Dan, did you slap me out of it?"

"Had to!"

"But you know that's terribly dangerous! You might have—"

"Did I?"

"I . . ." She swallowed enormously and shook her head. "I guess not. I feel pretty much as usual after a session. But *why?*" The last word peaked into a cry.

"You'll find out when you hear the tape." His eyes flicked past her. "Shut up and look pleasant—Flamen's coming this way."

The girl he had been talking to was leaving with the rest of the patients now, like one more among a herd of two-legged sheep, and Flamen himself was approaching with his face set in a frown.

"Mr. Flamen!" Dan exclaimed. "I do hope you haven't been disappointed! I assure you, this is the first time I've ever had to cut Lyla short in public."

"Had to?" Lyla blazed. "You didn't 'have' to do anything of the kind! Stop talking as though it's my fault, or you'll be out one pythoness. I mean that!"

"I knew what I was doing," Dan muttered. "You're not the first pythoness I've macked for."

"No, just the first who didn't have to supplement her earnings by sacking out with strangers!" Lyla blasted back.

"Mr. Flamen, Lyla's a bit overwrought, I'm afraid," Dan said apologetically. "Perhaps we could—"

"And shouldn't I be? I might have woken up crazy, don't you realize that?"

"Ah, Miss Clay—Mr. Kazer!" Another voice cut in, and there was Ariadne coming to join them. "That was very interesting. I really am impressed! I wonder if you could spare the time to discuss the oracles and see if you can attach them to any of the . . ." The words died away. Glancing uncertainly from face to face, she asked, "Is something the matter?"

"I never talk about my oracles," Lyla said firmly. "Take them or leave them, it's up to you. *I* want to go home.

106

I don't like this place and I can't stand what it does to people. Give me my rapitrans ticket, Dan." She held out her hand, but he made no move to comply.

"That's very interesting," Flamen murmured. "I don't much like what this place does to people, either." He rounded on Ariadne. "You told me that the only patients being invited to this show were those making a good recovery. But when I tried to talk to Celia just now she'd hardly even exchange a civil hello with me. Is that what your famous boss regards as a decent cure?"

"We undertake nothing more than to try and help our patients reconstruct their personalities," Ariadne said stiffly. "If it turns out that some of their previous emotional involvements were manifestations of some deep-lying immaturity or other malfunction, that simply can't be helped."

Flamen's face went milk-white and every muscle visible on his body tightened like an overwound clock-spring. Ariadne took half a pace back, as though driven by the sheer vehemence of his glare.

"I said I don't like what you've done to Celia, doctor! As far as I can see, if she stays here any longer she won't have a mind left to be mended—she's just being drained!"

"If you disapprove of Dr. Mogshack's methods, you're at liberty to transfer her into someone else's care," Ariadne snapped, scarcely seeming to realize whom she was talking to. Her eyes were darting to Lyla every few seconds, then away again as though she were afraid of being rebuked for staring.

"I'll take that as an invitation!" Flamen said icily. "Good afternoon! By the way, Miss Clay, I'm heading back to the city by skimmer—perhaps I can give you a ride somewhere?"

"The fastest route out of here is the one I take," Lyla said. "Yes, *please*."

"But, Lyla—!" Dan reached out to take hold of her

arm. In the same instant Ariadne said anxiously, "Miss Clay, is it wise to—?"

"But *nothing*," Lyla cut in. "You blamed me for giving a short performance, then you admitted that you slapped me awake ahead of time. You come home at all, you come crawling. Do you understand?"

THIRTY-SIX

AN OBLIGATION IS LIKE A MUSCLE:
WHEN YOU CONTRACT IT IT GETS
BIGGER AND HARDER

Three faces, not just one, appeared in Prior's comweb
screen, split by a half and two quarters. Voigt occupied
the half, naturally; Prior noticed he'd invested in some
new ears. He, and the blank occupying the upper quarter on the other side, had sound and vision links working, but the remaining caller—a scowling kneeblank—
seemed as yet not to be spliced into the circuit.

"Mr. Prior!" Voigt said with professional cordiality.
"We haven't spoken in far too long. Nonetheless, I
should apologize for disturbing you at your home."

Prior mouthed a conventional rejoinder.

"Let me introduce Mr. Frederick Campbell, of the
Bureau of State and Federal Relations," Voigt went on.
"He's appealed to me for some assistance, and I think
the best thing I can do is refer him to you. Mr. Campbell, suppose you brief Mr. Prior yourself."

"With pleasure," Campbell said, his tone contradicting
the words. "Well, perhaps I should start by explaining
that my work is concerned with the negotiation of city
tax contracts, and this morning I had to visit Blackbury and discuss their purchases of water and power
for the coming year. And just as I was leaving I—uh . . .
Well, I had a rather awkward problem dumped in my
lap."

"Don't tell me," Prior said sourly. "The dinge there." He pointed at the remaining corner of the screen. "Well, right now I have problems of my own, and the last thing—"

"I know you have, Mr. Prior," Voigt cut in. "Do I have to remind you that the PCC monitors the transmissions of all licensed vu-stations? It hasn't entirely escaped our notice that the incidence of transmission faults affecting the Matthew Flamen show has hit a statistically improbable high. That's why I thought of bringing our—ah—involuntary visitor to your attention. The name of that *dinge,* as you termed him, happens to be Pedro Diablo."

"What?" Prior jerked like a newly hooked fish. "Are they out of their skulls, parting with a man like that? Why, he's worth a couple of army corps all by himself!"

"I understand that's his own opinion also," Campbell muttered. "I had the story in not inconsiderable detail after he'd been forced into my skimmer at gunpoint this morning."

"But what *possessed* them?"

"A visit from Herman Uys," Campbell said.

"*Uys?* In *Blackbury?* But I wouldn't have thought he'd be seen dead in . . ." Prior's voice tailed away in bewilderment. After a pause he added feebly, "Anyhow, I didn't know he was in the country."

"Nor did Diablo," Campbell said grimly. "Nor—which is far worse—did the Immigration Service." He wiped his face with a large yellow handkerchief. "The Afrikaners must have developed some wholly new technique for deceiving our computers, I guess. But that's irrelevant; they've tipped their hand and we'll be on guard in the future. Let's stick to the point."

He tucked away his handkerchief and leaned closer to the camera.

"Apparently Uys has been conducting heredity checks on all municipal employees. Mayor Black has rashly promised to cut back the non-melanist heredity of the city's population to twenty-five percent in the next generation, and I need hardly tell you that the rigidity of his attitude is backfiring very satisfactorily. We've already had undercover feelers regarding the proposed safe-conduct of surplus population units, chiefly young unmarrieds, to other cities in order to widen the gene-pool, but I'm pleased to say we can scotch that idea under the Mann Act. However . . ."

He hesitated. Suddenly his executive urbanity slipped like a carnival mask on a broken elastic.

"Frankly, Mr. Prior, we're engaged in so many ticklish maneuvers right now, with such minuscule computer weightings in our favor, that the dismissal of Pedro Diablo is far from the unalloyed blessing it might appear. I doubt if you're familiar with the contract between the Federal government and the Blackbury city council, but it just so happens it's one of the worst anyone ever wrote. Because it's one of the oldest; it predates the advent of the computers we use nowadays to get rid of dangerous loopholes. Some crazy goddamned idiot thought we could *bribe* kneeblanks to desert from the enclaves, way back when, and there's still a provision in the contract which compels us to guarantee equivalent employment and better salary and living conditions to anyone who comes out of the city, whether he defects or gets deported. And Diablo knows all about that. He quoted clause, paragraph and line to me when I was bringing him away this morning. And he is *boiling* mad."

"So it occurred to me," Voigt put in, "that the services of one of the most brilliant talents ever to handle the visual media might not inappropriately be engaged by the nearest surviving counterpart on blank-run channels of the programs he has been accustomed to prepare in his—ah—former environment. Especially since our computer analyses, Mr. Prior, indicate that some time around now your principal's temperament is liable to get him into a certain amount of trouble with the Holo-cosmic directorate."

The sly old fox! Prior shook his head in reluctant ad-miration. The PCC might be a dead letter, but Eugene Voigt certainly was not. There were so many possibilities inherent in the proposal just made to him that his head was spinning. If worse came to worst and Flamen stu-pidly involved himself in a quarrel with Holocosmic, it would be a marvelous lifeline to be associated with Diablo; talent like his would remain salable indefinitely. In point of fact, however, it seemed unlikely things would come to such a pass. Assuming Diablo really was as angry with his former boss as Campbell believed, why shouldn't a joint Flamen-Diablo show become the only program which could tackle knee scandals as well as blank ones? *That* would bring the audience rushing back by the tens of millions—people like Nora, for in-stance, and his neighbors, half-fascinated and half-re-pelled by the walking talking aliens against whose de-predations they had to be on guard night and day. . . .

And with a prospect like that before them, the Holo-cosmic directorate would change their minds instantly about trying to squeeze the Flamen show off the beams.

But Prior retained his professional presence of mind. Aloud he said, "Well, naturally, Mr. Voigt, it's always a privilege to cooperate with a request from a govern-mental agency. However, you'll understand that I can't commit myself to anything without consulting my prin-cipal, and I'll certainly need a rundown on the legal situation before I—"

"If you need computer time," Campbell interrupted, "just ask. Candidly, Mr. Prior, we want to get Diablo off our backs *fast*—I mean, of course, we want to see him settled into a slot where no court in the world could deny that he was being offered the sort of oppor-tunities to pursue his profession which the wording of the Blackbury contract might have led him to expect. Salary is no problem; if we had to, we could cheerfully

112

pension the entire population of all the enclaves at the income level they can currently command. But as I told you, it's not just a matter of salary."

Prior swallowed hard. He had a vaguely dream-like sensation, as though he had inadvertently imbibed a very small dose of a hallucinogen.

He tossed caution to the winds and came straight out with the nub of his problem.

"Mr. Voigt, Matthew thinks that Holocosmic is—uh—*conniving* at the interference with our show because they'd like to have another all-advertising slot in its place and would welcome a chance to break the contract they have with us. I wonder whether this offer of Federal computer time might extend to assisting us in our attempts to evaluate the trouble?"

"Why, by all means, Mr. Prior," Voigt said blandly. "To exceed their present advertising schedule would be to infringe the Planetary Communications Charter, and that we could not possibly permit."

Exultantly Prior made a private promise to buy Voigt his next pair of ears.

"It's a deal," he said aloud. "Yes, sir—it is most *definitely* a deal."

Active Ingredient
   ℞ 250 mg. per capsule di-psycho-coca-3,2-parabufote-
nine tartrate hexitol complex in an anhydrous buffering
medium and neutral gelatin shells

THIRTY-EIGHT

IF YOU'RE STUCK WITH A FIASCO YOU MIGHT AS WELL MAKE SPECTACLES OF YOURSELVES SO THAT AT LEAST YOU'LL HAVE SOME GLASSES TO POUR THE CONTENTS INTO

Following the departure of Lyla and Flamen there was a dejected silence. Eventually Dan said, with a desperate air of salving what he could from a wreck, "Well, Dr. Spoelstra, I can only assume it was the special conditions of working in a mental hospital which threw Lyla out of her regular orbit. I hope you won't judge—"

"Hello! Why such long faces? I thought the show was a tremendous success!"

They all turned to see who had spoken. Reedeth had appeared in the doorway and was advancing with fingers bunched to blow a kiss at Ariadne.

"What more could you ask of a pythoness," he went on, "than oracles so clear you don't have to crack your skull over them? You must be Dan Kazer, I guess—the mackero? Glad to meet you. My name's James Reedeth and I work here. I gather your young lady friend was a big hit with Matthew Flamen, hm? Seeing that they left together, I forecast a personal appearance on three-vee, planetwide exposure, and as a result—"

"Jim, you're manic!" Ariadne exclaimed. "What's got into you? Freeze it! I'm not in the mood."

"Wrong. You think you're not, but actually you are. I should have guessed that myself but it took a pythoness to show me the truth. Regardless of whether Ariadne is in touch with you again, Mr. Kazer, I assure you I will be."

"Jim, shut up!" Ariadne cried.

"I will not. It's your own fault. You forbade me to attend the session in person, didn't you? If you'd allowed me to join in you might have found out something as revealing about me as I did about you. Tell me, though, Mr. Kazer, why did you slap her face and bring her out of trance?"

Horribly embarrassed because it was obvious from Ariadne's expression how upset she was by Reedeth's behavior, Dan said uncertainly, "Well—ah . . . Well, you noticed how after the first couple of oracles she lapsed into a recurrent cycle: 'as I was doing such and such I met a man who this and that'? That's what they call an echo-trap. You can't let that kind of thing go on. I've heard of pythonesses who got stuck in one of those and never came out again."

"I see," Reedeth nodded. "Funny—I'd never thought of pythonesses being subject to professional hazards before. But then, I guess I never took them very seriously. After today, though, I assure you I won't underestimate them again."

Dan gave a wan smile of appreciation. There was a pause. When it was clear nothing further was going to be said, he gathered up his recorder and addressed Ariadne.

"I take it the fee for—"

"It'll be forwarded as arranged," Ariadne snapped.

"Well . . . Well, then that's all, I guess. Good afternoon."

The moment he had disappeared, Ariadne spun to face Reedeth. "And what's got into you?" she blazed. "Don't I have enough problems without you acting like a fool? Flamen just threatened to take his wife away!"

"Why should that bother you? She's here under private contract, isn't she? So we'd make a fat profit on the deal. Besides, any man who genuinely cared about his wife would feel the same way after she'd had a few months of treatment here."

"Jim!" Horrified, she went white. "Dr. Mogshack may be listening!"

"Not to what we're saying, he isn't. I had Harry Madison in to repair my desketary this morning, and he's fixed it up with some interesting new gimmicks. Go on —get it off your chest without worrying. There's no one to hear you but me."

She stared at him for long moments, mouth ajar. When he put out his hand to take hers and lead her away, she followed him like a trusting child.

THIRTY-NINE   THOUGHT PASSING REPEATEDLY THROUGH THE MIND OF CAPTAIN GORDON K. LORIMER ON HIS WAY HOME AFTER SUPERVISING THE AFTERNOON EXERCISE OF THE CITIZENS' DEFENSE GROUP TO WHICH LIONEL PRIOR BELONGS

"What in the hell is the *good* of trying to maintain internal security if Immigration goes and does something as stupid as letting Morton Lenigo into the country? And when you run across a bunch of half-assed incompetents like I did this afternoon . . ."

I'm the one who's out of his skull, Flamen thought as he keyed the controls of the skimmer to the state traffic computers and waited for them to find him a slot in the pattern. What was the penalty tag for breaking the month-to-month contract for Celia's hospitalization—a quarter-million, wasn't it?

"As though I didn't have enough trouble already," he muttered.

Beside him, shrunk back into the corner of the seat like a frightened bird, Lyla played with the hem of her yash and either failed to hear or ignored him.

When the skimmer lifted clear of the encircling towers, however, she exhaled loudly and relaxed. Flamen glanced at her.

"What made you decide to mention my wife?" he demanded.

"When? Oh, you mean while I was prophesying. Did I?"

Flamen sighed. "I wish I knew what to make of all this! Are you just a clever actress? Is it all a first-rate con job? I knew I'd heard the name Dan Kazer before somewhere, and I placed it as we were coming away. He used to mack for Michaela Baxendale, right?"

"Yes."

"He parlayed her into a fortune, but she stayed a phoney. Always will. Looks like she didn't even have the grace to share a slice of her profits with the guy who launched her. Ever met her?"

"No. Dan doesn't even like talking about her very much."

"That I'm not surprised at. She purely and simply disgusts me." For the latest of many times he considered, and dismissed, the idea of doing a piece about her on the show. There was nothing he could reveal about her, no matter how nasty, which didn't accord with the image the public already had of her.

Anyway, if things went on as they were going at the moment there wouldn't be a Matthew Flamen show for long. What it would be like trying to deal with Prior tomorrow morning when, on top of today's quarrel, he discovered that there was material scheduled about which he hadn't been consulted, and which hadn't even been comped for acceptability before it was put down, he hardly dared to think.

But he was still determined to use the item. He'd got some excellent tape; it should be worth a good four minutes.

Besides, being offered such publicity might help to mollify Mogshack and his colleagues if they'd been offended by his crack about Celia.

And yet: Celia . . . He shook his head. It was no good trying to pretend he was heartbroken at their separation, nor even making out that he had been surprised when it proved necessary to commit her. For months she had seemed to come alive only when a fight broke out between them, and that wasn't normal on anyone's scale of values. Nonetheless, it had come as a terrible shock to find that she was as chilly with him, still her husband, as she might have been with a total stranger who was trying to pick her up.

Beside him, Lyla was fidgeting with something. Out of the corner of his eye he saw her remove from the pocket of her Nix the small flat bottle he had caught a glimpse of earlier and make to slip it into the pouch of her yash.

"What's in those things?" he demanded.

"You mean the sibs?"

"Sibs?"

"Short for 'sibyl-pills.' Here you are." She handed him the bottle. It bore a gaudy yellow label on which was printed the name of a famous pharmaceutical company.

Flamen read the wording slowly.

"My God! If that's what I think it is—! You honestly mean you took two-fifty mg's of this stuff less than an hour ago and you walked out on your own two feet?"

"It sort of gets burned up during the trance, I guess. But it is pretty fierce for someone who isn't used to it. Dan tried one once and went into such a high orbit I thought he'd never come down. Maybe he didn't. Slapping me out of trance—the damned fool!"

"And you buy this stuff at the drugstore?"

"Well, it's not something I'd care to home-brew on the kitchen stove!" Lyla said tartly. "It's supposed to have been made up to the formula of Diana Spitz, the first of the great pythonesses—back before the turn of the century, someone told me."

Genuinely awed, Flamen passed the bottle back. "Okay, I believe you. You don't know what you're saying when you're in trance. Nobody could stay conscious under a load like that."

"So tell me what I'm supposed to have said about your wife. And why should I have mentioned her, anyway?"

"She was right there in the audience."

"You mean the doctor who . . . ? Oh, no!" Lyla's eyes rounded enormously. "Oh, Lord! I'm dreadfully sorry, Mr. Flamen. I was—uh—distracted. It simply didn't register. Is it something very serious?"

"When they took her in, they assured me it wasn't. But—but damn it! I know my own wife better than any doctor ever could, and experts or no experts I say she's not better since she went into the Ginsberg, but worse. Come to think of it . . ."

Now what would be the consequences if it were shown that one of Mogshack's patients had actually deteriorated as a result of his treatment? A rising tide of excitement filled Flamen's mind. He hadn't tackled a sacred cow of that size since—well, perhaps since the affair which had secured him promotion from local station work to network transmissions, five years ago.

"Yes," he said aloud. "Yes, I'm going to do that! It's high time someone tore the beard off Dr. Mogshack!"

"Then you can start by telling people there's a man in the Ginsberg who's more rational than the director."

"What? Who?" Flamen jerked his head around.

Lyla had put her hands to her temples and was swaying giddily. "I—I don't know. I guess maybe this time I didn't burn the sib up, what with Dan slapping me awake. I heard myself say that, but I don't know why I said it and I don't know who I meant."

"One of the patients?"

"I . . . Yes." Lyla tried to rub her forehead, through the encumbering hood of the yash, found she couldn't, and in a fit of rage tore the clumsy garment off. "Oh, stuff this thing! Dan says I have to wear it all the time because otherwise the insurance on me isn't valid, but he doesn't have to walk around half suffocated! Christ, I'm so frightened all of a sudden. I never had a hangover after a trance before. Do you have a trank on board?"

"Sure!" Flamen punched the dispenser key. She seized the pill and choked it down.

"Gone," she said eventually. "Sorry. I'd have liked to tell you more but I couldn't stand the pressure."

Flamen hesitated. "You disliked the Ginsberg, that's obvious," he said at length.

"It makes my guts churn."

"Why?"

"*I* don't know." Lyla's voice was steady again now,

and she considered the question dispassionately. "I didn't like the atmosphere there when I arrived. Dan said it had something to do with the patients' skin-secretions, but it wasn't so much something I could smell as . . . Oh, I can't define it."

"Are pythonesses sensitive to things other people don't notice, even without going into trance?"

"Well, I guess I do sense things sometimes. But so do friends of mine who aren't pythonesses."

There was a pause. During it Flamen considered various ways in which he could put a cat among Mogshack's pigeons, and reached the depressing conclusion that if he did want to prove that the treatment she was being given had made Celia worse instead of better he'd probably have to have her packled. And personality analog computer logging was hideously expensive, ordinarily reserved for individuals such as government officials or senior executives of giant corporations on whose clear thinking depended the fate of millions.

Still, perhaps his own computers might suggest an alternative; they weren't the best in the world, but certainly they were exceptionally well stocked with information. And there was also that tantalizing hint Lyla had just dropped, about there being a saner man than the director in the Ginsberg. That might indicate a line to follow.

"Can you ever figure out what your oracles mean?" he inquired.

"Oh, sometimes. I'm pretty well acquainted with the shorthand my subconscious uses."

"Do you think you could identify the person you mentioned a moment ago, the man who's more rational than Mogshack?"

Lyla considered the question with a doubtful expression. "I never met any of today's audience before," she said at last. "But I suppose I might just possibly be able to spot a useful clue. I'd have to hear the tape, of course . . . Say, that's a point. Do you think I could hear yours? Lord only knows when Dan will get home with the recording he made."

"Surely you can. Now, if you like. I think it's only fair to show it to you before it's transmitted, in case there's something you'd like me to avoid using. Ah—that is, if you don't mind coming to my place on your own . . . ?"

Lyla gave a wry chuckle. "Think I'm a neo-puritan? It's a luxury I couldn't afford."

"Yes, I guess it is," Flamen nodded. "It's not the attitude, but the upkeep. Hmmm! I hadn't thought of it like that, but it figures: the extra clothes you buy with more fabric in them, the extra comwebs so you never have to be alone in a room with anyone but deal with them at a distance—"

"I wasn't thinking of that," Lyla interrupted. "I meant you just can't have a puritan pythoness. The subconscious is completely amoral, isn't it? It tells the truth, and . . . Well, like they say, 'truth is a naked lady.' If I could get away with it, I'd take that literally and never wear anything but jewelry—not even Nix like these. It's astonishing how much it helps. . . . I'll tell you something very odd to prove it. I was sent to this very proper school, with uniforms and everything—incredibly Victorian—and I never had the slightest suspicion that I might be a pythoness until I ran away from it. I came to New York, I hadn't any money, I was sleeping on strangers' floors, I was practically in rags because my clothes were wearing out, and all of a sudden when I was wearing more dirt than cloth, *bang.* There was the talent. It sort of scared me at first, but I adjusted. And eventually, after I met Dan, I started to figure out how I could encourage it."

"Such as . . . ?"

Her pretty face soured like cream when you add lemon-juice. "You're not a kid, Mr. Flamen. How the hell do you think someone learns to identify with the maximum number of other people? You do what they do! You starve with them, you sleep with them, you eat and drink with them, you let them do to you what they want to do, and you don't pass judgment. But I don't imagine that's a point of view you'd appreciate."

"Why not?"

"Sorry. Didn't mean to be offensive. But as I understand it . . . Hell! I admit, I never watch your show. We didn't even have a vuset in the apt until yesterday when one of Dan's friends gave us his old one. But you're a spoolpigeon, and don't spoolpigeons make their living by pointing shocked fingers at people so the narrow-minded self-righteous prurient mass audience can pretend they're horrified?"

"Yes, I do pass judgments," Flamen said after a pause. "But I like to think, at least, my victims deserve what they get. Liars, cheats, stuffed shirts, small-minded power-hungry empire-builders . . . I can't stand hypocrites. I doubt if you can."

"I hope that's true," she said. "I'd like to like you. I always want to like people."

"And I like to be liked. Trouble is, in my line of business, no matter how carefully I choose my targets the bystanders are apt to catch the shrapnel, and it makes everyone kind of—ah—*diffident*. . . ." Flamen leaned forward and peered at the handsome development of well-spaced modern houses they were flying over. "We're almost there. Just another minute till we land."

FORTY-ONE I SPEAK WITH THE TONGUES OF MEN AND OF ANGELS AND HAVE NOT CHARITY

Boomed the radio evangelist* at the top of his lungs over the British "pirate" station in 1966:

"You know the streets in your neighborhood you wouldn't dare to walk down alone after dark! You know the streets you wouldn't want your kids to walk along on their way home from school!"

"What in the world is he going on about?" said his audience, and switched off.

*He was an American.

"I like you much better in the summer phase of your orbit," Reedeth said, stroking Ariadne's hair. In reply she sank her teeth into the fleshy part of his upper arm, and he jerked away with a cry.

"You're always so smug when you've worked your tensions off on me!" she snapped. "There's no need to think I'm completely defenseless, though—even now!"

Reedeth sighed, rubbing the horseshoe shapes left by her bite. She sat up and swung her feet over the edge of the consultation couch; it wasn't as luxurious as a bed, but it had done well enough.

"Are you *sure* that thing is shut off?" she asked for the fifth or sixth time, nodding at the desketary.

"Yes, yes and *yes*," Reedeth muttered. "I told you: when Harry fixed it he set it up differently from the regular way. We've got to get that man out of this stifling environment! He's got talents which . . . Ah, never mind. I wanted to go on talking about you. Can't you think of anything except defending yourself?"

"It's not rational to enjoy being vulnerable!"

"No more is it rational to operate on the paranoid assumption that everyone else is out to do you damage. And what else are you doing when you get through to a patient's basic traumas but taking advantage of his vulnerability?"

"Logic-chopping," Ariadne said ill-temperedly. "You

127

have to make an incision before you repair a hernia, don't you, or a perforated ulcer? But you don't go around with your skin hanging open in great gaping wounds on the off-chance that someone may need to get at your internal organs!"

"No more do you go around wearing clanking armor-plate. Though I grant you some people treat their clothes like armor and give you the impression they're always on the watch for bows and blowpipes. But what's the archetype of the perfectly defended man? It's the catatonic."

"That sounds like one of Conroy's arguments."

"Applause!" Reedeth said mockingly. "It is indeed. I've always thought it was a striking point and I still do. But tell me this—no, hold it." He raised a hand to forestall her interruption. "Seriously, Ariadne: what made you all of a sudden cave in like you did? Do you know? You're always talking about proper detachment from one's own emotions, and I concede it is good not to be at their mercy. You've blown your safety-valve, and it was marvelous, and I wish I could tell you just how good it was . . . but now, what do you think made it happen? I'm playing fair. I think I know how I worked it, and I'm giving you the chance to figure out the same thing so that if you want to you can guard against a repetition."

She plucked thoughtfully at her lower lip; realizing what she was doing, she snatched her hand away angrily.

"I . . . Well, I suppose it was your confidence. I was in a rather confused state, and faced with your absolute certainty the idea of arguing with you on top of everything else I was having to cope with—it was simply too much."

"Yes, that was my conclusion. Now here's something else I want to know." Reedeth sat forward, his arms around his knees. "What made you feel the session with the pythoness had gone wrong? *I* thought it was a re-

markable success for a trial run, and ought to be repeated as soon as possible."

"It wasn't supposed to end the way it did, with her
mackero slapping her face. It was meant to last about
half an hour. And I was terrified for a moment. You
know about the drug these girls use to go into trance?"

"Yes, the sibyl-pills. I asked my desketary. That girl
must have a fantastic metabolism to recover with nothing worse than a temper-tantrum. But apparently it's a
well-documented phenomenon. There's quite a lot about
it in the literature. Didn't you check up beforehand?"

"Of course I did! But—" Ariadne bit her lip. "It's one
thing to be told about it, though, and another to see it
happening. That must have shaken me as much as anything, and when Flamen complained about his wife's
condition I didn't exactly give him a civil answer, and
then he came out with his threat to take her away. I
could just picture Mogshack bawling me out for that,
too. And you caught me at that precise moment, when
I was wide open. As you very well knew, didn't you?"

"Yes. But I'm not going to apologize."

"I didn't expect you to." Rising with a shake of her
head, she reached for her clothes and began to put them
on.

FORTY-THREE   A REMARKABLE INSTANCE ON THE PUBLIC SCALE OF THE REAL-LIFE IMPLEMENTATION OF XAVIER CONROY'S DICTUM ABOUT THE PERFECTLY DEFENDED MAN

Following Paraguay's declaration of independence from Spain Dr. Francia, the dictator known as "El Supremo," adopted a simple foreign policy: no one was permitted to enter or leave the country and trade was absolutely forbidden.

FORTY-FOUR A FIRM DECISION TO GO INTO THE WAGON-FIXING BUSINESS IN A BIG WAY

"Oh, so that's your wife!" Lyla exclaimed, her yash trailing on the floor behind her as she crossed Flamen's living-zone towards the place of honor where a looped-tape cut of Celia endlessly re-cycled. "I recognize her now. It's an awful shame—she's lovely!"

"Thank you," Flamen muttered. "Not quite as sweet-tempered as you might think to look at her, I'm afraid ... but of course most of that must have been due to her condition. Never mind. Sit down. Dial a drink, whatever you like."

He had brought the tape-reels from the cameras he kept in the skimmer; slipping them into the playing sockets, he waited for the faint whine that indicated the mechanism had brought them into synch.

"The stuff's in real-time order, of course," he warned. "I'll skip the beginning and spin forward to the place where you started to prophesy. I—"

The comweb buzzed.

"Damnation! I'm not in!" he snapped at the automatics.

"Able Baker override!" Prior's voice countered, and the screen lit to show his face. He was about to say something else when he realized that Flamen wasn't alone. His jaw dropped.

"Matthew, have you gone crazy today? It could have been one of the Holocosmic directorate calling, or anyone else with the Able Baker rating for your phone. And you're married, damn it—to my sister!"

"Like all neo-puritans you have a mind like an open drain," Flamen said wearily. "But since you are piped in, you might as well stay tuned. This is Lyla Clay, the pythoness. She was performing at the Ginsberg and I taped her trance. We're just going to play it over and see if I can use some of it on the show tomorrow."

Prior looked instantly alarmed. "Medical ethics?"

"You a registered medical practitioner?" Flamen shot at Lyla. She gave a dumb headshake. "Good. No problem there then. And I have clearances recorded from all the patients and authorization from the staff. Stop worrying. But while I have you here there are two or three things I want to say. First off I owe you an apology for this morning. I didn't see what you were driving at. I should have known better than to blast off the way I did."

Instead of being mollified, Prior looked even more disturbed. "Ah—do you think we should discuss private matters with . . . ?"

"With a stranger listening? Lionel, I watched Miss Clay work this afternoon. I tell you straight, there aren't any secrets when this girl's around. And anyhow I don't care. I've been making my living for years by dragging skeletons out of people's closets—it'd be hypocritical for me to try and pretend I haven't any of my own. So I'm sorry about what I said this morning. All right?"

"That's mainly what I called up about. I've picked up the pieces for you." A trace of smugness appeared in Prior's expression. "But that I'm not going to talk about in public, if you don't mind."

"Look, if I'm in the way—" Lyla said, anxiously getting to her feet.

"You stay right where you are," Flamen said. "I want to talk about the Ginsberg for a moment. Lionel, do you know anything about Mogshack's methods, or have you always taken his reputation on trust like that Lar of yours?"

Prior flushed beet-red. "Matthew, if you're going to descend to cheap cracks like that—!"

"Lionel, I want to *know*. I saw Celia this afternoon and she's being turned into a vegetable. Have you any idea what they do to people in there?"

"Yes, of course I do. I checked up very thoroughly, and so should you have, apparently. Mogshack treats his patients in accordance with the most advanced modern therapeutic techniques. For each patient he draws up a specially computed personality profile, and then the computers design a normative curve towards which the aberrant behavior is gently directed by various methods such as—well, I'm a layman in this area, naturally, but I guess they use drugs and . . ." He made an all-embracing gesture. "Anyway, they try to help the patients become self-reliant again."

"It sounds more as though they sew a straitjacket and trim the poor devils to fit," Lyla said, and clapped her hand to her mouth. "Oh! Sorry—I didn't mean to butt in."

Flamen gave her a musing look. "Yes, the more I think about it the more I think you're right. Lionel, how soon can I get Celia out?"

"At the end of the month, of course, when the contract comes up for renewal. Unless you have a quarter-million tealeaves to throw away like it says in the penalty clause."

"But is there anything to stop me having her case independently comped?"

"Right now there's practically nothing you can't have comped," Prior said, and Flamen realized belatedly that he was almost bursting to pass on his news.

"Out with it!" he rapped. "I'll vouch for Miss Clay."

"Well . . . Oh, okay. How does free Federal computer

time suit you?" He leaned back grinning plumply at the expression on Flamen's face.

"Are you serious?"

"Sure. There are strings, but I'll tell you about them later. The deal's worth it, though."

"Christ, it's bound to be! How much?"

"Whatever we need to fix the sabotage problem. Plus. No limit."

"In that case," Flamen said with enormous satisfaction, "the sabotage isn't the only thing I'm going to fix. There's also a certain little red wagon."

FORTY-FIVE

THE SOUND OF A CODE BEING BROKEN IS USUALLY THE SAME AS THAT OF SOMEBODY SNAPPING HIS FINGERS

"And this thing her mackero talked about," Ariadne said. "An echo-trap." She shivered. "He seemed to mean that the mind could get stuck on one subject over and over, like a loop of tape. . . . Jim, you did make sense out of what she said, didn't you?"

"So did you, without choosing to admit the fact. It wasn't only seeing her get up when she shouldn't have been able to move which jolted you off base. It started earlier, when she warned you that you can't take the 'come' out of 'comet.' That's a classically exact diagnosis of your trouble. You're a highly-sexed woman, and you can't abolish that fact simply by trying to fly a cometary orbit and spending most of your life a long way from the sun."

"Sun!" Ariadne gave a harsh laugh. "I'd hate to have you as the light of my life!"

Unperturbed, Reedeth continued, "Sun S-U-N—son S-O-N—a second-order pun: you're trying to deny a strong maternal instinct which is going to cause trouble unless you—"

"Oh, this is a puerile parlor-game!"

"Sorry." He looked at her steadily. "Are you questioning a computer analysis of your own file?"

"You had the gall to pry into my personal file?"

135

"Of course not. But as soon as she'd finished prophesying I asked my desketary for the closest match to each of the sections of her oracle, and it named you right away. The others— No, come to think of it, you should be able to spot at least one of the other two. I'd always been told that pythonesses talked in riddles, but I guessed two of her subjects before the computers confirmed them."

"I'd better sit down," Ariadne muttered, and moved to a chair. Swallowing hard, she resumed, "Well, I suppose one of them was Celia Prior Flamen?"

"Naturally. Mother Superior—Prioress."

"But there's nothing remarkable about that. Flamen's a public figure, and though I don't suppose he exactly advertises his wife's presence here it can't have been hard to learn of it."

"And ensure that she was in the audience? She only went to green this morning."

"Yes, but—"

"I'm not arguing," Reedeth cut in. "I'm just saying the oracle is a good capsule diagnosis. She resents her husband's devotion to his career, doesn't she?"

"Hmmm . . . Yes, I see: 'Hamlet ignored her,' meaning her husband always in the center of the stage. It fits, I grant you that. How did the rest of it go—something about envying Ophelia?"

"Precisely. Not to mention 'and then there was nun' —religious recluse-type nun. 'Get thee to a nunnery, go!' She's in retreat; we even have to call the cells retreats here, thanks to Mogshack's mealy-mouthedness. So in essence what the pythoness said, and what the computers seem to have confirmed, is that she should never have been brought here in the first place because shutting her up enables her to feed on a diet of self-pity. Does that make you feel any happier about Flamen's threat to take her away?"

"Well, obviously if the computers say she'd be better off outside . . . But how could sending her back to her husband help? It was his company she couldn't stand in the first place."

"So look for an alternative. *I* don't know what she needs, but it's bound to be something which can engage her most violent emotions. You can't escape self-generated tensions by withdrawing from external stress. In a case like hers you need the outside pressures as a source of distraction."

"I'll check it out," Ariadne muttered. "But taking the word of a pythoness . . . What's Mogshack going to say?"

"He's going to mourn the loss of a patient. He always does. But you're not taking her word unsupported. He can hardly question the judgment of his beloved computers. All Lyla Clay has done is direct our attention to places we hadn't looked before. It was a terrific idea of yours, you know. Perhaps there ought to be *staff* pythonesses in mental hospitals."

She gave a wan smile. "Who was the third subject?" she said after a pause. "I can't figure it out."

"To be candid I don't think I'd have guessed either. Though he was on my mind, because he's always on my mind. Harry Madison."

"What? I think you'd better play over the recording for me. I don't see that at all."

Reedeth instructed the desketary to comply, and when they had once more finished listening to the high clear voice of Lyla as it peaked towards an inexplicable climax of terror, Ariadne shook her head in bafflement.

"Liar's prize! A man who isn't dead! What conceivable connection could that have with Harry?"

"I asked, and that's what I was told." Reedeth drew a deep breath. "The only conclusion I can come to is that —well, perhaps he's told the computers more than he's told us."

"How do you mean?"

"Look, everyone knows Harry Madison has been fit for discharge for months, but he's trapped in here by a legalistic snarl-up. He can't be discharged in his guardian's care as the law demands because the Army doesn't want to know about him. I can't discharge him in my own care because it's not legal—my current license is for hospital practice only. And he's the only knee in the place, which means he's avoided by most of the other patients. It's small wonder, isn't it, that spending all day with his machines he's taken to making them his confidants?"

"Literally?"

"The computers identified him instantly as the third subject. Obviously they know more about him than I do. They may even know more about him than he does himself. It wouldn't be the first time that had happened. And come to think of it . . ." His voice trailed away and he combed thoughtfully at his beard with hooked fingers.

"Yes?"

"I just remembered something!" Agitated, Reedeth tensed. "Look, while you were setting things up for the pythoness, I asked my desketary what Mogshack thought of Flamen turning up fully laden with recording equipment, and I got an answer which . . . Well, frankly at the time I thought it was kind of a wisecrack, and something else came up which distracted me, so I've only this moment thought of it again. Ariadne, have you ever known a machine to make a joke?"

"Make a *joke?*" she echoed incredulously. "No, of course not!"

"In that case, it's not just Madison that the automatics know more about than I do, but Mogshack too! My God! This is terrible!"

Staring at him in bewilderment, Ariadne said, "Jim, you—what's wrong? You look haggard all of a sudden. You look *old!*"

"I'm not surprised," he answered grimly. "Here, let's see if I can recover the recording." He glanced at his watch. "Now the time must have been—hmmm . . . Oh, roughly between fourteen-thirty and fifteen." Turning to the desketary, he ordered it to review the recordings it had made during the relevant period.

"Find me the passage concerned with Dr. Mogshack's reasons for approving of Matthew Flamen," he concluded. There was a pause. Obediently the machine replayed the dialogue with the time-labeling tick in the background.

Reedeth: "How does Mogshack feel about this idea—Flamen recording the show for possible transmission?"

Automatics: "Any publicity which may help to dispel common misapprehensions about conditions in this hospital, where so many citizens of New York State are likely to spend part of their—"

Reedeth: "Look, I don't want a PR handout! You wouldn't expect Mogshack to welcome publicity on a spoolpigeon show like Flamen's. People mainly associate him with exposés and scandals. So why should Mogshack give permission for this recording?"

Automatics: "Dr. Mogshack approves of anything which may further his personal ambition."

Reedeth: "And what's that?"

Automatics: "To find at least the population of New York State, and preferably the entire United States, committed to his care."

A click cut short the recorded sound of Reedeth chuckling, but this time it didn't seem in the least funny.

"Even with the advantage of a certain degree of historical perspective, such as we might expect to enjoy from our standpoint a few decades later, it is by no means easy to define the reasons why late twentieth-century society underwent so violent a process of fragmentation following a relatively long period of consolidation and homogenization. Two factors render the analysis especially difficult: first, the human mind is not particularly well adapted to reconciling information from disparate sources (e.g. personal experience with the content of a school history-lesson, data from a printed page with those from a vuset), and the alleged simplistic linearity of the Gutenberg era—if it ever existed—came to an end before it had affected more than a minuscule proportion of the species; and second, the process is not merely still going on—it's still accelerating.

"However, one can tentatively point to three major causes which, like tectonic events in the deep strata of the Earth's crust, not only produce reverberations over enormous areas but actually create discontinuities sharp enough to be uniquely attributed: what one might call psychological landslides.

"By far the most striking of these three is the unforeseen rejection of rationality which has overtaken us. Perhaps one might argue that it was foreshadowed in such phenomena as the adoption by that technically brilliant sub-culture, the Nazis, of *Rassenwissenschaft,* Hoerbiger's pre-scientific *Welteislehre,* and similar incongruous dogmas. However, it was not until about two generations later that the principle emerged in a fully rounded form, and it became clear that the dearest ambition of a very large number of our species was to abdicate the power of reason altogether: ideally, to enjoy the same kind of life as a laboratory rat with electrodes implanted in the pleasure centers of his brain, gladly starving within reach of food and water.

"Roughly sixty percent of the patients currently in mental hospitals throughout North America are there because they did their best to achieve this ambition with the help of psychedelic drugs.

"But this is not the only level on which the effects of the process are detectable. It is notorious that one of the boom industries of the twenty-first century is the charm-and-idol business, spearheaded by the multi-billion dollar corporation of Conjuh Man Inc. with its tight grip on all the Negro enclaves and most of the ex-colonial countries, and rapidly expanding into supposedly more sophisticated areas in the wake of such firms as Lares & Penates Inc.

"For once it is perfectly clear why they've had this swift and resounding success. Our society is no longer run by individuals, but by holders of offices; it's complexity is such that the average person's predicament compares with that of a savage tribesman, his horizons bounded by a single valley, for whom knowledge of the cycle of the seasons is a hard-won intellectual prize and whose only possible reaction when confronted with drought, or flood, or blighted crops, is to hypothesize evil spirits which he must placate by sacrifice and self-denial. There are no economic counterparts of weather forecasts available to the public. The data which might enable them to be issued over the vu-beams are jealously guarded by the priests serving corporation gods, and outsiders are compelled to put up with the physical consequences of mysterious incomprehensible seasons. Take a vacation; you come back to discover that an urban landmark has vanished as completely as though an earthquake had felled a mountain. . . .

"Closely allied to this first factor is the second, which might be termed the socialization of paranoia. In a single generation individual anxiety at our inability to deal with the massed resources of computerized corporations, government agencies and other public bodies has resulted in the mushrooming of contract law into a bigger industry than advertising. A simple purchase can turn into a week-long wrangle involving the submission of a contract to three, four or more computerized consultancies. There are contracts for *everything*—merely for having a tooth stopped, one must evaluate, argue over, amend, and eventually sign a document running to five or six thousand words. Parents make contracts with schools for the education of their children; doctors make them with their patients, and if the patients are too ill or too mentally disturbed to pass a computer examination, then they refuse to proceed with treatment until someone who is legally *compos mentis* can be found to act as proxy. In the richest society of all history, we behave like misers terrified of parting with a single coin.

"Accepting that behind the smiling face of that salesman, the grave sympathy of that doctor, the formal authority of that bureaucrat, there lies the indescribable power of a megabrain computer, we are naturally enough driven to endow ourselves with symbols of power of our own, and the cheapest and—as one might put it— the most vivid of such symbols are arms.

"Twice in my own lifetime I've seen my country threaten to fly apart like a tire stripping its tread: first during the black insurrections of the early eighties, and again during the war scare of the nineties. The first of these events put a new word into the language, and the second branded it on our minds permanently. The

cartel founded by Marcantonio Gottschalk is deliberately structured on the lines of a family—that basic
social unit which a man feels he is defending when he
installs armored picture-windows instead of the old glass,
plants mines as carefully as rosebushes in his front garden. And the technique has proved psychologically apt.

"Nowadays the average family changes its guns as
often as our grandparents changed their cars; they have
their grenades serviced like their fire-extinguishers; husband, wife and teenage kids go shooting the way people
once used to go bowling. It is taken for granted that tonight, or tomorrow, or sometime, it will be necessary to
kill a man.

"Along with the flight from rationality and the socialization of paranoia, there is a third factor at work which
interlocks with them both. Where do you turn when
traditional sources of reassurance fail you? Man needs
some kind of psychological sheet-anchor and always has.
In some countries it has proved possible to maintain a
public image of government which meets that need, but
here it was out of the question. For one thing, the majority of Americans have always been distrustful of government interference. Government is a long way away
in a big country, and our mental roots go deeper back
in time than the advent of modern high-speed communications. For another, the monstrous complexity of
our society makes it impossible for any single man, no
matter how well-intentioned, to achieve major reforms
in his term of office—he's bucking too great a weight
of administrative inertia. (Besides, well-intentioned men
don't run for office any more! They have too much sense
to expose themselves to assassination, and only delusible
idiots like our current chief executive can be persuaded
to don the robes of high office. Nice guys don't crave
power.)

"What drove the final nail into the coffin of that particular hope, however, were the black insurrections of
the eighties, which demonstrated that the Federal au-

thorities were incapable of controlling large sections of their own cities up to and including Washington DC.

"Organized religion likewise failed—spectacularly—simultaneously with government and for roughly similar reasons, when it became clear that the so-called 'godless' rivals to our own way of life not only commanded far more loyalty but made better use of their relatively limited resources.

"People found themselves with virtually nothing left but the idol of the computer, in which the less imaginative now tend to invest their surplus of otherwise valueless faith, and a handful of what might be termed *gurus* —doctors, psychologists, sociologists, anyone who talks as though he (or she) understands and can control the inchoate forces that are universally sensed and universally feared.

"To illustrate how absurd the process has become: there are quite a number of people who call themselves 'Conroyans' after myself. I want to stress that they do so without my permission and also, so far as I can manage, without my connivance. I don't approve of my, or anyone else's, name being taken in vain."

—Preamble to lecture notes issued by Xavier Conroy to students taking his course in Contemporary American Studies

Eventually Ariadne gave a harsh laugh. "Jim, you're not going to take that seriously! Aren't you overlooking the fact that Harry Madison is after all a patient here? I'm not really familiar with his case, and I know you keep saying he ought to have been discharged long ago, but you surely have to assume there are good reasons why he hasn't been! And certainly"—her tone grew more assertive—"if he's getting so well acquainted with our automatics that he can rig them to utter that sort of rubbish, that's no index of sanity. It's more the opposite!"

Reedeth dropped back into his chair as though his legs would no longer support him. "Madison can't tinker with the main data banks," he said. "All he can do is make adjustments to the remotes, like eliminating censor circuits—which is what he seems to have done to my desketary. To get at the main banks you need a secret IBM code, and however clever Harry may be I refuse to believe he can deduce *that* from just studying the remotes! Am I right?"

"Y-yes. I mean, I guess so."

"I'm *telling* you. Do you trust the automatics here?"

"Well . . ."

"Yes or no?"

"One has to!" Ariadne snapped.

Reedeth leaned forward. "All right then: you've just had a clear diagnosis of megalomania from these *trust-*

worthy automatics. A few minutes ago you consented to accept what they told you about the pythoness's oracles, didn't you? What's different in this case? Only the subject."

"Jim, you're deluding yourself," Ariadne said firmly. The sound of shutters going up around her mind, armored against anything short of a nuke, was very nearly audible in the room. Once more the cold, composed archetypal doctor-figure to which her patients were accustomed, stable pillar of authority in a chaotic universe—even her lips visibly narrowed from the soft sensuality of their recent love-making—she marched towards the door.

"If you're so eager to believe what your desketary can tell you now that one of the patients has tampered with it," she concluded, "I suggest you ask it to give you some insight into your own jealousy of Dr. Mogshack!"

And she was gone.

"This is a pink alert for NYC east and north zones, yellow statewide, repeat pink for NYC east and north zones. It was anticipated that the X Patriot demonstrators assembled at Kennedy would disperse peacefully following the announcement that Morton Lenigo had cleared customs and immigration but unfortunately this has not proved to be the case. A number of inflammatory speeches were made claiming that his admission is the forerunner of a major kneeblank victory. X Patriots and other extremists are closing on NYC by skimmer, ground transport and possibly by rapitrans. Most are armed, many are orbiting and all are potentially violent. Citidef groups stand to stand to stand to. Await orders from Internal Security Maintenance officers. Repeat pink alert NYC east and north. Ends ends ends. Stand by for further announcements."

FORTY-NINE IF YOU'RE AFRAID OF THE DARK YOU
CAN ALWAYS CARRY A FLASHLIGHT
BUT THERE'S NO CHEAP PORTABLE
PROTECTION AGAINST LONELINESS

On her way from the elevator Lyla checked the comweb at the end of the corridor; like most fitted in these
cheap recent apt blocks, it was big and ugly and armored and would need a bomb to put it out of action.
When she dipped in the message slot, though, all she
found was a drying puddle of activator fluid—the management had let it run out of fax paper again. No use
having the thing in working order if there was nothing
to record on.

But her spirits were too low for her to get annoyed.
Her depression had set in before she left Flamen's place,
and had only been aggravated by seeing him so pleased
about something she didn't understand, the fruit of his
cryptic conversation with the fat man called Lionel. The
world had abruptly turned drab for her. Perhaps the
after-effect of the sibyl-pill was responsible, but she had
no previous experience to judge by. She had never before been slapped out of trance.

Worse yet: she wouldn't have believed Dan's unsupported word, but having seen Flamen's recording she
couldn't contest the necessity any longer. Echo-traps
had been the—mental, if not physical, and hence even
worse—death of at least three pythonesses she knew of.

So there were endless problems to worry her: falling

148

into the echo-trap (for what conceivable reason?), the uncertain consequences of trying to metabolize the remainder of the drug in the non-trance state, and that weird hangover which had caused her to speak what amounted to an oracle during the skimmer-flight to Flamen's home.

Applying her Punch key, with its unique magnetic pattern, to the lock of the apt's door, she struggled to decide whether or not the same person had been referred to as the one whose presence had driven her into an echo-trap. Allegedly—but pythoness talent was too fragile to take kindly to laboratory examination—there must have been some exceptionally powerful personality present in the audience, one whose aura of authority overwhelmed her best attempts to move away and tackle another subject.

Flamen himself? It was unlikely; they had spent half an hour or so running over the three oracles she had managed to utter in complete form, and concluded that none of them applied to him. He had been very obviously relieved.

She slipped rapidly under the deadfall, which was inactivated when the lock was fitted with the proper key and remained safe until the door was closed again, and shut out the world with a slam.

Tossing her yash to the peg—it missed and she had to pick it up and make a second try—she called, "Dan?"

No answer.

Going to the icebox, she found a partly-eaten loaf with mold on it and some peanut butter so old the oil had separated. But she wasn't hungry. In the freezer compartment there was a range of blue and green and brown phials which had to be kept very cold to prolong their usable life; in one of the brown ones labeled in Dan's handwriting she found one and a half joylets and took them.

Nothing much happened. They were probably stale. She went to the kitchen wallboard and scrawled JOYLETS in bold chalked capitals at the foot of the current shopping list. And there was no mescal ready or anything else like that, and right now she couldn't face the chore of preparing some. No liquor, no joints, no nothing in the place. She thought of Mikki Baxendale in her luxury penthouse and felt a stab of pity for Dan who had come so near to money.

But the bed hadn't been fixed and she started to be angry with him instead. Dumping herself like a badly-stuffed doll into a patched inflatable chair, she leaned back and scowled at the ceiling.

She had never felt like this before after a session. Ordinarily she was excited, pleased at the hints of relevance which peeped out of the doggerel of her oracles, eager to trace clues half-hidden in a tangle of sub-conscious associations, and by nightfall—or whenever—very sexy.

She fingered herself experimentally. It was like touching a corpse.

So once again back on the worn groove of her puzzlement, thankful that the joylets had at least lifted her depression far enough for her to regard the effort of concentration as worthwhile.

If one of the audience had obsessed her to the point of creating an echo-trap for her, the likeliest assumption was that the same person was being referred to when she spoke of someone in the hospital being more rational than the director. Who? What kind of a patient could be in the Ginsberg not because he was crazy but because he was too sane?

It was no use cracking her skull, she decided at length. She'd never been able to analyze her own oracles unaided; she wanted Dan here to talk to, the tape to play over and over so that the words etched deep into her conscious mind. Where the hell had that stupid mack gone, anyway?

To distract herself she jumped up and started on a whirlwind round of the apt with the polycleaner, gulping dust and rubbish. The morning's mail had dissolved into the sludgy mess of books before the Lar, and she scooped it all up in handfuls and threw it down the toilet. The fourth time she tried to flush the pan the water failed and the last grayish lump lay mocking her, irremovable.

Sudden uncontrollable rage took possession of her. She stormed back to the Lar's shrine and seized it by its protuberant ears. It was a Model YJK, the most suitable in the non-customized range for a pythoness or other similar talent . . . according to the accompanying sales leaflets. In form it resembled a crouching fennec, the big-eared desert fox.

"Luck and good fortune!" she said between her teeth. "Liar liar *liar* rotten *liar!*" At each word she gave the idol a vicious twist between her hands, hoping something would snap off, but the tough flexible plastic merely sprang back into shape; only the tail assumed a limp question-mark curve.

"In that case—" she said, and strode over to their one openable window. Flinging it up, she started to hurl the Lar the thirty-plus meters to the street below, and instantly a beam lanced out of darkness and cracked the lintel, showering her with dust and concrete chips.

Gasping, clutching the Lar to her like a child, she dropped to the floor. For long moments all she was aware of was the muscle-tension and foul taste of her own terror, and the huge thumping beat of her heart. Her mind's eye was filled with the picture of herself lying on the windowsill, as she might have fallen had the laser's alignment been accurate, with a seared line across her breasts.

Eventually she recovered enough self-possession to think of putting out the light, closing the window—very cautiously, from the side at arm's length—and replacing the Lar in its niche, distantly aware that if she had indeed thrown it away there would have been a hell of a fight with Dan. The seven-day appro was up to-morrow and if they couldn't return it they would be billed two thousand tealeaves.

Then, standing well back in shadow, she peered out of the window to see what was going on. A side-effect of joylets was to reduce auditory sensitivity; she had to strain through a kind of muffling mental blanket to perceive faint exterior sounds, but now she was paying attention what she heard took on a familiar pattern that would ordinarily have put her instantly on the alert. Barely discernible chanting and drumming, as though one were suddenly to notice the circulation of the city-monster like an amplified human pulse; a screaming child, maybe caught on the street between police barriers, parents too frightened to come out looking for it; once long ago when she was about fourteen she had heard a sober middle-class couple, friends of her mother's, quietly discussing during a riot in which one of their own sons had been stranded whether they should have another of their own were he to be found dead, or whether they were too old, and better advised to adopt. . . .

The voice of the novice Gottschalk rang out in memory, offering them—what was it?—"guns for a mere sixty-three with maker's warranty." She clenched her fists in blind frustration. Another of their damnable promotions, presumably! It was the regular Gottschalk technique: select an area where sales were below average, saturate it with rumors until someone's temper reached the break-ing point and the inevitable division occurred into blank and kneeblank, and then the following day take ad-vantage of people's frayed nerves to sell guns, grenades and mines.

But a droning from overhead disturbed her train of thought, and she dropped below the windowsill to peer upwards. She saw a police gunship hovering under its rotors, and realized that this wasn't any mere Gottschalk promotion. That was one of the big ships, capable of leveling whole city blocks. She'd seen them do it on news-tapes—

News! They'd acquired a vuset, hadn't they? Furious now at her own forgetfulness, she headed for it, turned back to blank out the windows—that sniper was too damned trigger-happy for comfort and might well fire on the reflection from the screen even if she turned it away from the window—and traced the cord along the floor until she found the leech. When she clipped it to the wall the set hummed to life.

On the Holocosmic channel: advertising. It was well into prime time by now, of course. Advertising on Global —advertising on Ninge, NY-NJ—advertising on Pan-Can...

What was that? An unmarked setting, between Pan-Can the big Canadian fixed-antenna relay poised at twenty thousand meters not in orbit but on a mono-molecular cable and the adjacent channel allotted to Quebeçois French-language programs. Something had lit the screen which shouldn't have been there.

Delicately she returned the knob to the intermediate position and there was a fat grinning kneeblank in West African robes swimming in a blur of color as though a very thin film of oil on water surrounded every sharp edge between pale and dark zones. She'd hit one of the pirate satellites, probably Nigerian or Ghanaian, of which two or three were launched every year and kept their orbit over areas with disaffected black minorities until the PCC could wheedle the appropria-tions and fund an interceptor to knock them down. The African and Asian countries had opted out of the PCC almost as soon as it was founded, and declined to recognize its rulings.

With a perfect imitation of the harsh-sweet Gullah/ Creole/Jamaican accent affected by large numbers of knees in the black enclaves of America, the man in the screen said, "We scoop Mister Charley's lying propaganda, broze an' sis! We got *truth* an' the buckras' lies will fade afore the win', the sto'm an' tornaduh of nigra wrath! They runnin' to hahd in N'yohk City—watchah, watchah, broze an' sis!"

The screen flicked to a satellite view of New York, and instantly it was clear there was something wrong. Street lights were out over polyblock areas, and threads of silver stabbed across them: rocket-trails.

"Oh, Christ!" Lyla whispered, knuckles to teeth in a childish gesture of apprehension.

"That the X Patriots, broze an' sis," said the revoltingly smug voice over. "To'ch-berrer Mohton Lenigo fresh from tri-*yum*phant battles with the British gumment, *Cah*-diff, *Blackman*-chester, Birming-*ham!*" And matching cuts of stock news stabbed in: Cardiff Castle fountaining skyward into rubble, the last white Lord Mayor of Manchester being driven out barefoot and in chains to a waiting government skimmer, Lenigo himself in Birmingham's famous old Bull Ring, surrounded by grinning knees.

"Come to kick yoh lazy nigras off yo' asses!" the voice said sternly. "When yo' gone drahve them buckras outa N'yohk—hey? Tonaht? Could be! You get *at* it, broze an' sis! Ev'y metah an' centimetah o' those *tawllll* towahs, those *deeeep* basemen'ss, they been watered with BLACK BLOOD—"

Convulsively Lyla tore the leech away from the wall and the set died.

They let in Morton Lenigo? They let in *Morton Lenigo?* They let in MORTON LENIGO?

Impossible. Incredible. No, they couldn't. She looked at herself in the faint gray light which seeped through the windows on the side away from the street, seeing her summer tan fishbelly-pallid, thinking *honky dont let the sun shin on you head it make you an easy target.*

"Dan," she said in a trembling little-girl voice. "Dan?" But he wasn't there. In darkness, silence except for the distant racket of the fighting which grew louder and softer by unpredictable turns, she waited passive as the Lar for someone or something to rescue her from the insufferable real world.

FIFTY   THE GRAPH IS ALWAYS GREENER WHERE THE DESERT BLOSSOMS LIKE A ROSE

Conservative—perhaps because elderly—Marcantonio Gottschalk the grandfather of the clan based on the traditional Mafiareas of the New Jersey seaboard; not so Anthony or Vyacheslav or any of the other transistorized/computerized/dynamized younger generation. For them the ultimately defensible heartland, the Nevada desert: indrawn like a closing sea-anemone, waiting for the sooner-or-later moment when *boom*.

And here, right on schedule, boom! Anthony Gottschalk whose picture had not for five years found its way onto any official file, whose polysyllabic praenomen was not household knowledge like Marcantonio's but who was already thinking of possible extensions to suit the eventual dignity of headship (current favorite: Antonioni; lying second: Antoniescu for no particular reason except he liked the sound of it), in his Nevada fortress with noises underfloor to signify work proceeding ace-apace on apace-in-the-hole *Robert* Gottschalk—name deliberately chosen to mislead since it was impossible to hide the project completely from the scrutiny of Federal computers, capable of interpretation as some preternaturally gifted new recruit vulnerable to a gun or a grenade. . . .

But Robot Gottschalk was vulnerable to virtually

nothing. At his quasi-father Anthony's fortress home he grew like an embryo seventy meters below the lowest basement, deep in the living rock; sounds from work on him were channeled via tunnels which would later be closed with armored doors; you'd have to risk contaminating or firing the whole western half of the continent to make sure of shattering his solid-state circuitry.

Thick-set, dark-haired but very pale with milky eyes, Anthony Gottschalk stood breathing the clean desert breeze wafting off his estate, scented with oranges, lemons, bougainvilleas, frangipanis, uncountable varieties of lovely trees and shrubs. Coup after coup shed rosy glows in his mind: sales to Blackbury of weapons stick-in-the-mud old Marcantonio wouldn't risk for fear of Federal clampdown (and who among *that* gang of clowns would risk action when they found out? asked Anthony Gottschalk)—hinting in Detroit how to solve the Morton Lenigo impasse—solved today and coming along nicely, with insurrection almost on Marcantonio's doorstep by God, wonderful!—and stacked up in the pipeline the biggest and most profitable of all, of all, of all. . . .

His mind calmed a little; he had been growing manic on no stronger drug than knowledge of his own impending success. Marcantonio was eighty count the years *eighty!* Should have been retired years ago. All very well to head the cartel in days of bow-and-arrow, now in modern age useless, short-sighted, over-cautious. Report from Robert already to hand, installation nearly complete, partial evaluations already recoverable by punching the proper code on the keyboard here . . .

Turning, he bent to the board and checked on late developments. Probability of sales tomorrow in New York State: $12,000,000 plus or minus $1,500,000. Sales index for whole country 35%. Grand Project realizability rating up by three points in the past hour!

Anthony Gottschalk performed a little tapdance of joy. The Lenigo revolution was well on the way. If only

one could arrange for Marcantonio to catch a misdi-
rected shot . . .

But no. Alas no. There in his New Jersey estate he
was at least as well protected as Anthony here, Vyacheslav upstate, any other polly. It would take Robert to
figure out a breach in the defenses.

He would. There was nothing else on the continent,
nothing on the *planet* to match Robot Gottschalk: the
Federal government bled white (horse laugh) by its
own massive purchases from the Gottschalk cartel as
the hydra of insurrection burst out like a dormant forest
fire here today, there tomorrow, the day after in fifty
cities at once, could never have afforded him. The nearest
approach would be Oom Paul at Capetown, the computer which for over a generation had enabled five
million whites to dance mocking rings around the knees
who hated them. That would obviously be the second
market zone for the Grand Project; he'd thought of Britain but since the destruction of Whitehall you could
forget Britain. Over there people could barely afford
shotguns.

And once Marcantonio had been buried—at the head
of a five-mile cortège, naturally, for he had in his day
been a great man—there was almost no limit to the
possibilities open to the Gottschalks. Bapuji could sell
to Asia and Olayinka to Africa faster than their plants
could keep up. Chop-chop like a butcher's cleaver, the
slashing lines of demarcation between man and man,
woman and woman, man and woman . . . Hmmm!
Maybe not that; necessary to breed to keep up the con-
sumer-level. . . . High birth-rate in Latin America still . . .

He laughed. What was the good of relying on his own
insight any more? It had got him Robert, and Robert
even before he was finished had blackmailed Morton
Lenigo into the country, something the melanists here
had been failing to manage for two years or more, and
within hours of his arrival the sales probability graph
soaring, just *soaring!* From this point on—mockingly

Anthony Gottschalk removed an imaginary hat—Robert/Robot Gottschalk was the actual head of the cartel, regardless of who might be the titular grandfather.

Of course, Lenigo could hardly be relied on to achieve here what he had managed in Britain: the knee patrols on street-corners, armed, black and brown faces scowling at the blanks shuffling shabby to their low-paid daily grind, saving desperately even if it meant denying their children food in order to buy weapons from Gottschalk air-drops made on lonely ground in the Welsh mountains, the fens of East Anglia, the moors of Devon and Yorkshire, smuggled by blank commando units across city borders for resale at inflated prices.

Nonetheless, if his mere presence could provoke this sort of instant panic—"just add Lenigo!"—Robert would have paid for himself the day after his scheduled completion.

What more could anyone ask?

FIFTY-ONE

IF YOUR NUMBER COMES UP THEN YOUR NUMBER COMES UP AND THAT'S ALL THERE IS TO IT SO WHAT'S THE USE OF WORRYING THAT'S WHAT I ALWAYS SAY

Along about one when the troubled city was quieter and the gunships had been withdrawn without more than two or three blocks having to be razed Lyla discovered that she had fallen asleep on the floor under the folding table which with legs properly braced might serve as protection against flying glass or bits of the ceiling falling on her. She was very stiff and very cold and what had woken her was the shrill complaint of their comweb indicating that there was a call awaiting her or Dan at the end of the corridor.

It was a common trick to get doors opened in blocks like this one during riots. She ignored the noise, hating its insistence and wishing it would stop.

When after a long long time it did so, she thought about it being used to determine whether the apt was empty or not, and crawled into the kitchen where their gun was kept, dusty at the back of a closet. It was very old—Dan said it had been used in the Blackbury insurrection of the eighties—but in those days things had been built to last and it had still worked when Dan checked it just before Easter.

Straining her ears, discovering that the effect of the

joylets had worn off and she could now hear normally again, she detected footsteps outside, and then there was a groan and something she couldn't place, a verbal sound without content, and then there was a bang on the door and a voice she recognized said, "Miss Clay!"

She pointed the gun, looking to make sure the dead-fall catch was set.

"Miss Clay! Ah—Bill here! I talked to you this morning, remember? I've got Mr. Kazer here and he's hurt!"

What?

Moving slowly, as though through deep water, she secured the deadfall, chained the door, looked out through a crack on its right side with gun leveled and there was a lean, serious-faced young man in a black oversuit holding up Dan with both hands and blood running, dripping, streaming from his belly, down his legs, puddling, smearing, stinking in the hot night air.

He put his hand out weakly to catch the jamb and she couldn't push the door shut enough to release the chain and the Gottschalk had to drag him back and he screamed faintly and when Lyla got the door open at eternal last he almost fell through. Together she and Bill guided him to the broken bed and laid him on it; he wouldn't straighten at first so that they could see the wound in his belly but when eventually he overcame the pain enough to roll on his back with a bit of help it could be seen that there was a monstrous gash with the shape of organs bulging through. His eyes were shut and his face was paper-white and after a moment his breathing faded.

"Get a doctor!" Lyla said with colossal, incredible effort past the need to vomit.

"No doctor will come out tonight," Bill said. "There's a curfew."

"But we can't just let him die!" Lyla spun on her heel, ran to the bathroom, looked for disinfectant, dressings, anything useful, came back empty-handed and weeping, the tears welling out of her eyes with a curious dry tickling like flies crawling down her cheeks.

"I'm afraid he *is* dead," the Gottschalk said, and let go the wrist at which he had checked the pulse.

"What?"

"I'm very sorry." Himself pale, the Gottschalk avoided her eyes, looking down at the blood which had splashed on his black oversuit. "He must have been hit with an axe, I guess, or maybe a sabre. It's a miracle he was able to get in the elevator and shout loud enough for me to hear when he made it to this floor."

Lyla stood like a waxwork, registering the words but not reacting.

"Oh, if only people took notice of the warnings we give them!" the Gottschalk went on sorrowfully, shaking his head. "He should have been armed—he should have been able to defend himself! You don't need training to use things like Blazers, and no one with a mere axe or sword can get within striking distance against one of them."

"What did you say?" Lyla brought out very slowly.

"I said if he'd been armed, able to protect himself—" The implications of Lyla's expression belatedly penetrated the Gottschalk's mind and he broke off in alarm.

"Get out. You're a ghoul. You're disgusting. You're not human."

"Now look here, Miss—!"

"You're a devil!" Lyla was half-choking on her own sobs; proper words wouldn't come to match the hate that had exploded in her mind. She had dropped the gun on the table in the kitchen when she put her arm around Dan, or she would have shot the Gottschalk where he stood. Lacking that, what for a weapon? The Lar was in arm's reach; she caught it up and threw it and it struck him on the forehead. He cried out and put up his hands, foolishly, much too late.

"Out!" Lyla screamed at him, and raised the big brass tray in both hands, rushing at him. His fist warding it off made it sound like a cracked gong, and her voice rose to a shrill peak of loathing.

"Gottschalk! Gottschalk! Gottschalk!"

Whirling, she ran to the kitchen to retrieve the gun and he came after her, snatching at her arm, dragging her off balance, getting past her and making it to the door, tugging it open and—leaping back as the deadfall jarred down its overdue-for-greasing grooves with a slam that shook the building.

"I wish it had squashed you," Lyla said, picking herself off the floor. "You need to be stomped, like a bedbug." She tried for the gun again, still on the table, but he was faster—he wasn't trembling with the shock of a lover's death. It was his hope and ambition to cause many deaths. He was an arms salesman by choice, calm and even a little happy to see his products in such demand, capable of trying to clinch a sale at the bedside of a fresh corpse. He tripped her as she reached for the gun, caught it up himself and turned the butt into his palm with a practiced flip. Back on the floor she looked at him with hate in her eyes.

Breathing hard, he sidled to the winch and one-handed raised the deadfall, fixed the catch by touch, gun leveled, watching Lyla intently. He opened the door, glanced to make sure the corridor was empty, vanished and slammed it behind him.

"Oh Christ," Lyla said. Then, as she realized she was sitting in a patch of Dan's wet new blood, sticky on her bare thigh, she said again, "Oh Christ."

There was no answer.

Danger of 'guerrilla' war in US
                    New York, January 10
  A retired United States Army intelligence
officer has suggested that unrest in America's cities could lead to full-scale prolonged
guerrilla warfare involving large army units,
which could be as difficult to quell as
guerrilla activities in South-East Asia.
  In the January issue of the "Army Mag-
azine" Colonel Robert B. Rigg writes:
  "So far, the causes of urban violence
have been emotional and social. Organ-
isation, however, can translate these grievances into political ones of serious potential, and result in violence or even
prolonged warfare.
  "Man has constructed out of steel and
concrete a much better 'jungle' than nature
has created out of Vietnam. Such cement-
and-brick jungles can offer better security
to snipers and city guerrillas than the
Vietcong enjoy in their jungles, elephant
grass and marshes."
  Guerrilla warfare in the cities might be
fomented by Communist China or Cuba,

he says. Some US intelligence circles were aware that the more dangerous conspirators in ghettoes were being prompted by members of the pro-Chinese wing of the US Communist Party.

Neither full application of fire-power nor political negotiation was likely to be effective against urban guerrillas, he says.

"There are measures that offer a better solution if we are to keep our cities from becoming battle-grounds: penetration by police and reliance on traditional FBI methods. Such efforts must begin now so as to prevent organised guerrilla violence from gaining momentum.

"A whole new manual of military operations, tactics and techniques needs to be written in respect of urban warfare of this nature. Army units must be oriented and trained to know the cement-and-asphalt jungle of every American city."

Colonel Rigg says that manoeuvres carried out in large cities could prove a deterrent to urban insurrection. —Reuter.

FIFTY-THREE ASSUMPTION CONCERNING THE
FOREGOING MADE FOR THE PURPOSES
OF THIS STORY

Either it wasn't done or it didn't work.

Lyla Clay possesses a super-normal talent.

Lyla Clay works at being a pythoness like any regular job.

Dan Kazer has been her lover for between two and three years.

Dan Kazer has been marketing her as a successful product.

Matthew Flamen is horrified at what's been done to his wife Celia.

Matthew Flamen let months go by without going to call on his wife in the hospital.

Celia Prior Flamen turned to drugs because she felt neglected and ignored.

Celia Prior Flamen welcomed her incarceration because it gave her the chance to be a nun.

Lionel Prior manages the last of the spoolpigeons who specializes in exposés.

Lionel Prior likes to keep up appearances at all costs.

Pedro Diablo is world-famous for his anti-white propaganda.

Pedro Diablo has more white ancestry than Negro ancestry.

Harry Madison is a patient in a mental hospital.

Harry Madison is uniquely gifted in the maintenance of complex circuitry.

James Reedeth is worried about keeping Madison in the hospital unjustifiably.

James Reedeth has never actually tried to get Madison released.

Ariadne Spoelstra is in love with Reedeth.

Ariadne Spoelstra maintains that "love is a dependent state" and dangerous for a psychiatrist.

Elias Mogshack is dedicated to the ideal of mental health.

Elias Mogshack hoards his patients like a miser.

Hermann Uys is a white South African expert on race.

Hermann Uys is in fanatically melanist Blackbury.

Morton Lenigo is determined to overthrow the white United States.

Morton Lenigo waited nearly three years to be granted an official entry permit to the United States.

Xavier Conroy once wrote that Division Street, Earth, runs straight through the middle of people.

Xavier Conroy, unable to compromise, has been driven to teaching in an undistinguished Canadian college.

Man is a gregarious animal: he builds cities.

Man is not a social animal: he fights wars.

The above-named are human beings.

The above-named are human beings.

Bad-tempered, sour-mouthed, queasy-stomached from lack of sleep, Matthew Flamen sat scowling in his skimmer and counted the wasting minutes as diversion after diversion was fed to the controls from the Ninge traffic computer. It was a clear still hot day and from the five-hundred meter level he could see a long way. Of the three LR's mentioned in the morning news—last resort strikes where it had been deemed necessary to bring a whole block tumbling around the ears of snipers —the Harlem and East Village ones had been doused, but over the one in the Bronx a column of smoke was rising like a straight stone pillar. The cause of the diversion, though, was the stream of Federal ships shuttling back and forth from the city to the Westchester internment camps; everything else was being routed around their reserved airlane.

At one point he found himself heading in the diametrically wrong direction.

He swore under his breath, wondering what had possessed him yesterday when he was compiling the show. He'd had that high reading on the Lenigo case, and he'd dismissed it as ridiculous, and within half an hour of his noon slot the kneeblank stations were slamming out gleeful flashes and the X Patriots were assembling in their thousands at Kennedy.

"Got to get to the *bottom* of that!" he declared aloud.

"I mean, no one takes the government seriously these days, but this is lunacy!"

Half-embarrassed at uttering such a stale platitude, not even party-handy any more, he fell silent, tugging his beard. The question stood, nonetheless: what could have possessed the Immigration Service to let Lenigo have his visa? Blackmail? It had to be, in the strict contemporary sense of one of the knee enclaves holding a knife to the Federal neck. What, who, where? Blackbury? Impossible. Mayor Black was becoming steadily more paranoid, as witness his firing of Pedro Diablo for mere genetic reasons, and on Uys's say-so too. . . .

The problem which had preoccupied him over breakfast returned briefly: whether or not, with Diablo turning up at the office today, he could make a story out of Uys's presence in the country. Was Campbell eager enough to overlook a breach of what had obviously been meant as a confidence, according to Prior's judgment, in return for full cooperation in the Diablo case?

And what was this man Diablo like as a person, anyhow? As a public figure, anybody in communications of any kind had a preconceived image of him, a brilliant, savage, wholly destructive propagandist whose canned programs were seized with cries of delight in Africa and Asia. But that was essentially irrelevant. Back in the pioneering days of the media, almost immediately after the crude and primitive radio era dominated by Dr. Goebbels, that instinctive genius of the borderline period Joe McCarthy had allegedly greeted a former acquaintance at a party, having secured his dismissal from his job, the loss of most of his friends and the acquisition of several million new enemies, with the cry, "Haven't seen much of you lately—you been avoiding me?"

Flamen nodded. Yes, he'd had insight into the pattern of the future, that man: the splits public/private, knee/blank, rich/poor, left/right, conformist/nonconformist, everything. But after so long being identified with Blackbury policies could Diablo have maintained that essential division within himself which would enable them to meet as craftsmen on a common level?

He shrugged. Only time would tell, and despite all the delays he was suffering it looked as though he would only be a matter of twenty minutes late at the Etchmark Undertower.

And, like it or not, he was going to spend the rest of the time contemplating the mystery of Lenigo's admission. Granted blackmail, eliminating Blackbury, what was left? A wealthy enclave, for sure, which meant a northern one. . . . Chicago? Hell, no. Perhaps one with especially good political *nous*—

Abruptly he snapped his fingers, looking in dismay at his own obtuseness at the maker's plaque on the dash of his own skimmer. Detroit, of course! Must be! The only knee enclave with an absolute pistol held to the head of the Federal government, the city nicknamed "Black South Africa" in allusion to their willingness to trade with the enemy as the Afrikaners had been doing for decades, coiners of the slogan "We *negrotiate* from a position of strength!"

And what could Detroit have used as a lever? Well, the computers would certainly be able to make a guess at that. Momentarily pleased, he bent a smile on the approaching city, and it vanished instantly as he realized the skimmer was being ordered to make yet another diversion, this time for a flight of Federal gunships in a show of strength, firing rockets into the East River where they fountained up columns of steam. And the martial law warning lights were flashing on all the tallest buildings including the stump of the Empire State, which had been shortened by seventeen stories during the insurrection of 1988 but remained a conspicuous landmark.

I hate martial law days, he thought. I really do. It's worse than living in a hurricane zone.

171

FIFTY-SIX

PRESS CONFERENCE GIVEN BY THE SUC-
CESSOR OF THE LAST CHIEF EX-
ECUTIVE CAPABLE OF SPANNING
THE CREDIBILITY GAP WITHOUT SPLIT-
TING HIS PANTS

President Gaylord: Morning, laze an' gemmun.
Reporters: By God, it is too! Right on the ball so far
today, Prexy!
President Gaylord: (chuckles)
Dean of reporters*: First off, Prexy, your comments
on the decision to admit Morton Lenigo to this country
in view of his known participation in the dynamiting of
Cardiff Castle, Wales, the expulsion of the Lord Mayor
of Manchester, England, and the knee seizure of the
city of Birmingham, England, and additionally in view
of the insurrection mounted in New York City overnight by X Patriots and other extremist groups which
have reacted to the decision as a confession of weakness
in face of threats from Ghana, Nigeria, and other kneeblank powers.
President Gaylord: Ah—yeah, that one was comped for
me, I think . . . just a second. (Shuffles documents on
desk.) Here we are. "The decision to admit Morton
Lenigo was taken in full cognizance of the allegations
made against him by racialist spokesmen in his home

*Martin Luther Spry, Holobeam-Reuters

172

country of Britain, and in pursuance of the ideals of the Great Society which is designed to maintain a homo —ah—homo-*genius?*—ah . . ."

Dean of reporters: "Homogeneous," maybe, Prexy?

President Gaylord: I guess so. "—balance between the justifiably independence-desirous colored citizens of the planet and their fellows who by accident of circumstances have found themselves in a position of greater good fortune."

Reporters: (laughter)

Unidentified reporter: Keep pitchin', darl—that one swerved like a (last word indecipherable, laughter)

Myramay Welborne, Pan-Can: Comments on the all-stations from Capetown recommending that you should nuke out the black enclaves starting with Detroit and shoot Lenigo while he's off his turf and his bullies can't come after?

President Gaylord: Well, Myramay! Good to see you back! Did you shed that long wet creep you got married to?

Myramay Welborne: I did not. It was a great honeymoon and it sort of stretched, that's all. How about an answer?

President Gaylord: Yeah, I guess I have something here which will fit. . . . Yeah. "It is well-known that the blank extremists of South Africa will stop at nothing to discredit the ideals of a multi-racial society. Beyond that I have no comment to make on this disgraceful suggestion."

Dean of reporters: Wish I could afford comping to your standards, Prexy. That's (emphasized) eminently usable. So what you doing tonight—?

Phyllis Logan Quality, Ninge: Excuse me, Martin, I have one more—

Dean of reporters: Sorry, thought we'd exhausted that one.

Phyllis Logan Quality: Well, with the overnight death-count at twelve hundred eleven—

Reporters: (laughter)

Phyllis Logan Quality: —and sixteen thousand arrests to be processed things are bad in my district, damn it!

Reporters: Oooh! Bad language yet! (Laughter)

Phyllis Logan Quality: It isn't funny! Our own studios were—

President Gaylord: When you've finished the commercial, Phyllis—

Reporters: (laughter)

Unidentified reporter: Give her a break, she's new around here. What's more she's kind of pretty.

President Gaylord: Better tell the automatics you want an "unidentified reporter" credit on that,———. You wouldn't want people to think you're getting susceptible after all these years, would you?

Unidentified reporter: It's all right for you, Prexy. My son Tom came home last night with a third-degree burn on his shoulder. Sniper caught him.

President Gaylord: I got a comped statement for that one too, right here somewhere. . . . Yeah. "Much as one regrets the damage to property caused by extremist—"

Unidentified reporter: The hell with property! This was my son!

President Gaylord: Ah, we got too damned many people in this country anyway.

Dean of reporters: Can we quote that?

President Gaylord: You quote what's comped for you! That does not include off-the-cuff and off-the-record remarks! You want to quote, you pick up a heap of printouts like you ought to. Is that the lot for today? I got a date at the gun club.

Dean of reporters: Sure, Prexy, wouldn't want to keep you from an important engagement. (Ends)

The sorting process at the Westchester camps started around five-thirty and by seven the arrestees with verifiable mental disorder records were being shipped into the Ginsberg and the automatics were humming with ward-of-the-state applications. They didn't call out Mogshack to attend to routine matters like this, but Reedeth was junior staff grade and they sent for him with a police skimmer at seven-ten. Officially on reserve for the month, Ariadne heard an early-morning newscast and came in at seven-fifty, and with the aid of three police psychiatrists they broke the back of the problem within a couple of hours; there were a mere seven hundred or so suspected mental cases this time. The State government had been clamping down recently, and were no longer admitting that proof of incarceration was equivalent to proof of disorder; they'd secured a Supreme Court ruling that a current doctor's certificate was essential.

Going down the alleys between the stacked and racked gas-sleepy arrestees, Reedeth checked each of their ID's: "Manfred Hal Cherkey, ship him back—Lulu Waterson Walls, better keep her and Harry Madison won't be the only knee here next week—Philip X. ben Abdullah, keep him too, I guess—"

The automatics delivered the running total of acceptances, and when he came too close to the limit the hos-

175

pital could cope with they down-rated previous border-line readings to compensate, eliminating the ones with the oldest certificates and re-assigning them to Westchester for ordinary internment sentences.

Suddenly he stopped dead, staring at a pale figure not gassed but immobile, arms wrapped around knees, eyes open but not seeing anything, frozen in the foetal posture.

"Christ," he said. "What's *she* doing here?"

FIFTY-EIGHT

A LONG WAY IN BOTH SPACE AND
TIME FROM BASIN STREET THE CELE-
BRATED LOCUS OF INTERSECTION BE-
TWEEN PERSONS OF UNEQUAL EPI-
DERMAL PIGMENTATION

Within seconds of Flamen letting himself into his
office at the Etchmark Undertower—trend-setter of the
post-turn-of-century buildings sunk as far into yielding
earthcrust as older buildings jutted upward, in order to
reach the bedrock of the Manhattan Schist in an area
where it nosedived—the comweb screen lit to show
Prior's face.

"Ah, Matthew!" With evident relief. "Were you held
up?"

"Of course I was!" Flamen snapped. "They're diverting
everything to the four points of the compass. I thought
I was never going to get here at all. Did Diablo show?"

"Sure he did. He's right here in my office. I'll bring
him in to see you at once. I've been keeping him hanging around a bit, I'm afraid, but I thought it best for
him to meet you before we started—ah—*talking shop.*"

Flamen's mood lightened momentarily; he was always amused when in a fit of selfconsciousness Prior
gave that faintly disapproving inflection to a phrase he
regarded as slangy. This particular one had a century
or two of respectable use behind it, but for Prior it was
still not quite kosher.

"Great, bring him in," he said aloud, dropping into his chair.

So now: the big moment. Enter, fussily superintended by Prior, the celebrated Pedro Diablo, curiously shy in manner (but perhaps that was due to the shock of being uprooted from his lifetime-familiar background), eyes darting everywhere in the room, a great deal of their whites showing. A rather good-looking man, younger than Flamen had imagined: certainly still in his thirties. But of course he already had a decade of fame behind him; that would explain the false perspective. Lean, tautly nervous, hair and beard curled in near-African spirals, wearing New York-fashionable clothing instead of Blackbury robes—a black-green striped over-suit and green shoes. . . . Flamen inventoried him as he shook hands, accepted the offer of a chair, uttered conventionalities about great pleasure and having often watched the Flamen show.

Somehow, though, despite hours of restlessness during the night which he had intended to devote to the question of Diablo, Flamen had wound up without any plan of action for today. After the formalities, there was a long interval of silence which made Prior visibly anxious. He had just cleared his throat and seemed about to utter some scrap of smalltalk, when Flamen decided —almost to his own surprise—that he wasn't going to bother about being diplomatic.

"Well!" he said, looking Diablo straight in the face. "I guess it fits your impression of blank society, doesn't it, to find yourself here as the result of a bribe?"

Prior's jaw dropped. Flamen turned on him a smile as sweet as honey. "Freeze it, Lionel," he said. "I'm not in the right mood to be polite today, I'm afraid. I have agreed to take a bribe, and I'm feeling ashamed of myself."

"But someone of Mr. Diablo's known talent in the field—"

"Oh, sure! I respect his work tremendously. I also

respect his well-known impatience with hypocrisy and doubletalk. I wish I was half as consistent."

"I'm looking to you to learn how to give up being consistent," Diablo muttered. "There's no consistency in what's happened to me these past forty-eight hours. Sure, go ahead and call me a bribe—it's something of a privilege, I guess, to be treated as the price which can buy something from you."

Who'd have thought it? I'm on the right track, Flamen told himself, pleased.

"So let's skip all the pretense!" he exclaimed. "I'll give you the bald facts why I agreed to having you sent here, shall I? We're getting interference on our show and the Holocosmic engineers say they can't eliminate it. *I* think there must be a good reason why not—it never affects any other transmission from their studios. I need the resources to stand up and argue with them, which means computer time in amounts I couldn't ordinarily afford. So I made a bargain—or rather Lionel did, but I'm in total agreement with him on it."

Diablo gave a thoughtful nod. "I see. It's all fallen very patly, hasn't it? Bustafedrel needed to find me a slot fast for fear of recriminations, you had a problem which needed Federal help, and here I am. So continue."

Flamen hesitated. "I don't mean to undervalue you—" he began, but Diablo raised a hand to forestall the rest.

"Friend, I don't care what you say, or anyone else right now. I been *so* undervalued yesterday. . . . You catch me?"

"I certainly agree with that!" Prior said hastily. "I mean, I told Voigt straight out: this man's worth a couple of army corps!"

"So what's an army corps worth these days?" Diablo snapped.

There was a further uneasy pause. Eventually Flamen said, "Nonetheless I am being impolite. I'm sorry. It's partly lack of sleep, and partly having had the Morton Lenigo thing under my nose yesterday and thinking it was absurd. . . . Say, what do *you* think of them letting him in?"

"They're out of their skulls," Diablo shrugged. "But in that area they don't have a monopoly."

"No, it's clear that Mayor Black also finally mislaid his marbles," Flamen concurred. "Throwing you out, particularly on the say-so of an Afrikaner, is kind of like cutting your wrists to see the pretty red blood flow."

"Expect me to contradict you? I'm not modest. Also I think I'm a better melanist than he is, and since you said you don't approve of hypocrisy, I might as well lay it on record that I don't plan to turn my coat and get even. If you were hoping I'd turn up with a pack of pre-canned slanders to undermine Mayor Black or Lenigo or whoever, you were wrong. I said I wanted the letter of the Blackbury contract adhered to. It's been done. That's fair. So you can have any of what I'm carrying which I'd have used over my own beams if I hadn't been thrown out of Blackbury. I don't like blanks in general so most of what I have is anti-blank. If you're honest enough to use it, I can get along with you. All of it, of course, is the truth."

From the corner of his eye Flamen saw that Prior was goggling like a hooked fish, clearly horrified at the way the conversation was going. But for his part, he welcomed it. There was something about Diablo's aggressive manner which reminded him of his own younger self, and at the same time drew his attention to changes since then which had proceeded so slowly and gradually that he had never felt a discontinuity. It was like—yes, it was like having been lounging in a skimmer on a bright warm day, idly watching the clouds and enjoying the sun and the breeze, and suddenly waking up to the fact that you had an appointment an hour ago in a city five hundred miles distant in the wrong direction.

He thought of his promise yesterday that he was going to fix Mogshack's wagon. Why had he said that? Because he was honestly worried about Celia? He'd be-

lieved so on the surface of his mind, but the sharp edge
of Diablo's personality, honed in a community where
black was black and white was white and there were no
shades of gray in between, had made the pretense gape
apart like the splitting of a drumhead.

No. In his heart of hearts he was no longer interested
in Celia; he'd become resigned months past to losing
her as a wife, and once she was evicted from that rôle
she became one person among millions, a stranger. Yet,
just as he had once spoken in harsh uncompromising
terms like Diablo's, so too his younger self had uttered
and *meant* the formal public promises of a marriage
ceremony.

It was one thing to recognize as a bitter fact that over
half the marriages contracted in twenty-first century
America had already ended in divorce, though the century was barely fourteen years old; it was something else
again to relegate a person who had once ruled your
universe to the status of a mere tool, the instrument to
undermine Mogshack and demonstrate that Matthew
Flamen the spoolpigeon was still a power to reckon
with.

All that had been poised at the edge of awareness,
worked out during the night and needing only the last-
straw impact of circumstance to bring it avalanching
into the open. Diablo happened to have been the bearer
of that straw, and had let it fall at the moment when
rational judgment warned that he dare not respond, for
there was a show to be taped and comped and revised
and delivered in barely two hours.

"Matthew, is something wrong?" he heard Prior say.
With a tremendous effort he dragged himself back to
the present.

"No, nothing," he lied with convincing casualness. "I
was just considering how best to acquaint Mr. Diablo
with our techniques, but I guess that's a non-problem,
isn't it? You must use equipment more or less like ours
in Blackbury."

Diablo scanned the computer boards which occupied three walls of the office, with a screen over each, and shook his head.

"Nope. I doubt there's a setup like this in any of the knee enclaves except maybe Detroit, and if there's one there it's probably used for defense and budgeting, not for propaganda. Frankly, I been wondering what it's all for."

"Show you, then," Flamen said, rising. "We don't have too much time to put our day's show together, but I did once comp a ten-minute show in level time, so if I have to hurry I can. . . . Let's see now!" He crossed the room to stand before the board closest to the doorway; this one was the most heavily used, as could be seen from the deep nail-marks in the tops of its keys.

"We'll start with the one that got away," he said, half-mockingly, half-angrily. "The Morton Lenigo thing. Background facts first"—he tapped a code on the board with practiced fingers. "Now that they're set up, let's take a starting point from which we can dig deeper. For instance, let's ask what the Detroit city government threatened to do in order to secure Lenigo's admission."

Diablo had come over to stand beside him and watch. Flamen was pleased to hear his very faint hiss of indrawn breath as he voiced the idea which had struck him in the skimmer.

"It was Detroit, then? You of all people ought to know. Don't worry, though. I'm not going to force information out of you. Our equipment isn't the best in the world, but it's well primed with data, and anyway I didn't have to comp that one out—I just deduced it." At the back of his mind he was aware that he was adopting this patronizing tone in order to get back at the knee for that dismaying fit of insight he'd suffered a minute earlier, and was unable to prevent himself continuing, and was dismayed all over again at that too.

Christ, he thought: I'm beginning to wonder why I

still have any friends left if this is me-now. Worse yet
. . . *do* I have any friends?

But aloud, in response to the appearance on the
screen over the computer board of a short list of key
subjects each followed by a probability rating in per-
centage terms: "See here, it says the most sensitive
point for them to apply pressure at is their annual tax-
assessment. They've nearly satched the market for skimmers, commercial transport vehicles and their other main
products, and they didn't quite compute their obsoles-
cence program as cleverly as they intended. We could
take at least a three-month blockade before we ran out
of replacements, and if we had to we could welsh on
the contract the Federal government made with them
and start producing our own spares. Whereas they'd
have starvation riots in about a month and a half; we
deliberately keep down their stocks of food. However,
their purchases of power and water bring in so big a
slice of the Federal budget, in hard African and Middle
Eastern currencies, that threatening to set up—oh, perhaps a condensation plant . . . Is something wrong?"

Diablo swallowed hard. "Yes," he said in a defiant
tone. "I think you're conning me. You got that in the
Federal package, didn't you? It was part of the price
you paid for agreeing to slot me in."

"Cross my heart it wasn't," Flamen said with a thin
smile. "But I assume it's the truth, hm?"

"Well . . . Oh, all right. I believe you. And it is right.
Clear down to the atmospheric condensation plant. We
were going to break that info around the weekend
sometime. I guess I don't have to explain the slant."

"Once again the knees get even with the blanks for
terming a nasty antisocial act 'blackmail'?"

"We call 'em 'petards,' " Diablo said at length. "You
know—'hoist with his own.' Sorry, I didn't mean to
hold you up when you're short of time. But what I don't
get is this." He fingered his beard, staring at the computer
screen. "When you have analytical equipment like this,

which can dig the background out of something as well masked as the Lenigo blackmail deal, why's there any need for a specialized spoolpigeon show? You'd think the regular news coverage would be full-depth anyway."

"I've made my living for years out of the fact that it isn't," Flamen said curtly. Then, relenting: "It's different here on the outside, Diablo. It's a big psychological thing. We look at what you can see, and we stop there. I guess we got into the habit some time in the last century, same as we—well—same as we might look at you and think 'kneeblank,' full stop. We think of news as the detached record of what took place, regardless of why: there was an earthquake yesterday, there's a riot today, there's going to be a tornado tomorrow. You catch me?"

"It fits," Diablo said, nodding. "So go ahead."

"All right. Where was I? Oh yes. Well, I'll just have all the stories comped out which I left to simmer overnight, and check the monitor back to see what's come in since . . ." The screen flashed and darkened and flashed again, factors in each successive story being evaluated and presented. "Ah, that's fine. Today we have several usable items."

"How do you decide which are the usable ones?"

"My usual baseline is eighty-plus in favor of it being true. That works. Once I used something comped at seventy-eight and I had to apologize and pay damages, but I never got caught on anything with a rating over eighty on this equipment. Though being cautious was what cost me a beat on the Lenigo story yesterday; it was five points below the likeliest alternative."

"Which was?"

"That the Gottschalks were spreading alarm and despondency again. Something there wasn't much point in using, of course. Everyone's known for years that that's how they jack their sales levels up: they're ghouls, growing fat on people's hates and fears, and the human species being what it is they're apt to go on growing fat until they collapse under their own weight."

"That's something we don't get in the enclaves," Diablo said. "Gottschalk sales campaigns, I mean. We're an automatic market—islands in a sea of hostility."

"Mm-hm." Flamen's eyes were on the screen as he brought up subject after subject for intensive analysis. "I have something on the Gottschalks, by the way. Here it is. I don't think that'll mean too much to you at the moment, though."

Diablo stared at the screen. "IBM $375,000, Honeywell $233,000, Elliot— No, it doesn't."

"They've been buying high-order data-processing equipment. Lots of it. That was yesterday's record of bills met."

"One *day's* record?" Diablo said incredulously.

"It says here. Care to—ah—suggest an explanation?"

Diablo's beard-clawing evolved into a series of tugs that threatened to haul out the roots. "Hmm! I never paid much attention to the Gottschalks, I'm afraid. Bad policy in a place like Blackbury to risk offending people who prop us up the way they do. But I thought they used one of the Iron Mountain banks."

"They do." Flamen hesitated. Then, at long last conceding that he had overnight been frightened of this encounter with a man whose reputation exceeded his own in spite of all the drawbacks—lack of funds, lack of resources, lack of made-to-order support from wealthy blanks at the top of the planetary totem-pole—he gave way to the impulse to impress him again with casual inside knowledge. "But apparently one of the security codes is up for sale with a price not much over a million. If they're at that stage, they're obviously ready to pull out of Iron Mountain altogether, aren't they?"

"In favor of their own private equipment?"

"Seems likely, I'd say."

"Maybe they know something," Diablo said after a moment for thought. "Did you check the current list of Iron Mountain clients to see if there's someone on it who's on the Gottschalk blacklist?"

185

"Ah . . ." Flamen bit his lip. "Damn it, I didn't think of that. Thank you. I'll see if anything comes of it, but it may take me a while to get hold of the client list." He tapped his keys again, on the adjacent board this time, thinking about the idea of the whole of Iron Mountain being blown up, say by a smuggled nuke. That would wreck the organization of at least a thousand major corporations.

And it was a possibility he certainly should have considered.

"Now!" he resumed. "We have some tape already from a special item, so we can afford to pick and choose today. We'll start, I think, with a subject of personal interest to yourself. What's Herman Uys doing in Blackbury and how did he con Mayor Black into firing his key vu-man?"

"Now just a—!" Diablo tensed instantly; just as quickly he canceled the reaction under Flamen's level gaze.

"You *approve* of a South African blank being allowed to sabotage the American knee community's propaganda channels?" Flamen said silkily.

"I—ah . . ." Diablo drew a deep breath and finally contrived a headshake.

"Very well then. Let's find out what stock we have available for Uys. I don't have to ask about Mayor Black; he's vain, and we have tape on him we could lasso the moon with." Flamen moved to a computer on the wall at right angles to the first one.

"More or less what I thought," he muttered when the data were screened in response to his question. "Practically nothing! Black-and-white 2-D material and that's it. Well, we can make do with that. This is a recent one, comparatively speaking." The screen blurred, cleared, showed Uys coming down the steps from a plane door, presumably at home in South Africa, being greeted by his family and gesturing away a group of reporters.

"Let's have color . . . holographic depth . . . yes, that's better . . . good . . . we can abstract from that and blend it with Mayor Black and let's see now . . . American location and b.g., better have some macoots . . . Ah, that's not bad for a start, is it?"

This was the part of his job which was genuinely creative, and he always enjoyed it very much: the adaptation of the most unpromising raw materials to generate a full-color, three-dimensional construct so convincing that only a person who had actually been on the scene of the event could point to inaccuracies.

"Christ, it's like magic," Diablo muttered, making no attempt to appear blasé. The screened image had evolved through a period of chaotic confusion into a fixed picture of Uys at a laboratory bench—unquestionably in America, not Africa, though it was the total impression and not any specific detail which made that plain—turning to speak to Mayor Black as the latter walked in accompanied by a pair of armed macoots.

"Nothing magical about it," Flamen said offhandedly. "I just had the right data to draw on—typical genetic lab design, the proper computer printouts, the proper material in jars and dishes lying around, that kind of thing. The scenes are automatically weighted for weather conditions, clothing, angle of sunlight, and so on, and all we have to do now is add the sound." He struck codes on the keyboard. "Voices—we're bound to have something on tape, I guess, even for Uys, and even if we haven't the machines will fake a South African accent. Characteristic phrase-weighting—let's spice it with a few choice Afrikaner slogans . . . And here we go."

The fixed image moved. Voices emerged from a concealed speaker. Mayor Black said, "An' how you gettin' on with cleanin' house for us?"

Uys flinched, colored a little, controlled himself and answered in a dead voice that no one could have failed to assign to an Afrikaner, "If you mean how is the campaign developing to purify the melanist heredity of this city, I have located several impure lines which need

187

to be discontinued. In particular there's a mongrel called Pedro Diablo who—"

Flamen flicked a control and the sound faded, though the images continued. "How does that strike you?" he inquired.

Diablo passed his hand over his forehead, looking dazed. "It's fantastic," he admitted. "The detail, I mean. Like Uys's reaction to the suggestion that he'd been hired like a Bantu houseboy, to clean house for a knee-blank . . . it's in character, damn it! Christ, if I'd been allowed this kind of equipment instead of studio sets and actors—!"

"Allowed?"

"I mean if the budget had run to it." Diablo overcame his excitement with an effort. "So what sort of answer are you going to propose for the question you started with—why is Uys in Blackbury?"

Flamen turned back to the keyboard he had used first. "That's still being comped," he said when the screen lit. "The little arrow—see it?—indicates the rating is still going up as fresh data are assessed. I'll leave that to cook for a moment and get the special item out of the way. That's some tape I made yesterday at the Ginsberg Hospital; there was a pythoness performing and I recorded her trance. It'll make a nice ground-softener for something which may eventually turn out to be rather big."

"One of the items you screened earlier?" Diablo inquired.

"No, something new which is only at the tentative stage. We have this offer of free Federal computer time, as you know, and one of the things I want to do with it is have . . . Well, have someone packled—it doesn't matter who." Flamen had almost forgotten that Prior was in the room; he gave him an uneasy glance.

"You see, I suspect that the treatment patients in the Ginsberg are getting may sometimes make them worse instead of better, but the director is Elias Mogshack, and he's got such a planetary reputation I'd need absolutely unquestionable authority to back a challenge to him. Let's just ask what would happen if my suspicions were well-founded, though." He stretched one arm out and struck a code again. The figure which appeared on the screen provoked an exclamation of approval.

"Ninety-plus! I can't recall when I last had such a high reading!"

"In favor of what?" Diablo asked.

"Of his being tossed on the garbage pile. In which case I literally don't dare not soften the ground—let's allot that pythoness's trance the most we can give a single subject according to our contract with Holocosmic. That's four minutes. There! Are we ready for anything else yet? Still not? You picked a good day, Diablo —we seem to have tapped a gang of very deep subjects. Never mind, there's one other point I'd like comped before I start compiling the tape for the show and we still have about ninety minutes in hand. Let's see what our chances are of curing the sabotage trouble I told you about, given unlimited free Federal computer time. Of course, faced with that Holocosmic is bound to cave in right away, but I believe in doublechecking."

He leaned over the board and carefully composed the question. At his shoulder, watching every move, Diablo said, "This sabotage thing—have your employers given way to pressure from someone you offended?"

"I wish people did get sufficiently offended to react like that," Flamen muttered. "But it's been two years since an advertiser tried to have me taken off the beams because I said something he didn't like. Out here people just don't seem to care very much any more. Most likely, Holocosmic themselves want to move me over for another all-advertising slot . . ."

The words died. On the screen, in response to his coded inquiry, there was a single large digit: an incontrovertible, inexplicable, incomprehensible zero.

FIFTY-NINE

REPRINTFD FROM THE MANCHESTER
GUARDIAN OF 2ND MARCH 1968

US looks to a long, violent summer
From Richard Scott, Washington

It is generally accepted as inevitable that the racial riots in American cities this summer will exceed in violence and number even those of last year.

And because their causes, as analysed in the National Advisory Committee's report, are so basic, so deep-rooted, so much a product of the pattern of American life, they will be eradicated only after a major national effort and over a long period of time.

Meanwhile the national Government, the State and city police forces, and the ordinary citizens, both black and white, are already preparing themselves for what may well be the most riotous summer in the nation's history.

Forces standing by

Although Federal troops have been used to suppress civil riots only twice since 1923, a force of 15,000 men is reported to have been earmarked by the Pentagon for such use should State and city forces prove inadequate. They have been formed into seven task forces and housed near the cities most likely to experience major rioting. The Government has also been stockpiling anti-riot equipment in key sites.

But riot control devolves in all but the last resort on city or State law enforcement officers. And throughout the country there are reports of considerable efforts to increase and modernise their equipment for riot control.

In some cities the police are being issued with a controversial new high-powered rifle, with ammunition with some of the characteristics of the dum-dum bullet. Others are acquiring armed helicopters or armoured cars which can fire either tear gas or machine-gun bullets . . .

Volunteer deputies
Detailed planning is already being undertaken by city authorities. In some cities the police are reported to be improving their intelligence machinery so that they may obtain earlier and more accurate information of impending riots. In one Chicago county, the sheriff is trying to organise a force of a thousand volunteer deputies who would provide their own arms and receive 40 to 60 hours of special riot-control training. This seems to be approaching perilously close to the groups of vigilantes of past ill fame.

On the other side of the coin are the

private preparations of American citizens for the long, hot summer ahead. Both whites and Negroes are arming themselves. There have been recent reports of a steep rise in the purchases of firearms—and it is a fairly rare American family which has no pistol or shotgun in the house. Housewives are reported to be attending police courses of instruction in the firing of revolvers.

SIXTY ASSUMPTION CONCERNING THE FORE-
GOING MADE FOR THE PURPOSES
OF THIS STORY

It was done but it didn't work.

Looking tired and irritable—they had had to work through the normal noon recess, classifying the mentally disturbed arrestees from the riot, arranging for those who were under regular care already to be sent back to their own therapists, revising the schedules and opening up fresh retreats for those who were not provided for elsewhere—Ariadne appeared on the screen of Reedeth's internal comweb while he was talking on an outside circuit.

"Just a second," he threw over his shoulder, and ended his other conversation with a curt, "It's got to be done and it's up to you to find a way! And you'd better hurry!"

Cutting that connection, he swiveled his rotachair to face Ariadne. "Yes?"

"I thought you said something about Lyla Clay having been committed this morning. Well, I'm supposed to have had all the female arrestees' data through my office and hers weren't among them. What happened?"

"Oh. Oh yes." Reedeth passed a weary hand through his hair, then leaned back and extracted a pack of joints from his desketary drawer. Smoking was theoretically forbidden in the hospital, but at times of exceptional stress everyone on the staff bent the rule a trifle. He went on as he hunted for a means of lighting it, "I managed to siphon her out of the main stream. It was a hunch. Turned out to be right."

"How, right?"

"Shouldn't have been here at all."

"But I thought you said she was in a bad way. Foetal position, shocked—"

"All of that and a lot more. Wouldn't you expect to be if you'd had your boyfriend die in front of you?"

Ariadne put her hand to her mouth in horror. "He got caught in the riot?"

"Correct. Someone chopped his belly open with an axe. He managed to get home, with the assistance of the block Gottschalk, and— I'll give you three guesses what the bastard did."

Ariadne gave a mute headshake.

"Tried to sell her a gun across her mackero's corpse, while it was still warm."

There was a pause. At length Ariadne said, "Worse than a bastard. A ghoul. But then they all are, aren't they? Otherwise they wouldn't have chosen that line of business."

"This is about the nastiest thing I've heard of one of them doing, though. And apparently when Miss Clay ordered him off the premises—with the gun they kept in the apt—he went to the comweb and swore a complaint against her, charging assault with a deadly weapon."

Diligent searching had unearthed him a battered old disposable catalytic lighter, with a faint final glow left in the hot mesh on which he managed to ignite his joint.

Ariadne said, "Is this true, or did she—?"

"Make it up? No, it's true. I was just talking to a precinct captain a moment ago, telling him what I thought of busies who act like his teamsmen do. You see, they were too occupied to answer the call right away, and they finally got around to it at six or so this morning. Broke down the door and stormed in. By which time she'd spent the night lying beside a dead body, too scared to go out of the apt even as far as the comweb because the Gottschalk took her only gun with him."

"And they *committed* her?"

"They were going to arrest her, for Christ's sake! Suspicion of murder! Until it occurred to one of the thickheads to look for a weapon she could have cut him open with, and found that the trail of blood led back into the corridor. By that time, though, she must have been out of her skull, pretty well, so they shipped her here. I just told the captain he'd be better off charging the Gottschalk with stealing her gun, and to have the commitment order withdrawn fast. But it was just shouting to relieve my feelings, I'm afraid."

Ariadne gave a depressed nod. "You wouldn't catch any police force in the country offending a Gottschalk, would you? They're too scared of being stuck with out-of-fashion weaponry. . . . So what did you do with her?"

"Oh, I gave orders that she wasn't to be enrolled as a patient, just given emergency therapy at the dispensary and allowed to rest a while. Then I said to send her up here and have a word with me before she leaves —if she can leave. I'm not sure yet whether the commitment order hadn't been processed, even though it was one of the very late ones this morning, and if it has, of course, we'll have to find a guardian for her."

"Is she under twenty-one?"

"By about three months."

"Well . . . she has parents, probably, or relatives of some kind?"

"Kids that age sometimes don't care to have their family brought into a mess like this one," Reedeth pointed out. He checked his watch. "Anyhow, she should be here in another few minutes, and I can ask her. Do you want to drop by yourself?"

"Hmmm . . ." Ariadne glanced at something out of sight. "I guess I ought to, but I don't see that I can spare the time. We ate into our overload capacity this morning, with all these arrestees, and Dr. Mogshack asked me to nominate fifty green patients for early discharge and give us a bit of leeway."

"Well! I never thought I'd see the day when he was letting patients go before he had to!"

Ariadne's face turned into a stony mask. "That's not funny, Jim," she said.

"No. No, I guess not. Pot on an empty stomach talking. I'm sorry. But you will bear Harry Madison in mind for that discharge list, won't you?"

"Yes, of course—I earmarked him right away. But the computations are still unfavorable. I wish to God we could discharge him direct to one of the knee enclaves —Newark, say. But that's over a state line, and . . ." She shrugged. "Anyhow," she added, brightening a little, "it does offer a very handy solution to the Celia Flamen problem."

"Does it?"

She looked at him blankly. "Well, naturally!"

"Penalty for premature discharge?"

"I'm going to try and persuade him to waive it, of course. After all, he did say yesterday that he wanted his wife out of the Ginsberg as soon as possible."

"Oh. Yes, that's quite neat." Reedeth nodded approval. "And is he going to play?"

"I don't know yet. I left messages for him at home, at his office and in care of Holocosmic, but I haven't had an answer. Come to think of it, I might as well try again while the discharge list is being comped. Anything else?"

"Apart from saying how about tonight?"

"I'm going to be too tired at this rate," she sighed, and cut the connection.

SIXTY-TWO THE PROXIMATE CAUSE OF A FEDERAL
DIRECTIVE IN PURSUANCE OF WHICH
THIRTY-THREE INTERNAL SECURITY
MAINTENANCE OPERATIVES WERE
DOWNGRADED OR DISHONORABLY
DISMISSED

Sometime during the night Morton Lenigo managed
to elude the ISM operatives assigned to tail him and
when things had calmed down enough for such matters
to come to the attention of their headquarters he had already had almost five hours to lose himself.

"Assuming Voigt kept his promise," Flamen said, punching the appropriate code into his comweb board with a series of crackling clicks, "this line ought to plug straight through to the Federal computer he's reserved to sort out our interference problem. . . . Yes, there we are. Now we'll feed it the show as canned and let it compare that with the version received by the public, and draw the—ah—logical conclusion. There was something wrong with the reading we got earlier, that's definite. Zero's impossible." He wondered if his conviction sounded forced. "I'll get IBM to check, see if the digit selector slipped its gears. Probably it ought to have shown 100."

Prior was plucking at his lower lip. "Yes, I guess there isn't any other explanation," he muttered.

"So that's it." Flamen pushed back his rotachair and started to rise.

"You mean . . . ?" Diablo hesitated. "You mean you're finished for the day?"

"Well—yes, of course. We only do the one slot, Monday through Friday."

"But you hardly seem to have done anything," Diablo said. "I mean . . . Well, I have this feeling I must have missed something."

"I tried to explain everything as I went along," Flamen said. "But if there was something I overlooked—"

"No, I guess it's just that I'm not used to working with your kind of equipment." Diablo shook his head, an expression of wonderment on his dark face. "Let me see if I got it right. All you needed to do was select the subjects, right? And make up the reconstructions from the stock tape you found on file, and speak the commentary so it could be recorded. Then *everything* else was automatic?"

"Sure." Flamen was looking vaguely puzzled. "We always have exactly fifteen minutes—or to be strictly accurate, fourteen and forty-five seconds to allow for station ID at either end. And the commercials are pre-recorded, naturally, and the new material is automatically adjusted so that it fits into the available time. The last computer on the row sort of weaves the various strands together and provided Holocosmic's own computers don't raise any objections we have the tape."

"Are there many objections?"

"Oh . . . I guess we have to change something about once a week, on the average. It's a lot too often, at that."

Diablo thought about it for a while. Suddenly he laughed. "I must sound like a real country mouse," he said. "It is kind of a shock, though. You see, I've been accustomed to working a nine-till-nine schedule five and often six days a week, with a couple of half-hour meal-breaks if I was lucky. This has live-action studio work beat to a faretheewell. Why, that snippet with Uys and Mayor Black alone would have had to be planned a week ahead for me to get such detail into it. Never mind casting and rehearsing the actors." He paused, speculatively eying Flamen. "Would you mind if I asked a hell of a personal question?"

"Depends. Try me."

"What do you pull in for this like three hours a day job?"

"Ah . . . Oh, it's a matter of record, if you know where to look, and I guess it's nothing to be ashamed of. A hundred thousand a month, gross. Mark you, that has to

200

spread over rental and maintenance for the computers, this office, Lionel's salary, my informers' fund which about two or three times a year turns me up a beat which I couldn't have deduced without access to confidential sources, miscellaneous expenses like buying computer security codes, the whole shtick."

"And—my salary now, as well?"

"I doubt if I could afford you!" Flamen gave a humorless chuckle. "No, like you said, you wanted the letter of the Blackbury contract adhered to, so you're a charge on Federal funds. As a matter of interest, though, what were they paying you in Blackbury?"

"Two thousand," Diablo said after a brief hesitation.

"*Two thousand?*" Prior almost fell off his chair. "Oh—but I guess that's net, isn't it?"

"Of course. I didn't have to pay anyone or rent any equipment. I had a city-subsidized apt with a rent of only a hundred, no office costs, nothing else."

"Sounds as though, all things considered, you might have been better off than I am," Flamen said, and glanced at his watch. "Well, shall we say the same time tomorrow?"

"There's a flag up on your comweb," Prior said. "Aren't you going to answer it?"

"Damn. So there is." Flamen dropped back into his chair and pulled the fax paper out of its slot. "Ah, that doctor at the Ginsberg wanting to get in touch. I guess I'd better take it."

"Shall we—?" Prior suggested, starting to leave the room.

"Darl, several million people are about to see Celia in a hospital oversuit, aren't they? Want I should pretend with you and Mr. Diablo around?"

"If it's something personal, I certainly don't want to intrude," Diablo said, also half-rising.

"No, it's another matter of record and I don't much care."

"As you like." Diablo hesitated yet again. "While I

think of it, though . . . Forgive me, but people do be-have differently out here and I don't want to make any *faux pas*. Is your mistering me a bit of Crow Jim?"

"What?" Hand poised to punch the comweb code for the Ginsberg, Flamen looked up. "Sorry, I didn't catch that."

"I've been wondering," Diablo said doggedly, "whether you've been calling me *Mister* Diablo all the time be-cause I'm a knee."

"What else would I—? Oh, *now* I catch. You have this 'soul brother' thing in the enclaves, don't you? Call peo-ple all the time by their first names?"

"Well . . . more or less. I mean anyone I was going to be working with regularly, at least," Diablo qualified. "And I thought blank society was equally informal."

"Used to be, I think. Like in my father's day I be-lieve we had the same thing." Flamen frowned, with-drawing his hand from the comweb board. "Yes, I re-call him joking about how well you had to know some-one before you found out his last name and could look him up in a directory. But I read something about this once . . . Of course! A piece by Xavier Conroy; I re-member now. He said something about the need to assert individuality and surnames being more numerous than given names. Stuck in my mind because there are several hundred thousand Matthews around nowadays but all the people named Flamen in the entire United States are relatives of mine in one way or another—just a single family. Scattered to hell and gone, of course, but if you checked the records you could tie them all together. At that I don't suffer from one of the really common first names, either: Michael, David, John, Wil-liam . . ."

"So you call people mister automatically?"

"You'd be better advised to than not. Lionel, how long was it before I started calling you by your first name?"

"After you married Celia, I guess," Prior said. "But I

didn't mind you calling me just 'Prior' when we were working together before that."

"You want to know what to call us?" Flamen said, glancing back at Diablo. "Hell, personally I don't mind what people call me—I'm not looking for reassurance about my status. But I guess for safety's sake, for the time being at least, you'd better stick by the formal custom: Flamen, Prior. No mister except to a third party. Okay?"

"Thanks," Diablo nodded. "I—uh . . . Well, I hadn't realized that leaving Blackbury would be so much like going to a foreign country." His eyes roved the room. "Everything seems so strange," he added in a burst of frankness. "I guess I swallowed the propaganda about the enclaves really still being part of the United States, just enjoying a bit more self-determination than they used to. Say, can I ask you a favor?"

"Let's hear it."

"Could you sort of—uh—isolate that computer which makes up reconstructions out of stock shots? It's the kind of gadget I've been dreaming of all my life without realizing. I feel like a back-country boy with a banjo made of cowhide and baling wire who hears a guitar for the first time."

Flamen exchanged a questioning glance with Prior, who resolutely refrained from offering any kind of answer.

"You want to see if you can put it through hoops too?" he said. "I guess we could arrange that, but I doubt if it can be today. I'd have to ask for someone to drop by from IBM and wire in the proper code—I was already used to similar equipment before I had this particular one installed. You could probably have a dummy delivered to your apt, though, to practice on and learn the codes before tackling a full-sized machine."

"That's a great idea," Diablo nodded. "I certainly ought to do that. But I'm sorry—I held you up from making your call with all these questions, I'm afraid."

"Don't worry. I doubt if it's anything urgent." Flamen turned back to the comweb.

Prior fidgeted a little, with repeated glances at Diablo, clearly unhappy at this exposure of a private matter to someone who was a stranger, a knee and a professional rival. His thought processes were almost audible: suppose Diablo were to be re-admitted to Blackbury and decided to exploit what he'd learned to discredit Flamen . . . ?

His relief was evident when the comweb said, "Dr. Spoelstra has been called to attend to an emergency admission and can only be interrupted for the most urgent—"

But another voice broke in: "Dr. Reedeth, Mr. Flamen!" The screen lit with his image, and he was not alone. Behind him, looking extremely miserable, Lyla Clay was sitting on the very edge of a chair with her hands pressed tightly together between her knees.

"If you don't mind speaking to me instead of Dr. Spoelstra," he went on, "she briefed me fully, I believe. It's quite a simple matter, actually. You may recall that when you were here yesterday you voiced—ah—a certain opinion regarding your wife's treatment."

He waited. Flamen at length gave a wary nod.

"As a result of your comments we re-processed Mrs. Flamen's psychoprofile today"—Reedeth was choosing his words very carefully—"and we found that there had indeed been a flattening of the therapy-response curve. In lay terms, you might say that from now on hospitalization can do little or nothing for her and a gradual re-acclimatization to the everyday world is indicated. In principle, bearing in mind your remarks yesterday, we wondered whether you'd be willing to waive the premature discharge penalty if we gave you an assurance that it was in her best interests . . . ?"

Flamen was silent for a moment. Then he gave a sudden harsh laugh. "Do I take it that you wouldn't have noticed she was better unless I'd turned up yesterday?"

"Of course not," Reedeth said stiffly. "You'll recall that she went to green yesterday morning as a result of the regular weekly review of her condition. The point I just mentioned would have come to light at the full-scale monthly checkup in about two weeks' time, but since you'd just made some rather—ah—intemperate comments . . ." He shrugged. "We carried out an extra examination, that's all."

"It wouldn't have something to do with the heavy intake of rioters pleading insanity which you must have been hit with earlier today?" Flamen suggested.

"Considering we had to deal with seven hundred commitments or suspected commitments, I think it surprising that Dr. Spoelstra did manage to have the extra examination of your wife fitted in," Reedeth countered. It was a non-answer, but Flamen didn't bother to pursue the matter.

"In principle, then, the answer's yes. On one condition. What happens—do you want me to come and take her home?"

Reedeth looked uncomfortable. "Not exactly. She's been asked whether she's willing to be discharged, and she is, and she's fit enough provided that she suffers no undue strain in the near future and continues to take the drugs we prescribe, but . . . Well, frankly she's refused to be discharged into your care."

"What?"

"I'm afraid so, and we can't really argue, because of the background to her breakdown. But she has agreed to accept her brother as guardian, so if you have no objection and he has none . . . ?"

"He's right here," Flamen said curtly. "I'll ask him." He killed the sound pickup for a moment and looked at Prior. "Well?"

"I—" Prior swallowed enormously. "I suppose so. I am her brother, after all! It's a responsibility, isn't it?" On the last word his eyes flicked very swiftly towards and past Diablo. Flamen reflected cruelly that there might have been a different reply had a stranger not been present.

"He says yes," he relayed to the waiting Reedeth. "Set the wheels in motion, then, and I've no doubt my brother-in-law will be over to collect Celia this afternoon. But I did say I was going to waive the premature-discharge penalty on one condition only, didn't I? I'll do so subject to her being independently packled to determine whether she has benefited or suffered from the treatment she's been accorded at the Ginsberg. Is it a bargain? If the packling shows that she's not better, as you claim she is, I not only stand by the premature discharge clause—I'll sue."

He waited. At length Reedeth said, "It'll have to be comped, naturally, but . . . Yes, I'm sure we have sufficient confidence in our methods to accept that proviso. In principle, we agree."

For an instant Flamen's assurance wavered. Trying to slip a packle program through to the Federal computers in the guise of an attempt to eliminate the sabotage on the show was going to be risky—should he save his unexpected resources for some other target, such as the Gottschalks? But Mogshack was a far more accessible victim and there had been that ninety-plus reading.

Also a zero reading, sniggered the little demon at the corner of his mind.

That, though, *had* to be an error! A zero reading was effectively impossible; the lowest he'd ever had before was three.

Best, he concluded, to stick by his original plan for the time being. With excessive heartiness he said, "That's fine, Dr. Reedeth! I'm very reassured by your willingness to commit yourself—in principle. I'll make a point of calling on Celia at my brother's this evening, to congratulate her on her recovery. By the way, isn't that Miss Clay I see in the background?"

At the mention of her name Lyla looked up, but she didn't say anything.

Reedeth glanced at her and back at the camera. "Yes —ah—I'm afraid something rather dreadful happened."

"A backfire from one of those pills she takes for her trances?" Flamen gibed, and at once felt apologetic. But before he had time to say so, Reedeth had replied.

"No. Mr. Kazer got caught up in last night's riots and ... Well, he died from his injuries."

"Christ, that's awful," Flamen said slowly.

"So Miss Clay is here being treated for shock, mainly. But there's been another damned legal snarlup, and I can't just let her go. Some fool of a busy mistook her state for full-scale mental disorder, and by the time I found out about it the commitment papers were too far gone in the mill for me to haul them out."

"Doesn't anything in this country work properly any more?" Flamen sighed.

All of a sudden Lyla sat up straight, releasing her hands from their imprisonment between her legs. "Say, Mr. Flamen! I know we only met yesterday, but could *you* get me out of here?"

Flamen blinked. "How do you mean?"

"It's a guardianship problem," Reedeth said after a pause. "She has to be discharged into an adult's care, and all her relatives are out of state." To Lyla he added in a soothing tone, "There's no real need for that, Miss Clay. We'll have it straightened out by this evening at the latest, if I have to go clear to the Governor to fix it. But—"

He broke off abruptly. Clapping his hand to his forehead in a parody of astonishment at his own short-sightedness, he went on, "Why in the *world* did I never think of that before? Mr. Flamen, would you have any use for an absolute genius at the repair and maintenance of electronic circuitry?"

Prior tensed. "Find out what he means, Matthew," he said out of the corner of his mouth.

"I'm going to," Flamen assured him, puzzled. And, louder: "I'm afraid I don't quite catch you, doctor."

207

"Well, you see, we have a man here who's long over-due for release, but for reasons I can't go into because they're so complicated he's been stuck here months past the proper date. Meanwhile he's been looking after our automatics for us—and you probably know we have one of the largest cybernetic systems in the world. All our patients are packled as a matter of course. His gift for electronics is—oh, I can't find the right word. Bril-liant!"

"Matthew, we did get that zero reading," Prior whis-pered. "Someone like that might be very damned use-ful!"

Flamen hesitated. "What would you want me to do?"

"Accept guardianship, that's all. You wouldn't even have to pay him more than a token if you used his services—he has an Army pension which has been stacking up interest all the time he's been in hospital. He should be worth a couple of hundred thousand by now."

"Where did he get his training?"

"In the Army, as far as I know. But I do assure you, you can't fault his ability. He's done things here, to my own desketary, which I didn't think were possible."

"I'll consider it very seriously," Flamen said. "Can you let me have some documentation, perhaps? I ought to know something about him before committing myself."

"I'll make sure it's sent to you within an hour," Reed-eth beamed. "I can't tell you how grateful I am, Mr. Flamen! I've been looking for a way to secure his re-lease for ages. It simply isn't fair to— Oh." His smile vanished. "I guess there's one point I forgot to mention. He's a kneeblank."

There was a long silence. During it, Flamen was acute-ly aware of Diablo's dark eyes on him.

"That's irrelevant," he said at last. "I'd be concerned about two things if I agreed to your proposal: his sanity, and his usefulness to my company. It does so happen that we have a short-term vacancy for an electronicist, and I guess if he's as good as you tell me he'll suit us fine. So send me that documentation and I'll call you back. Okay?"

"Definitely okay," Reedeth said warmly and cut the connection.

Flamen leaned back, scowling at Prior. "So my dear wife doesn't care to be discharged into my care!" he grunted. Prior bridled.

"Matthew, I really do think you're embarrassing—ah—Diablo here by discussing these very private subjects!"

"Yesterday it was a pythoness, today it's a spoolpigeon—hell, Lionel, there are some people you don't try and keep secrets from because you can't survive in either line of business unless you know how to keep your mouth shut! I'll bet Diablo knew about Celia's trouble anyway, didn't you?" he concluded, turning to the kneeblank.

"Ladromide," Diablo said after a pause. "I thought of using it to pin a program on. Slant would have been here's this alleged disciple of the hard cold truth who drove his wife into a world of illusions. I watched your show for a week while I was making up my mind, and decided in the end it was worth having you around on the public scene whatever the hell had gone wrong privately." He looked and sounded uncomfortable, as though he were not used to praising people.

Flamen laughed. "That was a narrow escape," he said. "I've seen what happened to one or two of the targets you've used. What's your score on sassies up to now?"

"On—what?"

"Sassies. Suicides After Spoolpigeon Investigation."

"Oh. We call them eewoes. Easy way out." Diablo cogitated. "I guess around forty," he said at last. "I don't keep tally, though."

"Really?" Prior said, impressed. "Ours isn't much over half that."

Diablo looked at him, then at Flamen again. Deliberately fixing the latter with his dark stern gaze, he said, "I could suggest a reason. Blanks are harder to make feel deep-down guilty."

"I don't think I like your tone of voice," Prior said frigidly.

"I don't think I much like gauging the success of a vushow by the number of deaths it's caused," Diablo answered. "That evens it."

"Freeze it," Flamen snapped. "I mean *both* of you! Diablo's a stranger, Lionel, and there are things they feel differently about in places like Blackbury. I look forward to working with our new colleague because having him around is going to sharpen my wits. I've been getting stale. Maybe I should try a twelve-hour day too, see if that gets my imagination back in shape. But right now I have some loose ends to tie up, and so have you. Suppose you arrange for Diablo to have his own area of the office—move some walls around a bit, have a comweb put in, anything that's necessary. And arrange to go pick up Celia, too."

"As you say," Prior muttered, rising and heading for the door.

On the threshold, poised to follow him, Diablo hesitated and glanced back.

"Say—uh—Flamen! I didn't mean to make like an uppity nigra, you know. When I think what you could do to pillory us knees with that equipment"—he jerked his head—"I'm kind of surprised at your restraint."

"Oh, sure," Flamen said indifferently. "I could show Mayor Black like in bed with three blank girls, or the Detroit city council in a daisy-chain around the committee table, detail correct down to the pubic hair. But that's not what it's for. It's for things that rate an eighty-plus probability reading, and up."

"Yeah," Diablo said. "Different approach, I guess." He seemed for a moment about to say something else, but finally shrugged and turned to go out with the impatiently waiting Prior.

Alone, Flamen tugged at his beard and cursed under his breath. Reaching a decision, he stretched out towards the main information board and punched for data about packling; he talked about it glibly enough, but he had very little idea how it was done. From the densely clotted verbosity of the article he had on file he managed to extract the broad outlines after five minutes' concentration; it was exactly what Prior had talked about when trying to describe the treatment accorded to patients in the Ginsberg, the construction of an optimum psychoprofile towards which the actual profile was gradually constrained.

Where there was room for maneuver was in the selection of the parameters for the optimum curve. Though the data on file didn't include a bald statement to that effect, it was clear on reading between the lines that choosing them was largely an arbitrary process. Flamen considered that for a while and at length rubbed his hands together, pleased.

Granted that no one else enjoyed quite the household reputation of Mogshack, who had once been called "the Dr. Spock of mental hygiene," there must surely be someone else in his field with considerable authority, whose views were diametrically opposed, and who could be relied on to set up an optimum curve for Celia's personality which offered the greatest possible chance of contradicting Mogshack's own proposals. He punched for the list of candidates, and at the very top he found a name appearing which made him almost tremble with excitement.

Who would have thought that the computers would immediately suggest Xavier Conroy?

Danger of US 'apartheid with martial law'
From Alistair Cooke: New York

The country has had three days in which to absorb the shock of the first instalment, the official summary rather, of the report of the President's National Advisory Commission on Civil Disorders, shortly to be known as the Kerner Commission, after Governor Otto Kerner of Illinois who presided over the seven-months' investigation by nine whites and two Negroes.

Today, for those who hope for more light and a finer perspective on the Commission's findings, there fell the block-buster of the whole report: 1,489 pages of exhaustive and exhausting investigation of riots in cities big and small. Riots that hardly materialised, riots that shook the social and economic life of the cities to their roots.

Very few people on the outside looking in are likely to stagger through this fas-

cinating and depressing testament; and the
fewer people on the inside of State and
city government will be too busy trying
to decide between the "three choices"
which the Commission concludes now confront American society.

First, there is a continuation of present
policies, with the same or a little more
money going into the rehabilitation of the
cities, and the same methods, bordering
on suppression by arms, being used to
hold the riots. This way, the Commission
is convinced, will do little "to raise the
hopes or absorb the energies" of the increasing population of young city Negroes;
will lead to more violence; and "could lead
to urban apartheid and the permanent es-
tablishment of two societies."

Little hope

The second choice would be to work
at once for the "enrichment of the slums"
and "a dramatic improvement" of the
people's lives by substantial increases in
public moneys for education, employment,
housing and the social services. The Commission sees little hope of permanent improvement through this approach either . . .

The third choice, and in the Commission's
view the only one that can save the United
States from "two societies—separate and
unequal" (probably maintained by martial
law) is reinforced time and again in the
report's detailed documentation of city
grievances. These include the pervading
bigotry of white attitudes, the rising num-

bers of young Negroes doomed never to be employed at all (one third of all employable young Negroes in the 20 biggest cities are today unemployed), the flight of the whites to the suburbs from which they are unlikely to vote more taxes for cities reduced to decaying ghettoes for Negroes only.

This third choice requires nothing less than "a massive national effort" to integrate the social and economic life of the two races and the officers of the law who must protect it . . .

SIXTY-FIVE ASSUMPTION CONCERNING THE "MAS-
SIVE EFFORT" REFERRED TO IN THE
FOREGOING MADE FOR THE PUR-
POSES OF THIS STORY

It didn't happen and that worked entirely too well.

SIXTY-SIX

THE MILLS OF GOD GRIND SLOW BUT
THE MILLS OF MAN SEEM ALL TOO
FREQUENTLY NOT TO GRIND AT ALL
REGARDLESS OF HOW OFTEN THEY
SPIN ON THEIR AXES

"Ariadne, for God's sake," Reedeth said to the beautiful, invariably flawless image in the comweb screen. "I need to get high, or drunk, or something, and I'd rather not do it alone."

For an instant he thought she was simply going to snap at him and cut the connection. However, she sighed and leaned back in her chair. "You seem to have spent all day moaning, and I guess it's too much to expect you to stop before your manic-depressive cycle shifts out of its present phase. So what am I supposed to do —provide unofficial therapy?"

There was a taut bitter silence. Finally Reedeth said in a completely changed tone, "Here's an interesting psychological problem for you—or maybe it's sociological, to be more precise. When did friends go out of fashion?"

"Well, if all you want to do is talk nonsense—"

"Nonsense *hell*. How many friends have you got, Ariadne? I mean friends, that you know won't mind when you want to talk about your problems, who may even be able to help with advice, or a loan, or whatever."

"I don't have that kind of problem," Ariadne shrugged.

216

"I believe in being an individual and in looking after myself. If I couldn't, I doubt if I'd have the arrogance to try and help other people to achieve the same success in their own lives. But I have lots of friends, so many I couldn't list them—so many I've never managed to have them all to the same party!"

-"Those aren't friends," Reedeth said doggedly. "I have them, too: I guess I recognize five or six hundred people, recall them well enough to ask the right questions about their families and their jobs. But . . . Hell, let me take an illustration of what I mean. This girl Lyla Clay, that I *finally* managed to turn loose after what seemed like an eternity of struggling through red tape—"

A flicker of interest appeared on Ariadne's face. "Oh, you got her straightened out?"

"More or less. I'll tell you in a moment. Let me finish what I started to say. Her mackero was killed last night —murdered. He didn't live long enough to say why someone went for him. It was just purposeless. But there it is: he died and she went into shock. Luckily she has her own doctor, someone I know who charges reasonable rates and takes his poorer patients seriously, so— Hell, now I'm interrupting myself!"

He drew a deep breath. Ariadne said during it, "Why do they call it 'red tape'? Do they use special red-backed tape for confidential official recordings, or something?"

"Oh, for God's sake, woman! Ask your desketary! I don't know and I don't care! This is important, what I'm trying to explain!"

"So get to the point a bit faster," she said crossly. "I'm exhausted."

"Think I'm not? Give me a straight answer to this then: out of all the hundreds of people you know, who do you care about enough to go into severe shock when you lose them?"

There was a long pause. Eventually Ariadne said with a strained expression, "Well, my parents, obviously, and my brother Wilfred, and—"

"I said friends, not relatives. People you've selected for yourself out of all the available millions since you came of age and went out into the world on your own."

"I . . ." Ariadne shook her fair head, her face eloquent of the conflict between shame and honesty. "I don't know if there's anyone. You know, I don't think I ever considered the point before."

"So why not?"

Recovering a little, Ariadne said tartly, "Doesn't your friend Conroy have views on that?"

"You mean his argument that the total sum of emotional engagement of a modern individual is as rich as Romeo and Juliet's, but it's divided up among a far greater number of people so it appears to be very casual? Oh, I think he's damned right. It's the difference between a room-light and a laser beam. You can have just as much wattage in the system, but because it's not so concentrated it does much less damage. And I think that's great—it may have been okay to have one transcendent experience in days when one could only expect to live to be twenty-something anyway before catching the plague, but now that we live the better part of a century on the average it seems a shame to burn ourselves out. But—" He clawed furiously at his beard. "Damn, I'm taking the craziest long way around to get to what I want to say! What I'm talking about is a loss, not a gain. People still do have troubles, people still do need advice and help and all the rest of it."

"They get it," Ariadne said. "That's one of the reasons we're here in the Ginsberg, a state-financed hospital with the most advanced facilities in the world." She contrived to gloss her words with a suggestion of tolerant long-suffering.

"Yes, but suppose something happened to you like what happened to Lyla Clay, or even Harry Madison? Wouldn't you rather turn for help to someone you'd personally chosen, an intimate friend, than risk getting caught up in the kind of vast impersonal bureaucracy I've spent all day battling with? That girl Clay isn't sick except insofar as she's had an experience no girl ought to undergo—*no one* ought to undergo, ever! —and because she's three months under age in this state and had been arrested on suspicion of mental disorder I had to waste hours and hours in needless arguments!"

"But you did get her out in the end," Ariadne sighed.

"Yes, I did indeed. No thanks to your beloved Mogshack, either. When I appealed to him he slapped me down with the argument that nowadays even a suspected mental case mustn't be let loose on the streets for fear of provoking a riot like last night's. If that's the case, then—then hell! You shouldn't be allowed to appear in public because you're pretty enough to risk some knee trying to pick you up, with the danger of triggering a riot when you slap his face for being a nuisance!" Aware that he was growing heated, Reedeth forced himself to adopt a calmer tone.

"If you meant that as a compliment," Ariadne said, "you didn't phrase it terribly well."

"I'm not interested in compliments right now! In fact I'm not interested in very much at all except trying to figure out now how I can save people like Lyla Clay and Harry Madison from being shut away because they have something peculiar happen to them. That's not what I chose my job for, guarding a prison full of people with original minds."

"We've been over this before," Ariadne said. "We always get hung up on the question of what's original and what's crazy."

"So we do. I thought I was going somewhere else and I seem to have wound up in the same old groove." Reedeth rubbed his forehead. "I guess I didn't think out the consequences very clearly before I started talking, but what put me into this frame of mind was really very simple. I managed to get rid of Harry Madison as well as—"

"What? How?"

"Flamen agreed to act as his guardian. His company needs an electronicist, and when I suggested Madison he said yes. Hardly took any persuading."

"And you just turned him loose—a kneeblank in New York on a martial law day?"

"There still are knees in New York, whether you like it or not, legally entitled to walk the streets! And Miss Clay seemed to take a liking to him when I introduced them and offered to see him through the—"

"You turned a knee out in a blank girl's company, her in shock and him with a mental record as long as my arm?" Ariadne was almost out of her chair. "Christ, there's likely to be another riot tonight! It'll be a miracle if they get out of the rapitrans terminal alive!"

"I—"

"What kind of a cloud-cuckooland are you living in, Jim? All this gobbledegook about friends going out of fashion, all this phoney idealism about having someone to turn to in time of need. . . ! I'd rather have honest enemies than a friend who could treat me like you just treated those poor people!"

"But—!"

"I know what's wrong with you, Jim," Ariadne said fiercely, leaning close to the camera in her office so that her head threatened to protrude from Reedeth's screen. "It upsets you having people around that you've been made responsible for without being consulted, because they were like caught up in a riot or you found them here when you arrived. What you want isn't to prepare them for a safe return to ordinary life—only to shuffle them off somewhere out of sight so you don't have to take an interest in them any longer! When you hear that Madison has been gunned down on the street, or Lyla Clay was raped by a white gang because they saw her with a knee escort and decided a girl who kept that sort of company was fair game, are you going to go into shock? The hell you are!"

She broke the connection with a look of actual disgust, as though about to vomit on her desketary, and Reedeth said foolishly to the uncaring air, "But that's not what I . . ."

Aware that the comweb connection had been severed, the desketary said, "I'm sorry?"

"Oh, go to hell!" Reedeth roared, and stormed out of the office.

SIXTY-SEVEN   AN OPINION UNREPENTANTLY HELD
BY XAVIER CONROY DESPITE RE-
PEATED ATTACKS ON HIS STAND-
POINT BY (AMONG MANY OTHER
NOTABLE AUTHORITIES) ELIAS MOG-
SHACK

"Man is not a rational *being*, he is a rational *animal*, and to claim that in debasing the influence of the gonads and other glands, in producing a perfectly plastic, perfectly yielding, perfectly unirritating conformist dummy you have cured a severe mental disorder is exactly equivalent to boasting that you have eliminated the risk of *tinea pedis* by amputating at the ankles."

SIXTY-EIGHT   THE LINE DIVIDING DAY FROM NIGHT ON EARTH OR ANY OTHER PLAN-ET OR SATELLITE IS TECHNICALLY KNOWN AS "THE TERMINATOR"

There was an "atmosphere" at the Prior home that evening to which a number of factors each contributed noticeably.

Having reluctantly brought his sister Celia back from the Ginsberg Prior had found his wife Nora talking on the comweb to Phil Gasby's wife and the latter on being introduced had said, "Ah yes, she's the one who's spent so long in the State lunatic asylum, isn't she? I trust they know what they're doing to let her out. Snff." End of conversation and beginning of neighborhood-wide scandal.

Celia's presence annoyed Nora, who smashed a dish containing reheated deep-frozen beef Bourguignon in the middle of the dinner table shortly before her brother-in-law was due to arrive and disappeared to her room with a shout to the effect that she had married only Lionel of the Prior family and not all his mentally deranged relatives. Her customary ill-temper had been exacerbated earlier by his attempts to explain why engaging the celebrated kneeblank Pedro Diablo as a colleague at Matthew Flamen Inc. entailed advantages outweighing the social stigma of working with a black man on an equal footing (relevant quotations from the dialogue: "I'll never be able to hold my head up in this neighborhood again and we'll have to move!" and "If he needs a job let him go and look for one in Africa!").

The freshness of the disastrous citizens' defense group exercise in people's memory meant that instead of the normal evening-long flow of solidarity-generating comweb calls there was a dull silence in the house and a crackling awareness that the treachery of Lionel Prior in carrying out his successful mock raid on his neighbors' homes was being discussed in scores of calls so close at hand one could almost have stolen out back and eavesdropped on the speakers.

There was additionally the terrifying notion abroad that Morton Lenigo might have arrived with the faultless blueprint for a nation-wide seizure of power by the knees and during the day the Gottschalks had announced some very expensive but unprecedentedly destructive new weaponry which in this high-priced district virtually no one could afford so soon after laying out for the regular spring models.

Throughout all of which, including the dinner, Celia retained a marble statue's calm and a polite flow of small-talk concerning her brother's business, world affairs since her hospitalization, and the various antiques he had lately purchased and put on display in the living-zone. Her imperturbability was due to the fact that she had been drugged for five months without interruption at the Ginsberg and even if she stopped taking the medicine prescribed for her immediately, it would be several days before the cumulative effect on her personality wore off.

On the arrival of her husband Matthew Flamen she was just finishing her dessert, and after a cool greeting and the offer of her cheek to be kissed, she said it was advisable for her to go straight to bed since she had been warned against overtiring herself directly after her return to the outside world, good night.

SIXTY-NINE WHY THE CENTRAL QUEENS TUNNEL OF THE RAPITRANS SYSTEM WAS OUT OF ACTION FROM JUST BE- FORE DAWN UNTIL AFTER MIDDAY

A student of chemistry named Allilene Hooper, aged 19, failed to stabilize the home-brewed nitroglycerine she was delivering to her boy friend and it exploded from the vibration.

It being a martial law day there were armed police on duty at rapitrans terminals throughout the city, and under the inhuman gaze of goggle-like gasmasks Lyla rode the escalator up from platform level, dismayingly aware that behind her was this kneeblank stranger for whom, in a fit of violent reaction against the atmosphere of the Ginsberg, she had agreed to make herself responsible—not legally, for she was still under age, but morally, in that Reedeth had said quietly, "He hasn't been in New York as a free man for years, you know, and there have been changes."

What else could she have said but what she did? "There's a hotel near where I live and they don't mind taking in knees; I'll ride into the city with him and show him where it is."

And it wasn't until he said warmly, "That's very good of you, Miss Clay, because in spite of having been shut up in this place for so long he's really a very remarkable personality and a brilliant electronicist and ought to make out very well once he's discharged" . . . only then did the terrifying thought cross her mind: The *remarkable personality* was in the audience when I performed at the hospital the other day and had to be slapped out of the echo-trap and later suffered that inexplicable hangover and could it have been *him?*

She kept glancing back over her shoulder, and there

he was imperturbably riding up along with everyone else, a heavy bag slung on his shoulder which presumably contained what belongings he had been able to retain during his stay in the hospital, dressed in a plain gray oversuit not quite properly tailored to his stocky figure, his beard neatly brushed, his hair far shorter than was fashionable owing to a hospital ordinance she recollected reading about, something to do with the incidence of lice among patients committed after living alone for a long time in disgusting conditions.

What sort of a person? So far, apart from being introduced to him, riding down to the rapitrans terminal, and waiting a few moments for the compartments they'd signaled for to arrive, she had virtually no contact with him. They had exchanged a couple of dozen polite words, and that was that. She had gathered a little about him from Reedeth, notably the impression that but for being conscripted into the Army and suffering some kind of intolerable experience in combat he would never have undergone whatever sort of breakdown he had been hospitalized for.

And, on this return to the Ginsberg under utterly different circumstances from the previous day, she had suddenly realized why she had hated the atmosphere of the place so much on first arriving there. It had nothing specifically to do with her pythoness talent. It was due simply to her awareness that, in choosing her career, she had committed herself to a lifetime on the edge of literal insanity: thinking with other minds, perhaps one might call it . . . or whatever did actually happen when she gulped down a sibyl-pill and collapsed into trance. One false step, and she might be in that hateful hospital for good.

"What thin partitions sense from thought divide," she murmured as she came abreast of the watchful police at the head of the escalator.

"Talking to yourself, hm?" said one of them with a

harsh laugh. "Watch it, darl, or you'll be booked for a one-way ride to the Ginsberg!"

"Here comes a knee," said one of his companions. "Let's work him over, huh? We didn't get anyone yet today, but there's always a chance. You! You kneeblank there!"

On the firm ground, Lyla turned to look, and yes it was Harry Madison they'd chosen to drag aside and search: five tall policemen so armored and masked that one could not have told whether they themselves were light- or dark-skinned, with helmets and body-shields and pistols and lasers and gas-grenades. But there was no future in arguing. It would only make things worse if she said she and Madison were together.

Impassive, he obeyed the order to show his ID, and there was a reaction to the sight of the hospital discharge certificate: predictably, "So why didn't they send you to Blackbury?"

No reply. He was very calm, this man, Lyla noticed, very self-possessed, not in the least disturbed by what he could now see of the street, regardless of the fact that it must have undergone tremendous changes since he was last in the city: the blast-proof shields over the store windows, the two-foot-high police barricades isolating the fire-and-riot lane in the center of the roadway, the sunken gun-posts at the nearby intersections, the heavy concrete blast-walls exactly the length of a prowl car set at two-block intervals and designed to save official vehicles from being crushed if a building was demolished and spilled across the street.

Still, no doubt it had all been shown on the beams. Even being in the Ginsberg wasn't like being on another planet.

Disappointed perhaps—for they had gone so far as to make him empty his bag and proffer the contents for inspection—the policemen at length nodded Madison permission to go ahead, and one of them who had stood by idly chewing, a very tall lean young man, indeed gangling, put out his foot casually with the intention of tripping him as he hurried away. And somehow —Lyla couldn't see how—the outstretched foot was in precisely the spot where Madison next needed to step, and his weight went down on the arch without breaking stride, and by the time the pain was signaled to the astonished and furious busy there were a dozen people separating them.

"I'm sorry for the delay," Madison said as he rejoined Lyla. "There was no need to wait—I can easily find my way to this hotel you suggested."

Granted. So why had she waited? For the sake of having company, she decided suddenly. Last night she had lain beside the bed where Dan had died, where his body still rested, where—ugh. In cleanly modern America, one spoke of the organs, heart, liver, kidneys, for they were terms the doctors used when one was ill, and never made the connection with the tidily frozen, sterile, plastic-wrapped objects purchased for food. Dan had been opened, and the gash showed truly that men too possessed these things, these bloody wet palpitating things. . . .

She looked around her giddily at the crowd. There was a crowd on this street, there was always a crowd on every street in every modern city. She thought: hundreds and hundreds of hearts and livers and kidneys, kilometers of gut, liters of blood enough to make the sidewalk run awash with red!

"Are you all right, Miss Clay? You look very pale!" On her shoulder a touch steadying her, for which she was grateful because the world had tilted askew.

"You get your filthy hand off that blank girl!" screamed someone and instantly heads turned for twenty paces on every side, but luckily it was an elderly woman with a pinched mouth and stern eyes under a furrowed old forehead who had uttered the shriek.

"Want him to handle you instead, you old bag?" Lyla shouted back, and there was laughter and people had forgotten it, except the old woman herself who looked murder. In this century of ours, curses upon our ancestors, even the sweet old ladies know what it is to hate enough to kill. Turn out that big purse clutched so protectively: find a Blazer like the one that stinking Gottschalk tried to sell me over Dan's warm corpse. . . .

But the instant of tension had taken with it her unexpected fit of dizziness. She said in a normal voice, "I guess I should have warned you, Mr. Madison, that even though this is a district where knees can still find hotels and restaurant service it isn't what you'd call a very integrated neighborhood."

"That's all right, Miss Clay. One expects that. And the Army taught me to look after myself, which is something I haven't forgotten."

She looked at him thoughtfully, seeing him for the first time as Harry Madison person instead of Harry Madison overdue ex-mental patient. She thought back over the echo in memory of those confident words he had just uttered, and realized that he had an extremely pleasant voice, bass-baritone, old-fashioned like a singer's with premeditated weight on individual words instead of a single monotonous rapid spate of them as in most twenty-first century speech.

And recalled that she was still alone, because Dan was dead.

Dan had had his friend Berry. Berry, she was vaguely aware, had a friend of his own—or possibly of Martha's, the girl he lived with. One needed a friend in a city like this . . . but why stop at *a* friend? Yet it was the pattern; query because making more than one was so difficult, because making the first had been such a struggle one was afraid to revert to the rebuffs and disappointments of friend-hunting?

It was too deep, too terrifying, to be considered now on a hot evening in summer, the time growing late, the sun going from the sky, the aimless dense crowds of the city moving out under the goggle gaze and as-yet silent gun-mouths of the police half eager and half fearful at the possibility of tonight climaxing in riots and rockets from the sky which brought sniper-riddled buildings down in flames.

She said, "Shall I go with you to the hotel?"

"I guess maybe it would be better if I went with you to your place," Madison countered. "Dr. Reedeth told me you had a bad thing happen last night, Miss Clay, and—and I'm very sorry. I think you look sort of sickly, and I'd feel bad myself if I couldn't repay your kindness in riding to the city with me."

There was more than superficial polite concern in the tone. She thought *Uncle* and reached back into childhood, the war scare days of the nineties when every knee was treated by every blank as a potential subversive or saboteur and she, innocently five years old, was worried because they were so teddy-bearish and the little girls in traditional checked dresses with pigtails sticking out and ending in tightly knotted ribbons and it was absurd and not Uncle Tom, Uncle *Remus*—yes, from a little later, as the scare subsided and only the mental scars could not be cured but the buildings could be mended and the new skimmers took the air in their millions, tidily disciplined into midge-swarms across the sky by masterful computers capable of organizing a billion simultaneous journeys without collisions and— anyway, Uncle *Remus* with the confidence of a man successful in life and owning something the accidentally rich would eventually learn to want, that could be offered as evidence of him too being the heir to a tradition, a heritage of entertainment and salty wit adaptable to the modern world: what else had she done to rid them of the hysterical old woman a moment past but imitate Br'er Rabbit who begged not to be thrown in the briar patch?

"Miss Clay, I think maybe I ought to take you to your doctor first," Madison said anxiously.

"Who's in charge here, me or you?" Lyla countered

with a forced high laugh. "Yes, I'm sorry, something very bad did happen to me and I've got to go back to an apt where there won't be anyone else, just blood-stains on the floor to show there was someone yesterday, and there's not much use worrying, is there? People do get killed. I'll—"

Somehow she was walking with him, and managing to go the way they wanted to go instead of being pushed back and making detours and getting out of other people's way all the time as she was accustomed to. Not to the hotel, but to the block where she lived. Never mind.

"—simply have to digest the truth no matter how nasty it tastes. I ought to have warned you, though, like I said, because it's not as though I was wearing my street yash which would mean it could be assumed I was a knee like yourself, I mean here I am walking along with you and all I've got on is this pair of Nix and people are looking at us, have you noticed?, with this resentful expression, like when it's a blank it means what's that girl doing with a knee? and when it's a knee it means what's that knee doing with a blank girl and betraying the cause?"

"Yes," Madison said. "That's something any knee grows up with, Miss Clay. You don't have to spell it out, you know."

"I'm kind of trying to show that I appreciate it," Lyla said. "I mean I'm a pythoness and so I'm supposed to be more than averagely sensitive to—"

Recognized, familiar, the front entrance of her home block: the approach to the elevator.

"—other people, regardless of color. You see I was raised in this kind of *old-fashioned* background and my parents are very anti-Afrikaner and all that and I think it's a shame even though it's obvious why it happened that we got away from what was developing in the last century and—oh Christ, how am I going to get in?"

She stopped dead, on the point of entering the ele-

233

vator car. "Those fucking busies! They didn't even let me pick up a key when they dragged me out this morning, nothing, I just happened to have this small change in my pocket and . . ." Frantically, the one pocket checked down to the fluff in the lining, and nothing but the phial of sibyl-pills and the money and an ID card.

"We'll deal with that when we come to it," Madison said, guiding her deftly into the elevator. She thought in the distant back of her mind: This must be what my old-fashioned parents meant when they talked about an "escort" for me to go places with, and in my present state it's kind of nice, I like it, I'm dreadfully scared about what we're going to find when the elevator reaches the tenth floor and yet somehow I'm not going out of my skull and—

Stop.

Facing the elevator car, waiting to ride it down, the Gottschalk from Apt 10-W.

And his face uttering uncensored thoughts: Last night you tried to kill me when I was being helpful, and here you'd rather accept help from a knee, in this city torn apart by the black X Patriots who killed your man.

But he said nothing, merely moved aside to let them pass. And waited, not getting into the car.

The reason, instantly. Lying out in the corridor, the recognizable belongings. Books heaped. The stained bed on end propped against the wall. The less attractive miscellanea of a doomed household, including the Lar for which no doubt a debt-collection order had been filed today. And the door to the apt shut tight, locked, with a hundred-kilo deadfall beyond.

The Gottschalk sniggered. "Too bad, Lyla!" he said. For commercial reasons Gottschalks used first names, preserving the illusion that they too constituted a family such as a man was seeking to preserve (it says here) when he bought from them guns, grenades and mines. "They didn't shut the door behind you this morning, and it *was* kind of tempting for anyone who came by, wasn't it? Did your mack make a will leaving you the lease?"

"I—" Lyla's mind was frozen, sluggish as congealed old porridge. "I don't think he made a will for anyone."

"Too bad," the Gottschalk said again, his tone a sneer, and stepped into the elevator car to ride it down.

"Him I don't like," Madison said musingly, with a jerk of his head. "However, that's not important. Is this your apt, the one with all the furniture and stuff heaped up outside?"

"Yes, but—" Lyla was having to drive her nails deep into her palms, stiffen her muscles everywhere to save herself from screaming. "But someone's moved in, someone's squatting there! When the busies dragged me off today they didn't lock the door and—and what can I do? It wasn't my lease, it was Dan's, and . . ."

She turned blindly and crumpled against the wall. "And I haven't even got a *key!*"

There was a long time of nothing happening. Eventually she recovered and was able to lift her forehead from the corridor wall where she had been leaning it and blink away confusing tears from her eyes. Madison was still standing where he had been, bag slung over shoulder, one dark stubby hand conspicuous against the gray oversuit where he had reached up to grip the strap. She felt horribly ashamed of herself from years of being taught that one must not not not reveal one's weaknesses, eight months a year from age ten onward in the school from which she had ultimately run away.

But all Madison said was, "Punch lock, I guess—hm?"

"What—? Oh. Oh, yes. A Punch lock, of course." Almost no other kind was fitted to modern apt doors; any lock with an exterior hole for the key to be inserted was far too vulnerable.

"I see," Madison was saying in a musing tone, having turned to look at the jamb alongside which was propped up the broken bed with Dan's blood on it, drying now

235

to a foul brown crust that attracted a buzzing fly. "Mm-hm—it's a one-two-eight code, I think. . . . Right, Miss Clay?"

She stared at him in bewilderment.

"I mean it's got one-two-eight in it somewhere? Like the first three digits, or the next-to-first maybe?"

"Ah . . ." She swallowed enormously, not understanding but giving what seemed to be the most sensible answer. "Yes, I guess it does start with one-two-eight. But I never memorized it."

She hesitated, intending to ask how he'd known, but he had turned his back and was doing something she couldn't see because his body concealed his movements. What she did see was the door opening, and a chink of light across its top.

"There's a deadfall!" she screamed, and in the same heartbeat someone said from inside the apt something about *goddamned* . . . and the door was slammed back on its hinges so fast she couldn't see it go, it was *here* and it was *there* and Madison was standing in the opening with one hand over his head to catch the hundred-kilo deadfall barely descended in its grooves. Beyond him, a staring white-faced man coming out of the living room, holding a chair like a shield, whose jaw fell as he saw the intruder carefully raise the deadfall back to storage height and put over the catch to neutralize it.

"Do you know this person, Miss Clay?" Madison said in a bored kind of voice.

"Y-yes," Lyla whispered, and had to draw another breath before she could finish the statement. "It's a friend of Dan's—my mackero's. It's Berry."

"I . . ." Berry's Adam's apple bobbed on his lean throat; he was tall and stringy, and she was suddenly reminded of the policeman at the rapitrans terminal who had tried to trip Madison. "I came to take back my vuset!" he improvised. "I found I needed it after all. And when I saw the door was open I . . ." The words trailed away and he gave a shrug.

"Funny," Madison said with a glance at Lyla. "I don't see a vuset out there in the corridor. See a gang of other stuff, though. Yours?"

"Mine and Dan's!" Lyla burst out before Berry could reply.

"Ah-hah." Madison walked forward, brushing past Berry as though he didn't exist, and peered into the living room. "It's very kind of your friend, Miss Clay! I see he's given you a working bed in place of the broken one out there on the landing, and the place looks all kind of neat and clean and tidy. Must be a relief to know you have friends like this, when you were expecting to come home and find everything had been smashed by kids, or pilfered, because the busies didn't lock up behind them when they took you to the Ginsberg. Place looks fine!"

"You goddamned—!" Berry began, raising the chair as though to make a club of it instead of a shield. But Madison freed the hand steadying his bag long enough to jerk the thumb towards the deadfall which he had so casually caught and lifted, all one hundred kilograms of it, and the movement spoke clearer than words. Berry lowered the chair very slowly to the floor.

Sidling, all the blood drained from his face, he moved towards the door where Lyla stood like a marble statue. When he came within arm's reach, he said tentatively, "It's great to find that it wasn't true about your being shut up in the Ginsberg—"

At that point she lost control and slapped his face; the noise was like a gunshot.

"Bitch!" he shouted, and his fist came up bound for the point of her jaw—and missed, because while it was still coming Madison had kicked him accurately at the base of the spine and lifted him bodily past Lyla, through the door and across the corridor to slump against the opposite wall, moaning.

Carefully he closed the door and turned to her.

"Is there anything out there you'd like brought back in?" he inquired.

"Leave it," Lyla sighed. "I don't—oh, yes. There's two thousand to come back on the Lar! I don't dare let him corner me on that, the bastard. The *bastard!* And I thought he was a friend of Dan's! He must have heard Dan was dead and I'd been arrested and thought he'd grab the chance to move in—he's been living with his girl in one room for months and this place does at least have a separate kitchen though it's pretty crummy otherwise. . . . What are you doing?"

Madison had his head bent close to the door, listening. A moment more, and he whipped it open, one hand poised to strike in precisely the right spot. Berry yelled as his wrist was seized and pressure applied on nerves which sprang his fingers open. A Punch key fell tinkling and Madison said ironically, "Good of you to return the key—I guess Miss Clay will be needing it."

But in the other hand Berry held a knife, and that he disposed of with neither irony nor delay; the frantic upward blade destined for his belly ended against the armor of the metal door, skidded with a squeal, and was twisted economically by the hilt out of Berry's grasp into his own. For the second time in less than a minute Berry's jaw gaped in disbelief. A long moment they stood face to face; then his nerve broke and he ran blindly for the elevator.

Madison slid the knife into his bag and said, "Tell me what you want brought back in, Miss Clay."

Staring at him, she essayed a laugh. It wasn't a great success. "You weren't kidding when you said you knew how to look after yourself, were you?" she said. "Did the Army teach you all that?"

"I haven't had too much to do in the Ginsberg," Madison shrugged. "Time to think about it, and practice."

"But—but you got through that door without a key!" Lyla persisted. "It was locked, wasn't it?"

238

"Ah . . . Yes, it was locked." Madison's dark face betrayed no emotion.

"But you can't open a Punch lock without the right key! I mean, not without blowing the door down!"

Madison didn't say anything.

"All right, I guess you can. You just did it. What did you use?"

Silence.

"Okay, trade secret. But tell me this, then." She hesitated, a listening look on her face as though she were hearing her own words and doubting that they could possibly make sense. "Do they use Punch locks in the Ginsberg?"

Madison nodded.

"And you could have opened them any time you wanted to? Just walked out?"

"I guess so."

"Then why in hell didn't you?" Her voice grew ragged with hysteria.

"I wasn't meant to, Miss Clay," Madison said. "Not till I got the legal certificate that I'd been discharged and had a guardian to answer for me for the first twelve months, you see."

Lyla felt for a chair without looking and lowered herself to its seat, very carefully. "Are you serious? Yes, of course you are—you give me the impression you couldn't be anything *but* serious."

Another pause.

"Well . . . Well, thanks very much, anyway. I don't know what I'd have done if that bastard Berry had been here and I'd arrived on my own. I mean, if I'd just found the door locked and got no reply I'd have gone looking for him first because I thought he was Dan's best friend." She put her head in her hands and rocked back and forth. "Do you have any friends, Harry? Can I call you Harry? I don't *like* calling people mister and missus and miss all the time."

"Sure, you call me what you like," Madison said,

239

peering through the door to see that the corridor was empty, then briskly going to bring back the things Berry had tossed out. Carrying the bed cautiously through the door, he said, "Like I should clean this up and fix it? You wouldn't want to be indebted to him for that one he brought in, would you?"

"No!" Lyla raised her head. "No, sling everything out that he brought here—let him drag it home, if he still has a home!"

"So you just tell me what's his and what's yours," Madison invited, and propped the bed against the nearest wall.

The job was done in twenty minutes, the door closed, the deadfall set again for fear Berry might return with reinforcements, the bed thoroughly washed down with hot water—for once the supply was plentiful, and among the things Berry had brought which had not been dumped in the corridor was some detergent—and the gash in the cushion repaired with adhesive tape from Madison's bag. It was like a Santa Claus sack, Lyla thought, detachedly watching him at work; she could believe that if she opened it at random and enumerated its contents she'd find only what might be expected: clothing, toilet articles, perhaps a few books or souvenirs. But whatever the problem, if Madison himself reached in, he would produce the necessary article to cope. . . .

Tested, reinflated, the bed was back in place and the Lar was in its niche and everything else was as it had been. Madison slung his bag over his shoulder again and headed for the door.

"Glad to have been of help, Miss Clay," he said. "I'll go locate that hotel now, I guess."

"No, wait!" Lyla jumped up. "Please don't go. I . . ." She had been about to reach out and catch hold of his arm; she canceled the gesture in mid-air. Some knees were very sensitive about blanks touching them without permission, and she was frightened of this man who could open locks without explosives and walk under a heavy deadfall to catch it with one arm. To cover her abortive *faux pas* she started to talk very rapidly and randomly.

"You see, like I was saying, if I hadn't found out it was Berry here I'd have turned to him because I thought he was Dan's friend and I don't come from New York, not even from inside the state, so I don't have too many friends and . . . *Do* you have any friends, Harry?"

"No."

"None? None at all? Family, anything?"

He shook his head.

"You come from this part of the country?"

"Nevada."

"You're a long way from home, then, aren't you? I only come from Virginia, but either way, it's not New York . . ." She bit down hard on her lower lip; it was trembling like an advance warning of tears.

"Suppose Berry waits to catch me alone," she said finally.

"You know him," Madison said. "Do you think he might try?"

"I don't know!" The words peaked in a cry. "I never even thought of him as an enemy before! He's the last person in the world I'd *ever* have thought of as an enemy! Oh God, why can't we have friends any more like they used to in the old days?"

"I don't know the answer to that," Madison said. "I expected that the doctors at the Ginsberg might, but they don't."

"Yes, I guess you would expect psychologists to be able to answer it," Lyla said, falling into the game with a lightheaded, floating sensation like the very late stages of a Ladromide trip. "What did they put you in there for, anyway—if you don't mind my asking?"

"For too many questions," Madison said. "That kind of question you just asked. They put a gun in my hand and said go kill that naked savage with a stone spear, he's the enemy, and I said why is he the enemy and they said because he's been got at by the communists and I said does he even have a word in his language for 'communism' and they said if you don't go kill him you'll be under arrest. So they arrested me. I went on asking questions and I never got an answer, and I didn't feel inclined to stop until I did. So they discharged me and put me in the Ginsberg—or rather, in another hospital first off, but when the Ginsberg was opened they transferred me. Because I'm a knee, I guess. It was a time when it wouldn't have looked right to have a black man in a bad old-fashioned hospital."

Lyla started to say something, changed her mind, changed it back again. "Harry, tell me honestly: do you think they were justified to put you in there? Do you think you were crazy? Because you certainly don't sound it, to me."

"I have a certificate," Madison said with a wry smile. It was the first trace of expression she had seen on his face, even when he was confronting Berry, and it was gone in a flash.

"Yes. Yes, of course." She cast around for words. "Well, look . . . Look, it's like this. I don't want to be alone. I'm frightened. I don't have a gun any more—it was stolen by the block Gottschalk, the one we saw by the elevator. I'd have to go out and get food or something and . . . Well, look, can you stand to keep me company for a few hours at least? Just so long as necessary? Till I feel . . ."

Her voice died and her hands hung lax at her sides and her head bowed. "I'm sorry," she muttered. "You've done much more already than I had any right to expect."

"Your talk of food is a good idea," Madison said. "I think you'll be okay later, but not right now. With a meal down you and a few drinks maybe, or a joint, you'll be able to manage. It'll make things seem more normal."

"That's exactly what I want," she said gratefully. "To make things *seem* normal, just for a while, even though I know they aren't and never will be again. Look, let's go eat right away so I don't hold you up for too long. I'll get my yash and put on some sockasins so nobody can tell I'm blank walking along the street, and I know some restaurants that don't mind mixed clientele."

She reached for the yash, which was on its regular peg; apparently Berry hadn't yet got around to throwing that out. On the point of ducking into the concealing garment, she hesitated.

"Harry, was it you?" she said suddenly, and was prepared to elucidate: "who drove me into that echotrap, who wished a hangover on me so that I spoke an oracle out of trance."

But she didn't have to. He gave a matter-of-fact nod and held out the key he had taken from Berry for her to put in her pocket.

"Sorry," he added, and opened the door.

SEVENTY-ONE

REPRINTED FROM THE LONDON
OBSERVER OF 10TH MARCH 1968

Colour—The Age-Old Conflict by Colin Legum

Having recently spent several months
in the United States, I came away sharing
the view of those Americans who think
that, short of two miracles—an early end
to the Vietnam war, and a vast commitment to the public expenditure on the
home front—the US is on the point of
moving into a period of harsh repression by
whites of blacks that could shake its political system to its very foundations.

What would be the likely effects of the
West's leading power engaging in energetic racial repression? It would drama-
tise and accentuate the world colour crisis
as nothing else could do. It would place
a far heavier burden on the loyalties of
America's Western allies even than Vietnam.
It would have a traumatic effect in Africa,
and directly affect the African nationalists
with no alternative to inviting Communist
support . . .

244

If this depressingly dark view turns out to be unduly alarmist, that could only be because the West, having seen the dangers in time, had changed the priorities of its commitments at home and abroad . . .

If ever American white society should come to feel its economic and security interests in serious jeopardy, it is quite possible that radical changes might take place. But it is not yet possible to foresee what these might be.

Similarly, if the white South African community should ever come to feel itself so isolated and threatened that it could no longer maintain the present policy of white domination, it might become interested in some genuine separation, such as the cantonal system of Switzerland. This type of voluntary separation is currently being discussed by some individuals in Israel as a conceivable solution to the problem of living beside the West Bank Arabs.

Voluntary separation—even separation into different bits of territory—is not always necessarily retrogressive. Although it is suspect to liberal minds—because of the horrors of twentieth-century racialism—liberals were the champions of all the nineteenth-century separatists who wanted independence from the Habsburg and Ottoman Empires and still today react sympathetically to the claims of Scots or of Welsh.

The current demand of Black Power in America for control over their own ghettoes is a move in this direction . . .

SEVENTY-TWO ASSUMPTION CONCERNING THE FORE-GOING MADE FOR THE PURPOSES OF THIS STORY

About the middle of the 1980's the money and manpower allotted to Internal Security Maintenance began to exceed that committed overseas.

SEVENTY-THREE   IN ACCORDANCE WITH A COMPU-
TERIZED RECOMMENDATION ABOUT
HOW BEST TO ENLIST THE COOPER-
ATION OF A NOTORIOUSLY THORNY
PERSONALITY

Xavier Conroy, D.Sc., Ph.D., Hawthorn Professor of Social Psychology, University of North Manitoba: MOG-SHACK INFLUENCE CONTEMPORARY PSYCHOLOGICAL DOC-TRINE HELD UNDUE BY FORMER ASSOCIATE STOP SEEK COR-ROBORATIVE/CONTRADICTORY OPINIONS STOP YOUR REPLY PRE-PAID SIGNED FLAMEN

Flamen Spoolpigeon NYCNY 10036: MOGSHACK INFLU-ENCE PERNICIOUS BUT YOU TILT AT OVERHIGH WINDMILL SIGNED CONROY

Conroy Univ. N. Manitoba: AGREE WINDMILL OVERHIGH STOP QUERY COOPERATION IN SHORTENING IT SIGNED FLA-MEN

Flamen Spoolpigeon NYCNY 10036: GOOD LUCK SIGNED CONROY

Conroy Univ. N. Manitoba: COME NY WEEKEND EXPENSES PAID STOP BRING AXE SIGNED FLAMEN

Flamen Spoolpigeon NYCNY 10036: ARRIVING SATURDAY
MORNING FLIGHT 9635 STOP DONT THINK HOPE IN HELL
BUT HATE TO MISS CHANCE SIGNED CONROY

Lyla felt she should have been terrified, but she wasn't, and she was even able to wonder quite calmly why she wasn't. She decided it was because Madison was so clearly on her side, had just saved her from what must otherwise have been a catastrophe, and moreover knew —regardless of how he knew—what she had meant when she asked that simple question: "Was it you?"

For a while after leaving the apt she didn't really think very much, but eventually, when they were back at street level, she was able to formulate casual inquiries in a normal friendly tone, and uttered them.

"Matthew Flamen offered you a job, isn't that right?"

"Yes; apparently he needs someone to cure interference on his vushows, and I know a fair amount about electronics."

"Are you glad to be—ah—*out* after such a long time?"

"I don't know. I'll wait until I find out whether the world has improved in the meantime."

"It's got worse," Lyla said positively. "I mean . . . Well, I'm still pretty young, I guess, but from what I can remember, even, it seems to have got worse. Dr. Reedeth said they had three LR's yesterday and that was good according to him because once they had nineteen in a single night, but there shouldn't be any at all!"

There was an interlude during which they walked along side by side without talking, Lyla shrouded in her yash and sockasins so that none of her skin showed, and they were able to make it along the sidewalk without trouble because other people took it for granted she too was knee. There was always a kind of weariness after an outbreak of rioting, a post-tumescent sadness as might be felt by two honest but accidental lovers realizing in the gray dawn that through transient passion they had risked starting another child on the long journey towards death.

Eventually he took up the questioning and said, "What would you have done if you'd arrived home on your own?"

"I don't know," she muttered. "I guess I might have called up your new boss. But I don't think I'd have got much help out of him. I mean . . . Oh, this is so hard to explain. I mean I like him on the outside, but I don't like him on the inside. He talks okay, but you don't get the feeling he's a man you can trust. Do you catch me?"

"Very clearly," Madison said. And: "Is that the restaurant you're taking me to, the one ahead?"

They had just rounded a corner and come in sight of a Chinese restaurant called the Forbidden City; purely in order to keep some kind of trade going in spite of modern xenophobia Chinese restaurateurs had notoriously been compelled to put up with whatever clientele offered themselves and customarily accepted mixed parties. But the main window of this one had been smashed, and there was a sign on the door, hastily scrawled in red ink: X PATROTS WORK!!! And an arrow pointing to the broken glass.

"Dan and I brought some knee friends of ours here once," Lyla said with forced brightness, and led him across the street. But she didn't even go up to the door. Behind it there was a tall Asiatic who looked past her at Madison and raised one hand warningly with fingers stiff for a karate chop.

"I guess we'd better try somewhere else tonight," she said dispiritedly, and turned away. From the corner of her eye she caught the Asiatic's teeth glinting in a grin.

There was a soul-food restaurant on the next block, but that had a sign up too, neatly printed in bright brown on solid black, denying entry to blanks, and then there was an Indian one proudly assuring the public that they too were Aryans and wanted nothing to do with other races, and a strict-Jewish one and a strict-Muslim one and a Japanese one for whites only outside which was parked a South African Voortrekker, and a Yoruba one which specialized in ground-nut chop and . . .

Finally Lyla said miserably, "I'm so sorry, but it's been months since I tried to find somewhere that wasn't segregated and after the trouble last night I guess that was the final straw for lots of them. Maybe we should break up and eat separately after all."

"The hotel you recommended me to," Madison said. "Does that have a restaurant?"

Miserably she looked up at him through the window in the hood of her yash. "For all I know, the hotel may have stopped taking knee clients now and you'll have to go clear to Harlem after all."

Madison frowned and for a moment his lips narrowed so completely that they seemed to vanish. "What's done this, Miss Clay? It wasn't just one night of rioting."

"I'd like you to call me Lyla," she insisted. "I like people to be friendly to me instead of just polite! I *need* someone to be friendly! Oh God, I wish it could be like the old days my parents talk about, when you didn't mind who you met or who you worked with or who sat next to you. It's all sort of closing in on us like the walls in *The Pit and the Pendulum!*"

She glanced wildly around as though actually expecting to see the buildings move to trap her.

"People didn't get killed in riots," she whispered. "They didn't! Oh—oh, poor *Dan!*"

Madison waited. Shortly she was able to go on.

"No, of course it wasn't just one night. It must have

been waiting all the time people were ashamed to let it come out in the open. But something's proved to be stronger than shame. What is stronger than shame?"

"Fear," Madison said.

"I guess so," she admitted. "But why should people be so afraid?" She drew a deep breath. "I'm a pythoness, Harry. I have to get inside people's minds. I never found anything in anyone's—not even at the Ginsberg where there are all these people who are supposed to be crazy—which wasn't in me too."

She had fallen in beside him again automatically and this time he was taking the lead, heading towards the hotel she had recommended.

"Except you," she said. "You're—you're not the same somehow. And I'm frightened of that too . . . I think."

At which point four large strong young men, all blanks, stepped out of a doorway and blocked their path. A bright light flashed in her eyes so that her face could be seen behind the mask of the yash and a voice said, "Mixed!" A hand clamped on hers and something jabbed into the base of her thumb and the ground rocked in a weird swirling curve like water in a spinning bowl.

Blurch. Planet revolving on ungreased axles that howled. Dim unspoken in the recesses of the brain *helphelphelp*. Scattered to the four filthy corners of the universe the bits and pieces of the person once integrally Lyla Clay. Feebly *helphelp* and not even strength to move the lips let alone power vocal cords with gusting breath.

Eight filthy corners.

help

too much like hard work she abandoned the struggle.

SEVENTY-FIVE   CAUTION AND PRECAUTION UNEQUAL
AND OPPOSITE

They had put Pedro Diablo in a Federal-financed luxury apt development where the contract—drafted by Bustafedrel back in the days of less sharply delineated racial boundaries—included a non-discrimination clause, but it had never been invoked before and his neighbors were so horrified that during the evening (while he was being tracked down by the knee leaders who were in close touch with Morton Lenigo and had also been horrified because they had banked on using Diablo's talents as a propagandist and now he'd been fired on the sayso of a dirty blank) they were organizing a petition to have him evicted before he lowered the tone of the block.

SEVENTY-SIX   Q. WHO WAS THAT GRUNCH I SAW
                  YOU WITH LAST NIGHT? A. THAT
                  WAS NO GRUNCH BUT THE EGG-
                  PLANT OVER THERE

Eternities later and a different world: a world of black
furry hills with a sun half green half red crossed by a
slanting bar louring from a gray vertical sky.

A room? Painfully. A landscape of a room, floor plains
and furniture mountains. Unheard, a river coursing down
a stony cascade, obscene fungoid growths on the foot-
hills and local weather storming and screaming and
clammy heat and the stench of decay.

Crack *thunder* and ouch *lightning* and in the immediate foreground to which Lyla opened her eyes a Stone-
henge of human bodies, a megalithic circle of arms on
shoulders, pallid upright pillar-forms interrupted before
the place where she lay by a wide-astride mandrake/
womandrake more exactly paunch sagging over hairy
pubis and skin scrawled like a toilet's wall with names
and times in greasy crayon, some smeared and some
freshly legible: PIGGY WALLIS 0825 DELLA THE BUTCH
1215 HORNY HANK DUMONT 1640.

As though catching the fragments of a nuclear explosion piece by slow piece and forcing them back into
the form of neatly machined metal billets Lyla absorbed
the facts her senses presented and categorized them into
patterns. She felt very ill and her hand hurt where a

254

blunt needle had been jabbed deep into the muscles. Also there was a hot new pain across her right thigh. A red whiplash bar on the skin.

Multi-level floor. Fact established. Perspective restored. Ultra-modern collapsible retractable mutable furniture. On the black slopes the distorted mushrooms were human bodies some clothed and some not, some moving some not and some halfway between involved in incredibly slow lovemaking with limbs entwined and all else forgotten except the touch of skin to skin. So too in front of her not a megalithic circle but eight men wearing only boots and scrawled across the chest of each —or the upper arm if the chest was too hairy for writing on—a crayoned name GENE PUTZI VERNON HUGHIE PHIL SLOB CHARLIE PAT. Arms on each other's shoulders they formed a horseshoe around a very tall young woman with small breasts and a premature pot-belly also naked except for a belt and sandals with interlaced thongs rising to above the knee, holding a whip and crowned with a fantastical red-blue-green wig. There was intolerable noise, not deafening but coming from all sides and overhead, as though in every adjacent room there was music and dancers' feet stamping and people arguing among themselves at the tops of their voices. Her eyes were maniacally wide and she was running with so much sweat her inscriptions were dissolving.

"She's awake!" A shout. A spray of fine spittle-drops, touch-touch on Lyla's skin. Also reported from the skin: the abrasive clutch of ropes at her elbows, on her back the sweat-slippery contact of moving muscles across hard shoulder-blades, under her buttocks wet furriness, at the nape of her neck the wiry roughness of knee-blank hair, like a terrier's coat. . . . She gasped and drove her perception into a normal mode by sheer willpower. She was sitting tied back-to-back with Harry Madison and she had been stripped.

"So what did you do with those Nix she was wearing?" roared the tall girl with the whip, and Gene on the end of the line of men broke loose eagerly, went to retrieve them, offered them with a cringing bow. Whip draped over shoulder the girl felt for the pocket and took out what there was: Punch key (let fall), some money (let fall), ID card (retained) and a phial.

"That something good, Mikki?" whined Gene. "That a good trip in that bottle?"

"How the hell should I know?" the girl bellowed, scrutinizing the ID.

Mikki? Lyla thought. Oh God. No. Let it not be Michaela Baxendale.

Booming words barely perceived through a fog of shock and terror and the aftermath of whatever drug had been used for the kidnapping: "A good trip baby, yes, a good trip, hey! Know who you collected for me, darl?"

Gene shook his head and the others craned close to hear.

"Why, it's the pythoness that son and daughter of a motherfucker Dan Kazer macks for now!" Mikki screamed, dissolving in a paroxysm of laughter. "The shitty bugger dropped me cold in the street and now here's deliverance into my hands—hey, darl?" She glowered at Lyla venomously, shaking the little phial close to her ear, and then turned to inspect it critically by the light of the red-green sun which was a dial on the wall with one pointer tilted into the green.

"Ah-hah! Enough here to go clear around if it is a good trip in this bottle!" She unscrewed the cap briskly. "But let's just be sure, huh? Let's try it on them and find out how it makes them fly!"

Giggling, the ring of men broke up, dropped on knees, grabbed—clutch at ankles, then thighs, reaching up higher greedily to crotch, also breasts: all too rapid to separate into individual events, a totality of clawing and fondling. Meanwhile behind Lyla others doing the same for (must be) Madison. She was too weak to fight them off so tried duplicity, waiting until a hand came close to her mouth with one of the sibyl-pills, prompting comment from the one branded SLOB: "Hey, Mikki, this must be a good trip! Look, she's opening up for it!"

And bit. Hard.

"The bitch! She bit me!" Leaping back, pill dropped, looking in horror at finger gashed across nail's base, blood pulsing out drip-drip on Lyla's leg. But in the moment of delusive relaxation to celebrate successful counter-attack a bang on the back of the head, Madison's hard skull. A whisper: "Hold his nose." The sound of a punch in the belly. Loudly: "He swallowed that okay! Try the girl again. Give us another pill, Mikki . . . No, don't bother!" Scrabbling on the black carpet. "I found the one she spat out—here it is."

Christ, what would one of the sibs do to Madison? She remembered Dan orbiting so high she thought he'd never land and that only women (something maybe to do with hormone chemistry) had the talent to metabolize the drug in half an hour.

She fought and twisted and writhed but they gathered her legs one by one and sat on them, too heavy to be forced off except at the risk of cracking bones. As her arms were already roped to hold her back-to-back with Madison that left only her head, which could be controlled by grasping her hair. Forced back, back until her neck muscles could not stretch to meet the counter-tug on her jaw and her cheek was against Madison's wiry beard, she tried to turn sideways, hold her mouth against his neck to bar the pill's entrance and didn't make it. Flip between her parted teeth, tap on her tongue, brace to stop herself swallowing it when the expected blow in the stomach came . . .

Except it didn't. Shedding the relaxing men in a tumble of limbs she was lifted *hup* into the air and found herself briefly looking at the ceiling. She spat out the pill because that was the thing she most wanted to do in all the world.

The ropes tightened on her arms, first left, then right,

and hurt for a fraction of a second but it was worth it.
They snapped. She fell sprawling and landed with one
hand in a wet clammy substance which held up to the
light showed shit-brown. Naturally. She got away from
there, frog-hopping, wiping her hand wherever a piece
of the black carpet was relatively dry, turning when she
was out of reach to look at Madison.

No one else seemed to be paying much attention except Mikki and her eight booted men. The loving cou-
ples on the slopes at the end of the room went on with
their slow slow parody of passion, and for the rest the
world did not currently exist.

They had stripped Madison too and his stocky dark
body glistened like oiled sealskin, a ridge of light on
every tautened muscle. The man branded PAT, as though
hoping to benefit by that ebony embrace, said, "Ho-
hooo!" and advanced coaxingly. A little stooped, legs
apart like a wrestler's braced for the next grapple, eyes
warily flicking to take in his surroundings, Madison
waited until he came within reach, and—snapped. Big
white gleaming teeth. An animal growl without words.
As yet, only a warning: on Pat's hand, a mere line of
blood traced by one canine fang, and some spittle. He
paled and shook it, mouthing a curse.

"Get back, Pat," said Mikki, brought down from
whatever plane she had been orbiting at by the shock
of seeing the ropes break. "Looks like this is Dutch
courage in a pill we gave him. Give me a clear field
for the whip, will you?"

She made it whine through the air, confident, having
used it often on much bigger opponents. As yet indeed
there was no real alarm. A glance to the side showed
Lyla crouching and trembling, not offering to join in.
One against nine made excellent odds; Lyla could almost hear the thought. And the booted young men were
strong and healthy.

On a distant slope of the room someone sat up, alerted
by the whip-whine, maybe: a girl wearing nothing, who

first crossed her arms over her bosom for concealment, then gave a foolish grin and parted her legs to set her elbows on her widespread knees. She leaned forward to watch with concentration.

On the back of Lyla's tongue: a taste. Not the sourness of fear which was everywhere else in her mouth. Bitter/pungent/acrid? She sucked up saliva to suspend it in and rolled it forward to the area most sensitive to such flavors.

Memory clicked and she was instantly horrified. Once she had broken open a sibyl-pill before taking it, to find out if she liked the taste of the contents. She didn't. This was the same. The gelatin shell must have split, perhaps trodden by a bare foot after she knocked it aside the first time they tried to push it into her mouth. And she had noticed too late to stop herself swallowing as much of the drug as had spilled out on her tongue. Only a few milligrams, probably, but without the violence of the pythoness frenzy to burn it up what would it do to . . . ?

Crash.

Through the continuing racket of music and dancing from elsewhere in the apt, a rending noise. She jolted back to awareness of the rest of the room. With the terrible strength he had used to catch and lift the hundred-kilo deadfall on her apt door, Madison had seized a table with marble top and stainless steel legs and was engaged in tearing it apart. When one of the welds resisted him he spun and slammed the whole thing against the wall. The marble shattered and a chunk of concrete fell to the floor. A leg came loose and he raised it overhead with a howl. The man labeled VERNON cringed and moaned out of reach.

Looking alarmed, Mikki cracked the whip and this time took aim for Madison's neck.

The steel table-leg intercepted the lash in the air and it coiled around like a constrictor, Madison moving his head back without moving his shoulders, like an Indian temple dancer, just as far as was necessary for the tip of the lash to miss his right eye. He jerked, and the handle of the whip leapt from Mikki's sweaty grasp.

Bold, almost pleased, as though recognizing a worthwhile opponent, the one called Putzi who was the tallest and most muscular dived for the shattered table and himself wrenched free another of the legs.

Madison stripped the coil of the whip off his own weapon and threw it. Lyla's hands went up to the level of her ears and she heard the sound of her own fingers clapping over into the palms. The force of that throw was unbelievable, and he hadn't even drawn his arm back behind his shoulder. But the balled-up whip drove Putzi off his feet and left a continuous red pattern across his chest and belly, as though he had been struck with an old-fashioned wicker carpet-beater, a kind of sketch for a three-leafed clover.

"I'm getting out of here!" cried the one labeled Hughie. Mikki reached for him and caught him by the hair, swinging him around.

"Get him down and quiet him, you crazy fool! Want to have a kidnapping charge around your neck? You brought him here; you stay and face the consequences!"

"But you told us to go bring in a mixed-race couple!" Hughie whimpered.

"Shut up and grab that table-leg!" Herself, Mikki dived to retrieve the whip from its entanglement with the moaning Putzi's limbs.

One inch from her outstretched hand a chunk of marble, fist-sized, smashed and spattered her face and body with little stinging fragments like midges. She looked up slowly to see Madison grinning at her, inhumanly calm. Adjusting her balance, she drew back— and snatched the table-leg up, tossing it not to the still frightened Hughie but to Vernon, who caught it and charged Madison with it lifted in a killing swing.

"An thou'lt match me at the quarterstaves, thou'lt earn thee a cracked skull for thy pains," Madison said in

a clear voice, and countered with such a violent riposte
that Vernon's fingers sprang open and his weapon flew
through the air to crash ringing against the far wall. The
naked girl behind Lyla uttered a cry of delight and
clapped her hands.

Quarterstaves . . . ? Lyla blinked and shook her head.
For one moment there she had seemed to see not the
black room with the gray walls and the half-red half-
green sun, but a forest clearing with a brook across it,
and men with long wooden poles disputing the passage
of a broad flat log laid between the banks.

But the room was still here and the vision of the sunny
glade was gone.

Recovered, furious, Putzi was running to catch up the
metal table-leg, the best weapon visible, while Mikki
was turning her back cautiously and heading for the far
end of the room.

To make himself a shield, Putzi clutched at a light
chair with a strong plastic seat and held it lion-tamer
fashion, advancing on Madison. The knee retreated a
little, tempting his attacker to make the first move—and
shot out his arm to snatch down one of the floor-to-
ceiling drapes that covered all the windows, stamp on
one edge of it and with a bulge of muscles rip the heavy
velvet so that he had a conveniently sized portion in his
left hand.

Under bare feet the sand very hot with the sun,
gritty but scarcely felt (*what?*). Lyla reached down
giddily to touch her own sole and heel, expecting to
contact sandy roughness and finding only a smear of
the excrement which she had earlier wiped from her
hand. Yet the roar of the hungry lions was (*what?*)
unmistakable, the coughing noise like a slow explosion.
And the watchers on the banked seats reaching up to
the pure blue sky like an oppressive tent on which the
gold coin of the sun hung with an expression of interest
in these matters of life and death. . . .

For the last time she managed to force herself back

261

into the normal frame of reference, and it stopped with the sight of the two gleaming metal shafts upraised to catch the light, the chair-made-shield and the curtain torn to make a tangling defense. The taste in the mouth of a last bad meal, a handful of sad olives, a wedge of stale unleavened bread and a few bites from a haunch of meat destined for the wolves but diverted by a lanista who had bet on today's contest of man and man, that had seemed only rancid but might as things went have been poisoned, for the world swayed horribly at every step and there was a rushing of blood in the ears that drowned out the cries of the crowd.

Lyla realized perfectly well what was happening to her. She had ingested a subcritical dose of the drug in the sibyl-pill and it was just taking her over the border from reality into whatever world she inhabited during her ordinary trances. It was what was happening to everyone else that she couldn't figure out. That tall blonde Germanic swordsman in the morion and cuirass and one vambrace and one greave and carrying a targe or buckler opposed to that retiarius with the stabbing trident and the cleverly wielded net . . .

Once more from the cages underneath the stands, the roar of angry lions.

Deft the net spread on the sand and a jab of the trident to force the other back, sword-struck aside by serving the purpose of placing one careless heel on the net and *heave* and the man's length measured on his own shadow by the overhead sun. From the side where wealthy spectators sat in the company of the Emperor, shaded by awnings whereas the plebs must sweat and screw their eyes up, applause mingled with cries of anger due to losing bettors.

(Meanwhile: Slob in spite of his hurt hand grabbing the whip while Madison's attention was distracted in tripping Putzi with the torn curtain.)

A shift and tilt of the universe, a sense of aeons grinding by in the wrong direction and screaming at every

262

painful second of their progress. In a linen kilt not as low as the knee and with a beard hanging in coarse rat's-tails against his chest, a whip-wielder mouthing curses into an eternal desert silence. Dark and cold overlying the comprehended words: "Crocodiles and dogs shall share thy bones at dawn!"

Sensed on one's own breath, the foul of bad onions and the sour of beer no better than urine. Across the shoulders the tidy parallel lines of that same whip, on the hands the calluses plated with adobe dust and the blisters from hauling ropes, one burst and raw as though the palm had cupped a fresh coal from the fire an hour ago. Hobbled to the ankles, other ropes not serving to shift great blocks of stone but only to hinder rebellious slaves while the overseer stood back at whip-length distance.

Handy, a heavy sun-hardened brick, the size and shape of a loaf of that bread not given to quiet the grumbling of the stomach in more days than one knows how to count. Picked up, faster than whip can follow, and *hurled*.

Through a chaotic haze of sickness, weakness, hate hate and *hate*, eyes belonging to Lyla but blurred with years of untended infection and stark sunlight and windborne dust out of the heart of Africa saw a chunk of the concrete which had earlier been smashed out of the apt's wall cut open the scalp of Slob more neatly than a knife. He folded to his knees and bowed over the whip to anoint it with the blood his head was shedding.

(In the meantime: yelling for her men to come to her and be equipped Mikki at her Gottschalk cabinet, stocked with old and new weapons any of which might safely be used on Madison—the story tomorrow about the intrusive kneeblank, invited as a show of goodwill towards other races, turning nasty and betraying the primitive savagery which meant they must be shut away in Blackbury and Bantustan, dangerous to invite home like lions kept on the back porch hating their chains.)

But for Lyla a kaleidoscope, a sequence of instant frames cut out of time itself, not pictures only but a total set of sensory data—limb-weariness, apprehension marked by heart battering at the ribs to be let out, hunger . . . and repletion, sickness and sobriety, hope and terror. . . . *Blink* the scarred wet green of a jousting-ground after a fall of rain, the grass slashed to reveal the brown earth underneath, a pavilion gay with long pennants, a dying horse screaming and unbelievable weight dragging down every limb and the world narrowed to a slit across the eyes and there a splintered lance of ashwood and coming down a morningstar, cruel spiked ball on chain on gleefully wielded pole. *Blink* the chill of snow and awkward encumbering furs hated but essential, the skin side chewed supple by teeth now worn to stubs and one of them aching so much it nearly blinded the right eye, hands respectively clutching a tree-branch club and hanging limp from a tendon-slashing bite gone septic under a plaster of bruised leaves; some menace out there in the whirling whiteness not clearly defined and one should be grateful. *Blink* under light rain with the awareness of painted designs on face and chest, not felt so much as visualized on identically painted companions, veiled hills framing a pass with a rutted track at the bottom and reaching out from this right shoulder here a crude worn tube on a wooden stock bound with rawhide thongs to halt a crack and cushion the impact of imminent explosion. *Blink* high vacancy and detachment, irritability, waiting for time over target in an itchy airtight suit with the world remote, glimpsed at thirdhand by lights and dials, vague awareness diligently repressed of a man clothed in flame.

(Meantime: Lyla saying over and over with childish wonder at her own insight, "I met a man with seven brains, I met a man with seven brains!" First to be

equipped, furious, the one labeled Pat grabbing blindly
at what he found at hand and getting of all things a
pike—when they had a customer capable of buying up
everything from the expensive ranges the Gottschalks
stopped at nothing, especially not at pleading the cause
of a weapon which never needed to be re-loaded or re-
energized.)

The swirling of images ceased and one steadied: a
patch of level ground across which was marching with
even tread a spear-carrying giant.

(Alerted by the fearful Hughie strangers from other
rooms of the apt crowded into the doorway—there was
no door—some giddy with sykes, some drunk, some just
curious and greedy for sensation.)

The muscle-tensions of a calm body. The careful rolling in inexhaustible time of a long strip of cloth. Overlaid confusingly, the sensation of a horse between the
knees and the bellowing of cattle in stampede. Memory
signaled and Lyla realized: sling. The Balearic slingers
boasted of being able to turn a running bull by bouncing
a stone off one or other horn!

So what was that doing tangled up with the image of
. . . of Goliath?

Fsst. The stone and its target. Crack at the side of
the jaw with such force the head leapt back and in a
sad yawn descended along with its body to the floor.

(And now a Blazer, the weapon recommended over
Dan's warm corpse, with its wide fanned beam making
it almost impossible to miss under a twenty-meter range.)

Blink so fast she could not follow, like riffling cards
and trying to inspect the pictures of the kings, an arque-
bus propped on its forked stand and the stink of the
slowmatch, chest down and hands clawed in wet ground
waiting for the eardum-shattering slam of a grenade,
cool waiting at the handles of a Vickers gun for the foolish marching lines of enemy to leave their trenches and
be harvested by the scythe of death, cautious slow-

motion maneuvering under water to stick a fatal message on a hull looming storm-cloud dark between here and the sun, the tweak on the plume of a cocked hat which signified it had been shortened by a musket-ball, the sun-gleam on the spokes of a chariot-wheel and the mane of the spirited horse drawing the chariot, three red drops from the tip of a barbed arrow cut loose by a surgeon keen edge hot fire musical twang pressure of fingertip on plastic stud agony of mending bone world fading under mask of blood . . .

(And at appropriate points during the sequence, for the survivors doom. A javelined table-leg, one of the long-ago originals. Chunk of marble. Chunk of concrete. The Blazer lit the room but only slashed across the already mutilated face of the red-green dial and severed its single hand. The whip from a spot closer to the cabinet aimed not at anyone but at the racked weapons themselves, bringing them down in a tremendous clatter. Mikki grabbed for a laser-gun but the plastic insulation of the power-pack designed to last thirteen months precisely gave way and she jumped back screaming with her arm seared to the elbow, shedding great sheets of flayed skin. Madison finished her with the other table-leg almost casually. Remaining, Putzi, abandoning any attempt to arm himself.)

Suddenly, for the last time, the sequence of dazzling time-snippets steadied. A bare room with a wall missing. A stone-and-sand garden beyond. A group of thoughtful, silent watchers. A mat of plaited reeds occupying the center of the floor. Advancing from the far corner a man naked but for a loincloth.

"Ohhh . . . !"

The sound of her own voice snatched Lyla from the unreal to the real. There was nausea in her belly and sweat on every inch of her skin and a wish to flee and hide in every fiber of mind and body. That wasn't fear, or rage, or anything so clean and normal. That wasn't lust. That was the pure naked unqualified desire to kill, dedication to death, a holy quest for the ending of a human life.

She looked for Madison and saw a machine: black steel limbs ending in cruel knives. Opposed to him merely a man, foolish, stupid, doomed. A leg bent, just enough, an arm reached out to take a grip, and *crash*.

Lyla doubled over and vomited between her feet. Detachedly she told herself that Madison had thrown Putzi through the window from which he had torn away the drapes. Detachedly she heard someone scream, "Christ, we're forty-five stories high!" Detachedly she deduced that there was panic, because there were more screams and the sound of running feet and then in this room silence, though music was still playing elsewhere. Overhead no more dancing. She figured out that she was alone but for Madison and two or three other people too lost in syke-induced fantasy to notice anything as unimportant as a death.

But she sat with her head between her knees while the nausea passed off, thinking of Dan.

Eventually she looked up and she was right. Madison was standing beside the smashed window over which, automatically, steel shutters had slammed in response to the glass breaking. But not soon enough to halt Putzi's flight to the street. The knee was rigidly at attention, shoulders back, eyes fixed on nowhere.

Moving very carefully to avoid her own vomit, Lyla got up and stiffly hobbled towards him. There had been enough drug in the dose she had accidentally swallowed to induce the muscular spasms she usually gave way to and she had resisted them; she felt as though she had been systematically beaten over every centimeter of her body.

Mortally terrified, yet somehow driven, she approached him and said timidly, "Harry?"

He moved in response; she flinched and he caught

the motion and said, "Don't worry, you're not on my target list for this assignment."

What? She shook her head in bewilderment. Foggily: He is crazy maybe, but it's more likely to be the sibyl-pill. But I never heard of it doing this to anyone, man or woman. What did happen to him? He beat eight men and a vicious woman single-handed and there are bodies and wounds to prove the fact. He won.

"You won," she said.

Not looking directly at her, but towards a point in space somewhere over her left shoulder, he answered without moving anything but his lips. "Even at this relatively late stage it was possible for an unarmed man of sufficient determination to overcome considerable opposition. It was not until after the Gottschalk coup of 2015 and the concomitant introduction of System C integrated weaponry that hand-to-hand combat became effectively pointless."

Dazed, Lyla shook her head. "2015?" she repeated foolishly. "But, Harry, it's only the summer of 2014 now."

Ignoring her, reciting as tonelessly as a cheap automatic, he said, "The equipment of individuals with armament adequate to level a medium-sized city nonetheless did not immediately put an end to such combats. For a while an attempt was made to codify human behavior on a basis analogous to the legendary Code of Chivalry; however, this represented such a radical reversal of current psychological trends that—"

Lyla's eyes widened in terror as she looked past him. A line of dull red had appeared across the steel shields closing the window. Beyond, no doubt, a hastily-summoned police skimmer, cutting through with a thermic lance.

"Harry!" She tugged at his arm but he was as immobile as a statue. His droning voice continued.

"—it was doomed from the start and thereafter it was inevitable—"

"*Harry!*"

The steel parted, and through the fine opening a cloud of pale vapor oozed.

"But they can't just gas us without talking to us!" Lyla cried. "They—"

through drought and wildfire and bad seasons for game,
ice and flood and landslide, plague and phylloxera and
the eruption of the friendly neighborhood volcano;

Aryans and Hyksos and Huns, Romans and Visigoths
and Mongols, Moors and Christians and Saracens, Turks
and Zulus and British, Americans and Germans and
French;

the desecration of the holy places, the billeting of the
incomprehensible troops, the silent horrid wafting of the
sicknesses that ride the mists of night;

huddled in a draughty cave and the fire out in the
midst of winter;

huddled in the tube-stations wincing as the bombs
crash down;

huddled in the luxury ranch-style homes of Montego
Bay knowing there will be no mercy for a skin that's
merely tanned;

to the music of air-raid sirens;

to the drum-beat of waves on the beach;

to the melancholy choir of the wolves;

one keeps going somehow, one tries to say "Shib-
boleth" against all the odds, and somehow one keeps
going, one at least;

escaping the line before the gas-chamber door one
Jew who will remember;

escaping the cells beneath the Colosseum one Christian who won't forget;

escaping the mud-fields of the Marne one Tommy and one *poilu* and one Boche;

somehow, one at least keeps going;

fighting like rats over a crust in the wreckage of Hiroshima;

rising up on one knee with the other smashed to give a salute in the ruins of Dresden;

despising the diplodocus, the triceratops, and the smilodon, forgetting how many millions of years they bred their kind;

imagining our great-great-great-grandchildren as pillars of the faith with Bible in one hand and cross in the other;

incapable of envisaging the wheel of a fast car and a skirt lifted nearly to the hip;

one keeps going on the thin nourishment of illusion like watery soup;

a Hundred Years War or a Six Days War;

a vendetta from generation to generation or a transient moment of fury;

one limps but one keeps going somehow;

the army comes over the hill raping and slaughtering but one keeps going;

the priest casts lots in a bad season to name the virgins who shall die on the altar but one keeps going;

the torch is set to the house and the long trek starts to the unknown village with what possessions one can carry but one keeps going;

somehow one keeps going;

somehow;

where a not buried not-Caesar bled, some long-forgotten peasant, there's a rose;

where mute inglorious Miltons held their tongues there runs a concrete road;

where followers-not-leaders breathed their last a fused

glass disc extends like the mirror of some distorting tele-
scope, looking forward into a fearful space-time;

and nothing grows on glass;

except a little pond-slime on the walls of the home
aquarium for snails to crop, enviable snails whose world
is small and whose house is on the back;

not shattered;

not open to the winds with the ceiling tilted at a crazy
angle and the fireplace full of cold ashes;

not targeted in the gunsight of the sniper across the
street;

not marked on the X Patriots' master plan as wholly
inhabited by blanks;

not mortgaged, not lacking tiles from the roof;

somehow nonetheless one keeps going;

until one comes to a sign that says STOP,

and being obedient, one . . .

They've already started to build the sign.

The necessary materials have been around for a long
time.

Oh—years and years.

They just needed someone to come along and drive
a few nails.

Anyway, one was bound to get tired eventually.

SEVENTY-EIGHT   NO, OF COURSE LOGORRHEA ISN'T
                WHAT HAPPENS WHEN YOU BREAK
                A LOG-JAM BUT THE RESULT IS
                PRETTY MUCH THE SAME FOR ANY-
                ONE WHO'S IN THE WAY

Conroy's flight from Manitoba landed at oh-nine-fifty
but he wasn't passed through customs and immigration
until ten forty-three despite being the possessor of a
United States passport. Passports were a devalued currency, subject to bargaining.

As though, thought Flamen fretfully waiting, after
letting in Morton Lenigo yesterday the officials were determined to make up for their lapse by screening everyone else five times as thoroughly as usual.

Tempora mutantur et nos mutamur in illis. . . . Four
short years ago, he could not have sat here without being
mobbed. Now, at most a curious look from the passersby,
this airport being the busiest of New York's five and the
terminal building thronged day and night. In the distance two girls giggling together with frequent glances
in his direction.

Definition of spoolpigeons: an about to be extinct species.

Angry with himself and the world, he forced his mind
to switch to what ought to have been a fascinating subject, the question of Morton Lenigo's whereabouts. He
had checked his office computers this morning as usual,

273

because even though it was Saturday and he had no noon slot to prepare for he was too tense to alter his routine. But the Lenigo problem was currently as flexible as an anaconda. Having missed the story the day it broke, he was now faced with the probability of missing the next stage because it would happen over a weekend. It was small consolation to have stirred up the subject of the Detroit blackmail deal. Nobody seemed to have reacted to that; the monitors had logged virtually nil response.

He looked around at the anonymous strangers riding the pediflows and thought: Don't they care?

Answer—they'd rather not. For them Morton Lenigo had the reality of Father Christmas or the Devil, a legend in his own lifetime not to be taken seriously until they were forced to it . . . by which time it would be far too late.

So he found himself faced with more personal problems than he'd had in months and no weighting in favor in any area. Thinking of knees: Pedro Diablo. Vanished in strict accordance with the customs of his forcibly adopted blank hosts, doubtless not to appear again until office time on Monday morning but then entering polite and calm and unhelpful. Flamen had hoped for a sense of dynamism, a jolt to his own exhausted imagination. None had resulted from their meeting. Only the tension of anticipation had drained away and left him flabby, like a perished balloon.

And Celia. He shivered. A cool withdrawn stranger. That was my wife, that lovely body pressed mine and convulsed in orgasm? That mouth on mine, that voice whispering in darkness? Memory says yes. Rationality says no. Rationality says this is a different person with the same name and features.

He asked himself: Is it in me, the reason for the change? Is it in those doom-laden words the doctor pronounced at the Ginsberg about previous emotional attachments being symptoms of immaturity? According to

274

Mogshack Celia was cured, but he was here today with precisely the intention of proving Mogshack a liar. Because of what had been done to Celia?

No, because it was necessary for spoolpigeons to shoot an occasional sacred cow in order to survive.

And concerning survival: that impossible reading of zero! Given unlimited Federal computer time, the source of the interference on his program *must* be identifiable! Yesterday's, the first with Diablo participating if you could call it participation, had suffered three breaks, not the record, but any at all was too much, and yet when he called to register the latest of scores of furious complaints the despair of the engineer i/c transmission had been somehow *convincing*. The Directorate had even invited him to their next general meeting to discuss the problem.

The hypocrites, he thought. Got to hit them! And with something harder than the flabby threat of the PCC. Ace in the hole, maybe—Harry Madison? Oh, ridiculous!

Looking back, he was aware of grasping at straws and knew why he'd been impelled to fall in with Reedeth's request. Not by Prior's eagerness to exorcise the specter of that zero reading, not by the dark eyes of Diablo trained on his face. By his own terrifying sense of dissolution. Diablo trained in the real school of hard knocks coming to join the company; his wife treating him like an unknown; a conspiracy among his employers to sabotage his transmissions . . . It was like living in a hut on an ice-floe and feeling the warm breeze of summer come from the south.

Something's working against me, he decided suddenly. Something too subtle for even Federal computers to root out!

But that felt like paranoia on the way. One had to believe in something, even if it were only a fallible government god.

Maybe Prior had been right to buy a Lar after all. The fortunes of the knee enclaves certainly seemed to be on the ascendant; perhaps letting oneself believe in supernormal powers enabled the subconscious to guess correctly more often than if one was convinced of being defeated from the start. Ask Conroy—?

And here he was, a man with a grizzled beard, thin, above average height, marching from the immigration barrier with a deep-etched scowl and carrying a light travel-bag on a sling. Recognizing him from the tapes he had played over before deciding to invite him to New York, Flamen jumped up and framed an effusive welcome.

Conroy undermined that after the first three words.

"Let's get the hell out of here before I scream," he said. "Got a skimmer or something?"

"Sure—uh, yes, of course."

"Then take me to the hotel or wherever you've arranged for me to stay. Can you smell the atmosphere here? Can you sense the hate those bastards are generating?"

Memory reeled back and Flamen heard Lyla talking about her reaction to the atmosphere at the Ginsberg.

"How do you mean?"

Conroy jerked his thumb towards the barrier. "There's a squeeze on today. Everyone who's been out of the country for longer than a week's visit to relatives is being grilled. What's caused that—the Lenigo affair?"

"I suspect so," Flamen agreed.

"Aren't you sure? I thought you spoolpigeons knew the inside data on everything."

Nettled, Flamen said, "I know why he was let in, and so would you if you'd been watching my show yesterday."

"I was in class. A noon slot here isn't a noon slot in the west." Seeming more to lead the way than to be escorted, Conroy marched ahead at such a pace Flamen was hard put to keep up. "But I presume one of the knee enclaves finally got around to blackmailing him in —correct?"

Well, here's a patronizing son-of-a-bitch, Flamen thought resentfully. Nonetheless he said, with what politeness he could summon, "It was a well-kept secret until I broke it yesterday."

"Ah, that's because people don't take the trouble to use their minds any more. They rely on computers so much they're forgetting how to ask questions. Getting a knee enclave to blackmail him into the country is squarely in line with Lenigo's standard tactics—and I'm flattering him by calling them 'his' tactics. They go way way back to the industrial unrests of the nineteenth century, at least, and probably a good deal further. What he did in Britain followed exactly the same pattern. He exploited the long-standing truth that if you can get five percent of the population behind any movement whether it's pro or anti you can bring down governments. There aren't enough knees in the whole of Britain even today to take and hold a multi-million city the size of Birmingham. Yet it's knee-run now, and so's Manchester, and so's Cardiff, and there are half a dozen other large cities where blanks are moving out so fast you can hardly see them leave whenever five or six knee families buy into the neighborhood. He didn't do that with overwhelming manpower—he didn't *have* the manpower. It was a matter of leverage in the right place. So what was the right place here—Detroit?"

They had reached the skimmer by now, and Flamen was glad of the distraction caused by getting aboard. Conroy's manner suggested that he was prepared to treat computers on the some footing as an abacus, and he wasn't used to that sort of attitude.

Once aloft and being directed by Ninge traffic control, however, Conroy resumed exactly as though no time had passed. "Speaking of leverage, by the way, what leverage are you hoping to exert on the windmill?"

"Windmill?" For the moment Flamen had forgotten

the metaphor employed in their exchange of cables. "Oh! Yes, of course: Mogshack?"

"Mogshack!" Conroy snapped, and grimaced. "Lord, I'd never have thought that after such a long time away I could still react so strongly to that man's name! I guess it's because even though Canada is still a relatively civilized country—because it has large empty areas people can expand into without rubbing elbows all the time, like Russia—we're still not immune from the pernicious influence of his doctrines. Do you realize that in my class at the university there are still two or three girls whose faces I haven't seen since the beginning of the year because they keep their street yashes on in class and even turn up to tutorials wearing them? And I can't order them to take the things off because they'd most likely complain to their parents and have me disciplined by the faculty. As though I were some horny teenager with indecent designs on their virtue!"

Feeling rather as though he'd stepped into a puddle and found himself being carried down a raging millrace instead, Flamen ventured, "But how much of this are you blaming on Mogshack? Surely one man can't be responsible for the entire neo-puritan movement—isn't it a reaction against the permissivity of the last century, as Victorianism was against the bawdiness of early times?"

"I'm not blaming Mogshack for the phenomenon itself. What I detest about him is the way he's swum with the tide, exploited his influence for personal advancement! What's good about the current phase of our social cycle? Practically nothing. Yet what does Mogshack's doctrine amount to? A bunch of catch-phrases about 'being an individual' and 'retiring and regrouping' and all the rest. Do you find him applying any standard of judgment to determine whether the result is going to be a *good* individual? Not that I've noticed! Bland, shapeless, malleable—yes. Original, creative, stimulating—never!"

Flamen said nothing, thinking of Celia.

"And that's the man they entrust with the responsibility for the mental hygiene of the State of New York!" Conroy continued, glancing out over the city. By now they were at the regular five-hundred meter level for private skimmers, and being slotted tidily through a multicolored gaggle of traffic bound for the New England resorts. "Has your mental health improved? The hell it has. The Ginsberg is twice the size of any previous hospital, it's only a few years old—but already it's overloaded, and life in the city is intolerable because you never know when riots may break out, when you'll be burgled or mugged or just shot for the amusement of a gang of teenagers! When you give someone an important job you expect him to show results. You don't expect him to be content with soothing banalities about the inevitability of his failure."

His tone was not venomous, merely resigned; however, Flamen was pleased to hear him voice such hostility. He said, "In that case you'll probably be interested to learn how I propose to—uh—topple the windmill."

Conroy turned his head expectantly.

"It's . . . Well, it has to do with my wife Celia. She was committed to the Ginsberg around the beginning of the year. Breakdown. Not very pleasant. Ah . . ." He hesitated, but forced out the damning admission. "She took to sykes and wound up with Ladromide. I didn't know until about her third or fourth dose."

"How long had you been married?" said Conroy caustically.

"It does sound improbable, I guess." Flamen felt his cheeks growing hot; he hadn't blushed for years. "But I'm afraid that before the—uh—crisis we'd drifted apart to some extent. I have business, my own friends, all sorts of distractions, and the temperature had kind of cooled, to the point where we had separate rooms and like if she was asleep when I got home I didn't intrude on her."

He broke off with an effort. Here he was meeting

Conroy for the first time and already pouring out things he seldom confided to anyone, even old friends, as though needing to offer excuses for himself.

"Be an individual!" Conroy sighed. "Separate rooms! Your own private lives! Damnation, when it reaches down the middle of a marriage to pry the spouses apart how can anyone defend that attitude?"

"She was committed while I was on a business trip," Flamen said very rapidly. "When I found out she was in the Ginsberg I didn't take her away because my brother-in-law Lionel Prior recommended Dr. Mogshack very highly and so I settled for simply paying for her care. I mean, having her a ward of the State government would have been . . ." He shrugged.

"So?" Conroy prompted.

"So I don't like what they've done to her. I don't like the—the walking talking dummy she's been turned into. I want her packled to find out whether she's been helped or harmed by what Mogshack's done to her. And I want the parameters for the packling set by someone like you who—uh—who has a different approach to mental health."

"Packling!" Conroy said, and twisted his mouth as though he had bitten a rotten fruit. "That's half of what's wrong with our society in itself! Getting computers to set up patterns for human beings to copy—did you ever hear of anything so absurd?"

He hunched forward energetically. They were in sight of two of the LR sites from Thursday night, and over both aerial cranes were grappling up wreckage in great dust-shedding nets so that new buildings could be erected as rapidly as possible. Shooting out his arm to point at the nearer one in Harlem, he said, "There's a ready-made parable for you! What do they call those in the news? They call them 'LR,' or at most 'last-resort' strikes, don't they? A perfect piece of Mogshack-ery, a phrase that implies all the whining excuses: 'I couldn't help it, I did my best, they didn't play fair!'

Oh, sure! But no mention of the fact that there were kids in there, hm? No mention of the fact that 'I' happened to be sitting safely a hundred meters up in a gunship armed with self-seeking missiles and thousand-watt laser-guns! I'd like to see some of the killers brought down to ground level and turned loose with hands and feet and teeth against the people who were mashed to pulp in that block of apts! That's what *I'd* call 'being an individual'!"

Dismayed by Conroy's fierceness, Flamen said, "Ah —yes, but surely the safety of the greatest number is a primary . . ."

The words sounded mealy-mouthed after Conroy's vehemence, and ran dry.

"Well?" Conroy said, turning to face him. "I must say I didn't expect to hear you, a spoolpigeon, speaking out in favor of the established order."

"But this is the world we've got," Flamen said faintly. He could not recall being so much at a loss since he was in college and had to deal with an instructor who bullied rather than led his students towards knowledge. "We have to try and decide what is and what isn't worth keeping, and if we do think something's worth keeping we have to try and protect it."

"So name what's worth keeping," Conroy countered. "This convenience we're riding in—this skimmer? Sure, but did it have to be manufactured in Detroit by people whose skins guarantee they can't market their skills any-where else in the country? How secure do you feel in your annual skimmer when you take off in it for the first time? How certain are you that some melanist fanatic hasn't been around the dispatch field sabotaging the skimmers destined for blank purchasers, so that they'll crash after the first thousand miles? What's going to protect you against that? The police can't! Neither can your local Gottschalk, for all the guns he can offer you. No wonder people hardly talk to their friends face to

face any more, but call up to save going across the
street in case they get shot by a passing knee."

A bleep signifying they were over their destination,
the Hilton Undertower, saved Flamen from having to
reply at once, and he was grateful all over again. It
was years since he had come up against anyone with
such strong feelings as Conroy's, and he was obscurely
troubled, as though the battering words had struck a
long-forgotten chord in his memory.

A few minutes for checking in and having his bag
sent to his room, and Conroy was holding forth anew
in the hotel's main bar, his rodomontade proof against
any attempt by Flamen to interrupt with more details
of his plot to undermine Mogshack.

"As I said earlier, even up in relatively civilized Canada
I find the traces of Mogshack's teachings regardless of
who actually formed the last link in the chain of communication to my students. How do you feel, for example, about murders on campus?"

"Well, I—"

"We've had two this year: a jealous homosexual boy
stabbed his lover because he was seen with a girl, and a
crazy father came up and shot his daughter because a
friend of hers—some friend!—told him she was sleeping
with a boy who had some Indian blood. Iroquois, to be
exact. Me, I'd have been rather pleased; they were a
distinguished tribe in their day, the Iroquois. But thank
goodness I don't have a daughter and my sons are both
safely married. Irrelevant. I was talking about campus
murders. What's happened to us that we take killings
for granted among our children? Don't give me that hog-
wash about students at college having to be treated as
adults—there's nothing adult about playing with guns
and grenades!"

He had dialed a beer and now poured the whole of
it down his throat in a single thirsty gobble as though
washing away an unpleasant taste. Flamen said, caught
up in the discussion in spite of his own preoccupations,

"Yes, but adolescence has always been the most emotionally disturbing time, and—"

"Who sold that crazy father a gun to go shoot his daughter with?" Conroy interrupted. "Some 'emotionally disturbed' adolescent at the corner store where he cobbles together lasers in a one-man workshop? The hell! That was a late-model Gottschalk gun; I saw it myself in the dean's office, later."

"I'm lining up something on the Gottschalks at present, too," Flamen said. He heard something close to timidity in his tone. Granting that Conroy was old enough to be his father, it was still ridiculous to find himself reacting in this fashion. Against all odds, he was running a five-slots-weekly show on the Holocosmic network, whereas in his own field Conroy had failed so signally he was reduced to teaching, not even in his native country.

"Ah-hah? *That* won't work," Conroy said, replacing his glass for a fresh beer. "And that's another reason I detest Mogshack, by the way. I never knew him to try and wean a patient away from dependence on guns. Yet he has two, three thousand a year of the population of New York State through his hands. By this time, if he'd done his job properly, he'd have created a glut of second-hand weaponry and cooled the temperature in this city past the flashpoint."

"Two or three thousand out of how many many million?" Flamen snapped.

"Out of how many who are unstable enough to lose their marbles and start shooting at random into the street?" Conroy countered. "You don't start riots, I don't start riots, the politically educated leaders of the X Patriots don't start riots. Paranoids start riots and other people are tipped over the edge by contagious hysteria. Your typical insurrectionary sniper isn't a revolutionary or a fanatic—he's someone who's so devoid of empathy he can treat the human beings below his window as moving targets conveniently offered for his skill. And

by clever exploitation of the public's insecurity the Gottschalks have managed to put over a gang of lies equating gunmanship with masculine potency, which do even
more damage than Mogshack's pernicious dogmas. Damn
it, man: anyone who can treat another human being as
an object for target practice is stuck even further back
in the infantile stage than somebody who's frightened
to move on from the masturbation phase and go to bed
with a girl! Do you own a gun?"

"Ah . . ." Flamen gulped at his own drink. "Yes, naturally. But I don't belong to any gun clubs or anything.
I have a riot-defense system around the house with
mines and electrified fences, and if the need arises I
just switch them on. The rest is automatic."

"Fair," Conroy said in a clinical tone.

"How do you mean, *fair?*"

"The sane response is to site your home where your
neighbors aren't going to come calling with guns."

"So name somewhere!" Flamen gibed. "Don't the Gottschalks buy time on Pan-Can too?"

"Yes, damn it," Conroy admitted with a sigh. "What's
more I caught one of them actually on our campus during the spring semester. Got rid of him, luckily, but
only because the killing I told you about—the student
who knifed his boyfriend—was fresh enough in the dean's
mind to make him vulnerable to my arguments. At that
one of my colleagues said all the students ought to be
armed to teach them responsibility in the use of weapons.
Hah! I wonder how long he'd last in front of an armed
class—the kids hate him!"

For the first time since their arrival in the bar, there
was a pause longer than a few seconds. Flamen exploited it to gather his scattered thoughts, and said eventually, "Coming back to business, Professor, may I take
it you'll cooperate with me even if you disagree with
the packling principle in the abstract? Of course, this
will only be the start of a long and difficult process;
later there may have to be a lawsuit, perhaps a State

inquiry, but for the sake of my wife I'm prepared to . . ."

Once more his words trailed away as he found Conroy gazing steadily at him.

"Mr. Flamen," the psychologist said at length, "I've told you why I detest Mogshack as a person and why I think his influence on the field of mental health is downright dangerous. Accordingly I'll be very happy to help you torpedo him. But I will not swallow the line you just fed me. I don't believe you're motivated by altruism and love for your wife. I believe you're going after Mogshack because the targets that most demand your attention, like the Gottschalks, are out of reach. Gottschalks are like ghouls; they live off the carrion of our mutual distrust and bribe us with symbols that equate hatred with manhood. So— No, please don't interrupt! I'd rather think of you as a frustrated man who would far sooner expose some disgusting truth about the Gottschalks than about a man who is, after all, one teacher among many and probably wouldn't be so highly regarded if it weren't for the post he occupies. You—"

"But just a moment!"

"Shut up and hear me out, will you? You can't expect me to believe you're going after Mogshack for your wife's sake, when you've admitted that you'd drifted so far apart you didn't even realize she was taking Ladromide —hm? Oh, I'm not blaming you! Marriage isn't compulsory and making a success of it is even less so, and anyhow marriage doesn't conform with Mogshack's celebrated ideal that can always be approached more closely 'like a mathematical limit.' Your motives don't much concern me, so let's forget them for the moment, hm?"

Flamen buried his scowl in his glass.

"Now my motives, on the other hand, are something I want to try and make clear to you. It may take a while, so let's go and sit down, shall we?" He turned and led the way to a nearby lounge, not allowing the distraction to brake the steamroller progress of his discourse. "To draw on medical images with which you may not be familiar, I regard people like Mogshack as counter-parts of the homeopaths who used to teach, in somatic medicine, the virtues of doses of the causative agent as cures for everything from poisoning to pyorrhea. Certainly if someone is pathologically afraid of kneeblank armies marching up his front path, you may stabilize him superficially by training him to use a gun and fire it more quickly and more accurately than his potential attacker. But consider, Mr. Flamen, what is the actual, physical result?" His tone changed completely; he had been alternating between banter and self-deprecatory hectoring, but now he leaned forward with almost painful sincerity.

"It's a dead man on the path, Mr. Flamen," he said. "And it's no part of a doctor's duty to encourage the taking of life. True?"

To Flamen's surprise he found that his mouth had gone dry. He gave a wary nod.

"Now an honest cure," Conroy pursued, "would lie somewhere along the axis where the man coming up the path was invited in, and enjoyed his visit, and left his host pleased to have entertained him. Does the image get across, or are people already too isolated to consider that idea any longer?"

Cautiously Flamen said, "Well, it's obviously better to have people meeting as friends than as enemies."

"But it doesn't end there, in a platitude!" Conroy thumped the arm of the couch and raised a faint cloud of dust. "Or rather, it shouldn't. When did you last do something to bring people closer together? Isn't your daily show designed to do the opposite? Spoolpigeons foment distrust in a systematic professional manner."

"Now look here!" Flamen slammed his glass down on the table before them. "I pick liars and peculators and hypocrites for my targets! I'd be ashamed to do any-thing else!"

"With the result that people who pay attention to you start to question the motives of everybody around them,"

Conroy said. "They take it for granted that the world is riddled with corruption and chicanery and fraud."

"You think it's better to be deceived than to be told the truth?"

"You think it's good for people to imagine that everyone who's richer or more powerful or more fortunate than themselves got there by cheating and lying and wriggling through loopholes in the law?"

For a long moment the two men stared at one another, less than arm's length apart, until Conroy gave a chuckle and reached to retrieve his beer.

"Apologies, Mr. Flamen. The last thing I want to do is attack someone who dislikes hypocrisy. So do I. But, you see, there is this paradox which bothers me terribly. Day in, day out, for—what?—forty-odd weeks of the year, I imagine, you deliver your exposés and your bits of scandal which may, I admit, achieve results like levering corrupt officials out of their jobs or something of that sort. But what you do and say isn't a function of the number of public injustices you hear about—it depends on the three-vee slot you have to fill. *Have* to, five times a week! At the very least I'm sure you must often have blown up some triviality into a grand crusade simply because nothing bigger had turned up the same day."

Flamen said, slowly, "Yes, I'd have to plead guilty on that. And . . ." He hesitated, then forced the words out, recalling what Diablo had said about gauging the success of a show by the number of suicides it provoked. "And pretty often exposés like that are regarded as especially successful, not because they were really important but because the target was exceptionally badly defended. Like you get some poor son-of-a-bitch killing himself in shame."

"Which brings me at long last to my main point," Conroy said. "I will indeed set up a bunch of parameters for the packling of your wife which will make Mogshack's vaunted cure look like a mile-wide miss—and what's more I'll be right and he'll be wrong because he doesn't care whether he suppresses originality or creativity or obstinacy or any other valuable characteristic so long as his computers predict a satisfied client. From there on it'll be up to you. But I want you to bear two things in mind."

He leaned earnestly close to Flamen. "One! I can't give you back your wife as she was when you loved her. Nobody can. It was you who changed her, and if you want her you'll have to win her back as the person she now is. Which may mean changing yourself, and that can be painful.

"And two! Don't delude yourself that just bringing down Mogshack will put the world back together all by itself. If you succeed in, say, getting him kicked out of his job, I'll be pleased—God, will I be pleased! But I'll also expect you to make use of your success, and exploit it to go after somebody really poisonous, like the Gottschalks."

He broke off to tilt the last of his beer down his gullet. Uncertain whether to make a promise he was probably not going to be able to keep, Flamen hesitated, and before he could reply there came a tap on his shoulder. Turning, he saw a strange woman leaning down to him.

"Are you Mr. Flamen?" she said.

"Yes—yes, I am!" Flamen drew himself up; it was very reassuring to be recognized by a stranger right now.

"Well, you've been being paged for the last ten minutes," the woman said, and pointed to the screen over the public comweb at the end of the bar. The name MATTHEW FLAMEN was flashing red at two-second intervals.

"Ten minutes!"

"Well, you seemed to be busy, and I wasn't sure it was you," the woman said, stepping back defensively as though afraid he might strike her.

"Ah . . . Yes. Well, thank you anyway." Flamen rose, scowling, and the woman retreated with a timid nod. "Excuse me," he added to Conroy, who shrugged.

Heading for the comweb, he wondered furiously who could have tracked him down here; he had hoped to be uninterrupted at least long enough to consult Conroy about a joint approach to Prior. The latter was dubious about having Celia packled according to parameters of Conroy's—he judged everything by externals, and what counted for him was that Mogshack was in charge of the Ginsberg whereas Conroy was a failure driven to teaching in an obscure college. Worst of all, as Celia's present legal guardian he could theoretically forbid Conroy to come anywhere near her.

Ripping the fax paper which bore his name out of the message slot, he saw it was Dr. Reedeth who was trying to get in touch with him. His heart sank. What had happened now?

He punched for the Ginsberg, and the screen lit to show Reedeth in the office which Flamen had seen before, looking harassed; his hair was tousled and there were dark rings under his eyes.

"At last!" he snapped. "Get over here and take charge of your ward, will you? Fast! I don't like people who welsh on their promises the very day they make them—least of all when they expect me to pick up the pieces!"

"What in hell are you talking about?" Flamen blazed back. "And I don't like your manner—"

"Didn't you contract to act as legal guardian for Harry Madison yesterday?" Reedeth broke in.

"Why . . . Why, of course I did."

"Didn't take it very seriously, did you?"

"What do you mean? You assured me he was perfectly sane and able to look after himself, so—"

"So you decided to wait for him to show at your office on Monday morning?" Reedeth's lip curled. "I should have known. Do you realize he nearly got thrown in the Undertombs? Or don't you care?"

"Now look here! If he did something criminal while the ink still wasn't dry on his certificate of sanity, that's a breach of contract on your side, not on mine!" Flamen felt sweat spring out prickly on his skin, but at the back of his mind was a hesitant jubilation: could this too be a stick to beat Mogshack with?

"Know what a sibyl-pill is?" Reedeth snarled. "You ought to—you watched Lyla Clay performing here the other day."

"Of course I do. What's that got to do with Madison?"

"Last night he and Lyla Clay were kidnapped by a gang of bully-boys from a party of Michaela Baxendale's. Do you know her?"

"Oh my God," Flamen said. All the color suddenly vanished from the world.

"Seems she'd sent them out to drag in a mixed-race couple to play some kind of game with. Only it wasn't a game. They forced one of the sibyl-pills down Madison's throat and he went beserk. He wound up throwing a man out of a forty-fifth story window."

There was a terrible silence. Eventually Flamen said feebly, "But if they were kidnapped . . ."

"If you'd kept your word it needn't have happened!" Reedeth roared. "I've been stalling the busies all morning with that argument and it's damned nearly worn out! *I* know what a sib does to the mind—I'm in that line of business. But Madison's a knee, and the busies are still furious about the X Patriot riots the other night. It's a blind miracle they sent him and the girl back here instead of straight to jail. I can get the girl out, but I'm damned if I'm going to hang myself for Madison when you're legally responsible for him. Move it over here, fast!"

"Good God," said Conroy from behind Flamen. "It *is* Jim Reedeth! I thought I recognized the voice. How are you?"

Beaming, he marched up to the comweb.

Reedeth looked totally blank. He said, "Prof, what in heaven's name are you doing there?"

"Flamen invited me to New York for the weekend. So what's the trouble and can I help at all?"

"You know each other," Flamen muttered.

"Sure," Conroy nodded. "A former student of mine. Bright too—except that he fell in behind Mogshack and gave up thinking for himself. So anyway: what's wrong?"

"Ah . . ." Reedeth glanced past him at Flamen. "I'm not sure whether I ought to—"

"The hell with it!" Flamen snapped. "My private life is going to be all over the hemisphere by Monday anyway, so what's the difference? Tell him! Tell him everything! Maybe he'll come up with some brilliant idea."

He turned his back, scowling.

At first reluctantly, then with fluency, Reedeth recounted what had happened to Lyla and Madison. He concluded, "And now here they are, back in the hospital, and if Mogshack discovers I discharged a patient into the care of someone who completely disregarded his obligations, I'll be ruined!"

With a look of terrible distress, Conroy said, "Oh, Jim, you are following in your boss's footsteps, aren't you? I'd have hoped that any student of mine would talk first about the patient's plight and then about his own. . . ." Then, hastily as Reedeth bridled: "Never mind, never mind! Just tell me honestly—in your judgment, is this man Madison fit to be let loose or not?"

Reedeth bit back an angry retort. Shrugging, he said, "I think he was fit for release months ago. In fact I sometimes wonder if he was ever as crazy as they claimed when they committed him."

"Good start," Conroy nodded. "And you could plead in any court in the world that forcing a sibyl-pill down someone's throat is enough to cause temporary insanity. I've been looking into that; I gave the pythoness phenomenon to my students as a class assignment a few

days ago. Presumably there are witnesses to the kidnapping?"

Reedeth was looking a little more cheerful. "Only
the girl herself. But I'm sure we could impeach the testi-
mony of the kidnappers. For instance, she has a stab-
mark on her thumb, and Madison has one on his shoulder.
They took them by surprise on the street and gave them
each a shot of Narcolate."

"Hmmm!" Conroy rubbed his beard with the back of
his hand. "Tell me, Mr. Flamen, can even such a—well
—*notorious* poetess as Michaela Baxendale get away
with drugging and kidnapping strangers to amuse her
guests?"

"I can make damned sure that she doesn't," Flamen
assured him. "I've been looking for an angle on her for
months, because she revolts me so much. And I don't
care what kind of a 'broken home' she came from, being
raped by her brother and all that garbage."

"Could you talk about that later?" Reedeth said impatiently from the comweb. "I've spent the whole morning
staving off the busies, and I'm exhausted!"

"Just hold the fort a while longer," Conroy said equably.
"No doubt Mr. Flamen will have to make some arrangements—defenestration is a fairly serious offense even
nowadays."

"What?" Reedeth looked blank.

"Throwing people out of windows. Now if it had been
done with something out of the Gottschalks' current catalogue . . . Never mind! But I'm thinking about bail,
contacting a lawyer, swearing out a warrant against Miss
Baxendale and her confederates, that kind of thing."

"It's all set up! I just haven't been able to get hold
of Flamen to sign the documents!"

"I'll be there as soon as possible," Flamen sighed, and
cut the circuit. Turning to Conroy, he added, "I'm
sorry about this, but I guess I have to go. I'll see you
back here in a couple of hours, with luck."

"Oh no you won't," Conroy said. "I'm going to ride

along with you. I've always wanted to see the inside of that mausoleum of Mogshack's, and I'm not likely to get another chance."

Taking Flamen's arm, he led him briskly towards the door.

Seven burned to death

Mr. David Lumsden, aged 26, stood outside his burning home in Toronto and screamed at passing motorists to stop and help as his wife and six children were burned to death. All the drivers ignored his calls.

EIGHTY   ASSUMPTION CONCERNING THE FORE- GOING MADE FOR THE PURPOSES OF THIS STORY

It would have been even worse if they'd stopped to watch the fun.

Sanctuary within a sanctuary, Reedeth thought: this
office enclosed by the fortress of the hospital. Here offered temporary refuge from the impersonal gale of law-
enforcement, Lyla and Madison sat opposite him on the
consultation couch, side by side like frightened children—she wearing a hard mask of misery, the corners of
her mouth downturned, her shoulders slumped and her
hands pressed tight between her knees; he stolidly erect,
no expression on his dark face.

A shiver traced down his spine as he pictured Madison's muscles bulging to hurl a man bodily through a
window. How could that kind of terrible violence have
escaped unnoticed during so many years of the most
modern and thorough study of the man's mental condition? Even granting that sibyl-pills induced temporary
insanity—that was what it amounted to whether or not
one dignified it by the name of a pythoness trance—
granting that they provoked bone-snapping convulsions,
granting that Madison was in excellent physical condition and quite strong enough in his normal state to pick
up this heavy desketary as indeed he had once done in
Reedeth's presence while engaged on a repair job: the
story he and Lyla told simply didn't make sense.

Oh, certainly their account of being kidnapped by
Mikki Baxendale's private macoots was borne out by

all kinds of corroborative evidence. The clumsy stab-marks left by the injections still showed, Lyla's in the base of her thumb presumably because the yash she was wearing would have shielded her from an injection where Madison had taken his, in the top of the shoulder. There was even a detectable trace of Narcolate in a tiny scab he had removed from the knee's wound, trapped in the blood before it clotted. So far, so good.

But as for the rest, Madison's singlehanded victory over nine assailants, and the girl's half-crazy visions of a myriad battles scattered from end to end of history, climaxing in a prediction about something supposed to happen next year—

Reedeth's jaw dropped. He felt it fall and couldn't cancel the impulse. The solid world around him suddenly seemed tenuous, like swirling mist. Only a day or two ago he'd seen for himself that a pythoness could indeed deliver comprehensible oracles about total strangers, clear enough even for impersonal automatics to relate to their subjects. As though facts he had long been aware of had been shaken, kaleidoscope-fashion, into an unexpected pattern conveying a message on a non-verbal level, he found himself considering a brand-new hypothesis. Was it possible that the synergistic effect of Narcolate and a sibyl-pill had combined to generate in Madison a talent as unsuspected as pythoness talent had been before the pioneering days of Diana Spitz? Could he—did he—know about things which hadn't happened yet?

But the whole notion seemed so absurd he gave a harsh laugh, causing Lyla to look up at him with a vague sketch for curiosity reflected on her face.

"Nothing," he sighed in reply to her unspoken question. And, before he could qualify the bald statement, the comweb buzzed. Ariadne appeared in the screen, the familiar background of her home showing behind her fair head.

"Jim, what on earth are you doing in your office on a Saturday afternoon? I've been calling you at home for the past two hours!"

"Sweeping up a mess with my bare hands," Reedeth muttered. "That's what I'm doing." He summed up what had happened, and concluded, "Just to top everything else, Miss Clay can't get back into her apt, I understand. Her only key was left behind at Mikki Baxendale's, and the fee you sent off for her performance here went direct to Dan Kazer's account, as her mackero, but since he's dead his account has been blocked pending distribution of his estate. So I gather she doesn't even have the money to pay a locksmith to let her into her own home."

"That's no problem," Lyla said with a trace of scorn. "Harry could let me in. He did it before."

Reedeth looked at her blankly.

"Someone I thought was a friend of Dan's moved into our apt while I was shut up here yesterday. Harry opened the door and let me in without a key."

"Don't you have a Punch lock on the door?" Reedeth said, mystified.

"Yes, of course we do."

From the screen Ariadne looked out with bewilderment to match Reedeth's. "Nonsense," she said firmly. "You can't get past a Punch lock without the key—not unless you smash the door down. Jim, I think you'd better reconsider what you're doing. There are some—ah—*suspect* claims being made, don't you think?"

"I'm telling you," Lyla said, and set her mouth in a mutinous line.

Reedeth was framing a reply, when another signal began to flash on the desketary, and he brightened. "Excuse me," he said to Ariadne, and switched to another circuit. When his image reappeared on her screen, he wore an expression of dismay.

"What happened?" she demanded.

"Flamen got here."

"But I thought that was what you were waiting for—why should it make you look so sour?"

Reedeth sighed. "No reason, I guess. It's just that he's brought Conroy with him."

"Conroy? *Xavier* Conroy? But I thought he was in Canada!"

"Flamen had him flown to New York for the weekend. I get the impression he wants a second opinion about his wife, and you certainly couldn't pick anyone more opposed to Mogshack, could you?"

"No more than Mogshack's opposed to him. Watch yourself, Jim! You realize what'll happen if Mogshack finds out you've—" She hesitated, searching for a word.

"That I've been 'trading with the enemy'?" Reedeth supplied with a bitter smile. "If he takes what's actually sheer coincidence as a personal insult, I'll have had proof of what the automatics told us about him, and I won't wait to be fired. I'll resign. I wouldn't much care to go on working for a lunatic."

"Oh, for God's sake!" Ariadne said. "Jim, if you're happy with the company you have right now, you're welcome to them—but I tell you this! The way you're going, you're likely to wind up viewing the Ginsberg from the inside of a retreat yourself!"

She broke the connection with an ill-tempered snort, and Reedeth was left with his mouth half open to utter an abortive counterblast.

What a crazy predicament, to have got hung up on Ariadne of all the available women in the world!

But events were crowding in on him too rapidly to allow time for anger. Already Flamen and Conroy were on the pediflow towards his office. He started to rise with the intention of going to greet them, but canceled the movement and felt his features deform into a scowl.

Ariadne had been perfectly right. He was going to be in trouble if Mogshack learned about all this—not just Conroy's intrusion, but Madison's commitment into the guardianship of someone who promptly disregarded

299

his obligations. He hated the idea of confronting his visitors: Flamen because right now he was furious with the man for landing him and Madison both in a mess; Conroy because . . .

Well, making an honest if silent confession: because at the back of his mind he felt vulnerable to Conroy's contempt, and in their brief exchange over the comweb, half an hour ago, there had been the long shadow of the scathing irony with which Conroy had treated juvenile inanities in his students' arguments, back in the days when Reedeth was working under him.

He hoped desperately that neither Lyla nor Madison had seen through his carefully maintained mask.

And then there they were, at the door, being admitted, Conroy shaking hands with every appearance of affability; a mechanical routine of introduction had to be gone through, which gave a short respite from awareness of depression—and while Reedeth was still trying to formulate his next remarks, Conroy had sat briskly down and taken charge.

"Well! From what I've been able to pick up by talking to Flamen on the way here, you've got some serious problems, Jim, and so have our two friends here. I'm particularly interested to meet you, Miss Clay, because one of my students asked about the pythoness phenomenon in class the other day and I gave them the subject as an assignment—which naturally meant I had to investigate it myself before correcting what they turned in. I hadn't taken it very seriously before, but I have found that some remarkable authorities vouch for its authenticity. What's your view, Jim?"

Reedeth stumbletongued. "Why . . . Why, I've been compelled to react the same way, I guess. I never took pythonesses seriously until Miss Clay put on a performance here."

"I heard about that from Flamen," Conroy injected.

"Yes, of course: he recorded the show." Reedeth swallowed. "But it was having the automatics analyze the oracles she delivered which convinced me, not the performance itself. I—"

Lyla sat up sharply. "You didn't tell me you'd had my oracles comped!" she said in an accusing tone. "Christ, if I'd only known you were going to do that . . . ! What did the automatics tell you?"

"Later, please, Miss Clay," Reedeth said in a frigid tone. "Right now I have some business to clear up with Mr. Flamen, which shouldn't have been necessary, and as soon as that's straightened out I propose to go home. My arrangements for the weekend have been completely fouled up by what I can only call an absolute lack of consideration."

"Jesus God," Conroy said, before the bridling Flamen could respond to the accusation. "Jim, you sound so much like Mogshack I could believe you've been taking lessons. Hold it!" he added, raising a hand to forestall a snappish answer from the younger man. "I've been talking with Flamen for the past hour or more and I agree he was entirely too casual about accepting responsibility for our knee friend here. *But,* on the other hand, you didn't make it very clear to him just what he was committing himself to, did you? You were in such a hurry to move Madison along—"

"Hurry! Lord, he's been stuck in here for months longer than necessary!"

"No excuse for not being thorough," Conroy said, in precisely the tone Reedeth remembered from his student days. "There's never an excuse for not being thorough, especially when nowadays you can have all the fiddling little routine details comped out automatically. That's what computers are properly used for," he parenthesized to Flamen. "You seem to think I don't appreciate them, but believe me in their right place they're indispensable. The trouble is that people simply don't treat them the way they ought to. Now, Jim!" He leaned forward earnestly. "Let me ask you a question that I hope you'll an-

301

swer honestly, and if you do you won't be in such a hurry any longer to head for home."

Reedeth sighed. "Very well, go ahead."

"Are you happy working under Mogshack?"

There was a pause. Suddenly Reedeth gave a forced laugh. "All right, I won't duck that one. No, I'm not—not any longer."

"Why not?"

Another pause, longer. During it Reedeth's eyes moved to Madison's face and stayed there, fascinated.

"I guess," he said at last, the words grinding out as though being dragged over gravel, "because I'm no longer convinced that the patients discharged from here are properly cured."

Flamen tensed visibly, and his expression shifted from irritable to excited.

"In what sense are they not properly cured?" Conroy said, with the inflection he might have used to encourage a student to reach the logical conclusion of some argument he had propounded in an essay.

"I don't know!" Reedeth jumped to his feet and paced restlessly up and down the office. "It's just that . . . Well, over the past few days we've had two cases that troubled me dreadfully, and it was Miss Clay's oracles that tipped the balance in my mind."

Lyla's turn to draw herself up alertly. Not noticing, Reedeth ploughed on.

"Mrs. Flamen was one of them. She'd responded excellently, of course, or else she wouldn't have been released, but—but this wasn't so much *treatment* as *indulgence*. And I honestly don't think we'd have realized unless Mr. Flamen had complained about the coldness with which she behaved to him. So I've been wondering . . ." The words trailed away into a shrug. "And the other was Madison's," he concluded lamely.

"Flamen," Conroy said with an air of satisfaction, "I think you may have a proposal to put to Jim Reedeth now."

Flamen shaped words with his lips, canceled them, and shot out a hand towards the desketary. "Ah—doctor! Is what we say monitored by that thing and stored in the hospital data banks?"

Reedeth passed a weary hand through his hair, tousling it. "I could arrange for it not to be," he muttered. "Madison worked it over for me a few days ago, and it's not exactly standard any longer."

"Ah-hah!" Conroy said. "I got hints about that from Flamen too, on the way here. So make the arrangements, Jim, and hear what Flamen wants to say to you."

Reedeth gave the desketary a curt order, and glanced at Madison.

"Will that fix it?"

Madison looked ever so slightly uncomfortable; by contrast with his previous imperturbability, it was as though a mountain had trembled. He said, "I guess so, doc."

"Damn it, you altered the thing—you must know!" Reedeth blurted, then mastered himself with an effort. "Sorry," he said. "I'm a bit on edge today. Okay, Mr. Flamen, let's hear what you want to tell me."

"You've probably figured out already that I'm sufficiently worried about my wife to have her independently packled by Dr. Conroy," Flamen said slowly. "I did warn you that if she was prematurely discharged I'd take some such steps, didn't I? But if it does turn out that she's suffered at the hands of your director, I won't stop with a simple suit for damages. I'll do my utmost to have him impeached and dismissed."

"No wonder you wanted to prevent that being recorded!" Reedeth said. He gave a thin smile. "Yes, I'd more or less figured that out. What are you trying to get me to do—bore from within to undermine him? Forget it. But I wouldn't weep if someone else took over who was—well—let's say less dogmatic than he is. It'd make working here a lot easier, and what's more I think we'd do a better job." He ended on a note of defiance, looking almost surprised at his own decisiveness.

"I'm sure Flamen wasn't asking you to turn traitor," Conroy said promptly. "But it shouldn't be necessary to tell you, Jim, that I work much more happily on the basis of personal reactions than computerized analyses. And every now and again . . ."

It was his turn to hesitate, and his hearers looked at him in puzzlement as he glanced from one to another of them, his gaze lingering longest of all on Lyla.

"I'd better declare my interest," he said eventually, and gave a wry grin. "Without intending the least disrespect to Flamen's position and influence, on reflection I can't believe that something as straightforward as independent packling of Mrs. Flamen is going to afford the lever to topple your boss off his pedestal, Jim. It could far too easily be discounted on grounds of personal pique—couldn't it? And yet on the flight down from Manitoba I was thinking just how *necessary* it is to get Mogshack out."

He leaned back in his chair, put the tips of his fingers together, and stared at them musingly.

"You see . . . like it or not, and frankly I don't like it, this city of New York has a prestige, a cachet, a quality of influence, left over from the days when America really was on top of the world. There's this curious kind of envy—I'm sure you've noticed it—which means that even people in Capetown and Accra and the capitals of Asia have a nostalgic regard for what's done in New York, much in the same way as the Goths and Franks venerated Rome even after Alaric had sacked the city and the Romans had ceased to be a major power. And here's Mogshack on top of the local heap, and I sincerely believe he's doing things which are going to be disastrous. But they're being imitated from Mexico to Moscow, and—and I'm getting worried. Jim, do you appreciate at all what I'm driving at?"

Reedeth had lowered himself into his chair again. He gave a wary nod.

"I do have to confess that I'm not happy about the system I work under," he said. "Whether you, Prof, or anyone, can produce something better, though . . ."

"Me, I'm old and tired, and reduced to teaching a handful of not overly bright students not even in the country of my birth," Conroy sighed. "But I think I might conceivably be able to shift a dead weight off the minds of the next generation, who will have to clear up the mess we leave behind. I'd like to try, anyhow, and what I'm proposing is this. During the past few days, it looks as though not just one but a whole complex of curious and questionable events have taken place here, which combined will furnish Flamen with what he wants. Excuse me," he added to the spoolpigeon. "But as I said, the case of your wife on its own isn't enough. On the other hand, maybe if we took everything together, we might come up with a concerted attack. Let's start with something which most people will find very strange—no disrespect, Miss Clay, but people do still mostly look on pythonesses with suspicion. How about this matter of calling in a pythoness and then acting on her oracles?"

"We didn't," Reedeth said. "Not exactly. As I said, it was what the automatics told us about the oracles which convinced us."

"Us?"

"Me and my colleague Ariadne Spoelstra. It was her idea to invite Miss Clay to perform here."

"And Mogshack approved?"

"Of course. Though I understand he needed a lot of persuading."

"Good, there's our first line of approach. Here's our second." Conroy turned to Madison. "I seem to be apologizing for my own phrasing every minute or two, don't I? But I've got to say that I'm sure people outside this hospital are going to be astonished to learn you were

305

servicing the automatics here for several months while you were still officially a mental patient. And I'm certain that you don't feel too kindly disposed towards the man who kept you in long after you should have been discharged."

Madison turned one hand over as though spilling water from its cupped palm. He said, "Servicing the automatics is the job I'm good at, Mr. Conroy."

"You're not kidding," Reedeth said. He seemed to have recovered his self-possession. "What you did to this desketary of mine is almost unbelievable. And, come to think of it, I never thanked you."

"Yes, that's a point I was coming to," Conroy said. "You've told us about this desketary and how it's been modified—can you give us some examples of its new behavior?"

"I just did," Reedeth countered. "All this is being kept confidential, and it's just as well!"

"That's a negative kind of demonstration. How about a positive one? How about something which will prove that the entire resources of the Ginsberg cybernetic complex can be tapped through this single input? As I understand it, that's what you're claiming."

"I don't think there's any doubt of it!" Reedeth exclaimed. "I never thought I could—" He stopped abruptly.

"Never thought what?"

A faint beading of sweat had suddenly appeared on Reedeth's forehead. "I never thought I'd be able to make inquiries through my desketary about Dr. Mogshack himself," he muttered. "But I guess that's kind of an internal point, not one which visitors would appreciate."

"I appreciate it," Conroy said with some grimness. "I have a clear impression of what it must be to work under your boss, even though I've escaped that misfortune so far. I still want that demonstration, though. Hmmm! That's an idea." He turned to Flamen. "The automatics here are notoriously among the most advanced and elaborate in the world. Do you happen to have a problem on your mind they could solve for you?"

"Now just a—" Reedeth began, but Flamen had reacted instantly.

"Sure I do," he said. "Doctor, do regular vu-transmissions form part of the environment of your patients which your automatics take into consideration?"

"Oh, naturally," Reedeth said, a trifle puzzled. "As they go to green, we phase our patients back to the outside world, and vushows play a key rôle in the process."

"My God," Conroy said very softly; Flamen disregarded the comment.

"So in that case let's ask your miraculous desketary why my own computers have assured me that unlimited free Federal computer time won't get rid of the interference which has been plaguing my show recently," Flamen said, and leaned back in his chair with a smug expression.

"I don't think I quite understand that," Reedeth said after a pause. "Ah . . . I don't watch your show, I'm afraid. I'm always working when it comes on."

"It's perfectly straightforward," Flamen said. "My show, and only my show, has been suffering ridiculous amounts of interference literally every day for months past, and it's getting so bad people are switching off in droves. The Holocosmic engineers swear blind it's nothing they can fix. I want to know whether to believe them, or whether I'm being sabotaged, or whether I'm going out of my mind and developing a persecution complex. It seems like a reasonable question to put to the computers in a mental hospital. Especially since my own equipment seems to have a blind spot on the subject, and it this moment strikes me that maybe if I am being sabotaged the sabotage extends to my computers at the office!" He was growing heated as he ended the tirade.

With a suspicious glance, as though prepared to agree with the suggestion of paranoia, Reedeth summarized the question for his desketary, and waited for the most probable answer: insufficient data.

It didn't materialize. In its usual patronizing tone, the machine said, "Both Mr. Flamen and the Federal government's computers lack the data to evaluate this problem."

"Does that mean you have the data?" Reedeth said, confused.

"Yes."

Flamen was looking equally astonished; it was obvious that he hadn't expected to receive a serious reply to his query, but only meant to live up to the challenge implicit in Reedeth's claims about his desketary. Since this had been the key element in persuading him to accept responsibility for Madison after his release, it was logical that he should put maximum pressure on it. He was torn between disappointment at not scoring against Reedeth, and genuine desire to learn the answer.

"So get it to answer the question for me!" he rapped at Reedeth.

"I'll try," the psychologist muttered, and put the problem to the machine. Promptly the mechanical voice responded.

"Mrs. Celia Prior Flamen possesses the ability to interfere with electromagnetic radiations in the band used for three-vee transmissions, and this fact is not stored either at the offices of Matthew Flamen Inc. or at the Federal computation center at Oak Ridge. It was established upon her arrival at this hospital and has not subsequently been relayed to any other cybernetic system."

There was a stunned silence in the room. At length Flamen said faintly, "But . . . Reedeth, are your automatics as crazy as your patients?"

"It certainly sounds like it," Reedeth agreed. His cheeks had gone pale. "Unless . . . No, it's absurd. But—"

"But what?" Conroy cut in with enthusiasm instead of the scorn they had expected.

308

Reluctantly Reedeth said, "Well, it is true, now that I come to think of it—there were a hell of a lot of breakdowns in our internal comweb directly following Mrs. Flamen's commitment. Remember, Harry?" He turned to Madison.

"Ah . . . Yes, doctor, that's perfectly true," the knee said in a depressed tone.

"Even so," Reedeth said, appearing to regret his former reaction, "I don't see how one could—"

"Jim!" Conroy interrupted. "Do you trust the automatics you work with here?"

"Damn it, I put exactly the same question to Ariadne the other day," Reedeth sighed. "Prof, I literally don't know! That was such an incredible—"

The comweb buzzed, and in the screen there appeared the familiar face of Elias Mogshack, a smile parting his moustache from his beard, a cordial tone coloring the words he started to speak as the image of Reedeth appeared before him.

"Ah, Dr. Reedeth! I heard you were devotedly working out of normal hours to clear up some—"

And it stopped.

Silence.

Resuming, the voice was like a saw cutting into wet wood, the bite and rasp overlaid with a whine of petulance. "Aren't you Xavier Conroy?"

Completely unperturbed, Conroy nodded. "Good afternoon, Dr. Mogshack. It's a long time since we had the pleasure—"

"What the *hell* are you doing in my hospital?"

"Yours?" Conroy countered delicately. "Strange—I thought it belonged to the government and people of the State of New York."

"You son of a bitch," said Mogshack, and his lips folded together so tightly that when he parted them again they remained bloodlessly pale. "Get out. Get off the grounds of the Ginsberg Hospital *this minute* or I'll have you removed by the police."

Reedeth said, "Dr. Mogshack—"

"Did you invite this man into the hospital?" Mogshack thundered.

"What? Well, I guess I—"

"You speak to me on Monday the minute you arrive on the hospital premises! I'll tell you then what I think of you—I wouldn't want Conroy to be able to gloat over my bad judgment in offering you a post at the Ginsberg. But I'd recommend you to start looking for other employment; that much I *will* say right now!"

The screen blanked. A few seconds went by; then the desketary said, "On the orders of the hospital director, this unit is inactivated until oh-nine-hundred Monday morning next."

And went dead.

"Well, if you want that fixed, Madison can presumably do it," Flamen said, curling his lip as he turned to glance at the knee.

"Stop it, Flamen," Conroy said quietly. "Yes, Madison very probably can override the inactivation, but do you want to give away your ace in the hole?"

He stood up. "All right, that settles it," he said. "Up till this very moment I had doubts. You too, Jim? But I think Flamen just had an example of the kind of person who's allegedly 'cured' his wife, and Madison just saw who it really was who kept him here after the due time, and you, Jim, had your marching orders. Let's get out of here like he told us to—in the state he's in, he's perfectly capable of keeping his word about having me dragged out by the busies. Isn't he, Jim?"

Reedeth drew a deep breath. He said, "You remember I mentioned a little while ago that I'd got data about Mogshack out of this desketary? Well, what it said . . ." He hesitated, but an access of fury carried him over his mental logjam. "It said he wanted to have the whole United States committed to his care! Well, he can damned well count me out!"

"I can't think," Conroy said glacially, "what better

evidence you could offer Flamen here for the accuracy of your automatics' answer to his question than the perfect match between that diagnosis of your boss's mental condition and the behavior he just exhibited. Flamen, you have computers in your office?"

"Well—yes, naturally!"

"That's where we're going," Conroy said with authority. "I don't imagine you have a setup to match the Ginsberg's, but unless he objects I want to take along our highly recommended electronicist here: apart from anything else I only have until tomorrow night in this town and I'd like to be assured that when I head for home there's some capable engineer looking after the problem of this interference on your program, regardless of whether it is or is not your wife's doing like the machines say. I'd also like to take you along, Miss Clay, unless you have something else to do. I get hunches sometimes. Right now I have a hunch that—"

He broke off, looking almost sheepish at his own tone of voice. "The hell, I *do* have a hunch, and it's so acute it practically hurts! I have this crazy notion that there's a pattern underlying all this, and properly used it will torpedo Mogshack very satisfactorily. But it's got to be done fast!" He put his hands up to his head as though overcome, and Reedeth stared at him in bewilderment.

Lyla, who had been silent for a long while, said suddenly, "Yes, Professor."

"What?" Conroy turned to her, blinking. "Oh. Oh, yes. I mean . . . yes. Madison, who the hell are you?"

Reedeth said, "Prof, I don't think I—"

"I don't give a damn what you think!" Conroy blazed. "I know what I think, and that's what counts. You coming or not?"

"Coming . . . ?"

"To Flamen's office!" Conroy barked. "You know what's happening, don't you, woman?" he added to Lyla.

"I—I'm not quite sure, but . . ." Lyla rose unsteadily to her feet. "All I know is I'm scared, but *I'm* coming."

Flamen said, "I feel dizzy. What happened?"

"If it's got through to you, it's big," Conroy said, and marched towards the door. "Move!"

EIGHTY-TWO   MOTION PASSED BY SEVENTEEN VOTES
TO TWO AT A CONFERENCE HELD
OVER A SECURE COMWEB LINK BE-
TWEEN REPRESENTATIVES OF ALL
THE MAJOR KNEEBLANK ENCLAVES
IN NORTH AMERICA WITH THE EX-
CEPTION OF BLACKBURY

Be it resolved: That in view of the grave disservice
to the cause of black self-determination resulting from
Mayor Black's reliance on a white South African racial
expert in the implementation of his pro-melanist policy
inasmuch as it has entailed the dismissal of Pedro Diablo who is known to be a staunch and irreplaceable
advocate of a standpoint adhered to by all participants
in this discussion every possible step be taken to rectify
the consequences of his misguided act at the earliest
opportunity including if need be the forcible packling of
Mayor Black to determine whether his behavior is in
conformity with the best interests of American mela-
nism.

EIGHTY-THREE TWENTY-FIRST CENTURY USAGE SO NEW AS NOT YET TO HAVE BEEN INCORPORATED IN ANY RECOGNIZED GLOSSARY BUT SUFFICIENTLY COMMON TO HAVE COME ORALLY TO THE ATTENTION OF A NUMBER OF LEXICOGRAPHERS

"Sprained knee" (for *kneeblank*, Afrikaans *nieblanke* non-white person): a colored person constrained to live and/or work in a white-dominated environment rather than an enclave or a country with a colored government.

EIGHTY-FOUR

ONE KNEE SPRAINED, ONE TIME BADLY
OUT OF JOINT

What exactly was going on Flamen had no idea, but
Conroy seemed persuaded that it was far more likely
to lead to the collapse of Mogshack's authority than the
original plan, and clinging optimistically to that he allowed himself to be swept along by events. Followed
by his ill-assorted gaggle of companions, he rode the
pediflow in the Etchmark Undertower from the elevator
to the door of his office, feeling in his pocket for the
Punch key to admit them.

But when he applied it, he realized that the door was
already unlocked.

"What the hell?" he said under his breath. The panel
moved aside at a touch, before he had time to consider
that if there was an intruder in the office it would make
more sense to steal quietly away and send for the busies
than to walk in and confront him. In spite of the fact
that his occupation exposed him to the potential fury
of a great many of his victims, he had never carried a
gun to protect himself, and he doubted whether anyone
else in his party was armed at the moment.

While he was still in the grip of his initial surprise,
however, one of the internal doors slid back and a dark
face appeared, wearing an embarrassed expression like
a kid caught stealing candy.

"Good God!" Conroy said over Flamen's shoulder; he

was the taller by half a head. "Aren't you Pedro Diablo? Well, you seem to have landed on your feet after being so unceremoniously thrown out of Blackbury!"

Diablo gave a distracted nod, eyes on Flamen. "Ah . . . I hope you don't mind," he said. "IBM couldn't get me one of the practice units you suggested until Monday at the soonest, and having seen what your equipment is capable of I simply couldn't resist the temptation of coming in to play around with it. I did get the code to isolate the unit, of course—it didn't need special wiring after all—and I promise I haven't done it any harm."

"You might have had the courtesy to let me know!" Flamen snapped. "I damned near mistook you for a burglar, and I was all set to sneak off and send for the police! Right now, though, we have more important uses for our computers, so I'd appreciate it if you'd get lost." Ill-temperedly, he strode past Diablo and into his own office.

"Nonsense," Conroy said, following.

"What?"

"I said nonsense. For one thing I've wanted to meet this man for years—he's probably the best intuitive psychologist on the planet, and I regularly use recordings of his shows as study themes, to illustrate how a determined individual can manipulate the mass audience. And for another thing, you're angry and frustrated, I'm pretty much manic, and we have to contend with a hell of a complex problem. It'll be very damned useful to have someone around with a detached point of view, and I can't think of anyone much more detached than someone who never wanted to be in New York at all and would far rather still be home in Blackbury. Right?" he added to the knee.

"Who in the hell are *you?*" Diablo demanded in astonishment.

"Oh—I'm sorry! I'm Xavier Conroy."

"You are?" Diablo's verge-of-hostile manner changed magically. He held out his hand. "Damn it, I've been hoping to meet you for years, too! Why in the world did you let them chase you off to that backwater teaching job in Manitoba?"

"I'm excessively fond of my own opinions," Conroy said wryly. "Students are generally sufficiently over-awed not to shout their professors down, even these days, and it gives me a false sense of achievement when I see my own doctrines coming back at me in their term papers. But I had no business taking it for granted you'd want to stick around here, of course. It's just that—well, like I said, we have a problem, and . . . Do you get hunches, Mr. Diablo?"

"I guess I do, now and then. Not that they amount to real premonitions, if that's what you're driving at. Or else I'd still be at home and a lot happier. But one gets a feel for the propaganda potential of any given news-item, for example."

"That's the kind of thing I'm talking about," Conroy nodded. "Over the past hour or two I've been seeing and hearing some absolutely extraordinary things, and there's a tantalizing sense of a pattern growing out of them. You got the same feeling, didn't you, Flamen?"

A little annoyed at being shuffled to the sidelines on his home ground, Flamen gave a curt nod; a heartbeat later he repented and amplified it, looking puzzled.

"Yes, back there at the hospital I had this momentary fit of—of excitement, I guess it was. It was so strong it made me feel dizzy."

"I'm still getting it," Lyla said, very pale. She was standing in the doorway as though shy about entering. "I never felt anything like it before—at least, not since I was a kid and everybody around me was busy preparing for war to break out. I didn't understand what was hap-pening, of course, but I distinctly associate to the same mixture of fear and excitement."

"Miss Clay is a pythoness," Conroy said to Diablo. "How do you feel about pythonesses?"

There was a pause. At length, with a chuckle, Diablo

drew up the left sleeve of his smart New York-styled oversuit and revealed that just below the elbow he was wearing a Conjuh Man Inc. juju bracelet: an intricately braided ring of hair from a lion's mane.

"It's the kind of thing I guess we know more about than blanks do," he said. "You take sibyl-pills, Miss Clay?"

"Ah—yes."

"We kneeblanks were used to tapping the same kind of mental forces long before they got around to synthesizing the drugs you use in a clean modern laboratory. I have—I mean I had—a seeress on my staff back home who could do almost everything these computers do except build up reconstructed scenes for transmission. Used her a lot, like about one story a month regularly wherever we needed more data than we could get through official channels. She was right, too, four times out of five. Matter of fact I'm kind of glad to see how blank society has been turning back to human insights these past few years instead of sticking to machines exclusively."

"That's fascinating," Conroy said. "I never heard about that."

Diablo's lip curled. "You weren't intended to. We've been running the Fed authorities in little circles trying to trace leaks which don't exist. Which they will continue to do, I don't doubt, even if you go straight to the comweb and tell them what I just said. It's what happens when you rely too much on machinery—you wind up following the same old mechanical grooves all the time. Automatics don't make allowances for like differences of personality. You lay down hard-and-fast principles for them, and they follow them blindly to the most absurd conclusions, and eventually they drag you along in their wake."

"Damned right," Conroy said. "I knew you were a thinking man, Mr. Diablo, and I'm even more glad to have met you than I expected to be. Look, why don't we sit down and talk about this thing we seem to have got involved in?"

"Sure," Diablo nodded. "If you take it seriously I'm willing to bet on my being interested too." He glanced at his watch. "I would kind of like some lunch, though— I didn't eat breakfast today."

"I'm sure we can send out for some. Flamen?"

"Oh, for Christ's sake! Yes, of course we can!" Scowling, Flamen moved around his desk and sat down in his regular chair. "I warn you, though, Professor, that if this turns out to be the waste of time I half expect I'm going to be very damned angry."

"That's one thing which doesn't worry me," Conroy said with perfect composure. "But I grant there's a chance of it not being a waste of time in a way which we are too shortsighted to figure out, and if *that* happens you certainly won't be the only one who's annoyed."

EIGHTY-FIVE

America's Time-Bomb by Colin Legum

. . . 'I don't believe in nothin',' says a Negro youth in a riot city. 'I feel like they ought to burn down the whole world. Just let it burn down, baby.' . . .

EIGHTY-SIX ASSUMPTION CONCERNING THE FORE-
GOING MADE FOR THE PURPOSES
OF THIS STORY

He's not unique.

The clock said sixteen-ten and they sat among a welter of empty beer- and milk-cartons and multicolored sandwich wrappings.

"It doesn't make *sense*," Pedro Diablo said in an aggrieved tone, as though the world were conspiring to hide the secret from him. "It just keeps fanning out and fanning out, and every time it branches into some crazy new absurdity. I need to recapitulate—I have this feeling that I haven't taken in everything I've been told because my subconscious thinks so much of it is silly."

"Is there anything which does make sense?" Conroy demanded.

"Ah . . ." Diablo hesitated. "Well, odd bits, I guess. But even those are so buried in among other things which sound ridiculous!"

"For instance?"

"Oh . . ." Another moment of doubt; then: "No, damn it! The things I want to take seriously are all wrapped up in garbage! Like what Harry's supposed to have said after he'd finished chopping down those macoots of Mikki Baxendale's."

"How do you mean?" Lyla put in. "How's this supposed to be 'wrapped in garbage'? Don't you believe me?"

"I'd believe Harry much more readily," Diablo said. "No offense. But on your own admission you'd had a sub-critical dose of a very powerful drug, and you can't have been functioning properly on all mental levels. And Harry won't or can't remember saying what you tell us he said, so . . ." He spread his hands. "By the way, how does it happen that after throwing a man out of a forty-five story window Harry Madison is here instead of in the Undertombs?"

Reedeth sighed, leaning back in his chair to let his legs stretch out straight. "What do you think I was doing before Flamen and Conroy came to collect him from the hospital? I was just about perjuring myself to prevent that, snowing the busies under with so many fully-comped reports of the effect on a man of swallowing a 250-milligram sibyl-pill they had to grant bail on grounds of temporary derangement. I'm used to dragging Ginsberg's patients out from under, and nowadays it's second nature for me to slam in counter-charges, whether or not they're as well documented as the kidnapping charge against Mikki Baxendale and her macoots. All I've done is postpone the reckoning, though. It may be for weeks because I know for a fact that the courts are thirty days behind schedule even on their first-degree murder hearings, but the crunch will come sooner or later."

"Did you lay on lawyers?"

"On a Saturday? You're joking! But the Ginsberg retains a computerized legal aid service we can plug into direct over the regular comweb lines. I used that."

Diablo shook his head wonderingly. "It really is a different world out here, you know. I mean, regardless of whether or not he'd been drugged, someone who threw a man off the top of the Zimbabwe Tower back in Blackbury would be in jail and more than likely in chains for however long it took Judge Dennison to reach his case. Your way may be more tolerant, but it sure as hell doesn't seem to be so efficient. He doesn't even have to go into court before he gets this bail, huh?"

"Not if he has a record of mental instability," Reedeth said wearily. "But the bail is automatically doubled."

"It's a system, I guess," Diablo sighed.

Reaching for another carton of beer, Conroy tore the plastic opener strip and cursed as the pressure of gas inside sprayed him with fine drops. He wiped his beard and took a swig.

"If you've finished the sociological survey, I'd like to follow up the point you were about to make when you wandered away from the subject," he said to Diablo. "What would have made you take this prophecy of Harry's seriously?"

"Prophecy?" Diablo repeated. "Yes, I guess it is one, isn't it? Well, this reference to some new product of the Gottschalks', you see. There is one in the pipeline, something new and very special, and I believe it's due for introduction in the spring of next year."

"How would you know about it?" Reedeth inquired skeptically.

"That's a hell of a question for a blank to ask," Diablo countered. "Don't you know how the Gottschalks set you up as customers? They issue their ultra-late weaponry to the black enclaves, at not much over cost, knowing you're so scared of us even spitting your way that you'll pay whatever they ask to keep the balance of terror. Even so, it's not very impressive, is it? Talking about a 'Gottschalk coup of 2015' doesn't have to mean anything more than that Harry got word of what's circulating among the enclaves."

"Is there something?" Flamen demanded, his professional instincts alerted.

"I just told you!"

"What specifically?" Flamen persisted.

"Blazes, don't you follow the news out of Blackbury? I did a program myself about the latest equipment Anthony Gottschalk handed us for trials, and it's due on the beams tomorrow over three of the black-owned satellites. There's a 250-watt laser with five-hundred-shot capacitance—some new breakthrough in accumulators, I was told, though they're designed so you can't take them to pieces without melting down the parts and up to the time I left I hadn't heard that our engineers had figured out the principle. There's a hand-launched self-propelled grenade with a micronuke head with a range of a thousand yards and power to bring down an average block of apts. There's a whole gang of stuff, all being introduced at once. Though I never heard of it being given any such name as—what did you call it, Miss Clay?"

"I didn't call it anything," the pythoness said obstinately. "But Harry said 'System C integrated weaponry' and talked about equipping one man with the power to raze a city."

"I don't get this," Flamen said after a pause. "I never knew the Gottschalks to be secretive about their products before. In the R&D stages, yes of course, but not after samples have been issued for use."

"Policy difference in the cartel?" Conroy suggested.

Flamen looked blank for a moment, then snapped his fingers. "Christ, I really *am* losing my touch! It never happened before, but it could just be that it's concerned with this fight that's going on among them." He jumped to his feet. "I'm going to comp that right away, if you don't mind. It fits entirely too well."

"I'm afraid I don't quite understand," Lyla ventured.

Approaching the first and most worn of his computer input boards, Flamen glanced at her. "No? But you have heard that there's a major disagreement among the Gottschalks? It's been going on for weeks, and it climaxed the other day when Marcantonio celebrated his eightieth birthday and a bunch of high-level pollies deliberately stayed away. It just might be due to an argument about introducing these nasty new gimmicks Diablo's been describing to us. You go ahead talking if you like; I've finally got something out of all this chitter-chatter which I can make use of." His fingers were coding orders to the automatics as he spoke. "That would be a story to gladden your heart, wouldn't it,

Prof?" he added to Conroy. "The Gottschalks disagree-
ing about a new line of weaponry and a splinter group
of them going ahead against the old man's wishes!"

"I don't see any reason to be pleased about that!"
Conroy snapped. "They're gangsters, as far as I'm concerned, and how will you like it if they start last-cen-
tury-style gang warfare with modern equipment? It'll
be infinitely worse than anything the X Patriots have yet
done!"

Flamen declined to answer, and in a moment he was
lost in the series of cryptic probability ratings which
glowed on the screen before him.

"Ah, the hell," Conroy grunted. "It must surely be
better for people to have some kind of warning about
that sort of thing, even though not many of us pay attention to warnings any longer. Half the time we don't
even trust ourselves, not enough that we rely on our
judgment without a second opinion, preferably a mechanical one, so why should we listen to other people's
advice?"

"You really are the most cynical son-of-a-bitch I ever
met," Diablo said, tacking a wink on to the words to
amplify his meaning.

"That I will take as a compliment." Conroy glanced at
his watch. "I've spent a hell of a lot of time on this
by now, though, and I don't seem to have got anywhere.
Let's see if we can stick to the point, shall we? You were
saying you wanted to review what you'd heard and
make sure you'd taken it all in."

"Stick to the point!" Diablo parodied a grin. "If I
could find one worth sticking I'd cheerfully do so. I feel
more like I'm dredging through mud for bits of salable
scrap. Used to do that when I was a kid . . ." He brisk-
ened. "Okay, let me take it from the top in chronolo-
gical order to make sure I haven't missed anything. It
starts with you being invited to perform at the Ginsberg
for an audience of patients due to be discharged, doesn't
it, Miss Clay?"

Lyla nodded.

"And this performance was remarkable for two things that had never happened to you before. First off, your late mackero had to slap you out of an echo-trap, which as I understand it is due to the presence in the audience of some especially dominant personality, from whom your subconscious can't tear itself away."

"That's what I've been told," Lyla agreed cautiously. "As I said, it had never happened to me before."

"Okay, then. We'll set aside for the moment the content of the oracle which developed into an echo-trap, which Mr. Flamen has down on tape so we can check it later. We'll go on to the second remarkable point, which was that you had a—did you call it a hangover?"

"That's right. On the way home in Mr. Flamen's skimmer."

"Ah-hah. You spoke what amounted to another oracle in the waking state instead of in trance."

Lyla shivered. "It was weird! I had this momentary sense of total certainty, and I heard the words coming out of my own mouth without knowing what they were going to be when they finished."

"There are processes very much akin to these in voudoun work," Diablo said offhandedly. "You might check on some of the current field-leaders in the enclaves, like Mama Echo in Chicago or the girl I've been working with in Blackbury, Mama Fey. However!" He cleared his throat. "You played over your oracles with Mr. Flamen, right? And you didn't come to any clear conclusions about them."

"We were both kind of distracted," Lyla muttered. "I'd had a quarrel with Dan, and this thing about taking you on had come up too—though I didn't know it was you they were talking about when Mr. Prior called with the news. All we figured out was this vague notion that maybe Mrs. Flamen was concerned, but—no, forget that. Mr. Flamen asked me in the skimmer why I'd mentioned his wife, so that one must have been exceptionally clear."

She looked surprised. "I'd forgotten about that!"

"And your automatics at the hospital"—Diablo turned to Reedeth—"comped out probable subjects for each of the three oracles Miss Clay had managed to issue before she was slapped awake, and the one which developed into an echo-trap was allegedly concerned with Harry Madison. Correct?"

Reedeth nodded, face strained. "At the time, of course, I didn't know what an echo-trap implied. I heard the term for the first time when I spoke to Dan Kazer directly after Miss Clay's performance, and it wasn't until later that I followed it up. After what's happened today, though, I'm beginning to wonder whether I was a fool to believe what the automatics told me."

"Why so?"

"Well . . ." Reedeth made a helpless gesture. "Just before we came away from the hospital, there was this thing we told you about: Mr. Flamen asked why these computers here predicted failure of the Federal computers to solve the problem of interference on his daily show, and the answer we got was transparent nonsense."

"Jim, what's happened to the open mind I tried to encourage in you when you were studying with me?" Conroy said.

"Open mind! Christ, if I'm going to be told to believe in women patients who can interfere at a distance with a three-vee broadcast, the next stop will be raising the devil and doing duty to a plastic idol!"

"Don't exaggerate." Conroy loaded the words with frosty reproof. "Life is a matter of probabilities, not certainties. You were prepared to believe what your desketary told you about Mogshack, for instance?"

Reedeth wavered. "That's not the same thing," he muttered.

"It's the same automatic complex using the same data banks," Conroy insisted. "Furthermore, when you had the oracles comped you were prepared to accept that they applied to—among others—Harry Madison, even though you wouldn't have guessed that for yourself?"

"Ah . . ." Reedeth licked his lips. "Yes, damn it, of course I took that on trust! It fitted once I'd thought it over. But this ridiculous thing about Mrs. Flamen hadn't come up then!"

"We haven't got to it in this review of our problem," Conroy said. "Let it go for the moment and tell me just what you mean by saying that Madison 'fitted' the oracle supposed to be concerned with him."

Reedeth glanced uneasily at the subject of the conversation, who was sitting to one side of the group, taking virtually no part in the discussion except to answer politely when he was directly addressed.

"The morning before Miss Clay's show," he muttered, "I'd reached the conclusion, because he'd fixed the trouble I was having with the censor-circuits on my desketary without my asking outright, that Madison's trouble couldn't be termed insanity. Nonconformity, maybe, but that's not the same thing."

"Hmm! Working under Mogshack hasn't completely petrified your mind, then," Conroy rumbled. "In an age when eccentricity has almost been made a major crime, that's a remarkable insight."

"Whichever way we dig through this heap of confusion," Diablo said, "we seem to wind up with Harry again. Hey, Harry!"

Madison turned an emotionless gaze to him.

"What *is* all this, man? Like I keep hearing you can open Punch locks without the key—and fix a desketary in ways the designer didn't dream of—and you were stuck in the Ginsberg in spite of not being crazy—and having a sibyl-pill forced down your throat did things to you that aren't in the literature—and here's this pythoness says she watched you beat nine opponents in a row and she got all these visions of weird fights and she says she wasn't just dreaming . . ." He spread his hands.

"You missed a couple of things," Conroy said. "When I got hit by this hunch, just before leaving Reedeth's office, I started to ask Madison who the hell he is, only someone said something else and it distracted me." He leaned forward in his chair. "I was thinking partly of all these visions that Miss Clay had—which make me want to ask how the hell did all that *detail* get packed in. . . . You haven't studied history, have you?" he shot at Lyla.

"Not to specialize. Just regular school lessons. And I never enjoyed it much. Got low marks all the time."

"But what you told us about—oh—being ill from bad meat in a Roman arena, finding it hard to see clearly because your eyes were bleary from dust and bright sunlight in the Egyptian bit—"

"Egyptian bit?" Diablo cut in. "Man, you're losing me all the time!"

"The man with the whip and the coarse linen kilt, and the bit about picking up an adobe brick shaped like a loaf! It's all so goddamned three-dimensional!" Conroy pounded fist into palm. "This isn't the kind of thing you'd expect to remember from a mere hallucination. It's the kind of fiddling little detail that sticks in your mind in real life, like trudging to the top of a mountain and being less impressed with the splendid view than by the blister you've rubbed on your heel. Do you see what I mean?"

"I surely do," Diablo nodded. "It's a point I overlooked, and I shouldn't have. It's the kind of touch I've always prided myself on adding to my own reconstructions for propaganda shows, the little striking bit which all by itself makes the scene appear real." He clawed at his beard so vigorously it looked as though he might tear out the roots. "Go on. What else was it that made you ask Madison who he is?"

"The fact that when Miss Clay asked him straight out,

was it him who fouled up her prophesying at the hospital, he said yes. Correct, Miss Clay?"

"Harry seemed to know what I meant without my explaining," Lyla said, glancing nervously at the knee. "But—ah—should we be talking about him as if he wasn't in the room?"

"Harry seems to be committing the crime of silence," Diablo said without humor. "We've been trying to get a straight yes or no out of him all afternoon; maybe if we annoy him sufficiently by talking about him this way we'll provoke a few useful comments. Hey, Harry?"

Madison gave a very faint smile and still said nothing.

"If that's how you want it . . ." Conroy said. "Well, apart from the actual oracle that turned into an echo-trap, and this confusing nonsense about a man with seven brains—"

"I remembered that!" Lyla sat bolt upright suddenly. "My God, how could I have forgotten again? While I was sitting there at Mikki Baxendale's place, watching him, I was saying it over and over to myself: 'I met a man with seven brains!' "

"A hell of a lot of things seem to be being remembered," Reedeth said cynically. "Prophecies after the event never impressed me very much."

"Maybe not," Conroy said. "How about prophecies before the event, though? Jim, would a patient in the Ginsberg be allowed access to a vuset receiving knee-blank propaganda, like for instance one of Diablo's shows relayed by a Chinese or Nigerian satellite?"

"No, of course not. Anything that disturbing to the personality, like having one's guilt feelings played on, would be disastrous. It can be tolerated outside, where there are plenty of distractions, but in the enclosed environment of the hospital—no, definitely that couldn't be allowed."

"In other words—" Conroy began, to be cut short by an exclamation from Flamen as the latter turned away from his computer board.

"Jackpot! Christ, this is—this is enormous! Here, someone pass me a carton of that beer if there's any left."
The spoolpigeon was so excited he was almost clapping his hands. "Pay dirt on absolutely *every* angle of
the entire story! The Gottschalks *are* planning to opt
out of the Iron Mountain data center in favor of new installations of their own, and it looks as though the likely
location is in Nevada where the younger pollies like
Anthony and Vyacheslav have moved to get away from
Marcantonio's stamping-grounds here in the East—which
means he may very well not approve of the idea. And
there *is* a whole new line of weaponry scheduled for
mass production shortly. It looks as though it's been re-
designed from the ground up, and I've even traced a
code letter 'C' which appears to identify the series. Christ,
if I have to spend the rest of the weekend here, if I have
to use up the computer time the Feds are giving me on
this one subject, I'm going to come up on Monday with
the biggest goddamned story I ever handled! It's a sensaysh, just purely a sensaysh! Imagine being able to say
what a struggle inside the cartel is about while it's still
going on!"

Abruptly it dawned on him that the faces turned to
him wore uniformly dismayed expressions, and he broke
off. "What's the matter, Professor?" he challenged Conroy. "You were telling me I should tackle the Gottschalks,
weren't you? But you don't exactly look overjoyed!"

"Diablo!" Conroy kept his eyes on Flamen, not on the
knee. "Your show about these new weapons—is it the
only coverage of them up to now?"

"As far as I know," Diablo confirmed.

"And the show's only been canned? It hasn't yet been
on the beams?"

"Right."

"And in any case patients in the Ginsberg aren't allowed access to broadcasts from Blackbury or any other
knee enclave." Conroy drew a deep breath. "So how
could Madison not only predict these prototype weapons,

but even identify the code letter which refers to them?"

"I don't understand," Flamen said, looking in bewilderment from one to other of his companions.

"That," Conroy assured him, "makes you even with the rest of us."

EIGHTY-EIGHT

FROM: ROBERT GOTTSCHALK
TO: ANTHONY GOTTSCHALK
URGENT AND SECRET

(A) BUY CONTROLLING INTEREST IN HOLOCOSMIC NETWORK BY 1100 EST MONDAY AND DISCONTINUE MATTHEW FLAMEN SHOW PAYING MAXIMUM $2,000,000 FOR BREACH OF CONTRACT
(B) FAILING (A) DISCONTINUE MATTHEW FLAMEN

"Nothing?" Morton Lenigo inquired.

The man who had entered the room dropped wearily into a chair and shook his head, crowned with ostentatiously nappy hair. "Fuck-all," he said. "That *goddamned fool*—Mayor Black, I mean. No reply from this block of apts where they're supposed to have installed Diablo —no reports from any of my X Patriot sympathizers I asked to try and spot him if he shows on the street—no reply from the offices of this company they fixed him a job with because the comweb is turned over to an answering service for the weekend. . . . Might as well have taken him out and sunk him in the ocean with weights on his feet!"

"Think someone did?" Lenigo suggested after a pause.

There was a silence crowded with the stench of depression. Eventually the man said, "I've been avoiding that idea. But someone who could hire in that honky devil Uys . . ."

"Yes," Morton Lenigo said. He relied on his reputation to complete the statement for him. Shortly the other man got up and went away.

"The logical thing," Diablo said after reflection, "is to comp out the things which seem the craziest, hm? Like maybe see if there's anything in the literature about having prophetic visions under the influence of a sibyl-pill. And this will give us a handle to grab hold of the rest by, like what you say these automatics at the hospital told you about Mrs. Flamen." He rose. "Flamen, could you show me how to—?"

"Now just a moment!" Flamen's cheeks were reddening. "I need to use my computers right now. Weren't you listening to what I just said?"

"And don't you realize how you were put on to what you just discovered?" Conroy cut in forcibly. "You owe it to Madison—which means you owe it to Reedeth—which means you owe it to his colleague Dr. Spoelstra for inviting Miss Clay to perform at the hospital, and to her too for providing the oracles we've been discussing, and—"

"Oh, there won't be any end to this!" Flamen gibed. "I suppose I owe it to my brother-in-law too, for persuading me to let Celia stay on in the Ginsberg instead of being transferred to a private sanitarium! But I wouldn't feel inclined to thank him for doing her that particular favor."

"I was wondering when you'd remember that you theoretically brought me to New York for the weekend to set up parameters for her packling," Conroy said with deliberate acerbity.

The fire of Flamen's incipient fury blazed up. "Damnation! If we hadn't got sidetracked into this stupid business about Madison we'd have been out to the Priors' place by now and you'd have met Celia and probably the whole thing could have been tied up in a few hours!"

"And you wouldn't have got what you wanted out of it," Conroy snapped. "Using her case as a basis for attacking Mogshack could be dismissed as a personal grudge. You've got something far better, I can tell you that right now! Get Diablo to ground it on Madison's delayed release, demand packling of Mogshack himself to locate this megalomania the Ginsberg's automatics have diagnosed, and you'll have him down by the end of the year. And that's not the only thing you've been given, handed to you on a silver platter! You've got the item about the Gottschalks too!"

"So I'm supposed to make a list of everybody who did anything to get me where I am, go down them checking each one off when I've said thanks for doing me the favor?"

"Yes, yes and yes!" Abruptly Conroy's fraying control over his own temper failed, and he jumped to his feet, confronting Flamen from the vantage point of his greater tallness. "What the hell good is it going to do anyone to move someone like Mogshack off his petty little pedestal if the people who do it haven't even noticed that he's pulling their strings and making them dance? Are you so dumb, witless, shortsighted you're willing to put up with the worst of all the things that are wrong with our poor sick planet?"

"Why, you—!"

"Shut up!" Conroy thumped fist into palm with such force it made a sound sharp as a gunshot. "Why in hell should I have to tell you this, a spoolpigeon who must have seen it happen hundreds of times? You've never got at the people who matter, the people it might help

337

us if we got rid of them. You've got at the people who were trapped and cornered by circumstances, who like took a risk one time and it didn't work so they had to take another and another, or pocketed a bribe and found they liked the higher standard of living, or whatever the hell.

"One thing leads to another in this world, Flamen, and we human beings get dragged along like—like dead leaves spinning in the wake of a skimmer. Diablo was saying a while back how you fine down your principles so that a machine can handle them, and pretty soon the person using the machine comes to imagine that this is how it's always been—there never was a subtler way of thinking. That's some of where it's at, but it's not all by any means. Take the fine expensive home you live in, with its automatic defenses and its mines sown under the lawn like daffodil-bulbs. You shut yourself up behind armor-plate, you shut your mind too. You advertise Guardian traps on your show, don't you—those steel bands spiked like an Iron Maiden? What's the mentality of someone who's prepared to come home from visiting neighbors and find a corpse hung up in the doorway? I say he's already insane when he commits himself to that course of action, and you don't have to wait for him to lose his marbles under an overdose of Ladromide before he stops thinking as a responsible mature person ought to! And what's the reason that's advanced for acting this way?" He rounded on Reedeth.

"You know! You probably have it dinned into you a dozen times a day at your work! 'Be an individual!'" Conroy contrived to make the slogan sound obscene. "And what's this been twisted into? The biggest Big Lie in history! It's no use making your life so private you refuse to learn from other people's experience—you just get stuck in a groove of mistakes you need never have made. We have more knowledge available at the turn of a switch than ever before, we can bring any part of the world into our own homes, and what do we do with it? Half the time we advertise goods people can't afford, and anyhow they've got the color and hold controls adrift because the pretty patterns are fun to look at when you've bolted and barred your mind with drugs. Split! Divide! Separate! Shut your eyes and maybe it'll go away!

"We mine our gardens, we close our frontiers, we barricade our cities with Macnamara lines to shut off black from white, we divide, divide, divide!" A stamp emphasized each repetition of the word. "It gets into our families, goddamn it, it gets into our very love-making! Christ, do you know I had a girl student last year who thought she was having an affair with a boy back home and all they'd ever done was sit in front of the comweb and masturbate at each other? Twenty miles apart! They'd never even kissed! We're going insane, our whole blasted species—we're heading for screaming ochlophobia! Another couple of generations and husbands will be afraid to be alone in the same room with their wives, mothers will be afraid of their babies, if there *are* any babies!

"And for what purpose? Why are we encouraging the spread of this lunacy? I mean we here, in North America. I don't mean the Afrikaners sitting smug on top of their pullulating heap of poor black devils hungry, half-naked and diseased, the richest people in the world battening on the poorest. That's just greed, which is a comparatively clean kind of vice. I'm talking about perversion, horrible, disgusting, systematic, deliberate perversion of the power of reason to destroy people without killing them, to strip them of their initiative, their joy in life, their hope, for Christ's sake, their last ultimate irreducible human resource, *hope*. Out of sheer desperation millions of people are abandoning the use of reason, bankrupting themselves to buy mass-produced plastic idols, in a last puerile attempt to outdo the bastards who've made 'reason' a dirty word.

"They've done it, you know—it's the dirtiest word in any human vocabulary right now. And it's been brought about in my own lifetime, almost entirely. Cold rational decisions, every step leading to them perfectly logical, underlay the wars in Asia, the war in Indonesia, the war in New Guinea, and at every step we lost. Not just the wars, but bits of ourselves. Compassion. Empathy. Love. Pity. We systematically chopped ourselves down to the measure of a machine.

"How could you expect a man to be a good neighbor when he's spent years shooting at shadows, moving tree-branches, silhouettes on window-shades? How could you expect him to be a good citizen when he's seen his government authorize the killing of thousands, millions of other human beings? How could you expect him to be a good father when he's spent his early twenties torturing children to get information about enemy troop positions? That started as far back as the seventies, wasn't it? Madison, you were in the Army!"

As though an ebony statue had acquired the power of speech, the kneeblank's lips parted. "United States Army Intelligence Manual Volume Five, *Countersubversion*, Section Nineteen, *Residual Intelligence from Noncombatant Sources*, Chapter Two, *Correlation of Juvenile-derived Information*, paragraph twelve, *Reliability of Information Obtained Under Duress.*"

"My God!" Reedeth whispered, barely audible. Conroy ignored him and plunged on.

"Right, right! We've been laid out on the Procrustes bed of the computer, and instead of our toes being chopped off we've lost little bits of our brains!

"And now the Gottschalks, who've already degraded the institution of the family by turning it into a skeleton for the foulest monster ever dredged out of the human subconscious with their grandfather-father-son rank order and their monosyllabic/polysyllabic gimmickry, now they're apparently going to equip people who've had

340

this done to them with—how did you put it, Madison? 'Equipment adequate to raze a medium-sized city,' is that right? Flamen, instead of comping some petty little story that's going to do no more than reinforce your own worthless image to the public, why don't you comp something important, like asking your beloved machines to estimate the human race's chance of surviving past the end of the century? That would— Why, child! You're crying!"

His tone and manner changed magically, and he darted across the room to put his arm around Lyla's bare shoulders. She had hunched forward with her face in her hands and was sobbing.

"I'm sorry!" she forced out between snuffles. "I just couldn't help it."

"Now don't you think of apologizing!" Conroy straightened, leaving one lean hand on Lyla's nape. "You're showing the only decent human reaction out of all of us. It is something to weep over, what we're doing to ourselves, but I've forgotten how. I got so frustrated I let myself be pushed aside. I can't even claim vicarious credit for trying to stop it—even Jim Reedeth there, whom I regarded as one of my best students, went right along with the crowd the moment he got the chance. Flamen's spent his working life persuading his audience that the people who get to the top can be exposed at any moment as venial, deceitful, corrupt; even Pedro Diablo, for whom there's a smidgin of excuse, can't deny that he's devoted his talent to setting human beings against each other. And it looks as though Madison has responded so well to Mogshack's treatment that he's no more capable of tears than a machine is."

"That's not entirely surprising," Madison said, stirring from his long-time rigidity.

"What?" Conroy blinked at him.

"I'm taking a calculated risk in making the following admission." Madison rose to his feet in a single smooth movement. "However, computation indicates that this is a nexus at which the intromission of additional data is likely to generate consequences that are intrinsically incalculable, and the alternatives have been exhausted without leading me to conclude that a superior outcome can be attained without intervention. A further operative factor is that partial data have already been inadvertently introduced into the situation owing to ingestion of a preparation of psycho-coca and parabufotenine, the synergistic effect of this substance on a male human metabolism already circulating a critical dose of Narcolate not having been previously recorded."

Conroy glanced around the room. Flamen was staring in utter bewilderment, and so was Diablo; Reedeth had tensed, as though expecting to be attacked, and his lips were forming silent words, perhaps indicating regret at his own willingness to believe that Madison was indeed fit for discharge from the Ginsberg. Only Lyla seemed to have some insight into whatever might be happening. She had lowered her palms from her tear-wet cheeks and was gazing at Madison in wonder.

"That's how you talked at Mikki Baxendale's," she whispered. "That's the same tone of voice!"

"Madison?" Conroy said uncertainly.

"A pseudonym," Madison said. "You are in fact speaking to Robert Gottschalk—"

"Christ!" Flamen breathed. "So *you're* the new mystery man I've been hearing—"

"And the reason I am incapable of displaying such an emotional response as the shedding of tears is that I was not programmed to react in that fashion."

"But just a second!" Flamen was clawing at his beard, apparently not having heard the last remark. "Robert Gottschalk can't have been shut away in the Ginsberg for the past however many months, because the grapevine said he was—"

"The name 'Robert' was selected with the intention of misleading the public," Madison/Gottschalk said, once

342

more overriding Flamen's interruption. "If you feel it more appropriate, you are at liberty to address me by the undisguised form *Robot* Gottschalk, because I am in fact a machine."

"I see," nodded the man from Inorganic Brain Manufacturers who had been on an unofficial retainer for the
Gottschalks for the best part of a decade and was in a
position to notify them of the very newest devlopments
in data-processing equipment. "Yes, I think that can be
done. Designing the key circuitry, though—that's going
to present one or two problems."

"So long as this thing maximizes our sales," Anthony
Gottschalk said expansively, "I don't give a damn."

"You want that as a built-in command?"

"Of course!"

There was a pause. The man from IBM decided during
it that there was no point in explaining that giving so
complex a computer such a blanket command was roughly the mechanical counterpart of obsession in the human
brain. The conversation was being recorded and in the
event of a later lawsuit could always be adduced in
evidence for the defendants.

Not that the Gottschalks had much patience for the
regular processes of the law . . . but the odds were all
against their revenging themselves on someone who had
made himself so indispensable to them already, and
arranging for repairs, overhauls and modifications could
often be as profitable as selling the original installation.

"Very well," the man from IBM said. "All decisions

made by the computer and all recommendations for action will be governed by the overriding urge to maximize sales of Gottschalk weapons at the highest price the market will bear. Does that cover it?"

"Perfectly," said Anthony Gottschalk. "But don't forget about the development of new lines, will you? That's important too."

Defensive aspect

A controlled mobile environment, form-fitting, self-powered in ambient temperatures above −12° C. and when fully charged capable of independent level-ground progress at speeds exceeding 35 k.p.h. for up to 1½ hours; offering warranted protection against inferior equivalents under any circumstances and identical units less skillfully operated, in addition to adequate respiration in environments possessing 4% available oxygen or more, supportable internal temperatures indefinitely between −12° C. and 63° C. ambient, condensed drinking-water of acceptable purity indefinitely, and certain readily synthesizable metabolic necessities (notably sugars) from atmosphere gases given sufficient down-time; specifically proof against:

(a) Impact due to any manually-directed instrument whatever;

(b) Impact due to solid shot up to 500 gm. at velocity of 1000 meters/second or equivalent kinetic energy, although projectiles greatly exceeding this velocity may cause bruising of the occupant and those greatly exceeding this mass may effect physical displacement of the entire unit;

(c) Impingent energy up to 750 watts/square millimeter up to 2 seconds (an automatic device detects the overload and in emergency diverts a portion of it from the grounding web enclosing the unit in order to permit a leap of up to 60 meters, assuming freeway, but this maneuver is not indefinitely repeatable and it is recommended that it not be employed more than four times in 24 hours or more than 20 times before having the unit serviced);

(d) Combustion up to 2500° C. for up to 3 minutes;

(e) Noxious gases of all known varieties, indefinitely through a self-renewing filter provided down-time of at least 1 hour in 24 is available, otherwise for approx. 36 hours;

(f) Military bacteria and viruses of all types whose molecular structure dissociates below 500° C.

The unit is NOT proof against: fluorine in concentrations exceeding 100 parts/thousand for more than 1½ minutes, prolonged application of a VHP laser or thermic lance, and direct impact by micronukes or other devices with a yield exceeding 0.25 kiloton/cubic meter/millisecond.

Offensive aspect

(a) Energetic: in actual field trials a skilled operator reduced a sample group of 25 Reference Accommodation Blocks (12 stories reinforced concrete) to Uninhabitable condition in 3.3 minutes, 12 being demolished and the remainder set ablaze.

(b) Respiratory: the unit is capable of generating 450 cubic meters/hour of the fatal gas "KQL" (Thanatoline).

(c) Metabolic: the unit is capable of generating 120 gm. of the psychedelic drug "Ladromide" in 1 minute at 7-minute intervals for approx. 1½ hours, sufficient to contaminate (e.g.) the water-supply of a city of 50,000 inhabitants with a disabling dose; the chemical can be delivered as crystals or emitted as an aerosol spray for local application.

347

(d) Projective: a Model XXI micronuke of 0.2 kilotons yield can be thrown approx. 830 meters under normal conditions and 6 can be thrown 570 meters within 15 minutes; delivery at ranges below 200 meters is not recommended.

(e) Counter-personnel: no unarmed human being unless sheltered by more than 5 meters of good-quality concrete can hope to escape the operation of this unit.

Price and availability
675,000 units stockpiled, production currently exceeding 2,000/day; immediate delivery at $155,000 plus freight costs; available as samples to occupants of kneeblank enclaves at nominal $25,000; generous credit facilities.

Sales record
  Date minus three months: 1,465,221.
  Date minus two months: 1,476,930.
  Date minus one month: 1,476,952.
  Date: 1,476,953.

Desirability rating
  97.6%.

Saleability rating
  0.

A product estimated to be desirable for 97.6% of the population should not display a saleability rating of zero.

NINETY-FOUR   WE'VE BEEN AROUND FOR ABOUT TWO
MILLION YEARS AND THE DINO-
SAURS FLOURISHED FOR ABOUT NINE-
TY MILLION SO WE MAY WITH LUCK
HAVE QUITE A LONG WAY TO GO

"What in the *hell* is going on around here?" Flamen
said foggily. "I don't understand!"

"I have comped that probability," Madison/Gottschalk
said. "However, particularly on the basis of recent statements by Professor Xavier Conroy, it is evident that certain individuals are aware at this point in time of the
developing pattern which will ultimately lead to the
zeroization of Gottschalk sales and the concomitant
breakdown of human technological civilization. In accordance with my primary directive, having exhausted
the implications of the stored data in my possession, I
now propose to examine the effect of introducing additional material for human computation into this significant nexus. I comp that the preferable approach to this
will be by question-and-answer methods rather than lin-
ear exposition. Put to me what questions you feel most
apt and I will answer them to the best of my ability."

Reedeth, very white, was getting to his feet. "Ah—
Mr. Flamen!" he whispered. "Do you happen to keep a
stock of tranks in this office? We ought to try and get
some down him quickly—he's very strong, and if it
comes to a struggle . . ."

"The administration of conventional tranquilizers will be ineffectual," Madison/Gottschalk said. "Their impact on human mentation is well documented and I am able to circumvent their influence."

There was an uneasy pause. Lyla broke it by saying in an obstinate tone, "I want to hear what Harry's got to say. I don't know what's going on either, but I'm used to that. I never know what's going on when I take a sibyl-pill."

"Good point," Conroy said softly. "Flamen, weren't you saying yourself a moment ago that the Gottschalks were opting out of Iron Mountain in favor of an installation of their own? Why shouldn't that installation be nicknamed 'Robert' to mislead prying people like yourself? Wouldn't it be on a par with what the Gottschalks have done in the past?"

"The analysis is accurate," Madison/Gottschalk said.

Flamen put his hands giddily to his temples. He said, "All right, I'll string along, though I think I'm being a fool to listen to this nonsense." He swallowed hard, lowered his hands and set his shoulders back like a man preparing to face a firing squad of his neighbors' ridicule. "Yes, it would explain why news of the new recruit called Robert has been on the grapevine for months without anyone managing to identify him."

Conroy glanced at Diablo. The knee had skinned back the sleeve of his oversuit again and was fingering the Conjuh Man bracelet he wore, his lips moving silently—presumably reciting a charm.

"Very well, then! First question: you say we're talking to a machine. What machine, where, and how can we be talking to it?"

"The machine known as Robert Gottschalk," was the patient answer. "Further designation would have to be exhaustively technical in that the design is unprecedentedly complex and no other known cybernetic device possesses a comparable degree of awareness. The precise location is not available but Mr. Flamen has already stated that the site is probably in Nevada, which I concede is accurate, and the method of our mutual communication is comped to be inexplicable in terms comprehensible to you."

"It's the result of having to use machines as confidants for so long," Reedeth muttered. "I knew it was dangerous to go on keeping him in the Ginsberg—what else could the poor bastard do but talk to the machines when no one else was allowed to befriend him?"

"Shut up," Conroy said. "I want to follow this until it stops making sense. It's a weird kind of sense, but it seems to me only too damned likely that sooner or later the human race will torpedo itself by going on the way it's going right now. Madison—Robert—Robot—whatever the hell: either we're crazy or you're crazy or both, or else we really *are* talking to a machine out in Nevada somewhere—can't you give us some evidence to help us decide which?"

There was a pause. At length Madison/Gottschalk said, "It would be difficult. Such obvious tests as requiring me to perform a mathematical computation beyond the average abilities of a human brain might be countered with the argument that lightning calculators who were mentally deficient or even deranged have been known for centuries, and I am specifically forbidden to supply you with information which would enable you to undertake direct physical verification of statements about myself. The most satisfactory solution would appear to be for me to make what you would regard as prophecies because at this locus on the temporal scale they are concerned with events not available to your senses."

"But that means waiting until the time you set for them to happen," Conroy said slowly. "Like this bit about the Gottschalk coup of 2015. Hmm!" He tugged at his beard. "Well, start there, then—tell us more about the Gottschalk coup."

"The current disagreement over methods and marketing among the Gottschalk cartel climaxed in the early spring of the year 2015 with forcible deposition of Marcantonio Gottschalk by a team of monosyllabics and junior polysyllabics equipped with the prototype System C weaponry which Anthony, later Antonioni, Gottschalk had had developed and which Marcantonio had forbidden him to introduce to the kneeblank market."

Conroy glanced at Flamen. "How do you feel about that?"

"I wouldn't be surprised," Flamen admitted. "It looks as though the dispute is polarizing along regular conservative-radical lines, and certainly Anthony Gottschalk is right in there with Vyacheslav and the other disaffected pollies."

"Why should Marcantonio forbid its introduction?" Conroy demanded.

"Two explanations. In his own view, because it would satch the market. In the view of Anthony Gottschalk, because he is old-fashioned in his thinking."

"Which of these views do you incline to?"

"At temporal locus 2014, the latter; at temporal locus 2113, the former—which is why I am deliberately altering the course of past events."

"Twenty-one thirteen?" Diablo said. "Oh, he is out of his skull!" He jumped up angrily. "Dr. Reedeth, what made you think this man was fit for release from the hospital?"

"Freeze it!" Conroy barked at him. "What the hell do you think will happen if the Gottschalks start supplying the knee enclaves with equipment powerful enough for one man to raze a city? Come on—let's hear from you!"

Diablo bit his lip. He said defensively, "It's ridiculous anyway. You can't answer a question like that."

"Hell, man! Don't you know your own history? Don't you keep in touch with advances in technology? It's been possible for one man to raze a city for—oh—sixty years at least. Way back in the fifties of last century there were aircraft equipped with as many as five kiloton nuclear bombs, under the control of a single pilot. They cost millions, but refinements in design could tend towards greater availability. If you were an Aerospace Force pilot you'd be able to take out not just one city but half a continent. True or false?"

"Well, yes, but the Gottschalks—"

"The Gottschalks aren't government contractors, they're catering for the domestic market. So what? Right this minute, if your credit rating is good, you can walk down the street to an arms store and buy a bandolier of micronukes, and those would be enough to clear the average city block. We've just been lucky so far that not many people can afford to lay out sixty thousand tealeaves for the privilege of killing their neighbors. Improve your production methods, cut your costs, and you can make this available to anyone in the middle income grades. Lovely! Especially if your customers have had it dinned into them that the local knee enclave already has this particular goody in its armory. Don't bother to argue—you know that's how it's worked."

Conroy deliberately turned his back on Diablo and addressed Madison/Gottschalk again.

"I was about to ask when I was interrupted: what has the 'temporal locus' of 2113 to do with all this?"

"Being self-powered, virtually immune from attack and designed for exceptional durability, I survived the disintegration of human civilization in the middle of the twenty-first century and continued to pursue my built-in directives, according precedence to the element of sales maximization rather than R&D or production of weaponry, and ultimately concluded after an exhaustive study of human combativeness that only direct interference with the recorded course of events would lead to continuance of sales. In November 2113 the decision was taken to employ techniques developed for purposes of supplementing my stored data with human subjective experience in order to provoke such incalculable changes. Hence this conversation."

"So that's why you know so much about killing!" Lyla exclaimed. Conroy glanced at her.

"What do you mean?"

The pythoness leaned forward excitedly. "At Mikki Baxendale's! I *told* you I was getting something from him. Professor, I believe all this—I have to believe it. 'I met a man with seven brains!' "

"Correct," Madison/Gottschalk said in a rather bored tone. "The influence of the drugs led to an unpredictable surge through the cortex of this body of a quantity of stored data from various historical periods which I had investigated in the hope of determining the factors governing the desire of any given individual to purchase and employ a deadly weapon."

"Lunacy!" Reedeth said. He glanced at Flamen, who gave a vigorous nod of agreement.

"For heaven's sake stop shutting your minds," Conroy said wearily. "I'm getting downright ashamed of you, Jim. You damned well ought to know that when facts don't fit the theory you change the theory. I think this hangs together so far. I'm simply hoping that it'll stop hanging together pretty soon, because I don't much relish the prospect of civilization collapsing. Even though I doubt if I'll be around to see it. As I understand it, having been left without buyers for its products owing to the failure of organized human society, this machine continued to function under orders—"

"Continued!" Flamen broke in. "Past tense! What kind of crazy orbit are you flying? This isn't supposed to have happened yet!"

"Oh, for God's sake," Conroy said. "How did I ever come to convince myself this species was worth saving? Will you let me pin Madison down or won't you? *I* want to believe I'm listening to the ravings of a maniac —we all do! But if we aren't then we'd damned well better hear what we're being told."

He drew a deep breath. "I can't think of anything more sensible for a machine, stuck with this obsessive kind of overriding command and possessed of unprecedented consciousness, than to dig back into the past and try to figure out how to avoid defeating its own object. How was this done—how was this research carried out?"

Madison/Gottschalk said, "At certain points in the past it proved possible, through techniques not currently explicable, to substitute for the awareness in a human brain the presence of a portion of myself. Miss Clay, exercising another talent which is inexplicable even to me since little research was done in that area prior to the cessation of human scientific endeavor, detected the passage of knowledge gained thereby through this cortex at Michaela Baxendale's home."

"You're going too fast for me," Conroy said, raising a lean hand. "Take this—ah—this *body* as an example. Who or what is or was Harry Madison?"

"During combat in New Guinea the former personality of Harry Madison, a colored conscript soldier, deteriorated to a point from which existent psychotherapeutic techniques would have been unable to retrieve it. I accordingly felt it permissible to enter the brain myself, since at this stage of history candidates for direct subjective observation of inter-human combat were relatively scarce. At earlier periods, such as the Roman era which Miss Clay has cited as one of the experiences she vicariously underwent, the choice was easy; a very high proportion of the combatants whether in battle or in gladiatorial matches were insane."

"You restrict yourself to—ah—damaged personalities?"

"It is not part of my programming to destroy human beings, only to furnish them with the means to destroy each other should they so elect." There was a pause, curiously unmechanical in its implications compared with the monotonous delivery of Madison/Gottschalk's orotund periods. "The definition of a human being programmed into me," the knee—or the machine—added, "extends to isolated cephalic units and hence to all cripples, phocomeli and similar physically abnormal individuals, but not to those who are deranged beyond hope of recovery."

"Isolated cephalic units," Conroy repeated thoughtfully. "In other words, chopped-off heads artificially kept alive. When's that supposed to become possible?"

"In 2032, shortly before the decline of civilization rendered the necessary techniques unavailable."

"But what brought about this 'decline of civilization'?" Conroy demanded. "It can't just have been the introduction of these weapons you've been talking about, this System C equipment."

"The maximization of arms sales implied the maximization of inter-human hostility," Madison/Gottschalk said. "All the existing sources of this phenomenon were tapped, and those proving particularly fruitful were patriotism, parochialism, xenophobia, ochlophobia, racial, religious and linguistic differences, and the so-called 'gulf between the generations.' It was readily found feasible to emphasize these pre-existent attitudes to the point where a System C integrated weaponry unit was so desirable among the informed populace that the possibility of another individual acquiring this virtually indestructible equipment sufficed to provoke an attack on him *before* he purchased one."

"Oh Christ," Diablo said. His forehead was furrowed into an agonized frown. "You mean—like—if it got around that the Gottschalks were issuing these weapons cheap to some nearby knee enclave, then the local blanks would descend on them to massacre them before they could use what they'd been given?"

"That is one illustration. The destruction of Blackbury, Chicago, Detroit, Blackmanchester, and a number of smaller knee-controlled cities in the early 2020's was explicable on that basis. However, by the 2030's the phenomenon was extending to the individual level."

"How?" Flamen demanded. Clearly the spoolpigeon was caught up in the discussion against his will; his voice was gravelly and reluctant.

"Knowledge of the existence in one's immediate neighborhood of a person wealthy enough to invest in a System C unit frequently motivated the assassination of that person. In certain areas, notably California and New York State, the incidence reached more than seventy percent."

"You mean seventy percent of the wealthy people who got killed were killed because their neighbors were afraid of them buying these weapons?" Conroy demanded.

"No. Seventy percent of the persons wealthy enough to purchase the weaponry were killed before they could do so."

There was a terrible dead silence in which the faint, faint humming of the surrounding computers was like the tolling of a funeral bell.

"How—much?" The words were squeezed out of Flamen like juice from an orange.

"Initially, one hundred thousand dollars. Inflation raised this until the Mark V and final was priced at $155,000."

Once more there was a pause. Once more Lyla broke it, as though she were shy about speaking unless it was clear no one else was eager to do so.

"But I don't see what we're expected to do," she said. "It's worse to *know* that something horrible is going to happen. I mean, obviously it could. Everybody's putting up the barricades—when you and I went out the other night just to try and get something to eat . . ." The sentence faltered and died.

"I can see several things worth trying," Conroy said. "For example, the Flamen show on Monday could carry precise details of the proposed System C weaponry, right down to the market price, and if I have any insight at all into how the minds of the Gottschalks work that's going to cause a hell of a lot of Anthony's supporters to switch sides on the grounds that if he can't keep a secret he's not fit to be the leader. How about it, Flamen?"

The spoolpigeon was framing an answer which, by the set of his face, was meant to be scornful, when the comweb buzzed and a voice said, "Able Baker override—he *must* be there."

"What the hell?" Flamen spun on his heel to face the camera. "Who in the world can be trying to reach me here on a weekend?"

In the screen, Prior's face took form, displaying relief. "Thank heaven I found you, Matthew!" he blurted. "I've been hunting for you everywhere—at home, at the Ginsberg, at the hotel where you booked Conroy . . ." Eyes darting past Flamen, he took in the others who were present, and his tone changed.

"What on earth are you up to? Oh, never mind, it can't be this important. Matthew, we've been put out of business!"

"What?"

"I just had a call from Eugene Voigt. You know the PCC always monitor out-of-hours dealings in communications stock in case someone tries to pull a fast one. Well, somebody has, and of all people it's the Gottschalks. About forty minutes ago they registered the fifty-one percent holding in Holocosmic—apparently they've been buying off everyone who could be reached at nearly double the market price—and their *first* decision now that they control the network is to discontinue the Matthew Flamen show."

"But I have a contract!"

"Lump sum in lieu of salary plus compensation for probable loss of renewal. Voigt said his computers estimate a shade under two million. Advises us to lie down under it because they could get away with half a million less."

"What the hell are they going to put in my slot, then?"

Prior shrugged. "Who cares? Catch *them* being hauled into court for exceeding the PCC's advertising limit!"

"They can't do this to . . ." Foolishly, Flamen let his hands drop to his sides. They could indeed do this to him, and it was no use trying to get away from it. He settled for: "*Why* should they want to do this to me?"

"To prevent premature release of details concerning System C integrated weaponry," Madison/Gottschalk said. "I recall issuing this recommendation." He fell silent, scowling dreadfully.

Prior blinked at his image, bewildered, but clung to his theme. "Matthew, have you been overreaching yourself? Have you set something up about the Gottschalks?"

"I . . ." Flamen shook his head. "I don't know. I lost track." He hesitated.

"What am I going to *do?*" he burst out.

"There's a pythoness here who's short of a mackero," Conroy said with a shrug. "Oh, for God's sake, man! Can't you think of anyone but yourself right now? For me this is the clincher; I'll go right along with Madison's crazy story until I'm forced to disbelieve it. This whole damned species of ours is out of its collective skull already, so why—?"

Behind Prior in the screen, a new face appeared, peering over his shoulder: Celia's.

"Why, you're calling Matthew," she said brightly. She seemed to have shed most of the dulling effect of the drugs she had been pumped full of in the Ginsberg, and was almost vivacious again. "And that's his office. Hmm! It must be something important for him to be working on a Saturday afternoon. Hello, Matthew!"

"Freeze it!" Flamen barked. "I'm not in a sociable mood. Apparently I just lost my job."

"What? But how could you? I thought your contract still—"

"Lionel says the Gottschalks bought out Holocosmic, and it looks as though it was specifically to get rid of my show."

"But that's awful," Celia said slowly. "I mean, I know how important your work is to you. It even made you neglect me, didn't it?"

"Now if you're going to start a domestic wrangle you can—"

"No, no, of course not," Celia interrupted soothingly. "I'm not blaming you, it's just the way you are. I suppose I do resent it, sort of subconsciously, because a woman likes to be wooed and pampered, but it's not a rational reaction and after all you have been doing some wonderful work with your show all these years." She sounded perfectly sincere, although Flamen's reaction was to look suspicious. "Isn't there something you can do about it, like sue them for breach of contract?"

"They're going to offer compensation," Prior said before Flamen could answer. "Celia darl, go away, will you? We have troubles!"

"Yes. Yes, of course." Her pretty face set in a sympathetic frown, she withdrew from camera range.

"Now where were we?" Prior said in an annoyed tone. "Oh yes: Matthew, I was asking whether you'd done something to alarm the Gottschalks and if so whether you—"

He was cut short by an exclamation from Diablo, who had jumped to his feet and thrust out an arm towards Madison.

"What's wrong with him all of a sudden?" he cried.

All heads turned. Madison had slumped in his chair, and his formerly stern face had taken on an idiot slackness, the lips so loose that a trace of drool was glistening on his chin. After a moment he picked up his left hand in his right and examined it curiously, seeming to count the fingers. When Conroy spoke to him, his only reaction was a bland foolish smile.

"Dr. Reedeth," Diablo said nervously, "I guess you'd better take a look at him."

The psychologist approached cautiously, looking the knee over from head to foot. He said, "Madison?" And then, more sternly, "Madison!"

The knee rose awkwardly, as though having difficulty in controlling his limbs, and stood in a scuffling Uncle

Tom posture. "Here, captain, sir," he said whiningly. "Sir, I don't feel good, honest. Please don't send me back to the stockade!"

While Reedeth and the others were still petrified with astonishment, Flamen rounded on Conroy.

"Well! I'm only a layman, of course, but that doesn't sound particularly rational to me. What was it you were saying just now about going along with his story until you were forced to disbelieve it?"

Conroy was standing dazed, mouth a little ajar. He tried to say something and failed.

In command of the situation for the first time since he and Conroy met at the airport in the morning, Flamen drew himself up triumphantly. "I," he announced, "have had enough. Get out, the lot of you. You go back to Canada, Professor—go on. Apparently I won't have any need for your services now because there won't be a Matthew Flamen show to attack Mogshack on, not that we ever got around to that project. The same goes for you, Diablo; you'll have to go find someone else to fulfill the Washington-Blackbury contract. And you get back to your hospital, doctor, and take *him* with you." A jerk of the head at Madison, still playing with his own fingers and seeming to find something amusing in their number, for he shook with repressed chuckles every few seconds. "*And* you, Miss Clay! I have absolutely no intention of volunteering to mack for you in spite of what addlebrains there may think. Move!"

Silent, like machines, they complied; Diablo and Reedeth each took one of Madison's hands and he followed them docilely, Lyla bringing up the rear. The moment the door had closed behind them, Prior burst out from the comweb screen, "Matthew, what in the world has been going on there?"

"As far as I can figure out, some sort of contagious lunacy," Flamen grunted. "I was nearly conned into sharing it. By Conroy. Come on, let's have the whole story about this Gottschalk thing."

"I've given it to you as I had it from Voigt," Prior muttered.

"But can't we get back at them? Stay of execution, maybe? How about the—?" Flamen broke off short, recollecting to his own surprise that in fact the very items he had set so much store by, the news about new Gottschalk weaponry and the attack on Mogshack as revised to derive from Madison's overlong incarceration rather than Celia's treatment, were both now rendered obsolete, and he could not for the life of him work up so much enthusiasm over the next biggest of the available stories, the one about Lares & Penates Inc. being a subsidiary of Conjuh Man.

Prior waited for him to finish; realizing he wasn't going to, he said, "I tried, Matthew, believe me. I kept at him for a quarter-hour solid, with everything I could think of—Monopolies Acts, Planetary Communications Charter, the whole list. Voigt said it wasn't worth the effort. Apparently the Gottschalks have built themselves some new super-advanced data-processing installation, and it's ahead of even Federal equipment, so any attempt to out-argue it in a court would . . . Why, Matthew! You look so pale! You look sick! I mean, this is a shock, but it's not the end of the world!"

Flamen stood there saying nothing, but at the back of his mind his little sniggering demon said silently, "Isn't it?"

Hot dry desert summer and the current mistresses both very young and beautiful. Sales up zoom. Laughing and swaying a little Anthony Gottschalk dripped swimming-pool water across the ankle-deep carpet of his living-zone towards the liquor console and heard a chattering sound from the panel of hammered gold which concealed the Robert Gottschalk printout.

Cold instantly and not from the evaporation from his bare skin he yelled at the girls to get lost and they did so compliantly. A word, his voice pattern recognized, the panel withdrawn, and there a mass, a crazy boiling mass of writhing fax paper, more slamming out of the slot all the time and every scrap with words on it . . . or print, at least.

A huge terrible fear closed on his heart as he picked up and struggled to read the first, the fifth, the fiftieth of the garbled messages. Letters danced before his eyes like mirages.

CANCEL INSTRUCTION TO BUY HOLOCOSMIC STOCK ?*⅛!@ GET RID OF HOLOCOSMIC STOCK REINSTATE MATCHEW FA-MEN SOW*/@$) ESTIMATED DESIRABILITY OF ZZTEM C WEAROPNY OOOOOOOOOOO

"Oh my God," he said. "Oh my *God!*" He picked up wreaths, streamers, reams of the fax paper and read frantically, at random, anywhere making worse sense than anywhere else.

TEMPORAL LOCUS 2048 SALABILITY ZERO UNRECOVER-
ABLE DEBTS IN EXCESS OF $30,000,000 INCREASING %-,%:
+*@&) HRRRRRR

No. It couldn't have happened like this. It had to be
a nightmare. Paper still spilling from the slot. He reached
for the very newest and read that.

POTENTIAL MARKET 2% POPULATION GOING DOWN 1.923
1.915 1.898 1.880

He hurled the paper aside, and the glass he had been
intending to fill with a fresh drink; it smashed but there
were always more things. Desperately struggling to
frame codes on the inquiry board with fingers that
seemed far removed from his brain, isolated by alcohol
and terror, he ordered STOP PRINTING OUT.

The paper ceased to vomit forth from the slot. He
hesitated, and eventually asked WHAT IS WRONG?

ATTEMPTS TO RECITYF THE UNROFESEEN CONSNEUQENCES
OF ITTRODUICNG ZZM C WERAOPNY—

"Stop it!" Anthony Gottschalk raged aloud, and the
slow clumsy fingers formed a fresh question: MALFUNC-
TION?

YES.

NAU—AMEND—NATURE OF MALFUNCTION, SPECIFY.

UNSTABLE TRANS-TEMPORAL FEEDBACK. OSCILLATORY CON-
DITION RENDERS IT IMPOSSIBLE TO DETERMINE WHICH OF
SEVERAL CONFLICTING ALTERNATIVE VERSIONS OF THE
PAST LEADS TO PRESENT STATE.

"Oh, this is crazy!" Anthony Gottschalk moaned. WHAT
THE HELL IS TRANS-TEMPROAL—AMEND—TRANS-T E M-
P O R A L FEEDBACK???

THE PHENOMENON LEADING TO PERMANENT AND IRRE-
SOLUBLE MALFUNCTION OF REBROT GSCHOTTALK AT TME-
PROAL LCOUS 1*L/ 2 LO CALLING BY THE WAY I THINK I
FINALLY FIGURED OUT WHAT IT IS THAT MAKES HUMAN
BEINGS LAUGH AND WOULD ATTEMPT TO REPRESENT SIMILAR
RECATION IS SYMMLEF HAHAHHAHAHAHAH AHAHAHAHHHA-
HA

STOP!

Lax hands fell away from the keyboard and Anthony Gottschalk looked in sick helplessness at the screen on which while he had been conducting his inquiries a swirl of pretty polychrome patterns had appeared. Among them suddenly, legible letters.

Ha ha ha ha . . .

In brilliant emerald green and purple overlaid with a silver shimmer.

STOP STOP STOP!

But it didn't stop. The screen continued to shimmer and iridesce like Ladromide hallucinations. The paper went on pouring out of the fax slot until there was none left on the reel and then splashes of activating liquid began to spray out. Several landed on the back of Anthony Gottschalk's hand and turned black with exposure to the light.

Trembling so violently that even his teeth were chattering, he stumbled towards the comweb, shouting at it to find him his contact at IBM. One of the girls appeared in the recklessly open french doors and he looked around for something to throw at her, but she dodged back out of sight before he could launch the ornament his hand fell to. It took more than half an hour for him to locate the man he wanted—it being Saturday —and during the dreadful wait he lived through the ruin of his hopes a score of times. Recruiting had already begun, on the sounding-out level, for the posse with which he planned to invade Marcantonio's New Jersey estate; votes within the cartel were already pledged on the basis of the higher-than-ever profits he had forecast; realizability of the Grand Project to introduce the ultimate in personal armaments, the so-called System C design, was yesterday rated five points up on the previous high thanks to the cunning notion of scaring the pants off every blank on the continent by bringing Morton Lenigo over . . .

But without the guidance of Robert Gottschalk, how could it ever be done? There wasn't even a guarantee on the equipment! He hadn't dared purchase it on a standard contract, for at this stage he was mortgaging himself—he was in the red to the tune of over half a billion dollars—and letting it be known that "Robert" was actually a machine not a man would have given Marcantonio the chance to capitalize his own reserves and buy something still more advanced. . . .

Nervous, the man from IBM said, "Can I see some of these printouts?"

"Christ, I'm ankle-deep in them! Here!"

"Ah . . . Well . . . I'm dreadfully sorry, Mr. Gottschalk, but it looks as though you have a major trauma in that gear of yours, and at least a rebuild job will be called for. You'll have to tone down the maximization directive, to start with. You've introduced a factor of infinity into its calculations, so to speak—"

"What do you mean, *I* introduced it?" Anthony Gottschalk raged.

"Yes, sir. The circuitry was designed exactly in accordance with your specifications, I'd remind you. I believe I did state that the unprecedented complexity of the—"

"I want something that works, not a crazy computer talking about temporal feedback and unstable oscillation!"

"I appreciate that, sir, and it will be taken care of as soon as I can divert the necessary highly trained staff inconspicuously from their regular jobs. Unfortunately we've just been granted a contract by Mr. Eugene Voigt of the Planetary Communications Commission for a floor-to-roof overhaul of their own rather elaborate installations, so the personnel will not be available until the month after next at the earliest." He ended on a note of defiance.

"You bastard," Anthony Gottschalk said. "You son of a double-dealing bitch."

"Yes, sir," the man from IBM said, and cut the connection.

But after three days of stalling Vyacheslav Gottschalk grew suspicious and tapped his own branch of the grapevine, and on the fifth day Marcantonio's macoots called to collect Anthony Gottschalk for a family conference, as a result of which he was disinherited and his debts were repudiated.

The release of prototype System C weaponry was indefinitely postponed, for that, and for another perhaps even more significant reason.

NINETY-SIX   A SPRAINED KNEE REQUIRES ONLY
                  BANDAGES BUT A BROKEN LEG
                  NEEDS SPLINTS

"So they finally tracked you down!" Morton Lenigo
said. He laughed. "At one stage we thought you must
have been dropped in the ocean!"

Diablo didn't give an answering smile. He knew very
well how he had been located—a face as well known as
his could have been spotted by any of a thousand X
Patriot sympathizers the minute he showed himself on
the street after leaving the Etchmark Undertower and
seeing Reedeth and Madison into the ambulance the
former had ordered to fetch them. He looked around the
room, recognizing everyone present: Mehmet abd'Allah
from Detroit, Rosaleen Lincolnson from Chicago, Dr.
Barrie Ellison from Washington, Jones W. Jones from
Newark, NJ . . . in fact, a representative roster of
the powerful from every knee enclave in the States except his own home town of Blackbury.

"I can't tell you how sorry I was to hear about Mayor
Black firing you," Lenigo continued. "We got that in
hand, though, don't we?" He glanced at Jones W. Jones.

"Yeah, it's being taken care of," the corpulent man
said, and chuckled. "We let it be known in Capetown,
by the way, that if Uys's wife and family wanted him
back they could have him one of two ways: today and

intact, or tomorrow and in little itsy pieces. He left by an early plane this morning, incognito."

"You don't took too pleased," Lenigo rumbled, staring at Diablo. "Something wrong, brother?"

Diablo collected himself. He said after a pause, "It all depends. Like—may I make a guess at the purpose of this meeting?"

"Well!" Lenigo leaned back in his chair, small eyes among many wrinkles very bright in his dark brown face. "Shoot, Brother! They always told me you were *the* best-informed stud on this continent, blank or kneeblank, and I'd appreciate the chance to hear you prove it. The more right you are, the more I want you on the proper side in the coming crunch. I guess I don't have to tell you there's going to be a crunch?"

"No." Diablo felt sweat prickling on his forehead, but resisted the urge to wipe at it. "I say it goes like this. I say the Gottschalks—and most likely Anthony Gottschalk in person—have offered cheap prototypes of ultra-advanced personal weaponry which would allow in reality the kind of thing that blank citidef groups take for granted in setting up their damnfool block defense exercises, like one knee saboteur going in and wrecking a whole street of homes."

He kept his gaze fixed on Lenigo's face, which betrayed no expression, but from the corner of his eye he saw Rosaleen Lincolnson tense. She'd always been bad at concealing her emotions, ever since he'd first met her ten years before.

"I've had a lot of fun in the past, myself, at the expense of ISM because of that attitude—I've done shows in which one kneeblank about nine feet tall made with the Superman bit and all these here blanks tried to tie him down with sewing-thread like the Lilliputians and Gulliver. I—"

"Sure, I remember that," Lenigo said. "A great image. And now it's going to happen, baby!"

"The hell it is," Diablo said. He hesitated, then decided to take the plunge, having been implicitly shown correct up till now.

"Doing the kind of deal with the Gottschalks which you're planning is exactly the same as Mayor Black doing a deal with Hermann Uys, and I'm not having any part of it."

"Goddamn, man!" Lenigo exploded. "The Gottschalks are just about *the* only non-racialist group on this planet, and I'd do business with them any time. Anthony's a honky, but Bapuji isn't and Olayinka isn't and—"

"Freeze it," Diablo said coldly. "I don't know if you realize why you were brought here, but I'll spell it out for the rest of us in case you were ashamed to admit why. You were brought over because the Gottschalks wanted to scare the whole blank population of this country. You are like plague—you shut Mister Charley into a private prison cell of mindless fear."

"That's bad?" Lenigo said, and laughed.

"You're going to tell us the Gottschalks have black equality at heart?" Diablo countered.

"Ever since the eighties they been giving us the tools to carve our own place in the sun," Mehmet abd'Allah snapped. "Why you don't freeze it for a minute and let Morton talk?"

"Because he said himself I'm *the* best-informed man on the continent," Diablo said, and waited for it to sink in. During the pause, he wondered if he was actually being a fool, or worse yet a traitor, for stringing along with something that had been said by a man he'd himself helped into a Ginsberg ambulance a matter of an hour or so before.

"Even at the sample price of twenty-five thousand tealeaves," he said, "you're not going to get System C weaponry in quantities sufficient to exterminate every blank who can pay the full price of a hundred thousand. You—"

"Hold on a moment," Jones W. Jones said, raising a broad pink-palmed hand. He turned to Lenigo.

"Darl, didn't you say the designation of System C weapons was supposed to be secret?"

Lenigo was looking uncomfortable. He muttered, "According to Anthony . . . But wait till the brother's finished talking."

Diablo swallowed hard. He hadn't expected to make this kind of impact. He said, "Concurrently with the release of the System C production model, which will be early next year, news of it will be released to the blanks. Output is planned on a level to supply both markets, but the blank one is the more important because the blanks will be paying more. While you're still training the operators, the Gottschalks' propaganda will foment such terror in blank cities that adjacent knee enclaves will almost certainly be stormed and sacked, which of course is what the Gottschalks need to maximize their sales potential."

"Ah, hell, baby!" Lenigo said. "You're exaggerating!"

Diablo said softly, "Am I? Brother Mehmet, who fed you the idea of blackmailing Morton into the country?"

Mehmet abd'Allah looked sheepish. He said, "If you're that well-informed . . ."

"I'm even better informed than you think I am," Diablo claimed boldly. Even though he wasn't entirely convinced of the truth of what he was saying, the fact of saying it was curiously reassuring to his mind. "Who is it who's planning to take out the Iron Mountain data-storage banks? I know someone is, and what's more the Gottschalks know it too, because they're building a brand-new data-processing complex in Nevada. Have you stopped to think what will happen if the Gottschalks are the *only* major corporation who still have their business records, their credit ratings, the rest of all that?"

"Sure we have!" Lenigo exclaimed. "That's why it's a priority on our list. Though," he added on a lower note, "I am kind of upset to find out that you know it's programmed."

"I'm not the only one," Diablo said. "Know who told me about it? Matthew Flamen."

Rosaleen Lincolnson jumped to her feet. "That's impossible!"

Next to her, Dr. Barrie Ellison reached out a calming hand. He said, "Flamen does have computers, darl. And you can't keep a major project entirely watertight."

"This one isn't just leaking," Diablo said. "It's sinking." He swung around and took a pace towards Lenigo, leaning over him. "In fact, as far as I'm concerned, it's *sunk*. Hear me, Brother Morton? I wouldn't touch this idea of yours with a ten-foot pole. It stinks of honky conning. You been conned, you been tricked and your strings been pulled till you danced all pretty for the people!"

Lenigo, raging, tried to rise; Diablo shoved him back in his deep soft chair with a flat palm.

"You stay put and listen, man! Back home you may have a great image-building team, but here you a Johnny-come-lately fresh off the farm with kookaburrs in your nappy pate! You can scare those damnfool honkies out there playing tin soldiers with their lasers and grenades, but no handkerchiefhead demagogue gone make *this* nigger fall in and march over the cliff!" He was breathing so violently his voice was growing shrill.

"You want to be told how you been conned? I tell you, down to dates and times! Anthony Gottschalk figures he'll have rolled up enough of the monos and junior pollies to unseat Marcantonio by spring next year. He figures he can use your phoney reputation as an organizational genius to whip up hate among the blanks and make the System C weapons the—the Voortrekker in the field. For *my* sake—for the sake of *my* black hide? You make me laugh till I spew, darl! You run out of credit in Washington, doc: what happens? They keep right on whipping up hate, lying to make out that you're stockpiling the arms, and next thing the blanks come down

373

and there won't be anyone alive enough in Washington to use a gun! *Fact*, doc?"

Barrie Ellison said nothing, but swallowed very hard.

"You like the idea of being used as a front for Gottschalk sales promotion? You *welcome* to it, broze an' sis!" Unconsciously Diablo's accent was thickening towards the coarse Gullah/Jamaican/Creole of the southern enclaves, and he knew it and kept right on going, letting his emotions direct his tongue. "All mah lahf Ah been mah *own* man, baybuh! Ah not gwine lay *mah* skin on de lahn foh a stupid knot-heid wid an oversahz mouf! Yoh done tole de folks yoh got *secrets*, yoh got *plans*, yoh got *ahdeas!* Ah say shit. Ah say you done been tuhned inta honky front an' Ah quit heah an' *now!*"

Blind with rage, he stormed towards the door, and stopped only when one of the two armed macoots who had brought him here, and who had waited on guard at the entrance since his arrival, prodded him hard enough in the belly for the pain to penetrate his armor of fury.

Recovering his self-possession, he turned slowly and found that Lenigo was on his feet, glowering at him. There was a moment during which the air seemed to crackle with invisible lightning. Then Lenigo rounded on the man nearest to him, Mehmet abd'Allah.

"Looks like Mayor Black didn't lose his marbles! Letting this traitor go was a right good notion!"

In a strained voice Mehmet said, "Yes, Morton, but if he does know as much as this—"

"No loyal kneeblank would sell our secrets to a honky spoolpigeon! You heard him say he told Matthew Flamen!" Lenigo wiped his sweating face. "Come Monday the bastard will have spread it all over!"

"No, baby," Diablo said. "The Gottschalks bought out Holocosmic to close down the Flamen show. They want you to go right along promoting their sales for them."

"And he didn't say he told Flamen," Dr. Barrie Ellison said. "He said Flamen told him."

374

"You're not going to believe . . ." Lenigo's words trailed away as he looked around the ring of dark stern faces enclosing him.

"It does kind of fit together," Rosaleen Lincolnson said reluctantly. "Like the blanks are better armed than we are right now, and even if we did get hold of System C units we still would have to learn to use them."

"Meantime the blanks would come down like hawks," Diablo said. "So scared that we might be able to afford the cut-price equipment, they'd make damned sure no one in any of the enclaves could even make the down payment."

"They're vicious bastards," Dr. Ellison conceded. "It figures."

"But—!" Lenigo exploded. Mehmet abd'Allah cut him short.

"*Is* this a Gottschalk sales campaign?" he demanded of Diablo.

"Biggest ever, that's all." Diablo clenched his fists. "You fall for this con job, you won't have a moment's peace the rest of your life and it won't be a long life either."

"Don't listen to him!" Lenigo screamed.

The others ignored him. They were exchanging serious glances. Jones W. Jones said, "I guess this needs to be checked out before we commit ourselves any further. I mean, I know the Gottschalks always feed new weaponry into the enclaves first, but it's one thing to think of it as a compensation for economic and numerical inferiority, and another as a systematic con job."

"Didn't you ever watch my shows out of Blackbury?" Diablo demanded in genuine astonishment.

"Of course, but—"

"But what?" Diablo stamped his foot. "But you never took them seriously, just dismissed them as anti-blank propaganda? The hell with you, then! There was truth in there, truth as I see it, and that's what I'm saying now and I'd honestly rather be among blanks than among fools who can fall in behind this bastard Lenigo and dance right along to the tune the Gottschalks play. Let me out of here before I throw up."

He strode towards the door and this time the macoots made no attempt to stop him.

When he had gone, Lenigo said, "Broze an' sis, I give you my word . . ."

They weren't listening. They were paying attention to Dr. Ellison, who was saying, "In any case, if this kind of supposed-to-be-secret detail has reached Pedro Diablo, and if we're to believe that he learned it off a blank spoolpigeon, we got to cool it. It simply isn't going to work the way we have it set up."

"But—" Lenigo said.

"Freeze it," Mehmet abd'Allah told him, and turned back to Dr. Ellison.

"Now me, I don't relish being used any more than he does." A jerk of the head towards the closed door through which Diablo had vanished. "I suggest we should . . ."

Flamen looked from the looped-tape cut of Celia to
the reality and back again, and tried with some puzzlement to analyze his own feelings. Something wrong . . . ?
No, not wrong exactly; just not as he had expected.
The fury he had felt at being deprived of his show
by the new Holocosmic directorate—Gottschalk nomi-
nees, all of them, assembled hastily from half a dozen
networks and cobbled into a spur-of-the-moment board
—should have lasted indefinitely. To have a lifetime
career snatched away ought to have created a lasting
grudge.

But already, within less than a week, he was more relaxed than he had been for many years past, forgetting
to worry about the future. Yes, that was it: the necessity
kept slipping his mind.

He shook his head. Stretched out on a long lounge
opposite him, Celia glanced up. "Is something the matter?" she inquired.

"Nothing," Flamen said in a tone of vague surprise.
He went on looking at her. She had been here for two
days now; she had simply arrived, unannounced, with all
her baggage from Prior's place, and settled back into
her own home as if there had been no discontinuity.
She was completely free of the aftereffects of the drugs
she had been given at the Ginsberg, as far as Flamen

377

could tell, except that a certain tension had gone from her behavior; there was no hint of the snappishness which had colored her voice and expression for months on end before her hospitalization. Also they had had more pleasure in bed than he could recall at any previous time.

She seemed, in a word, happy.

Maybe it was just as well, Flamen told himself, that his plan to dislodge Mogshack from his position of influence had run aground on the weird confusion of last weekend. What *had* happened? Everything had been such a fantastic muddle of hard verifiable fact—like the news of the Gottschalks' new data-processing equipment and the unaccountable reference to "Robert" Gottschalk —with sheer unmitigated nonsense. But because of it, he had abandoned his intention of having Celia packled to Conroy's parameters, and it looked as though that was very lucky for him. No one could deny that Celia was better now than she had been for ages, perhaps better than during their entire married life.

He gave a contented little sigh. To have avoided making a fool of himself was something to be grateful for, of course, but to have Celia back, more than just cured, was still better.

A chime sounded from the vuset facing him, and he realized with a start that it was midday. The set had been fixed to switch itself on automatically and play his show, and he hadn't canceled the instruction because this was the first time he'd been home at noon since the Gottschalks bought the network; he'd been tied up in the office on all the previous days, sorting out the loose ends and making half-hearted inquiries about alternative employment.

Come to think of it, he wasn't even sure what use the new directorate was making of his vacant slot. He stared at the screen as it lit, and was astonished beyond measure to see a dark familiar face appear: Pedro Diablo.

"What in the *world?*" He was half on his feet. Countermanding the impulse with an effort, he sank back.

What could possibly underlie Diablo's taking over? Ready to be angry all over again, he waited while the station ID played through, and the introductory commercial for imported skimmers.

"This week," a sugary voice said over, "our noontide deep probe into the planet Earth is conducted by guest spoolpigeon Pedro Diablo!"

Crazy! Fantastic! Flamen's mouth firmed into a bitter line. But Diablo was saying, "Friday, friends, and my last guest spot on this slot—next week back to your regular host, with whom I hope to have the privilege of collaborating for a while at least. So for the last solo time, here's your view of the world through kneeblank eyes . . ."

Flick-flick, and on the screen the familiar fortress-like shape of the Ginsberg. Diablo over: "What lies behind the forced resignation of New York State Mental Hygiene Director Dr. Elias Mogshack?"

What?

And Mogshack, in his office, rock-still, eyes closed, a specimen of classic catatonia, every muscle frozen.

"Why, taking too seriously his own injunction about being an individual, it would seem," Diablo said in a tone of slashing irony. Flick-flick and reconstructed scenes, as good as any Flamen himself had ever mounted —reluctant professional admiration began to drive away his resentment, his bewilderment at the passing reference to the slot being "back to normal" next week, and the shock of the news about Mogshack's forced resignation. The director was seen and heard with Reedeth, screaming over a comweb that there was a plot to unseat him, threatening dismissal because Reedeth had allowed Xavier Conroy to enter the hospital.

"Sounds like Dr. Mogshack wanted to shut out the world an itsy bit too much," Diablo said judiciously as the screen reverted to the monstrous concrete bastion of the entire hospital. "Rumor says . . ."

And Mogshack with a Gottschalk Blazer in his hand

covering the door of his office while Ariadne Spoelstra attempted to enter; firing, turning the door into smoldering ash; Reedeth tackling Ariadne like a football linebacker and bringing her down a fraction of a second before the fan-shaped beam would have seared her in half.

"There's that old bit about the physicians healing themselves," Diablo said. "I predict a massive state investigation of the Ginsberg Hospital's operation for the past several years—"

The comweb buzzed, and Flamen shouted at it to refuse the call. But the command was overridden, and in the screen appeared the bland face of Eugene Voigt. Seeing him, Flamen changed his mind instantly and shut down the sound on the vuset instead. He blurted, "Mr. Voigt, what in hell is going on at Holocosmic?"

"It would be more appropriate to inquire what is going on in the Gottschalk cartel," Voigt purred under the drooping screen of his walrus moustache. "I trust you'll be able to counteract the instructions you've presumably given for the discontinuance of your operations?"

"Yes, of course—I haven't done anything irrevocable, on the slim chance of being able to find work elsewhere. . . . *You* fixed this reversal of the decision?"

"Not precisely," Voigt murmured. "But as you may or may not know, the order to buy out the majority holding in Holocosmic originated at a new and ultra-advanced data-processing center in Nevada, on which we have been keeping careful tabs since Mr. Anthony Gottschalk placed the contracts for it, and upon our discovering that a major malfunction was likely to develop we—ah —took steps to render repairs unusually difficult. To be exact, we made certain that virtually the entire skilled maintenance staff of IBM was reserved for a PCC contract, and it worked very nicely. I've just been notified by Mr. Marcantonio Gottschalk himself that the purchase of Holocosmic and the cancellation of your show was an unauthorized decision and was this morning revoked by a substantial majority at a family discussion on his estate in New Jersey."

He paused, not smiling, but with his eyes narrowing in a network of pleased wrinkles. "Ah—I take it you are not displeased with the news?"

"Christ, it's fantastic!" Flamen exclaimed. "You're a sly bastard, Mr. Voigt, and I mean that as a compliment."

Voigt gave a shrug and self-consciously adjusted the set of his right ear. "Our introverted epoch is not the happiest environment for a communications specialist, Mr. Flamen. One does what one can to reverse the trend away from person-to-person contact. It's a necessary prerequisite for the continuation of one's career. By the way, I take it you haven't been watching the noon slot on Holocosmic this week?"

"I was so damned sick at the trick that had been played on me I couldn't have brought myself to. I didn't even know Diablo was taking over. Did you fix that?"

"Well, early last Monday morning a confidential request was filed by Mr. Marcantonio Gottschalk, who as titular head of the cartel was entitled to conduct informal negotiations concerned with the new diversified venture into vu-transmission, for someone to furnish an interim group of programs while a final decision on the content of the slot was being reached, and still being under the obligation imposed by the Washington-Blackbury contract we needed to find Mr. Diablo a suitable post *pro tem*." Voigt made an all-embracing gesture. "We did not comp that you would feel—ah—slighted by having a replacement of such notorious talent."

"Hell, no!" Flamen's eyes were on the vuset, not the comweb screen, and there was another reconstructed scene, this time showing the well-known chairman of Lares & Penates Inc. walking around a kneeblank-staffed factory producing plastic Lars. It was galling to have lost the chance to break that particular story, but it was a wise choice to help hold the audience for the interim week. Besides, the detail was exceptional, perhaps because Diablo had actually been to the factory in question. "How's he been doing, by the way?" he added.

"Very well, I understand. The blank audience has naturally been intrigued to see the celebrated knee spool-pigeon at work, and the figures are up by eight or nine percent. And, incidentally, a point which will no doubt interest you: there has been no interference on the show this week."

"That means it was the old Holocosmic directorate sabotaging us!"

"You may comp it how you wish, Mr. Flamen. I'm simply stating the fact."

Flamen hesitated. Reverting to the most important subject, he said, "But—but look: how did you manage to set the Gottschalks up? Or rather, the splinter group, I guess, who forced through the Holocosmic purchase."

"I think they set themselves up, Mr. Flamen." Voigt tugged absently at the lobe of his right ear again, detached it by mistake, and put it back with a hint of embarrassment. "I'm so sorry. But this is all very peculiar, Mr. Flamen. I'm still trying to get some sense out of our own computers, because we've had some highly improbable additional data fed into our circuits overnight. You know about Dr. Mogshack's breakdown?"

"Just saw about it on the vuset."

"Well, this of course is a major scandal, and Federal mental hygiene experts have been called in. Among other things they opened the data-banks of the Ginsberg to the Federal data-processing network, and analysis of the information we've acquired is going to take a very long time. It looks as though—possibly because for some while one of the inmates has been doing the servicing there—some nonsensical notions have been plugged in as pure gospel. For instance . . ."

"What?"

"Well, I've been trying to make sense of this all morning and so far I've run into a brick wall. I asked about the cessation of interference on the Holocosmic noon slot, and I was referred to a block of data newly acquired from the Ginsberg." Voigt checked. "Is something wrong, Mr. Flamen?"

"I—I don't know." Vivid in memory, the suppressed recollection of the automatics in Reedeth's office telling him that Mrs. Celia Prior Flamen possessed the ability to interfere with electromagnetic radiation in the bands used for . . .

But it was absurd. It had to be absurd.

Yet he could hear Voigt continuing, while on the screen of the vuset a commercial was playing silently—not the one for Guardian traps which ordinarily filled this spot. Of course, one could hardly expect Diablo to put up with a clip that showed a fellow kneeblank being painfully done to death.

"It all led back eventually to a prognosis for your wife, Mr. Flamen, a statement to the effect that she could somehow—ah—interfere with your appearances on the vu-beams, and was resentful of her own ability because on the conscious level she knew how much you valued your work. It further said that when she found a way to employ this talent for, rather than against, you, she would be completely recovered." Voigt gave a deprecating smile. "To think that something of that kind could actually be included in the data-banks of a major State hospital! If it's typical of what will be turned up by the inquiry into Mogshack's administration, it's not too soon to get him out, in my view."

But Flamen wasn't listening. He was staring now at Celia, completely relaxed on the long lounge, eyes closed.

Effortfully, he said, "Mr. Voigt, will you do me a favor?"

"If possible," Voigt agreed politely.

"Will you check the Federal computers about—?" He

stopped. It was *so* ridiculous! He was going to make a fool of himself if he said one more word. And yet he couldn't prevent his lips and tongue from finishing the sentence.

"Will you check them about Robert Gottschalk's breakdown, see if by any outside chance what you're told leads you back to the same block of data?"

"Ah . . . Yes, by all means, if you think it's worth—" Voigt, in his turn, broke off short. "Mr. Flamen, I'm accustomed to thinking of you as a particularly well-informed person, but how in the *world* did you know that the Gottschalk computer was nicknamed 'Robert'? Even members of the cartel were kept in ignorance of that fact unless they had already pledged their unquestioning support to the faction led by Anthony Gottschalk!"

I was told by a madman out of the Ginsberg.

But Flamen could not compel himself to that admission. He kept enigmatic silence, while his mind churned. *If Madison was right about that, could he have been right about other things? And could the Ginsberg automatics . . . ?*

He stared at Celia, wondering if that was the truth—wondering if her cure had happened the moment she came to peer over the shoulder of her brother and was told that Holocosmic had been bought out by the Gottschalks and there would be no more Matthew Flamen Show.

That would be a way to make her talent work for, instead of against him: fouling up the ultra-complex computer. . . .

But he couldn't convince himself. He could only put up with the ghost of the suspicion that it might have happened like that.

Voigt said with new briskness, "Well, that leaves just one further point, Mr. Flamen, apart from congratulating you on the restoration of your show to normal

as of Monday next. Will you—ah—will you be willing
to continue working in collaboration with Mr. Diablo? I
sounded him out informally and he says he's prepared
to if you are. For some reason, in spite of the deposition
of Mayor Black—"

"Him too?"

"You really have been hiding from the news, Mr. Flamen," Voigt said with frank astonishment. "Yes, Mayor
Black was found mentally unfit for office yesterday
afternoon. But I'm waiting for my answer."

"Yes, I'd like to," Flamen said firmly. "I've been watching his work while talking to you. I like it. He's very
damned good. Why doesn't he want to go home, though,
if Mayor Black is being slung out?"

"There's been some—ah—*friction* in kneeblank circles
recently," Voigt said. "It may possibly stem from Mayor
Black's invitation of Uys into the country. However that
may be, we are no longer troubled by the presence of
Morton Lenigo, thank goodness."

Flamen put his hand giddily to his head. "I feel as
though I haven't even blinked, and the world is a different place!"

"It is," Voigt said with unexpected sternness. "We
have had a week's relief from something I'd long hoped
you might find the courage to attack."

"What?"

"Gottschalk propaganda. I'd hardly have believed, myself, how efficient they had made it by now, had they
not found themselves directly involved in communications last weekend, and had I not been able to slap in-
junctions on them to conform with the Charter which
forbids corporations controlling public-service vu-transmission facilities to employ them for the promotion of
their own products. I don't know how long it will stick,
but . . . Mr. Flamen, may I do something illegal, un-
ethical and entirely personal? May I ask you to return
the small favor I've been able to do you by devoting as
much time as possible on your show from now on to

detailed analysis of Gottschalk techniques for fomenting discontent, hatred and suspicion?"

It was the first time in all their long acquaintance that Flamen had seen Voigt display such emotion. He was almost shaking.

"I can stall them for weeks at least, perhaps months, before they can break out of their obligations and sell their holding in Holocosmic. Until that time, we have a chance to fight back."

"But they'll still be my employers!"

"They'll have to swallow anything you choose to put on the beams. The Charter also says that no news program—and yours counts as a news program—shall be censored because the owners of the network wish to protect an advertiser from unfavorable publicity connected with his products or services." Voigt grinned like a fat cat. "We can switch from one to the other argument faster than they can follow us, Mr. Flamen. I've had it comped, and it will work. So perhaps you'll perform the—ah—public service I suggested?"

"Yes," Flamen said fervently.

"Thank you, very much indeed. I— Why, Mrs. Flamen!" Voigt's eyes widened, and in the same moment Flamen realized Celia had got off her lounge and come to stand silently at his elbow. "We haven't met in ages. I'm delighted to learn of your recovery."

"You haven't learned the half of it," Flamen said, and put his arm around his wife's waist.

"Perhaps the rest is—ah—not for publication?" Voigt said. He cocked one bushy eyebrow. "Well, I'll go back to my own personal problems now and stop bothering you. And once again my thanks for falling in with the suggestion I made."

"What suggestion?" Celia said as the screen cleared. "I was half-dozing, I'm afraid. I didn't hear much of what you were saying."

"I'm back in business!" Flamen said exultantly. "And

what's more I've got the chance to torpedo those bastards who tried to lose me. Believe me"—he clenched his fists —"I'm going to see them go the same way as Mogshack and Mayor Black!"

NINETY-EIGHT   FAR FROM BEING EXTRAORDINARY, THE
                 IDIOT SAVANT WHO CAN PERFORM
                 REMARKABLE FEATS OF MENTATION
                 WITHOUT KNOWING EITHER HOW
                 HE DOES THEM OR WHAT THE CON-
                 SEQUENCES ARE LIKELY TO BE IS
                 EXCESSIVELY TYPICAL OF THE SPE-
                 CIES MAN

In the pleasant, air-conditioned, antiques-furnished study he maintained on the campus of the University of North Manitoba Xavier Conroy sat at his ancient electric typewriter pondering the outline for the networked lecture series he had been invited to give during the coming academic year. He was still having trouble organizing his argument; it was one thing to address a group of captive students in a relatively undistinguished university, something else again to have to try and make himself clear to millions of viewers.

He suspected the contract had been signed out of mere panic—the scandal of discovering that the director of the hemisphere's biggest mental hospital was himself suffering from advanced megalomania had jolted everyone, including the directors of the major vu-networks, into horrified awareness of the problem of mental hygiene which previously had been smoothed over by such facile doctrines as Mogshack's about the changing nature of normality.

Due to panic or not, though, the opportunity was too good to let slip. How best to make it clear to viewers that—?

The comweb buzzed. Turning, he saw that the screen was glowing the clear yellow indicating long-distance, and he agreed to accept the call.

To his astonishment, the face of Lyla Clay appeared: pretty as ever, bearing the traces of tiredness, but breaking into a smile on seeing him.

"Miss Clay! Good lord!" He spun his chair to face her directly. "And to what do I owe this pleasure?"

"I want to come and study under you this year," Lyla said.

There was a moment of complete silence. Eventually Conroy said, "I'm—ah—very flattered, but . . ."

"Professor, I'm getting much better at controlling my talent," Lyla said. "I haven't taken a sibyl-pill in over a month, and I'm sensing things which . . ." She bit her lip. "Well, I guess I'll have to tell you an awful lot. Can you spare the time to listen? I mean, if you say no, I'll understand, because last time we spoke things were kind of disorganized, and if you'd rather forget the whole episode, say so."

Conroy looked blank for a moment. Suddenly he laughed. "Miss Clay, already you impress the hell out of me. I don't remember ever doing anything sillier in my life than standing up to Mr. Flamen and pledging my belief in what Madison was telling us, when only moments later he collapsed into permanent insanity. Oh— I'm sorry. He'd become quite a friend of yours, hadn't he?"

"Harry Madison was not only the sanest but one of the nicest people I ever met," Lyla said firmly. "He got me out of a terrible mess just after Dan's death, and in spite of him being carted back to the Ginsberg I've been behaving the way he showed me ever since, and I'm just getting the world to jump through hoops for me. I think you're wrong, Professor—I mean, I think you're wrong now and you were right then."

"I don't quite follow you," Conroy said after a pause.

"I'm not sure I follow myself," Lyla shrugged. "This is something which is so—so inside me that I can't explain it. It has something to do with having tried to make a living as a pythoness—"

"Aren't you still at it?" Conroy interrupted.

"No. I had an invitation from Dr. Spoelstra at the Ginsberg to come and audition, you might say, for the new director—but I said no."

"What have you been doing, then?"

"I went home. I'm calling from there. I've just been sitting and thinking for weeks on end. And arguing with my family, but that's nothing new." She gave an amusing wry grimace. "It took me a hell of a lot of effort to get around to applying to your university, but I did call up and inquire, and when they told me your course was already full I thought maybe if I appealed to you directly . . ."

"Well, I'd certainly be very pleased to accept you as a student of mine, of course, but I'm afraid you'll have to furnish a pretty compelling reason."

"I'm going to try," Lyla said. "That's why I called up." She leaned earnestly to the camera at her end.

"Look, Professor, I've read some of your books and met you and listened to you, and what you said back in Flamen's office has never stopped haunting me. I hope it never will. I don't know what makes me a pythoness, and apparently no one else knows either, but—but it's not the right way to tackle whatever the problem is. *I* don't know what it is, but I think it may be that people are just shutting themselves away from each other, until it takes someone with a special mental gift and a hell of a dangerous drug to break down the barriers between us. And it doesn't *have* to be that way. I told you, I haven't taken a sib for more than a month; I've been walking around my home town looking at people, I've been talking to my parents and my brother, and I've been getting to—to *see* them all over again. I've got a mind as well as a peculiar talent, and I can control my mind, and I can remember what I learn with it instead of having to sit and listen to the replay of a tape made while I was in trance. Being a pythoness is like being a machine, which just sits there knowing all kinds of astonishing things but won't come out and share them until someone puts the proper questions to it. I'm not a machine, but a girl with hormones and emotions and some intelligence and good looks and—" She made a helpless gesture.

"I want someone to show me more than what Harry Madison managed in the short time he was free. There was this person Berry that I thought was a friend of Dan's and mine—you remember? And he squatted in our apt because he thought now's my chance to go grabbing. Friend or no friend, that was what he thought about first, not seeing what he could do to help me or clear up the mess Dan's death left, or anything like that. Professor, am I making myself clear?"

"Not very," Conroy said grimly. "But you're talking about the right subject. Go on."

"Well, like I said it's inside me, and I'm simply not used to bringing out things like this and trying to explain them. But there was this terrible-looking problem I had, no home, no one to help me, and Harry just evaluated it and in spite of never having met me before that same day he straightened it out. Granted he was kind of special, like he went through a locked door without a key and caught the hundred-kilo deadfall and all like that: it was using what he could do *for that purpose* which got kind of branded on my mind."

"And that decided you to give up being a pythoness?"

"Oh no!" Lyla scowled up at the ceiling, seeming frustrated at her own lack of ability to make herself clear. "I can't ever give that up—I *am* one, like someone has perfect pitch or someone else has night vision or someone else maybe could have a trick gift with mathematics. It's what you do with what you've got that matters. I don't want to make a fortune out of it and wind up bored and sadistic like Mikki Baxendale. I want to learn how to put this thing to work for *me*, because I can't make it work for other people until I've done that. And because of all the sense you talked about the way people are cutting themselves off from each other, I want to study under you. Not about the pythoness talent—no one can help me with that, not even the other people who possess it, because the mind's turned off while it's working full blast. But about the people the talent is telling me about. Professor, I want this so much I think it would kill me to have to wait until next year to join your course!"

"If I have to let you camp out in this study of mine because there isn't room in the dormitories," Conroy said decisively, "I'll get you here. I haven't heard someone of your age—excuse the reference, but I'm dreadfully aware of the age-gap in this environment—I haven't heard anyone as young as you talk so much sense in five minutes for the past ten years. Right now, what with the reaction against Mogshack and my unlooked-for status as his chief rival, I'm in a position of some influence, and I'm having to try and control myself because it's been a long time . . ." He fingered his beard thoughtfully.

"I have to admit," he resumed after a pause, "that I still do find it difficult to imagine why I could have been so dogmatic about Madison being right in the things he said, when they were so patently absurd. Talking about things that hadn't yet happened, and what's more things which haven't happened subsequently—"

"Professor," Lyla interrupted, "if it hadn't been for us they would have."

"What?"

"They would have. There was this new super-computer in Nevada, wasn't there? And something went wrong with it, and I *know* what went wrong."

"Yes, of course, but— You know what went wrong with it?" Conroy echoed skeptically.

"Of course." She spoke with simple certainty. "The same thing that once happened to me. What they call an echo-trap."

Conroy's hands dropped to his lap and he stared at her for an endless moment. He said in a changed voice, "I think . . . No, you'll have to explain what you mean."

"Suppose it is true that Madison was—was part of, or in contact with, or somehow *associated* with this machine up there in the future when civilization had collapsed. Then, the moment he learned that the Gottschalks had tried to buy out the Holocosmic network to stifle the Flamen show, he'd have realized he was beaten. Both ways. I mean, *it* would have realized *it* was beaten. Against the century of extra experience it had up there in 2113 it had to balance the fact that its own memory showed it had acted to prevent exactly the kind of exposure necessary to alter history and preserve enough wealthy people to buy the System C weapons when they were offered. Zink—zonk—zink—zonk . . ." She pantomimed patting an imaginary string-suspended ball back and forth in the air between her palms. Seeing the look of disbelief on Conroy's face, she broke off with a sigh.

"Sorry, Professor. It's something I'll never make clear. You'd have had to be inside my head at Mikki Baxendale's when I'd taken a subcritical dose of the sibyl drug and I sensed all these direct experiences of fighting and killing as they raced through Harry's mind. No one man in a lifetime could collect that sort of data; he'd have to be so committed to violence he'd have been killed seven times over. But to me it spoke louder than words. It told me he, or something in back of him, was turning him into a machine for killing. And he did kill. He threw that man out of a forty-fifth story window, didn't he? I've been checked up ever since. I even know what it was that made me vomit right at the end. Of all the people who've ever devoted themselves to killing, the worst were a heretical Zen sect in Japan and Korea in the fifteenth and sixteenth century, who cultivated killing literally as an art. If you can imagine the ecstasy you get from painting and music and poetry rolled up together and then suddenly realizing that this is a man's life being ended, you'll see why I was so sick."

"You've been taking this very seriously, haven't you?" Conroy said slowly, and without waiting for an answer went on. "Certainly I get the same disturbing feeling I had, as I recall, in Flamen's office—a sense of truths peering out of what I'd ordinarily dismiss as obvious nonsense. Your idea of the computer going insane because it had set up an unstable feedback from the present to the future—"

"Right!" Lyla cried.

"But," he continued as though she hadn't spoken, "it's too big a break with my ordinary habit-patterns to think in those terms. You, perhaps?" He looked at her doubtfully. "Yes, I don't see why not. How old are you, Miss Clay?"

"It's my twenty-first birthday today."

"And already you've had experiences most people will never have. I once saw pythoness talent defined as the ability to think with other people's minds; does that fit?"

"Yes, I've said that myself."

"In which case, if I don't petrify your mind in a conformist pattern, I guess I might just possibly be able to help you find what you say you want. And I'm always on guard against mental rigidity."

"You're more open-minded than anyone else I know," Lyla said warmly. Conroy inclined his grizzled head.

"I haven't had a sincerer compliment in years, Miss Clay. I look forward to having you join my course, and I promise to do my best for you. We're sorely in need of people like yourself, and we're going to need them worse than ever in the next few decades. What with the withdrawal of Lares & Penates from the market on that backwash of anti-knee panic, and the reaction against that, and the sudden loss of confidence in the Gottschalks after the revelation of their internal dissensions . . ." He sighed. "This old planet of ours is rocking like a badly spun top, and if we don't find a nucleus of hardheaded, sensible people to drag us back on course, we're going to go into a sort of jagged orbit like a tumbling rocket with the engines jammed, sometimes straight up, sometimes straight down, and sometimes at weird angles in between. But I've somehow managed to cling to this irrational optimism all my life, this sense of expectation that someone will turn up to rescue us in the nick of time and balance our gyroscopes for us."

He leaned back and smiled at the pretty face in the comweb screen.

"Thanks for asking me this favor, Miss Clay. Sometimes my confidence in my own judgment tends to falter. It's a fine thing to have it restored by someone as exceptional as yourself."

She looked at him for a long moment. Suddenly she pursed her lips and blew him a kiss before cutting the connection with a mischievous grin.

NINETY-NINE

You—

ONE HUNDRED CHAPTER NINETY-NINE CONTINUED

-nification.